Black Kestrel

In Honor of

Joseph Maria Silva

Black Kestrel
A Story of Madeira

Ingestre Press

For information address:
Booklocker.com, Inc.
P.O. Box 2399
Bangor, ME 04402

ISBN-10 1-60145-022-2
ISBN-13 978-1-60145-022-7

Printed in the United States of America

Black Kestrel

A Story of Madeira

Don Silva

How shall a man escape from his ancestors, or draw off from his veins the black drop which he drew from his father's or his mother's life?

--Emerson

Leis em favor do Rei se estabelecem,
As em favor do povo perecem.

--Camoens

Preface

Ten years later, he sailed from New Bedford back to Madeira to attend the Festival of Saint Blaise in Campanário. The pebbled beach at the foot of the cliff rattled and roared, waves breaking on the rocks. That seemed centuries ago.

He and Pistola walked to the top of the cliff from the Sítio de Lapa e Maçapez and climbed down one step at a time, the old man cautious on the crumbling steps, supported himself with his cane and careful handling the decrepit handrails. Bearers no longer used this way when once it streamed with men carrying sacks of potatoes, baskets of cabbage, oranges, onions, and embroidery for the Funchal market. With an antique key, Pistola unlocked the door at the entrance to his cave where once he had stored merchandise for his shop and produce to be shipped by boat to his cousin in Funchal.

He and the old man sat on the quay, in the sunshine and talked about the Senhorio's tyranny, the day when the wherrymen stopped work and watched Pistola argue with the imperious Senhorio. Which man had the right to admit the Englishman who appeared out of nowhere in his sloop with its white sails?

His father's land, terraced gardens, banana plants, orange trees, and the field of sugar cane remained on the steep slopes below the village square. He had once toiled there and cultivated the porous volcanic soil. His family had difficulty growing enough to feed itself and meeting their obligations and they were in debt to the Senhorio, the feudal lord of their land. The young men at the age of sixteen had to serve six years in the army of King Carlos. Since childhood, he'd wanted to learn to read and write and never did receive the permission of the priest to attend school with his sisters. He admired his brother Henrique who lived in the mountains free of the Senhorio. His father beat him every time he left the land without permission and wandered off to the pebbled beach or sailed on Blandy's tugboat and spent the day in Funchal.

One day changed his life. Pistola had been much younger, a vigorous man who stood up to authority and assisted the poor in times of famine and gave young men reasons to dream of a life better than the island of poverty, famine, and disease. The day he worked before daybreak came back to him. He had rested on the handle of his hoe and gazed on the magnificent sea spread out before him, a dark blue expanse of water off which the sun reflected its light and the wind blew and made its patterns, like the ruffled feathers of birds, and the shadows of kestrels, the joy of flight, freedom far and away over the sea.

CHAPTER I

The night before he sighted the sail, Maria teased José about Rosa Castagna. The girl Rosa smiled and waved to him in the afternoon as he carried a stack of hay on his shoulders and walked by her father's cobbler shop across the square from the church of Saint Blaise in Campanário.

"She's a trick," Maria said. He'd never heard the word before and he dreamt that night with Maria close, her warm body wrapped against him, he was pressed between the stones of the sugar cane mill at Pedegral and blood streaming out and flowing down mingled with the raw sugar juices. He opened his eyes. The faint light of day fell on the ladder down from the sleeping loft over the kitchen. Maria tormented him about Rosa and he kissed her before pulling on his worn trousers and climbed down the ladder out of the loft and into the kitchen. Mother boiled coffee and toasted bread. He doused his face with water from the trough outside the kitchen and shivered in the brisk morning air. The cocks crowed in Sítio de Lapa e Maçapez
. Last week, the Senhorio had sent word. Once more Father learned José had left the land without permission. With the young men, he had played cards in the afternoon instead of working on the terraced gardens. They had gone down to the pebbled beach and drunk wine at Pistola's taberna. Again, José had left the land without the Senhorio's permission.

This morning, Maria and mother tied their kerchiefs under their chins before the bells pealed a missa and José yelled for his older brothers Silvino and João still asleep in the loft. He took up his hoe and walked through the banana grove and beyond the field of sugar cane and hoed new rows in the patch of sweet potatoes along the levada. Tia Nita, his old Aunt, sang and gathered herbs in her cottage garden and the hum of the water-mill cooled the burning in his blood. He resented the punishment, hauling stone for the Senhorio. He'd left the land without permission to see the sailing ship.

José Abreu worked the red volcanic soil in the garden patch of his Grandfather Abreu hewn from bedrock near the top of the cliff overlooking the pebbled beach during the reign of Dom Luís. He swore at the Senhorio for sentencing him to hard labor. His back hurt and he stood up and shined the dust off the worn handle of his hoe. At that moment, a sloop far on the

1

sea caught his eye. He wiped his brow and looked beyond the quay where the Blandy's steam-tug, Falcon, lay at anchor and wherrymen rowed out with cargo. A white sail in the southeast by the blue shape of Grande Deserta and its shadow islands, Bugio and Chão, a bright sail over the water loomed under banks of clouds and like a winged caravel tacked toward the pebbled beach.

The sail was rigged fore and aft with one mast and a single headsail jib, its lines not carvel-built like Madeiran boats that worked their way to Ribeira Brava and the southwestern villages, a strange boat tacking toward the campanário, the spire, the massive rock formation out of the deep waters off the beach where pebbles rolled up in the white surf and rattled down with the ebb. The men on the quay stopped carrying bales to watch the sailboat. Two wherrymen grabbed a line thrown by the sailor with his straw hat pulled down low over his eyes. He wore a white shirt and black trousers.

José moved out of the sunlight and into the prickly pear in the shadow of the outcropping of volcanic rock. He left his hoe stuck in the soil like a crosier.

Falcon's whistle blew and its sound echoed off Cabo Girão. The longshoremen scrambled out onto the quay. Blandy Brothers' tug eased off the quay and settled in the deep water. The early explorers had turned back when they saw the campanário, the steeple rock, a sign of danger. José would have sailed on.

Down on the quay, the sailor leapt ashore and walked along the cobbles in black soft-leather boots, strange boots never seen here before. The sailor held his arm in a sling, the dark arm visible against the light shirt.

The peasants, dockmen and fishermen dropped their work and gazed at the sailor. The men in Pistola's cave forgot sorting fruits for delivery to Funchal market and moved into the sunlight and sea air, away from the cave dug into the grey tuff at the foot of the cliff and observed the stranger.

The sailor hesitated before the inquisitive peasants and raised his head and looked at the cliffs and the gardens and terraces on the heights above the village.

From high on the ridge where he'd been grubbing in the soil when the sail appeared, José wandered to the cliff's edge and into the hut where he stored hand-cut hay for his goats and peered down on the sailor who shaded his eyes with his hand and scanned the hillsides.

The sailor wore a knife, sheathed in a metal case on his right hip. He paused and pushed back his hat, the sun reflected off his forehead, and his blue eyes stared at the peasants along the quay.

2

The stranger's appearance was "news" and the islanders moved closer, silent, curious and vulnerable. Pistola himself emerged from the cave aware of the change in activity on the waterfront.

Falcon blew another whistle blast and the wherrymen rushed to their boats along the quay jumping down into the barge-like vessels and manning the oars. They off-loaded boxes from Funchal and Lisbon and set aside those marked for Pistola's shop in Maçapez. The shoremen handed up stalks of bananas, baskets of fruit, vegetables and hampers of embroidery. One wherryman collected the mail bag and rowed ashore three villagers returned home from visiting their families in Funchal-town.

Pistola left the cave and moved down into the onlookers and José ran from his lookout and jumped off the precipice onto a narrow ledge, crawled into an opening in the crevice and made a hidden descent to the pebbled beach and ran to Pistola, the shopkeeper with the calm brown eyes, speaking with the sailor.

The stranger and Pistola were two meters apart. Pistola smiled and eyed the bruised arm, the black sling, the bright shirt, the tired face.

"I need a place to rest for a couple of days, some water and fruit," said the sailor.

"*Uma pausa preciso um pouco dias, por favor, e agua e fruita,*" I need a rest for a few days and water and fruit, please.

The words were familiar, the accent strange. Pistola rested his hands on his hips and smiled. The stranger spoke to him again now in French. Pistola spoke in French! The wherrymen left their wherries, their eyes darted and lingered on the two men facing each other.

The stranger's face in the shade under the brim of his hat was pale and wrinkled. He saw the wink and gesture of the wherrymen, their slight nodding. His deep-set, blue eyes, dark of the sea, turned toward Pistola. The lines at the corners of his eyes were kind and he listened to Pistola.

The Senhorio appeared on the cliff path and led his men after him in single file with bales on their shoulders. Álvaro and Segundo-of-the-chapel ran to meet António Gonçalves de Abreu, better known as the Senhorio, the feudal lord who lately fought with his tenants over authority and rights. The Senhorio directed the men with bales to store them in his cave. Two men carried a small barrel of wine. The Senhorio saw the stranger and Pistola on the quay and hurried across the beach to them, annoyed at Pistola, the village shopkeeper who supported tenants and even fishermen.

"Who's this stranger?"

"A stranger seeking bed and meals," said Pistola. "He sailed from Lisbon against the wind. He ran into a storm. His family has a quinta, an estate, and are wine merchants in Funchal," said Pistola.

The news surprised José. Pistola knew so much and was calm with the stranger.

"I'll question him, myself," said the Senhorio.

"He'll talk later. He's tired and hungry. He'll sail to the Bay of Funchal after he rests."

The Senhorio swore and hit his fist into his palm. He glared at the stranger.

"Who are you? What is your business here?" he said.

The sailor removed his hat and greeted the Senhorio. His black hair ruffled in the breeze. His arms were slender and his shoulders muscled from hard work. He extended his hand and smiled. He spoke in French.

Pistola said, "His arm is bruised. He needs assistance for a short time. He'll stay at Maçapez above my shop."

The Senhorio pointed his finger at Pistola. "Why sail to Funchal? Why alone? How do you know he sailed from Lisbon? There are questions, Senhor!"

"Your questions aren't my business," said Pistola.

"You have no authority to let him land at Campanário. You don't know his destination."

"Funchal, my good Senhor. Who knows where a man's home is?"

"The police and the customs know," said the Senhorio.

"He wants fruit and water. You can see he's an Englishman. The storm drove his sloop here. What do you want?"

"To invite him to my quinta in the Valley of the Melons and question him myself."

A wherryman brought a glass and wicker of wine. He poured the brown liquid for the stranger.

"Please drink with your new friends, sir," said Pistola. He repeated the request in Portuguese. "À sua saude," to your health, he said. The sailor tasted the wine. The wherryman refilled the glass and handed it to the Senhorio who poured the wine on the cobbles and it splashed on the stranger's boots.

"Treat my guest with kindness," said Pistola.

"He must speak. I'll drink when he accepts my hospitality. What does he wish?"

4

The sailor turned to Pistola. "What does this man want? I'll pay for food and I can sail this evening."

"This man wants you to be his guest on his fief. It's better to stay with me at Sítio de Lapa e Maçapez. You'll be safe."

The Senhorio understood a little French. He squinted and scratched his stomach under the old grey sweater. He wore the wide-brimmed hat and a white shirt with a maroon tie. His fingers fumbled at the buttons of his sweater.

"The stranger stays at my quinta. Later, he'll visit with you, Senhor."

Pistola raised his glass and drank the wine in one swallow. "I'll keep this stranger from," he said to the Senhorio.

One of the wherrymen cleared his throat. José leaned forward. Tatara, the one called caterpillar, jumped up. "Will you let a stranger say no to a prince, sire?"

Pistola laughed. The Senhorio didn't.

"Show the stranger you're boss," said Tatara.

The Senhorio grabbed the stranger's arm. The sailor jumped back and pulled his knife and pointed it at the Senhorio.

"I'm not overwhelmed," the stranger said.

The on-shoremen moved closer. The Senhorio leapt at the sailor and snatched the knife.

The crowd was silent. The sailor was bruised and tired from the long watch during the storm and wanted rest. The Senhorio's mouth was taut and his eyes followed the movement of the sailor. The sailor backed away from him and drew a small knife from his black trousers.

José hid himself amidst the onlookers where the Senhorio couldn't see him.

Tatara, the caterpillar, was sorry for the Senhorio. He pulled his ear lobe and shook his head.

The Senhorio crouched and about to set the knife on the pavement. He had forgotten the slight. His peasants often defied his authority now that he was older. The wherrymen waited.

The two circled and eyed each other. The sailor moved forward. The Senhorio edged away. They circled one another like the cocks in the pit at Ribeira Brava. They eyed sunlight and shadow, the ground beneath their feet. They leapt and swung.

The force sent the knife out of the Senhorio's hand, bouncing on the worn path and across the pavement. The Senhorio ran and reached down for it.

José dashed out and kicked the knife with his foot. It fell down over the pebbles and onto the beach landing at the water's edge.

"I'll kill you, scum of the lizard's tongue. You ungrateful bastard Abreu," said the Senhorio.

José ran toward the steps at the foot of the cliff.

The wherryman picked up the wine glasses. Tatara raised his glass and drank a toast.

"I didn't want a fight. You saw the knife," said the sailor. Pistola nodded.

José moved down the path closer to the men. The Senhorio shook his fist at him.

"What will he do to the young man?" said the sailor.

The crowd turned toward José.

"The lad can take care of himself. He lives on the fief and knows the Senhorio. He's safe with his own," said Pistola.

"I meant no offense," said the sailor. Pistola translated his gracious words.

The Senhorio cursed and waved his arms about and lost his breath.

The wherrymen made way for him. He called his crew on the pebbled beach near the cliff of the Smuggler's Cave and ordered them to load produce for Funchal.

The Senhorio disappeared into his storage cave and tallied boxes. The Senhorio hated the peasants and tenants resented him and resisted his authority.

José wished he were hidden in the mountains with his half-brother Henrique. He felt lonely and cold, for it would begin again, the relentless hatred of the landlord when he left the land without permission.

Blackeye and Twenty-Seven, servants of the Senhorio, asked where he wanted them that evening.

"Nine o' clock at Sítio de Porco Morto, Place of the Dead Pig," said the Senhorio.

The wherrymen and the peasants sang and drank wine. The Senhorio walked slowly across the beach climbed the steps to Sítio de Furnas e Amoreiras, place of the caves and mulberry trees.

José joined the wherrymen.

The strange sailor sat at the mouth of Pistola's cave on a pile of fishnets. He spoke slowly and clearly in Portuguese. "I'm happy to stay with you."

"Don't worry about the Senhorio. He has a temper," said Tatara. "He deserved the fight. He stole the land from us. His grandmother signed the deeds thinking they were papers to join the King's militia. It was a trick."

"Yes, he stole the land and my birthright," said José.

"The executor had papers and the Abreu lost their land," said Pistola.

"He'll punish me," said José

"You have a heart of maracuja. You did well. Fetch the knife."

José cleaned it on his shirt and handed it to Pistola. The longshoremen piled up wicker-ware for Blandy's boat. The stranger took another glass of wine and drank it down.

"Thank the lad," said the stranger. "I'm Garth Talbot, from Ingestre, nine days out of Lisbon. I'd set sail now. I can't manage very well with this arm."

Talbot took coins out of his leather purse and offered them to José. José shook his head.

"Take them," said Pistola.

"I don't want money. I need a boat," said José.

"You'll need both tomorrow. Show your manners to Senhor Talbot," said Pistola.

Muito obrigado, O Senhor," said José, Thank you very much, sir.

"I'm dead tired. I'll pay for my mooring," said Talbot.

"It won't be necessary. I know the men on this quay. You need soup," said Pistola. "His father beats him for leaving the land. Come, we'll climb to Maçapez."

Pistola ordered a barrel of flour, settled accounts and marked bales for his shop and told his men to lock the cave.

José crossed over the bridge at the foot of the waterfall and climbed the cliff. A kestrel hovered on the currents of air in the sunlight and swooped in an arc into the shadow of the clouds.

Only smoke from the stack of Hawk, the other Blandy tugboat, returning from the trip to Arco da Calheta, beyond Canhas and Ponta Do Sol, marred the sky.

CHAPTER II

Garth Talbot sat on stone steps cut from the rock of the cliff to catch his breath. He waited for Pistola and his men to gather their boxes and hampers. The village set atop the cliff across from an expanse of fields and banana groves and sugar cane. The steeple of the church rose above the tiled roofs of the cottages and the ruins of a medieval fortress stood overlooking the village.

Jaime Sousa played a ballad about the girl gathering chestnuts in the mountains who met the King's son. "Love never died while they lived." Sousa cradled the machete, thrummed its strings, closed his eyes and sang.

Garth refused the hammock ride. Virgilio Rodrigues stared, sad brown eyes, at the rare use of the hammock for transport. Garth was light-headed and steadied himself against the bed-rock. Hundreds of feet below on the surface of the ocean, the wind pushed against his sloop. The fragile craft leaned away from the wind steadied and righted itself.

José the knife kicker was on the steep trail beyond the cliff. The long body and short legs climbed without stopping and disappeared over the ridge.

Garth struggled up the steps. The face of the Senhorio was lighter colored than the villagers, with black eyes sunk into a head covered with thick black hair streaked with white, a heavy beard down his neck and tufts of hair grew in his ears.

Garth shook his head, breathed deeply and sat down. The village set on a slope above fields of sugar cane and banana groves. The brook became a waterfall and ran over the cliff into a pool at sea level. He sat on a ledge and listened to the waterfall until his heart quieted and he felt better.

The machete player stopped strumming when they crossed the rushing stream. The men smoked cigarettes and whispered about the fight at the pebbled beach. Pistola walked ahead in the shade of a custard apple tree. Garth hopped across the stream on foot-stones and caught up with the laughing band. They climbed higher.

José chopped soil with his long-handled pickaxe, his figure etched against the sky by the late afternoon sun. The enxada struck the soil with great force.

"The boy works well," said Pistola.

"My men in Funchal don't work as hard," said Talbot.

"The Abreu had worked hard. Their landlords were kidnappers during the settlement of Madeira. They kidnapped the Câmara family to redeem one of their women. They raided the town hall in Funchal and captured Simão Gonçalves de Câmara, first Count of Calheta, faithful to the land and people."

"How much further is there to go?"

"Across the field through the gardens, my shop is by that schoolhouse," said Pistola. He pointed to the vines he set for his father as a boy more than forty years ago.

José dug into the soil making up for the time he spent at the pebbled beach.

Talbot listened to the men and their gossip about the Senhorio. Many seasons in Funchal taught him the patter of sounds similar to those in Lisbon, more clipped and soft, at times lost on his ear, made him feel as innocent as a child learning a strange new language.

The shop set in a manicured garden of tropical and semi-tropical shrubs and fruit trees. Pistola supplied the villagers with staples and hardware from his shop. It was situated on the pathway from the sea to the church. The church on the height above his shop overlooked the market-square, half a kilometer away.

Beyond the village and the forests of Spanish pine, clouds built up against the mountains, great masses like the clouds of Salisbury and Norwich painted by Turner.

The men gathered in the tiny barroom that was separated from the shop by a doorway with a countertop across the entrance to keep them from wandering into the shop.

Pistola served glasses of wine, bottles of beer and orange soda, swapped stories with the men.

"We know the grudges of the Senhorio," he said. "Abreu wants his sons on the land to pay for the levy set by the Senhorio. The lad provoked Senhor António and he'll pay for it."

"Slavery was abolished in 1869," said Talbot. "King Carlos is happy with the republicans. I met him and Queen Marie Amelia once in Lisbon."

Pistola shrugged his shoulders and filled wine glasses for the hammock bearers. Outside on the cobbled path, women called their fisherman husbands, whispering to them before they went to sea.

Pistola gazed into the sunset, his large frame leaned forward over the counter, a short man as wide as he was tall. When he walked his feet pointed out a little, and with his short legs, gave him an amusing gait. He didn't waddle up the path, but edged along as if his torso were going to topple without his dainty side-movements.

"The Senhorio is landlord of Ribeira Melões, the Valley of the Melons," he said. "He worked for us back in the old days when I ran the shop out of my Father's doorway. It was a miserable location up there where you see that row of cottages. I was tired of working on the land, and that hovel beside the water-storage tank, poor as it was, made me barely a living. I bought a little salt, sugar and coffee to sell to the women. I saved them the long walk down to the pebbled beach where my Uncle had a shop. I made baskets and chairs from osiers, and sent them to Funchal. The women returned for small things--needles, thread, baking powder, beeswax, pepper, and even new pots when their old ones could not be repaired."

The men listened to Pistola's old stories though they had heard them before and drank their wine in silence.

"I sold rice in small bags, and spaghetti, which they'd never seen, in half kilos. The Senhorio used to come from his hovel at the bottom of the ridge there, Sítio de Fumas e Amoreiras, the Place of the Fires and Mulberry Trees. He wanted sugar but he had nothing to trade. He worked hard but he didn't make enough to feed the mouths in his family. I refused to do business and he'd walk to the beach and try my Uncle. He was young, about ten years old and never forgave me. Boredom and overwork! We lived on both. He and his men loved wine but couldn't afford it. They saved up credit for the Festival of Saint Blaise and drowned themselves in wine that week."

Bells tolled for evening Mass. Women in groups of two or three with kerchiefs tied under their chins walked up the path toward the church.

Pistola escorted Talbot onto the patio that looked out over the middle of the village called simply igreja, those families that lived in the shadow of church, the priest's house and the market-square.

While the women washed and dressed Talbot's bruised arm, Pistola set a bottle of green wine on the table. They drank with in the twilight and waited for Pistola's women to serve the evening meal. About half nine o' clock, the old cousin, Mariazinha, showed Talbot his bed. Without washing up, he fell onto the quilt, closed his eyes and fell asleep.

Talbot dreamed of the young Madeiran on the hillside chopping soil under the bright stars after twilight faded into darkness. Roosters crowed and church bells rang, echoing through the valley.

Footsteps on cobblestones, laughter, Talbot smelled Pistola's morning cigarette! He opened his eyes. He must reward the young man that kicked the knife. He'd speak to Pistola about a job. The rulers owned the land, the peasants, the animals, the crops and the produce of life. Exhaustion overtook him and he slept with the dreamy motion of his sloop rising and falling through the white caps toward the green island, kestrels hovering in the sky above the village.

The previous day, José had seen the hammock men and Talbot follow Pistola up the steep ridge from the bridge to the waterfall. They rested by the brook that flowed over the cliff into the blue pool and the twilit sea.

The setting sun cast long shadows and he swung his enchada, pickaxe, rapidly chopping away the hard red soil. He covered the old potato vines.   When he cut a new trench he filled it with compost carried from the pig pen by Silvino. He heard the machete on the evening breezes stirring and blowing away the sound of music and the men's voices.

He heard a whistle. His brother's head appeared above the shrubs. "I saw a beautiful boat tied up to the quay," said João.

"It belongs to an Englishman that lives in Funchal," said José.

"News travels your way, lucky fellow!"

"This sailor spoke with Pistola and the Senhorio. They had words and Tatara spoke for the landlord."

"You left the potato patch," said João.

"She's a strange boat without an eye painted on her bow."

João nodded and looked down where the quay lay outlined in surf. "She's not a carrick, yet she's beetle-shaped."

Silvino whistled from the valley of the melons.

"Give me a hand and we'll finish this garden."

"I'll help Silvino put the baskets in the cave before supper. Father's angry. You went to the pebbled beach."

"I'll hide. The Senhorio threatened the cave people. He'll not beat me," said José.

"Why did you leave?" said João.

"I'll go home after feeding my pet goats, Preto and Estrela, Blackie and Star."

"You'll run off to the mountains."

"Freedom is better than slavery," said José.

"There was a fight."

"The Senhorio drew his knife on the sailor. He dropped it. I kicked it into the pebbles."

"You're mad."

"I saw the sail on the sea and went down to the boat."

"You left the garden."

"I'll sail someday."

"What do you tell Father? The Senhorio knows."

"Nothing, I wanted to see the boat. This Englishman sailed from the continent, bruised his arm during a storm. He needed rest."

"Father heard from the Senhorio's men."

"Father hates the tail of the pig."

"He pays his taxes. The stranger doesn't."

"Go see him, João. Black beard and wears black boots with square toes!"

"Let's eat in peace," said João.

"The beans dried up. We'll be eating stone soup from Saint Blaise until spring."

Father sat at the table eating potatoes and beans. The lamp flickered and smoked. Luisa turned up the wick. José walked to the table and dropped to his knees.

"Father, give me your blessing," he said, and kissed his hand. His mother set a plate of boiled chestnuts on the table. The old man peeled a chestnut and refused to bless him.

He went to his place at the table where Maria poured cabbage soup into wooden bowls. João received father's blessing and took his place, looked and looked down in his lap. His sister passed the platter of potatoes and carrots. They ate with their hands, fingers shining in the lamplight. Mother brought cold, sliced cornmeal and set it beside Father.

She smiled at José and went to sit by the bright coals in the kitchen to eat by herself. Father coughed and blew his nose. He finished his boiled chestnuts. "You went to the pebbled beach," he said.

He demanded to hear the story. Each son spoke at once. When they stopped, Father said, "You were on the beach!"

"I saw the beautiful sailboat," said José.

"You had no authority. You were to work. I needed vegetables to pay taxes."

"He doesn't like us," said Luisa.

"Madness!" said João.

"A family needs sons," said Maria.

12

José said nothing.

"The Senhorio receives a day's work for leaving the land without his permission. It's an insult. I want you working," said Father.

José looked at mother beyond the lamplight.

"You work your share. We live on the Senhorio's land. We pay his tax."

"The Senhorio insulted the sailor, Senhor."

"I don't care. You disobeyed, work's not done and the family suffers."

"You taught us to be polite," said José.

"Rude to the Senhorio is one day's labor. Tomorrow you'll work for him."

"He's a bastard from the tail of the pig. He stole your birthright."

"I'll call him bastard but he's our bastard. Button our lips. Tomorrow, you'll work in the fields where the old Aunt gathers herbs."

"That's her haunt," said Maria.

"Silvino and I'll do his work," said João. "But it'll begin in the dark and end in the dark."

Father moved. He grabbed José's arm and threw him against the wall. José shook his head and pushed the old man aside.

Mother said, "António."

As he fell, José saw the chain hanging from the wall. Mother pushed father off-balance. Father jabbed at her with his left hand and clenched the chain with his right. He snapped it on the cobbles and caught José's ankle. José screamed and ran. He staggered. His left leg felt broken. The second blow cut his shoulder.

A scream shot from his lips. Running up the steps he hobbled and the old man came after him.

He leaned against the gate and regained his breath when another blow landed on his shoulder and back. He turned and took hold of the chain and yanked it out of his hand.

The land was darkening and the stars were bright over the ocean and silhouettes of the mountains loomed against the sky. He ran into the kitchen garden and fell.

The old man swore and trampled down the flowers and knocked pots onto the walkway. José fell where he stood on the edge of the embankment and rolled under the grape arbor into the New Zealand spinach. He didn't move. The old man cursed in the dark.

It was silent. He saw the chain hanging on the wall where it had hung since he was a child. It appeared in his mind and ever present reminder of his beatings. He felt cold and listened to the crickets and rustle of the night wind in the sugar cane. His shoulder hurt and he heard the sound of someone coming toward him.

A whisper rose on the air. "Where are you?"

It was Maria. He whistled.

She held him in her arms and covered his   shoulders with her burlap hood.

Back in the kitchen, she poured him a dram of brandy. She reached down and pulled him up the ladder into the loft. His left leg felt numb and it hurt when he put weight on it. She massaged his shoulders and kissed him on the neck. João snored. José crawled into the blankets beside his brother and sister, Maria snuggled up to him, warming his back with her arms and breasts.

He curled up in a ball in the darkness of the loft and the face of the Senhorio appeared at the moment on the pebbled beach when the knife fell and clattered over the pebbles and glinted in the sunlight. The Senhorio faced him at that moment. The mouth revealed teeth ready to bite him. The eyes were flat dull black with a spark of light for an instant where the irises usually outlined the soft brown interior. The Senhorio leaned forward and spit out a gob of bright green mucus and wiped his lips with his shirtsleeve.

Even with Maria beside him in the bed under the thatched roof radiating the heat from the sun he felt cold inside. The old feeling came back to him, the never ending relentless hatred of the lord of the land forever pursuing his every movement whether he spent the day in Funchal and returned on the night boat, or the day on the pebbled beach picking limpets and playing cards with Julio and Duarte.

He saw himself hauling stone, a long day in the sun in the field high above the village where Tia Nita collected herbs for her medicines carrying stone from the great pile left by the quarrymen of Quinta Grande to the line of stone laid out along the levada the foundation of the wall the Senhorio ordered built to keep the soil from eroding into the irrigation channel from the north. It took him away from harvesting the vegetables for the market and sitting around the table with Maria, Julia, Luisa and mother over a bowl of cabbage soup at lunch. A long day wasted alone without the gossip of the square and the cackle of the hens and the nuzzling of his goats when he fed them handfuls of hay after his afternoon nap. The penalty could be worse.

Being sent to the onion fields to chop weeds and listening to the men locked up in the old slave quarters for drunken brawls and refusal to work after hours of wine and card games, the men whose only enjoyment was the taste of wine and an afternoon of cards whose families lived on the edge of famine and the charity of the Senhorio.

The thought of fighting the Senhorio frightened him and he held Maria close in the dark bed but worse was imagining the beating his father would give him for breaking his bond with the Senhorio and the force of madness quieted him.

In a cave of silence he heard a cry coming from somewhere and listening heard it coming from himself. He hated being so weak and frightened that he cried, a child whimpering over the loss of his favorite wooden top thrown into the fire by his merciless father.

In his dream, a kestrel hovered over the valley. Its cry carried on the wind. The bird's eyes stared down on him, like the eyes of a fierce eagle.

From the high in the clouds, he saw the face of a woman, her eyes looking up. Her worn wrinkled complexion, old leather stretched over bone. He saw the rock-face of the cliff and an ancient cottage in the mists.

"Leave me alone."

He awoke in his sister's arms and she soothed him. Maria was the oldest sister.

"Can you move your arm?" she said.

He gritted his teeth. A bird-like cry rose in his throat.

Maria kissed him. "Relax dear, sleep."

Why live in bondage? Why be beaten? He slept once more.

The church bells rang in the early darkness. "Come to the mountain to see me," he said.

Maria nodded. "After embroidering and visits to Rosa and the Senhorio's house, I'll see you. The climb isn't steep."

"I love you, Maria."

"Joachim, Pistola's cousin, asked me to marry him."

"I'll love you always José," she said, "You'll not keep me from leaving home."

She and Mother walked up the dark pathway under the stars to attend Mass.

CHAPTER III

Maria opened her eyes to the sound of weeping. The early light filtered into the loft and revealed José's face, calm and as unmoving as the effigy of a saint. She heard the footsteps back and forth before the fire. Mother was down in the kitchen making cornmeal mush and coffee. The aroma of newly brewed coffee enticed her back into her dream of lying curled in the warm blanket until mother had to call her out for washing the clothes in the river.

While brewing coffee for her sleeping husband, Ana Maria of the Saints dreamed of giving her heart away to a loving man, unaware of the tears falling down her cheeks. In girlhood, she had swept the steps at the priest's house. She dressed before daylight, before Dona Alzira called her and washed the front walk and steps. For three years she worked for the Senhora Alzira in the rectory and took lessons with Father Segundo. One morning, Alzira's voice startled her. She looked at herself in the mirror and slipped into a dress, wearing nothing beneath it. She went out into the corridor and down the passageway to meet her housemother and followed her into the darkness before sunrise.

The candles illuminated the sanctuary and warmed her as she knelt before the altar and shivered. Her mind awakened at the sound of Reverend Father's voice and she lost herself in the Mass. She felt again his generous hands grasping hers at the confessional.

Now, Ana swept her worn kitchen floor and wiped her tears away. Sadness filled her heart when she dreamed of giving her heart away. The fresh breeze from the sea enlivened her dream and she remembered his voice and eyes when he ordered her to undress.

She went to the stove and stirred the coffee and moved it off the flames. She lifted the basket of leftover food to her head, and balancing it as her mother had taught her with baskets of washing down to the brook and back, she stiffened her neck and with the grace of a court dancer walked to the pig pen.

Her bare feet touched the cool dew-covered cobbles and she remembered hurrying back to the rectory to have breakfast on the table when Reverend Father returned from Matins. She threw scraps to the pigs. She kindled the Priest's fire daily and filled the porcelain pot with milk.

Alzira cut the bread in thin slices and arranged them on a blue and white plate with gooseberry jelly and packed the butter in tiny jars with fine drawings along their glazed sides.

Maria heard Mother sweep the kitchen floor and knew she wished her heart away in dream. Maria climbed down the ladder to see mother weeping, the handkerchief held to her nose. Maria smelled the coffee and dipped her hands into the bucket by the entryway and splashed water onto her face.

"You're sleep walking, mother," she said. Ana smiled, remembering her husband's temper when he caught her in sadness. She stirred the coffee and watched the joyous flames licking the pot.

"I was dreaming of mornings with Dona Alzira. Father Segundo arrived when I boiled the coffee, dressed in black and sat down at the end of the long white table, alone. White linens covered the smooth dark surfaces of the sideboards and serving tables. Your father knocked at the door to make arrangements on such a morning."

Maria shrugged and scratched herself on the shoulder where she had been bitten in the night. "I must clean out the straw and put fresh or I'll get lice."

"A tall dark man stood at the gate and didn't ring the bell. He knocked gently and waited to enter. Dona Alzira dressed me in white, for she'd heard from António, the Senhorio, that father was coming to speak for our Ana."

"I want coffee," said Maria

"We talked like magpies, and made up the beds with clean sheets. We drank coffee and watched the man talking by the gate in the early sunshine."

Maria heard the story before. She poked the fire and picked up a dried chestnut and peeled it.

"He was old enough to be my Father and he had a cast in one eye. Most of the Abreu have a squint eye. The banns were read three Sundays. He promised his dying wife to marry and raise their eight children. He never spoke to me until a month before Luisa was born."

"The young men hid in the mountains from the army. The captured ones served ten years in jail for not serving King Carlos. The others went into the militia for six years. By the time the young men returned, I was married to António Abreu. It cost many *reis* to have the priest write letters and make the papers for the proxy. I had no dowry."

Mother's face relaxed over the memory as if she could feel it like the heat of the fire and she pulled at the sleeves of her blouse as she talked of the old days.

Maria picked up the chain father had dropped the night before and hung it on the nail. She cleared the dishes off the table and dreamed of a man for herself.

The two women sipped coffee from their cups by the open fire and listened to the church bells ringing second matins. Maria looked for Father and found him dressed and shaving before the old mirror hanging on the wall by the watering trough. The mirror belonged to a Scottish soldier who had lived in Tia Nita's hut and had walked to Câmara De Lobos and had never returned.

The old man wore his stained shirt that needed bleaching in sunlight. He sat down at the table. Maria served the only bread they'd see that day and Mother brought the coffee and the goat's milk. Father blew on his fingers.

Into his cup, he put three spoonfuls of coarse sugar. Mother poured in the coffee and added milk. His black trousers were worn and wrinkled. He wore the boots sold by the muleteers that drove through the district once a year on their way to Paúl Da Serra. Mother waited on him and returned to the fire.

The first beating had surprised her. She'd been to Mass and walked home alone. She stooped and picked wild flowers. He pruned grapevines and didn't wave or smile at her.

The blows were rapid and their force paralyzed her and she stood unmoving. She remembered Dona Alzira saying, "He's too old and I want you to spend your nights with me." Dona Alzira said Abreu was strong and hardworking and that women needed men to protect them or they lived a sad life. She became his wife and her life was labor and sadness! She hadn't understood Dona Alzira.

"Mother, come to morning prayer," said Maria.

"I promised father to attend on Sunday. He doesn't want me to breathe without his permission. The family was too large to feed and the fields too small to provide their food, my dear. I picked wild flowers when he worked in the lower gardens."

"This one time come to the late Mass. I want to hear the prayers."

"No, the women will gossip. Like hens' feet, their tongues scratching away at me. They say I'm pregnant. They don't visit me. They don't sleep with me at night. What do they know?"

Maria caressed mother's cheek. She gathered up clothes to be washed in the river.

On the way to the kitchen, she felt her breasts, full and heavy, her nipples large and hard, no longer tiny and slender breasts.

Her dream was to live in a home like the priest's. She wanted to bathe every day and buy herself clothes to wear at the Festival of Saint Blaise. She lived on a garbage heap.

Mother often told them. "Each of you will have one happy day. I had mine long ago in the house of the priest. I was born in Amoreira in the house on the edge of the cliff. I was carried away from rubbish, and washed and slept in a clean bed. I was loved. Each night, Dona Alzira kissed me before I went to bed, and she kissed my ears and my cheeks. Never forget. They didn't beat me in that home."

Maria smelled the ashes and added wood to the fire to fry the cornmeal for the family. She looked across the valley toward Amoreira. The drought killed grasses along the ancient landslide glowed in the sunlight. Where would José live? He kicked the knife away from the landlord. The Senhorio would send him to the stone quarry for punishment.

She heard him climbing down the ladder and she went in to help him. She touched his shoulder and kissed him on each cheek. He was stiff and frightened from his beating. She helped him sit at the table and fried him strips of cornmeal and piled them on his metal plate.

Silvino and João hurried down the ladder and relieved themselves outside the house. They splashed water from the trough on their faces, spitting water and laughing. Damp air from the sierra blew in the doorway when Maria lifted the coffee off the fire. No one spoke to the old man. He still sat at the table and stared at his coffee. João threw a wood chip at the rooster and tossed coffee at him to keep him outside the doorway.

A band of light covered the eastern horizon, low over the ocean. José sat with his back against the wall above the outdoor kitchen, away from his father. He waited for his coffee and cornmeal. The mug warmed his hands. He smiled at Maria. She comforted him in the night and she smiled at him. The coffee touched his lips and warmth swirled in his stomach and he drank deeply of the sweetened coffee. He took up the last piece of cornmeal. Luisa spent the night with them. She was older and wiser. She fooled with the cat, tossing a ball of embroidery thread. Julia cracked a joke about the affair between the widow and the Senhorio's guardsman. Mother packed cornmeal and dried chestnuts in braided banana-leaves. She gave José one to carry for his lunch. He didn't want to work in the hot sun. He hated carrying stone for the Senhorio.

The old man left the cottage and took his sickle off its hook. Silvino and João hurried out and went off to haul baskets of carrots to Pistola's cave.

"You better be on your way, José," said father "The Senhorio sends a spy."

"You'll visit Tia Nita," said Maria. Luisa crossed herself when she heard the witch's name.

Mother crossed herself.

"António, I'll bring your lunch to Fajã Velha," she said.

"I don't want you near the witch woman," said Father. "This family doesn't need her curse."

"The Senhorio curses you and your family. He's the evil one," said Maria.

"Shut your mouth. You talk about the Senhorio and he'll hear it. He's raised the taxes. One more tax and we won't be able to pay. He'll throw us off the land and we'll have to live in Amoreira. He has dineiro to buy us off the land. He owns the rights."

"I pray we leave his precious land," said José.

"And be forced to live in Amoreira?" said Father. "Be blown by the winter winds, dried out by the summer droughts with no levada water, and long walks to the village. The Senhorio would laugh and enjoy seeing us there. I'd be miserable and the Abreu would laugh..."

The old man looked at his daughters and wife. They prepared the lentils for the festival. He laughed at João and Silvino hauling baskets of carrots and swore.

"You're mad, the whole lot of you."

"You don't know what you're saying about our land, António," said Mother. "I lived in *Amoreira*. It's the end of the world, the pit of the village, the edge of nothing."

"This land's worth our sweat. The Senhorio knows it. Once he loses the spirit of the land, it's worth nothing," said Luisa.

Maria promised to meet José and her lips brushed his and he went off in the rain.

"You keep away from him," said Father.

"Let's work in daylight," said Mother. "The rain makes the land sweet."

"Come and work before you talk us to death," said Father.

Father said to Mother: "The best families on this coast hold lands, strips of forest on the heights and down to the sea. God provided the land for them. A family with land lives like the King."

"I'll go to Maçapez," José had said.

"You're obliged to work for the Senhorio. He owns the land and every thing living on it."

José shrugged and pulled his biretta down to keep the rain off his head. At the bridge, he waved to her. She fed the pig and the goats.

From the outlook he peered down into the valley, he saw the tiny cottage and the smoke from his mother's cook fire. He looked over his valley at the cave where he'd been born. He saw the cottages of Fernandes, Abreu, Gomes, Mendes, Gonçalves, Silva, Brazão, Henrique, names, like a litany from the Mass, the spirits of his land. The chapel hung on the edge of the cliff and close by it Tia Nita's hut, obscured by the rain, and by the time he climbed to the Kestrel Rock the cottage was flooded in sunlight.

CHAPTER IV

From the goats' cave beyond his house, José waved to Maria and with sliced cornmeal and a handful of dried chestnuts for lunch. He had stopped by the cave and fed his goats. He caressed and kissed their noses and threw them bunches of hay. He gazed into their almond-slit eyes. What were they thinking?

The Madeiran canary's morning song cheered him as he groped his way up the slope toward Kestrel Rock. The view of the valley spread out below him. Maçapez with its orange-tiled roofs and great porcas reflecting the daylight, Pistola's shop with dark green shutters in the middle of the group of small cottages. He wished to visit Talbot whose sloop was tied up beside the quay.

"The sun won't fry my brains. I'll be limber by the time I reach the Witch's field and I'll work in the shade."

Kestrel Rock gave him a view of the coastline of the island, the clouds had formed on the mountains at day break and sun brightened the patch where he had dug yesterday on the edge of the cliff. Early clouds had thinned away in the northeast and new clouds boiled up and over the summits of Pico Ruivo and Pico Arrieiro and the wind blew the clouds into great masses, snow white steeples.

He walked through the field of the four sisters, "the old crows." Cotilia, Juana, Beatris, and Elena Gomes chopped the soil in their dead father's abandoned garden. They stooped over, black kerchiefs covering their heads, talking rapidly. The youngest dressed in black but wore a white skirt, bright amidst her sisters' black sweaters, skirts and stockings "Enough!" he shouted, and laughed when they shook their fists at him.

The village priest called yesterday at the house and scolded his mother for missing Mass. She never missed church unless she was sick in bed. He hated the priests and bitterness rose into his mouth like the taste of a dead limpet. He spit a white gob into the prickly pear.

 Father Segundo had refused him lessons. In the autumn, José went with Maria. They'd walked for a long time, the sun beating down on the walkway his mother used to sweep for the "black beetles" and the thought scalded his heart. He wanted to write his name, but his heart burned when he as much as looked at the crucifix. Father Segundo had told him to do the work of his father.

He looked across the valley at the chapel with its cross, a weathered symbol of death and suffering. He crossed himself and looked for the kestrel in the sky above Fajã Velha.

When he reached the last source of water, he dipped his foot in the icy current for good luck. The valley below was shaped like a cone split in half its base drawn along the cliff-edge, three hundred meters above the sea.

High on the ridge above him, at the head of the valley, water rushed white from the mountain and fell to the sea. Tears blurred his view of the old woman gathering wild geranium leaves.

Bent over and gnarled and rough as oak bark, the weathered hag in her eighties examined a specimen of herb.

"You startled me," she said. "It makes heart trouble and kills the spirit. It's a lovely morning, urchin."

"Good morning, Tia Nita. You rise early." He shifted his eyes and averted hers by gazing into the basket at her herbs.

"What brings you here?"

"It's punishment. I'm to haul stone for the Senhorio *'s* wall along the high levada."

"He's mad. It's a waste of time. The wall makes him no *dineiro*," she said.

"A stranger landed his sloop at the *cais*."

"Yes, my nephew. I got word. You left the land. Don't touch my bundles. I'll cover them myself."

"I'll haul stone today and return to the home land tomorrow."

"There's nothing here for you. You're the youngest. There's no living."

"I worked with Henrique in the mountains and with Pistola in his shop. Father took me back. The Priest said no school."

"I love the old religion," she said. "That chapel doesn't belong here." She pointed to the white square-shaped, orange-tiled roof way down in the valley on the edge of the cliff, the size of a domino.

"Who built it?"

"I've told you before, Beatris wife of the first António from Arco da Calheta. The King took back the lands of Gonçalves Zarco and gave this valley to the Abreu."

"The Senhorio rules it," he said.

"He robbed your family and gave nothing back. He's from the pig's tail. He's a bad Jew."

"We don't practice the old religion. The priest forbids it," he said.

"I whisper the Old Spirit," she said. She hummed over the herbs and dropped them into her basket.

"God's blessing, Auntie," he said.

The sea spread out, a great desert with winds moving over its surface, sunlight reflecting off its complexion and painting it rainbow colors. The wind blew from the heights, purple currents moved through silver clouds and across the water hundreds of meters below him.

A rabbit bounded through the prickly pear. He waved to the Fernandes brothers working in their sun burnt berry patch. They saw him talking with the old Aunt.

The Priest forbade her to chant over the water yet she chanted and threw branches into the river.

José hunched his shoulders and pushed himself against the cliff and felt the bruises of his beating, a dull pain across his kidneys. The sun was higher and he lifted a rock and carried it toward the wall. The sheep grazing-by ran off and up the slope above the *levada*. The noon-day sun baked the slopes. He worked his portion before noon. He sited along the foundation course and set flat stones along it. He saved the square ones for the next course. The crosspieces fit along the six meters of new wall and helped him tie the outside with the center.

He groaned as he lifted a large rock. He picked narrow ones that were light and rolled them end for end. He filled a sack with small pieces of rock and "chinked" the exterior along the face. The sun hurt his eyes and its reflection on the sea blinded him when he squinted at the fishing boats moored off the rock spire. The fishermen from Ribeira Brava moored their boats in the sea and returned home to the shore in the master boat.

He crawled into the shade to avoid the sun at its zenith blanketing the valley in heat. He knelt beside the water and making his hands into a cup scooped up a drink. He listened to the song of a rock sparrow. No other sound touched his ear. He tossed a few pebbles into the growth below the stream. He wished to be in Maçapez at lunch with cousins and talking with the Englishman. Someone moved in the brush.

"Stop throwing rocks," said João.

"You're throwing rocks," he said and threw a handful.

"Stone-thrower, stop your barrage."

"Carrot-hauler, appear before you disappear," he said.

João stuck his head above the mimosa and walked up the slope, sweat dripped down his face. He smiled and set his lunch sack down.

"We finished loading carrots. I climbed into the smuggler's cave and looked for your knife. You'll need it when the Senhorio sends his men for you."

"Father's as narrow-minded as the rest of his family."

"You anger him and expect leniency! That's absurd."

"You left the land, are you spying for the Senhorio?"

"News from the pebbled beach, Maria's going to marry Joachim. He's asked Father for her hand."

"You're joking." He threw another rock into the Mimosa trees.

"We'll have more work. She'll tell you soon enough. She's engaged and won't have time for us." said João.

"She can't marry. We need her in the gardens."

"She wants to marry in August."

He swung hard and knocked him down.

"Don't blame me for it," said Joáo.

He wrestled him, until exhausted by the heat he stopped and sat up.

"Father's angry."

"I don't care. He farms land he'll never own. He lives without title. The Senhorio takes away the fruits of the harvest."

He thought about his family. Luisa married and living in *Calçada*, returning home like last night, on mother's plea. Julia courted by Manuel Silva, though he hadn't asked for her hand, and Maria leaving home. Three left to work the gardens and feed the animals. Henrique lived alone in the mountains.

"How do you like the bone yard?" said João.

"You know the gossip. How they chased and cornered Tia Nita and stoned her to death. She died and the evil eye returned her to life."

"You don't like hard labor so crawl down there and obey the Senhorio. Our duty is to the land."

"Bullshit! Hundreds of men worked these *levada* walls. Many never finished the canal and didn't see water flowing into the valley. Sending men to die is the Senhorio's vainglory."

"Don't talk like that, brother. He'll hear it. I don't want to fight. You're wrong to fight. They're talking about locking you up and asking ransom for the sailor."

"The Senhorio is mad. Pistola invited *senhor* Talbot. The landlord took it as an insult." said José.

"Blackeye and Twenty-Seven told on you and asked Silvino to bring you in."

"The Abreu held captives for ransom in the old days and didn't get wealth or fame. The Senhorio has their pride."

"The stranger has friends in Funchal. The Senhorio can hold him until his family buys him back."

"That's madness. The stranger's British. They're favored by the King. Will the Senhorio visit Maçapez?"

"This evening they'll meet at the schoolhouse. They'll grab the stranger at dinnertime and take him back to the *Senhorio's quinta*."

"Warn Pistola." He said.

João shook his head from side to side.

"I'll go myself."

"You're bound to work," said João.

"I'm free as the kestrel." The terrain down the mountain and along the ridge had many points for spies to observe him. He'd be whipped for leaving the land. He must tell Pistola about the raid.

"I'll report you," said João. "You belong to us."

"João, warn Pistola. You've no excuse. They won't miss you. I'm duty-bound."

"I'm off to cut hay for the goats. Tia Nita saw me climbing here. She'll tell the women."

He had a sour cherry taste in his mouth. Henrique lived alone. Silvino was married with a family. The thought of no family brought tears. He'd work for his parents when they were old and couldn't pay the taxes. He'd never own land. João refused to fight.

"Pistola needs to know about the ransom," he said.

João shook him by the shoulder. "You ran down to the pebbled beach."

"I saw the sail on the horizon. It was coming to Madeira."

"You've told me, you live here in this valley and work these fields. You kicked the knife away from the Senhorio. You owe Pistola nothing."

"This is a chance for good luck."

"You're trying to show you're as great as the *Senhorio*." said João.

"Pistola once spoke with the Priest and he will again. I'll go to school like Luisa and Julia and Maria."

João laughed and slapped his thigh. "You insulted the *Senhorio*. You embarrassed him before a stranger."

He stood close, his biretta touching João's, nodding his head like a hoopoe. The tassel of the biretta danced like the head of a pheasant.

"You pushed me first that day on the mountain," said João.

João never forgot their fistfight. He surprised him with his first swing. They'd been carrying wood from the mountain. Maria threw her bundle on the ground and refused to carry it. She fell weeping and wouldn't stand.

He begged João to stop hitting her. When he continued, he jumped on him. They rolled over and over in the broken lava and rested more from exhaustion than wanting to stop fighting. They touched the cuts on their arms, breathed heavily and swore at one another. João shook his fist warning him that if he were ever jumped again, he'd slit his throat.

They eyed each other over the remains of their lunch. João had come to taunt him with the news of Maria's betrothal.

"Every peasant from here to Maçapez will see you going down there. The Senhorio will hear," said João.

"It's late. "When the sun hits the ridges of Ribeira Brava, I'll be free to leave," he said.

They scooped water from the *levada* and drank. Without a word João moved down into the thicket and disappeared, waves of heat dancing in the air. The sun shone into the valley. The verdure grew pale under its glare, the midday turning them pale and grey on the northwest ridges.

I'd cut my feet for honor. The sun-heated rocks burned his hands and the heated stones weighed more than when he was fresh in the morning. The heat filled them and added more weight. He cleared a space twenty-nine paces square.

Pistola worked well with folks. He wished to work with him. He worked alone as his father taught him to with patience. He grasped a great rock and heaved it into the air and it broke into bits when it hit the ledge. Pieces fell into the water flakes of grout spinning downstream. The brook trout swam away, black arrows in the current.

He took his *sesta* in the shade behind a great rock in the middle of Tia Nita's field. The sun moved down the sky and shadows grew on the rocks. When he opened his eyes he was in heaven. Far down on the sea he saw dark spider-sized creatures loading boats at the quay. The green canary sang its evening song along the edge of the water storage tank. He hurried toward Maçapez.

Blackeye surprised José. He checked trees in the timber on the slope. As he came around the slope José saw the spy. Blackeye checked to make sure the *Senhorio* was not cheated on the timber tax.

"Going to the pebbled beach?" he said.

José gave Blackeye the finger.

José ran down through the mimosa and eucalyptus trees. He must warn Talbot that the *Senhorio* planned to kidnap him.

CHAPTER V

The deepening twilight surrounded José. Darkness concealed the holes and sinks in the pathway from the heights down into the valley. He ran until his side hurt and he sucked air in great draughts to relieve the pain. The stiff jacket he wore aggravated his back where the wounds from his beating were fresh. He closed his eyes and the chain snaked through the air and he smelled his own blood. Though tired from hauling stone that day to satisfy his punishment, he didn't rest long and walked on to arrive at Maçapez before Pistola closed shop.

In Amoreira he passed the poor cottages, their willow thatch weather beaten and worn. He followed along the *levada* path, sections washed away by heavy rains. The caved-in wall hadn't been repaired and rock-slides crossed the way. He climbed over them and hurried on.

Twenty-Seven the card-player and confidant of the *Senhorio* leaned over the wall by the Fernandes garden.

"What're you doing in Amoreira?"

Surprised, José said, "I'm going to see Little Arturo, Senhor." He couldn't see the man's eyes in the gloom. Twenty-Seven was a member of the kidnapping gang. Had the gang been to grab Talbot?

"Who sent you?"

"I send myself. I'm free," José said.

"You were free on the pebbled beach and insulted the Senhorio," said Twenty-seven.

The *Senhorio* owned his men on authority granted landowners in the 15th century by the King. The Senhorio's men didn't own José.

"I don't want to see your face around here," said Twenty-seven.

At the fountain near Maçapez, he met Little Arturo of the Square. He embraced him and slapped him on the back.

"Comrade how goes the battle?" said Arturo.

"So-so. What do you hear in Maçapez? Have you seen the Englishman?" he said.

"I heard you saved his life."

"It was trouble," he said. "You saw him?"

"At noon, a few drunks sat around Pistola's *taberna*. I carried poles to make a new trellis in my grandfather's vineyard--too many. Epah! The sun was hot as Gehenna."

"I felt the sun. The *Senhorio* ordered me to work in the old Aunt's field. His men plan to grab the Englishman tonight. I'll tell Pistola."

He lowered his voice and whispered into Arturo's ear. Arturo whistled. "You don't say, those bastards!"

Arturo punched and pushed him, swearing and cursing the *Senhorio*. Their voices echoed along the *levada*.

"We'll speak to Talbot," said Arturo.

"More important to Pistola," he said.

"I saw Talbot at dinner. The *Senhorio's* men sat around played cards."

Arturo led the way into the square and over to the *taberna* that Pistola ran as part of his general store. He kicked the soft dust with his bare feet. He dropped his soccer ball and worked his way around the corner by Pistola's gate. The locals ate dinner, candles lighted on the tables. Three men sat at the side tables and played cards. One slammed down his cards to dramatize each hand of *dead man,* his favorite card game." The *Senhorio's* men were there to kidnap Talbot.

Garth Talbot sat alone with a plate of bread, tuna salad, and wine. The salad sat on the blue plate with cheese like a chunk of ice on green lettuce. The fresh tuna was pickled in olive oil, pepper, vinegar and garlic.

He smelled garlic. He rubbed his hands together and smoothed them along his trousers. Instead of tired and beaten, Talbot felt rested and smiled at the men who listened for the signal to take him.

Arturo led him up the steps and bowed to Talbot and retreated to the street.

José waited to be recognized. He stood with his biretta in his hand looking down at the Talbot sitting at the dinner table as he did when listening to the *Senhorio*.

Talbot nodded and chewed a mouthful of fish. He raised his eyes and smiled.

"It's you, the lad from the pebbled beach. I thought I'd never meet you again. I'm glad to see you."

Talbot's Portuguese words were odd sounds.

"I worked carrying stone for the *Senhorio*. I ran here, *O Senhor*." His words bubbled out in Madeiran. José knew the stranger wouldn't hear some words. He lapsed into the sing-song child-like lilt he heard spoken in Funchal."

"Thank you for kicking the knife. I won't forget it."

"Sir, the Senhorio comes to take you to his *quinta* and your family must pay him *dineiro* to get you back." Talbot frowned.

Talbot thanked him and forked another piece of tuna onto a piece of bread and shoved a piece of tuna into his mouth and offered José bread and fish.

José shook his head. He saw no alarm in the man's eyes.

Talbot cleared his throat and said, "Please tell Pistola. I don't understand your customs. I'm used to Funchal. Tell him what you said."

"Do you need a boy to work for you, sir?" he said.

"Sorry. I'm sailing for home in a month. Mother has many hands on her *quinta*."

José nodded and smiled. He leaned on one leg and waited for Talbot to dismiss him. Talbot continued eating. Finally, he said, "Speak with Pistola."

The shop closed and women left their goods cradled in their arms and heads covered with shawls. Pistola came out and Talbot beckoned him to his table in the *taberna*, but he stopped to speak with Arturo and José.

"Thank you for the tip, José. Now be off before the *Senhorio's* men catch you in Maçapez. Go back home and feed your goats," Pistola said.

"We want to fight the bastards," said Little Arturo, like he was six feet tall, strutted up to Pistola.

"I can handle these rogues. Off with you and let me talk with Senhor Talbot."

Pistola waddled up the steps to the bar and asked for his usual red wine. He drank it down without a glance at the card players. Talbot waved to the shopkeeper. Pistola joined Talbot at his table and Mariazinha brought their dinner, boiled potatoes, fried rice, *pargo*, sea bream, and cabbage.

Blackeye and Twenty-Seven walked in to the *taberna*.

José nudged Arturo. Pistola's white shirt shone brightly. The drunkards wore field clothes, faded shirts, patched and re-patched, worn trousers, and sang verses about the old whore. Egilio wore his *festa* hat and Jacinto his straw boater from his trip to the Azores.

Blackeye and Twenty-Seven ordered *vinho verde* and sat at the table in the corner where Pistola couldn't see them. They eyed Talbot and covered their lips when they spoke. Blackeye rubbed his palms. He shifted his feet on the paving stones as if to stand up and run.

José nodded to Little Arturo and they moved away into the shadows. They looked up the lane for the *Senhorio*.

"Where's the bastard?" said Little Arturo.

"He promised to meet them after dinner."

Singing and card-playing continued--arguments over feats of lifting, laughter and swearing. Rumor of the kidnapping traveled fast. Twenty-

Seven pulled at his Adam's apple. He stared as Pistola, drank his wine in quick sips and tapped the table with his index finger.

Pistola strolled to the bar. "I'll have another *tinto,* red."

"You never lifted two sacks of flour off the deck in your life," said Manuel, Pistola's wait-man, to Jacinto who leaned over the bar.

"Christ, you work in the *taberna.* You weren't there. I used all my strength and lifted them--carried them off the boat," said Jacinto.

"I'm tired of it," said Blackeye. "Get on to a new one." The men at the bar turned around and watched Jacinto.

From the darkness of the trees, Arturo and José saw the *Senhorio's* men. Tia Nita walked up behind José and pinched his arm. She cackled. He jumped and she shook her finger at him. She went over to the patio and walked up to Pistola. "Where's my sack of flour?"

"On the porch where I promised it," said Pistola. "We have Jacinto. He can lift your sack and carry it back home single handedly."

Blackeye sneered at Jacinto and grumbled.

"Once in awhile, a man lifts more than he will during the rest of his life," Jacinto said.

"You're tired of telling the story so why not go and lift the sack for the witch," said Blackeye.

"I'm thirsty and nothing to drink."

"Have one on me. I need quiet."

Twenty-Seven tossed a coin and it landed on the bar top, rolled in a circle and fell. Jacinto slid his hand over it.

"Two glasses of white," he said. He pushed the coin and it fell onto the floor clinking on the tile. The bar man poured two glasses of white wine paying no heed to the coin lying on the tiles.

Pistola whispered to Manuel. He slipped out through the curtain and into the alleyway beside the shop. In half a minute, he appeared with a dusty wine bottle and a towel. He wiped off the old bottle.

"Pick up the coin," said Blackeye.

"Please come home now and eat, Jacinto," said his wife from the street.

Blackeye was angry.

His wife's voice startled Jacinto. He raised his arm to drink the second wine.

"Pick up the coin your self," he said. "I'm going home."

"Lucky for us and better for you," said Twenty-Seven.

Jacinto burst into song, the one about the house in the tree, the beautiful giant chestnut growing on the *achada* of Campanário

"Where in hell is the Senhorio on this beautiful evening?" said Blackeye. He tossed discarded wine corks against the bottle and off the table.

Twenty-Seven shook his head and followed each move in the card game. He looked out into the street and at the old kitchen clock in the shop.

"You're welcome to drink as late as you wish," said Pistola. "You're my guests. I want you happy." He saw the *Senhorio's* retainers lounging on the steps. Jacinto stopped singing and pointed to a tall man that walked into the *taberna* and joined the card players. The *Senhorio* had arrived.

"Where's Talbot?" he said.

"We're friends, here." said Pistola.

Talbot's seat by Pistola was empty.

Blackeye jumped from his chair and ran into the street to find Talbot.

He stood very near Arturo and José. Little Arturo shrugged. When had Talbot left the table?

The men on the steps swore and searched the street and alley. "He sat with Pistola while we played cards," one said.

"I didn't see him move," said Jacinto.

"You were to keep an eye on him." said Twenty-Seven.

Pistola wiped his mustache with his napkin. He ordered another wine. "May I be of service to you, gentlemen," he said.

The *Senhorio* walked over to Pistola. "I came to visit your guest Talbot. I wanted to hear about his lands and winery in Funchal."

"With these men?" said Pistola.

"They heard about that day on the beach and wanted to meet him."

"They can see him tomorrow."

"Talbot should honor us with his presence."

"Sorry Gentlemen. He went to bed. I'm sorry you walked here for nothing. The bar is open and I'll buy you a wine. Another night," said Pistola. "Senhor Talbot has a bruised arm, fatigued from his journey and needed rest." Pistola signaled the barman to fill their glasses.

"Talbot drank at your table only minutes ago," said the *Senhorio.*

"How can you be sure? You weren't here."

"What do you say, Blackeye?"

"Yes sir."

The men waited for Pistola to answer when Talbot pushed through the beaded curtain.

"It's him," said Twenty-Seven, grabbing Talbot by the arm. Talbot shook off Twenty-Seven's grasp.

"You asked for me, I believe," Talbot said.

Pistola had sent Manuel, his wait-man, to warn Talbot and he smiled and offered wine to the men.

"I'm sorry about our meeting on the beach," said the *Senhorio.*

"It was nothing. I'm a stranger in Campanário. I didn't know you were the *Senhorio,*" said Talbot.

"It would be an honor to buy you a drink. Shall we?" Both men walked up to the bar. The other men crowded around the little bar.

José and Little Arturo listened to the chatter and the crickets singing and the sound of men's feet moving in the darkness

Blackeye and Twenty-Seven sat by Talbot's side, laughing and pushing, and moved him away from the bar. A circle of men slipped around the three and swept them off the patio and down the steps. Before they reached the street, Pistola jumped behind the bar and pulled out his shotgun. He lived up to his name. Few remembered how Pistola earned it. It involved a pistol and courage like a dream in the morning with sunlight on the cliff overlooking the sea. He saved his father's shop from three robbers some time during 1881.

"Wait! There's a mistake," said the *Senhorio.* He smiled and walked back toward the bar. The gun pointed at his chest. "We're excited. Have a good time. Sorry, my friend. We're going for a walk."

"Unhand him. You can't make Talbot your guest."

Twenty-Seven shook his head and released Talbot's arm and blinked. He backed away from the *Senhorio.*

The Senhorio spoke to Talbot, "I hope one day, you'll visit me in the Valley of the Melons, Senhor."

Talbot nodded and returned to his wine. Pistola lowered his gun. Manuel served drinks and the men calmed down and played cards, loud and profane.

"You need hospitality," said Pistola.

"Guns don't make friends," Talbot said.

"Neither does ransom," said Manuel the wait-man.

"It made money in the old days," said the *Senhorio.*

"We live in an age of telegraph and steamships. New ways are coming. Your people live in bondage, they're slaves. You may regret it," said Pistola.

Tia Nita listened at the entrance by the patio. She stared at Talbot's blue eyes.

"It's late for me, O Senhor. I'm tired from a long day," said Talbot. His Portuguese faltered.

"I'll show you to your bed. "Goodnight, gentlemen. See you tomorrow."

"You'll see me," said the *Senhorio*. He winked at his men and drank off his wine. He shook his fist in the air. Tia Nita spit on the cobbles.

The men playing cards were angry. They'd wanted a kidnapping or a fight. The old aunt's grunt surprised José and he ran over to the porch and lifted her sack. He carried it on his shoulder to her stone cottage on the cliff. His wounded back hurt worse and he had missed supper at home. She handed him a few dried chestnuts. She blessed him. On his way to *Fajã Velha*, he stopped at the cave on the ridge above his family's cottage and fed his goats and hugged them and arrived home in darkness.

CHAPTER VI

While walking in the darkness of the valley under the stars, José had planned his journey to join Henrique in the mountains. He had slipped into his house and climbed up into the loft where Maria slept. He whispered in her ear. She mumbled. He kissed her cheek. In the morning before light, he tiptoed down the ladder with his biretta and burlap cape. He'd be safe on the heights, away from father and the *Senhorio* but sadly be far away from mother, Maria, and Pistola. He'd avoid beatings and punishments and be free to wander in the mountains.

He took his bearing from the notch in the mountains, black silhouettes against the northern sky. The night wind blew his sack and he lost balance and caught himself. Where was the path in the pines that led to Henrique's hut? The dampness on his burlap chilled his shoulders. The stars faded in the dawn and he reached the summit.

He searched for the hut. Henrique built it the first time he ran away when he was twelve. He shunned women and never married content to wander the highlands of Madeira.   Villagers called him *little guy*. with affection, *dwarf*. Henrique was born in the goats' cave before father built the cottage. The bark of pines was rough to José's touch as he groped along the path. Where were the thatched hut and its stone chimney?

A cigarette glowed, a tiny sun in darkness. Henrique called out from the doorway where he smoked. The sun rose and he told Henrique of the *Senhorio*.

"Have you eaten?" said Henrique

"No, Senhor."

"There is *milho, bacalhau, laranjas*, corn meal mush, salt cod, oranges."

He laid a pine knot on the embers and held the old black pot over the fire and boiled codfish and corn-meal. He drank wine from the goatskin hanging by the door. The fish softened and the meal thickened. He poured his breakfast onto a plate.

"So, you've run away," said Henrique.

"I hate the *Senhorio*. He taxes more than we can pay. He enslaves us."

"Living in that valley, you need patience."

"I can't live there."

"He'll drive the folk away," said Henrique.

"It's better to die."

36

"And never live! Work for the family. Make life for them. Your running away makes them poorer."

He pled with Henrique to hide him. He showed off his muscles from working in Tia Nita's field.

"The land eats me up. I want to live in the mountains. The *Senhorio* argued with Pistola and wanted to be lord and host to Talbot."

"The *Senhorio*'s mad. King Carlos will send soldiers to free the land for the people of Campanário."

"Soon, the soldiers come for recruits and the young men hide," said José.

Henrique nodded and dozed. "This Englishman sailor will leave and you'll never see him again. You have to live with the *Senhorio*."

"I want to sail to Funchal and work on his mother's *quinta*."

Henrique coughed and spit. "You have goats and gardens. You can't leave. If the Senhorio discovers you are in the mountains he will send men and make life hell for me and you and the shepherds. Work the land and live."

"There's nothing to eat. I'm the youngest and no land will ever be mine. I've no house, no family, and no land."

"Patience, your word is your bond. Pistola gave me the land for this hut. He'll help you. He loves Campanário."

"Father beats me. When I leave, he'll worry me no more," said José.

"Ah! You belong to the land."

"No, I belong to the wild. I'm *francelho*, the kestrel, hovering over the cliffs."

You talk nonsense. You're a *francelho preto*, a black kestrel."

"I'll find Talbot and follow him."

"Dream of land, never the sea," said Henrique.

"Even seeing the Senhorio is evil."

"You'll grow older and forget the stupidity." The morning wind stirred. Henrique pulled his tunic around his shoulders.

"I'll run. The Senhorio duped our Grandmother for a few *real*. He lusted for the land and stole our birthright."

"Stay awhile. You can work," said Henrique.

"You've changed your mind!"

"I'm cutting and hauling timber to the mill in Quinta Grande. It's a job for one man on the mountain. You can help me, bright rooster."

"I can herd sheep with the old man of the *serra*."

"You belong in the family, little one. Work here a little and go back."

37

"You'll let me work but not let me stay!"

"I need a woman to make soup and bread, to dry chestnuts and split firewood," Henrique said.

"We know you and women. We have village girls but they want marriage. You don't wish to marry. Maria is going to marry Joachim Silva. Our sisters want us brothers working the gardens."

"They love you," Henrique said.

José felt tears and he made no sound so that Henrique wouldn't at him.

"I want to read books," he said. "Father Segundo refused me. He taught my Aunts not my Uncles. Tia Nita reads the Bible, and the Priests hate her for talking to God. She tells stories of the old religion when we believed in the Hebrew prophets.

Henrique told him to forget gossip and going to school. He knew that Aunt Eulalia helped the *Senhorio* read the papers when he stole their birthright. "Go to Funchal and you can stay with the family of old João Abreu by walking up the Caminho de Santo António."

Henrique rolled out the blankets. The wind died before first light and the only sound was the bells of Saint Blaise.

"You might study God," said Henrique.

"Impossible," said José. "I can't read and write."

"Father Segundo would let you join the church and become a black beetle. You'd be a big man in a *Minho* village in ten years."

"I don't want to be a priest. I would not be free."

"They get the first grapes and the best harvest of the sugar cane. The people bring trout from Ribeira Frio, and *Uveira da Serra*, blueberries, from the heights and give them to the priest."

He pointed southwest where the Abreu were granted estates at Calheta in 1497.

"The women complain to the priest every day. I don't want that," said José.

"You could ape the Senhorio. He won't live forever. One of these days someone will put a knife in his back."

"I can't go to him."

Henrique nodded. "I've spent my life outwitting that fox. I built this hut with my own hands. I paid for the privilege with honest labor."

"You live without family and friends and festivals."

"I miss them. That's the fee."

"I'll live here and we'll fight the bastard," said José.

"I can't change the valley. We suffer in life, like it or not. I pray I die on the heights and not as the prey of the Senhorio. Promise, I won't be trussed up like a turkey and spit on by villagers."

"I promise," said José. "Life here is freer and this hideout a place to live and fight the Senhorio."

"It's lonely on foggy days and during cold and windy winters."

The last thing Henrique said before they went to sleep was, "The church is a better life for you than wandering the mountains. In the Order, you forget land, family and fief. I want you to stay in the valley."

"I'll go to Mass and seek out Father Segundo."

José settled down in his rough blankets and dreamed of church. The divine light filtered across his eyes and when he opened them he saw faint breaks in the eastern sky and Henrique moving through the door-way. He closed his eyes and later the loss of circulation in his arm under the pillow awoke him.

Two bananas in the cupboard were ripe. He sat on the doorstep and peeled them, savoring their flavor. Across the ledge, he kneeled at the spring and drank water with the flavor of pine-needles. Where was Henrique?

The bells of the sheep sounded on the steep. He searched the slope where they gathered chestnuts in autumn. As the light grew he hoped to spy Henrique. No sound. No movement.

He gathered chips and with flint and steel kindled the fire. He boiled coffee and drank two cups. He ate slices of cornmeal and wiped his hands on his trousers. He hiked along the high *levada,* stream, and listened for the sound of his brother's axe.

He peered down through the plantation of Canary Island pine. He felt relaxed in the warmth of the sun and worked his way up the long ridge, keeping his eyes peeled for Henrique. Madeiran pigeons flew up, and he perked up his ears. He didn't move. The lizards crawled across the rocks and hid. The *Senhorio* would send Blackeye and Twenty-seven. The sun painted the trees with bright patches of pink and yellow. He listened for the song of the Madeiran pigeon.

One shepherd stood alone with his flock on the surrounding mountainside and signaled his companion, a mile away with a whistle. The wild call of the kestrel awakened the countryside. Ahead, the mountain pass loomed bright in the early morning light.

The land was bare and grasses and flowers grew in sheltered spots. The prevailing wind tore at his biretta as he reached the pass. Dusty clouds blew up along the path and he covered his lips. He saw the desolate land without water and cultivation. Shepherds devoted their lives to keeping sheep on this sparse grass. It was hopeless to track Henrique.

A high whistle pierced the morning air. A mountain man yelled. A sheep dog barked until he neared his shepherd.

He was Old Carmo, a short man with dark eyes, tanned face, with white lines where the sunlight missed the flesh around the mouth and whiskers.

"What are you doing in Hell?" said the shepherd.

"I'm looking for the dwarf."

The man closed his eyes. He leaned on his staff and listened to the sheep. He shook his head. He kneeled down and patted the dog.

"Where is he?" said José.

Carmo shrugged and reached into his pouch and flipped out a cigarette paper, poured fine tobacco into it and ran his tongue along the edge of the paper. His Lucifer flamed up and brightened his face when he lit the fag. He cleared his throat and spit out a gob of mucus.

"He's mysterious that one. I heard you've got a wall-building job forever."

"The Senhorio has us rebels work on his *levada* wall," said José.

"I heard the sound of an axe toward Ribeira Funda a couple of hours ago. I haven't laid eyes on my old friend, in two moons."

"Could I help with the sheep, O Senhor?"

"On misty autumn mornings, I need a boy. I've no money, no food to give. You've plenty of work in the valley, no!"

"I want to live with the mountain men. Henrique won't have me."

"Vincent Nobrega at the "Mouth of Hell, " or his man Gold Tooth, they have *Reis*, and they know the shepherds beyond Serra D'Agua and on the great plateau, Paúl da Serra."

"Thank you, Senhor. Where will I look?"

"Above *Boca do Inferno*, the mouth of Hell, in Jardim da Serra. You'll return home once you work with sheep. We walk and some nights through blinding snows cover our huts." He laughed and spit. "The sun dries out our brains and we live with bronchitis."

"You're free," said José. "You follow the sun and the moon and the stars."

"Free to die in the desert," said the old man. "We move the sheep or they eat all the grasses. The sheep love the places where the wind blows free and no hut is nearby to warm a man."

"I'm ready to fly like a kestrel," said José.

The dog wagged his tail. The man whistled and the dog trotted ahead of him. "I wish you good-by José and good luck."

"I'll see you."

He hunted the ridges and followed the sounds that carried far in the mountain air, and no Henrique. The sun blistered his lips and he rested in the shadow of the rocks. The hours dragged by and he heard no rustle of lizards. He dreamed of cabbage soup and women gossiping over embroidery. He found a spring with water flat and cold. His hands burned from the sun and abrasions from rock-carrying. The tips of his fingers were thin and smooth and the heat hurt them as if God burned the rocks for the hands of the stonemason.

The light and heat of the day danced in his brain, and he tossed in his blankets back at the hut. Sunlight washed over him and fire seared his skin. He wanted his brother Henrique. Without him he'd climb down to the village. Talbot was the man to help him. He'd look for him at Pistol's. In his sleep, he saw hounds and armed men and a cave. He slept alone amidst wild sounds in the darkness of the mountain.

CHAPTER VII

José woke early and hiked into the valley. Below in the square, Duarte Capelinha, waved at him. "I heard four people died in the village."

"Jaime stumbled around with a bad headache. He was thirsty and had pains in his arms and legs. He took to his bed and mumbled most of the night," Duarte said.

"Did he have red spots on his face?"

"Yes, and he had hiccoughs and a swollen belly."

"It was typhoid fever like with the other deaths."

José hurried down to Duarte and took hold of one of the two jugs the youth carried. "Is this water from the well?" he said.

"No, I carry water from the high levada. In our family only my mother drinks the village water. She drank it since she was a baby," Duarte said.

"She is ignorant. The water from that well will give her the fever."

José shook his head and turned toward the square and the approaching band from the Valley of the Melons.

The Senhorio stomped along the flowered path from his *quinta* to the village, heels hitting the basalt paving stones, buttocks jouncing, swearing.

The Senhorio said to José, "Scum of the lizard! Knife kicker, you are a pain in the ass."

José laughed at him and refused to pay his respect.

Duarte said, "O Senhor, the mother of Twenty-Seven is dead."

"I'll meet Father Segundo this evening to make arrangements for her service. Don't stare at me. It's Sabbath but we will cut the sugar cane today." He shook his fist at José.

Duarte said, "José meant no harm, Senhor."

José pulled off his biretta, bowed deeply, and asked for the Senhorio's blessing.

Duarte grinned at José and taking the cue from his fawning manner made a deep curtsey.

José bowed his head and nodded.

"You worked the stone and ran off!" said the *Senhorio*.

"To visit my brother Henrique," he said.

The Senhorio cursed. "The small guy, the wandering crow, the mountain dwarf, he'll burn in Hell."

"Henrique sends good wishes for the Senhorio's health."

"Yes, and Talbot sends me greetings and best wishes from Maçapez, eh!" said the *Senhorio*.

"I've not laid eyes on Talbot since dinner at the *taberna*," José said.

"He stays with Pistola and refuses my invitation to *Ribeira Melões*. My table is fit for a King."

"The village deaths are strange," José said.

"It's the spell of Tia Nita. She's a curse on the village. I'll lock her up and take her cottage."

The Senhorio glared at him.

"Senhor Talbot sent for the doctor in Funchal," said Duarte.

"You tell Pistola to send Talbot and the doctor to me. We'll talk about the deaths."

"I saw Talbot the Englishman's sloop at sea and went to the pebbled beach," José said.

"You left my land without permission."

"I worked my patch and saw the beautiful boat," he said.

The Senhorio waved his hand brushing José's words off like flies.

"What does the Senhorio wish for?"

José bowed over his biretta and gazed at the metallic eyes.

"You'll haul stone every time you leave the land without my permission." The Senhorio brandished his cane dismissing them and turned toward his estate.

The Senhorio's maid sat on the steps in her Sunday finery, red and white skirt, embroidered white blouse, white on white, and a vermilion sweater. She asked his blessing. He gave it and hugged her slim waist and touched her cheek.

"Elena! My pretty one, give me a kiss." She ran away to Dona Margarita.

On his terrace, the Senhorio laughed and clapped his hands. The houseman brought passion fruit cordial, goat's cheese and fresh bread, baked by Maria while the others attended Mass. Without ceremony, he stuffed bread into his mouth and drank off a glass of cordial.

He called for Maria. She presented herself and kissed his hand. The sunlight illuminated her blouse and figure.

"I heard you're going to marry Joachim. Father Segundo and I are pleased. I have a privilege as Morgado, before you marry this gentleman."

Maria looked away and said, "Senhor, the custom is from olden times and seldom practiced."

"I've watched you grow up. Since you were a child, I loved you, the way God loves the Virgin. I'd not force you to love me. I do have a right."

"Let me be, Senhor."

"It's for my favor. I've given reis to the Church. I arranged your dowry with Silva."

"It's no favor! I belong to the man I marry. You'll never be that man."

"Remember your family and custom. I'm Morgado. I've the right to spend one night with you, nothing more."

She stepped away from him, keeping calm, her mind alert, her feelings cold. He'd spoken with no passion.

He called for wine. She waved to the houseman and while he poured a glass, she skipped into the kitchen and out the door and avoided Dona Margarita.

She ran through the potato vines and the sugar cane along the levada. The breeze dried her tears.

He jokes about me and wants to sleep with me. I'll speak to Father Segundo. In the cave, she hugged the goats. Their warm bodies soothed her. She went into the house and in the dark bed she and mother cried together.

José and João brought home pargo, sea-bream. Mother and Julia boiled potatoes and broccoli, set out cabbage soup. José broiled the fish. João asked father's blessing and made the sign of the cross.

Mother kissed them with tears in her eyes. She touched his ear with her soft chin. She pointed at the hot soup and went back into the kitchen and sat by the oven.

The room flooded with light from the oil lamp and the smell of the laurel nut oil perfumed the air. Maria smiled and kissed him when she sat down to the table. He burned his tongue and asked for water. Maria gave him the pewter dipper-full. Father sucked his soup and his jaws snapped as he

chewed bread and swallowing sounds rose in his throat. With his fork, he stabbed slices of tomato and pepper, sprinkled with salt and olive oil.

"You disappeared for three days. You worked the stone in the witch's field and never returned that night."

"I went to Henrique," said José.

"You saw him?"

Father seldom spoke Henrique's name. He had vowed never to speak to him. Henrique and Father nodded when they met and made bargains together. Father never forgave him for leaving the land.

Father had asked for news about Henrique in the fall of the year and had sent him an invitation to the Festival of Saint Blaise in February. He made good on timber and firewood deals with Henrique but insisted his son obey the Senhorio and return to work on the land.

"Henrique cuts trees every day, even Sunday. He eats *bacalhau.* Life is good for him," said José.

"He's living without a family, a church, a wine shop. He's lived alone so long he can't count years. I knew the year he ran away. I've forgotten."

"He's your son, remember your eldest," said Mother.

"He's a stranger, living alone, no church, drinking no wine. I forgot him. He's a mystery."

José hunched over his plate toying with a piece of fish. He lifted it and set it in the bowl and lifted it and didn't put it into his mouth. He listened to Father. He didn't like father's Henrique. His penalty from the *Senhorio* was over and he was home.

"Tomorrow, pick the melons for market. I'm happy you're home. You'll do it!"

Maria sat, red-eyed, silent. She remained silent in father's presence. She stared. She squeezed José's knee, wrinkled her nose at him and ran to the kitchen.

"The *Senhorio* met with the Association of Saint Blaise. The water in the village is foul," said José.

"I drank from it on the way to Mass," said Mother.

"Four died from drinking. Father Segundo believes the water is bad and ordered us not to drink it."

"I drank the water before I remember drinking it. My Mother gave me cupfuls."

José nodded. Mother poured hot soup into his bowl. She kissed him on the cheek and patted his hand.

"I'm happy to be home. Henrique sends greetings from the mountains and will attend the festival. Where did you get fish for soup?"

"Uncle Jaime gave Father a chunk, the first fish we've had in months. João brought pargo. No fish! Now more fish than we can eat."

"It's the best water in Campanário and the only water for those living on the square and by the church. It tastes better than any water from here to Câmara da Lobos," said Father.

The lamp flickered and flared and the shadows moved like flames of a black fire. Maria smiled and burned her tongue on the soup. They finished the meal with melons--light green and sweet as sugar cane, fine market melons, ripened before picked. The poorest urchin starved before stealing a melon. His hands would be beaten bloody and he'd not dare to show his face at church or in the public square.

"José was sent to the high field to work at the *Senhorio's* pleasure. He returned to us smiling. God bless him!"

José watched the old man the one he called father eat his melon. Work had worn him down his squat figure, slender arms, sinewy and tough. He worked from dark to dusk. Darkness overtook him in the field. Father worked to eat and sleep and nothing more. Sometimes he bought wine and *espatada* at the festival.

"I'll use the well. The Priest doesn't tell me where to drink," said Father.

"Where is there good water?" said Maria.

"We'll use *levada* water on the schedule, or we can haul it from the fountains at Calçada and Amoreira."

Father rose from the table and reached for his black felt hat.

"Have more melon before you go to the *Senhorio*," said Mother.

"I've no time. I'm falling asleep," he said, and moved away from the lamp light. Maria beckoned to José to stay. She and Mother washed the bowls and wiped the table. João sat through the meal in silence except when he said, "Turkey Yucky!" sounds he'd heard from the cripple that spent every day in the church square.

"Father's stubborn. He listens to the *Senhorio*. He hates him and acts dumb and blind."

"Don't talk about it, José. The *Senhorio* is boss. He rules and does the talking. Someday he'll die and we'll be free," said Mother.

"The land is divided in odd shapes, and men never know where the boundaries were drawn by the original owners. When hatred remains, brothers fight over the land."

"It's none of your business. You're young. You're a man. You're free to speak. I'm without words," said Maria.

"Don't," said Mother. "We need José here on the land, not living with Henrique. He works for us. Anger him and he runs away."

Maria cried, "The *Senhorio*'s after me. He won't be put off. He wants me to sleep with him before I marry."

"Don't say it. Someone will hear. I was safe in the rectory when your Father arranged with the Priest to take me away. Don't speak of these things."

"I'll live with Tia Nita," said Maria, "don't refuse me."

Mother appealed to the virgin and returned to her embroidery.

"Go to Tia Nita. I hauled home her bag of flour. She's kind and we spoke in the high fields," said José.

"She's a witch and deserves the stake for practicing the old religion," said Mother.

"I can't gossip about the old woman."

"She's cursed."

"Mother, she gets nothing for midwifery and herb medicines except old clothes and leftovers," said José.

"She practices mysteries. She's makes signs and says words forbidden by Father Segundo. She hid herself on that scrap of land given by her grandfather and never kept her mouth shut."

"She has a right to live. She has little land. What can she sell to live?"

"Nothing," said Maria. "She tells the tales of the old Jews."

"If the Senhorio takes her garden, she'll starve to death," said José.

"Where would we be without the land?" said Maria. "When you die mother, who feeds us?"

She didn't answer.

"The old Aunt cried when I sent her a piece of salt fish and a skewer of beef on Christmas day. We'll end living on a scrap of land," said José.

The odor of cigarette smoke arose on the night air and the bells rang at the chapel on Fajã Velha. Father returned from the village and went to bed. Mother sat sewing by the lamp.

"You talk like Henrique. Purple's the color of bitterness and our color. My heart is purple when the Senhorio asks for more dineiro," said Mother. She wept.

"Please help me with the baskets, Maria," he said. Mother spoke as he went into the darkness.

"You're a good son, José. Be good to your Mother. I won't be here forever." She kissed them good night and went to bed. They carried the baskets down over the wall and set them out for the morning.

"You're going to marry, so soon, my love."

"João told you, I know he did. It's for the best. The Senhorio wants me."

He held her hand and felt her cheek next to his. They stood under the stars and listened to the crickets. She kissed him and they climbed the ladder into the loft.

The stars were shining in the west when he finished breakfast. José took his basket and looked for the ghost green melons in the dew-covered patch. He left his straw hat for Maria to find him at lunch time.

The rising sun shown on the sloop tied at the quay and José knew Garth Talbot still visited with Pistola. He remembered on the heights there was nothing to eat except chestnuts. The sun warmed the melons and he fondled one as he set it in the basket. He carried a full skep down to the path and met Tia Nita with a load of washing balanced on her head.

"How are the melons?" she said.

"Delicious," he handed her one. I take them to the storage cave, before Blandy Brothers' tug arrives to carry them to Funchal. They're ready for market."

"Our Maria is going to marry Joachim Silva."

"Yes, she told me herself," he said.

The old woman in the early light looked harmless. She stooped a little and wore a kerchief on her nut-shaped head. The villagers feared her. Her face and figure were bent with age and he felt no fear.

"Joachim lives in Alto. His family owns good land. You're getting a friend in the bargain," Tia Nita said.

José couldn't speak.

When he thought of Maria, a lump formed in his throat and he envisioned her slight figure slip away from home and into church for marriage vows and out of the family forever. He worked carrying stone during the morning hours while the old Aunt gathered herbs on the mountainside.

In the noon heat, Maria appeared on the path below carrying the lunch basket. She called to the old Aunt to join them for a bite to eat. She kissed the old Aunt on both cheeks.

"How's Henrique?" said the Aunt.

"He's free as a kestrel. He won't let me live in the mountains," said José.

"I remember him as a boy. He never grew tall. He followed the men into the mountains to cut wood."

"Tia Nita, I need help to prepare for my wedding. Would you assist me?"

"With all my heart, my dear, my first advice is never to forget your brother José, no matter what happens in marriage."

The old lady nodded and blinked.

"God bless you," said José. He lifted his basket of melons. "I'm not a slave of the Senhorio. I found courage in the mountains."

Maria walked a little ways with the Aunt who was going off to gather herbs and visit a newly-delivered baby at the place called, *Black Spring.* José watched them disappear, Maria along the ridge toward the village and the Aunt into the heights looking for roots and herbs. He took his nap in the shade of the mimosa trees and then began his descent down the heights toward the sea.

At the pebbled beach, he went into the little wine shop at the land's end of the quay.

"Ain't seen you down on the pebbles, since you kicked the knife," said Pistola's wait-man, Faca. "You made him look bad my boy."

"Have you seen Pistola and Talbot?"

"No, José, you need to go to Maçapez but first have a glass of wine with me and rest a minute. No need to pay me. It made my heart feel good to see the old bastard of a landlord lose face for a change."

Faca poured out a small glass of wine of the village. "We got trouble with that well and there's talk the soldiers come to seal it."

"Don't drink the water," said José. "My Father said he'll drink it, but three are dead and many ill." said José.

He drank the wine down in one swift movement. It tasted like vinegar, wine made from pressings.

"I watched the sloop. The *Senhorio's* men haven't gone near it. Blandy Brothers' captain asked about it the first week. He reported it to the Rock Fort at Funchal. The fishermen drink wine and play cards with nothing else to do when they are not at sea. They asked me about Talbot's sloop tied up at the quay. Your sister's marrying Joachim Silva, I hear."

"Thanks pal! Anything brilliant happens in the Valley of the Melons, I'll send word.

"The Priest ordered the villagers to stopping drinking water from the well. He said death comes from it. You better see the Englishman. He received letters from Funchal. His arm is without the sling and swings freely." Faca waved José good-bye.

Maria arrived with her basket of melons and he opened the cave for her to store them. She then went to gather limpets along the rocky shore and beckoned to him. The tide had risen and surf smashed against the boulders and made the best ledges difficult. She stood in a pool, smiling up at him. She held the black shell on the rock and sliced it away with a knife and shoved the limpet into her burlap bag. She peered down into the water to find each crack and crevice. "Come and help me," she said.

He rolled up his trousers and looked for shells. The surf pounded and the sounds of the gulls were lost in the wind whistling around the great rock spire, the *campanário*. She disappeared behind a large boulder recently fallen from the cliff into the sea. A wave moved in toward him and surf broke around him and he swam a couple of strokes to regain balance. "Come out, wherever you're hiding," he said.

Maria swam into sight, her hair streaming around her face, laughing and rolling her eyes. "You're wet. Have a little water," she screamed and sprayed him with a slap of water.

They collected a full bag of slimy limpets and returned to the beach, lay down on the pebbles until the sun warmed and dried them.

She held his hand and looked into his eyes. "How is Henrique?"

"He opens his eyes on open pastures and wanders freely over them. He never thinks of gardens and families. He'll never come back into the valley."

"And you?"

"I'd live there tomorrow, if he'd asked me."

"He's an outlaw and the eldest in our family, the first son of the first mother. He should be faithful."

"Tia Nita knew him as a child. He never lived at home. He grew up on the cliffs cutting grass for the animals and sleeping with the goats. Father sent him to the heights for wood. And beat him each time he left the land. They called him *silent one* before we were born."

Maria removed her skirt and spread it out on the rocks to dry. "He'll let you live with him?"

"Henrique was silent during my visit. I asked his permission to live in the hut. He wouldn't listen. I wanted to travel with him on the timber expeditions. I'd be free of the *Senhorio*. Henrique knows every shepherd and forester from the Grand Curral to Paúl Da Serra."

She said, "Henrique has freedom on the heights and has no family. If he loved us, he'd visit us on *festas*."

"You don't know him. He has nothing, no land, no house, and no woman. He misses his Mother but she died and we are his in name only."

"He's our blood and not an Abreu when he lives alone."

"He says we are what we are born and nothing in this world changes it."

Maria touched his nose. "I love you. And I'm happy with you. The family created me and I gained life from its blood. I'll marry Joachim but I'll remain in the family. I refuse to live by myself. I'd never live with the cousins on the Amoreira cliffs. Without a family, there's nothing."

"I want to own my land," said José. As long as I live under the *Senhorio* and in this family, I can't breathe. Joachim Silva owns land and you'll have the spirit as long as you live. The people are the spirit of the land and without it they're nothing."

"Henrique has no land. You admire him!"

"He lives by sunrise and sunset, the changing moon, rain and mist, sleet and snow. He loves goats and sheep and birds--they are his family. The eagle and the kestrel together, high above mountain streams and the air moving the mist through the mountain passes make him a family. Alone is freedom. Alone is happiness."

"Living with me is freer and healthier," laughed Maria.

"We have the *Senhorio*. He's our family! I give you the mad landlord as lover. He owns the air, the water, the plants and animals, us."

Maria pushed him away trembling and pale. "When Henrique's old and can't walk the ridges, he'll come down into the valley, crawling and beg us to care for him."

"He'll die alone. If I can't be free, I'd rather die." He kissed her.

"You don't die for yourself," she said. "I'll love you even after my marriage to Joachim. You'll be my José until I die."

The surf moved the pebbles up the beach and rolled them down, cold impersonal sound, empty and monotonous rising and falling, no seabirds' crying to soften the fall. Her hand remained in his warm one. She lay back and exposed her face to sunlight and sea wind.

Death belonged to the community and he couldn't change it. He loved family even the dead belonged to him. The Church taught he belonged to God and made his home in the family of God. The dead still lived in the family and they were better there than buried alone on the heights or in the sea. He pulled her closer.

"I want you to take me to Mass," he said.

"What on earth for? You haven't been for months. You'll meet Father Segundo."

"I'll talk to him about life," he said.

They climbed the path together and rested at the top of the ridge. Maria rubbed her nose and listened for the surf murmuring among the rocks, hundreds of meters below her.

"I sit with the women and embroider away the afternoon. I love the peace I feel with you. Maybe I'll fight the Senhorio. He'd send me off to the Witch's Field to haul rocks." She laughed.

She kissed him on both cheeks and he held her by the waist. She pushed him away and ran along Fajã Velha, her figure rising beyond the mass of prickly pear. She waved and pointed toward the heights. The wind caught her hair. He shaded his eyes from the sun and saw bright flickering in the distance toward Ribeira Brava. The strange light hurt his eyes and when he looked, it disappeared. He yelled.

Maria danced away, waving each time he waved, and she didn't wait for him. He rested in the shade of the ancient ruin, the Abreu fortress from the 15th century. In the dark shadows on the heights he saw a light flash along the ridge toward the Valley of the Melons.

CHAPTER VIII

Later that afternoon, José climbed from the beach up to his garden patch and dug furrows in the terraced soil and water rushed down and spread across the garden into the cabbage patch. A clanking echoed from across the valley. He looked for the flashes of light. He stood on the brow of Fajã Velha and searched the hillside for the source of the sound and saw no movement on the ridge. Smoke rose from the saw-mill on the far ridge. He waited for the sound, his grub-hoe poised in midair, his mind drawn tight like a snail in its shell, the sound like the slap of his leather cape against his back. He chopped a furrow and water fanned into the garden. Sea mists blew over the tide-soaked pebbled beach, the air tasted salty the landscape pale blue and gray mist, brightening to ghost-like white.

Voices drifted over the garden along with the clanking sounds. He dropped his hoe and climbed the steps beyond the garden. Two men and a donkey moved along the trail, the men's voices clipped and smooth, Funchal accents, urged their beast forward with whistling and laughter, surveying the vineyards and gardens. They wore King Carlos' coat of arms sewn to their foot-soldier uniforms. A mortar strapped to the animal's back caught the sun's rays and reflected mirror-like into José's eyes.

The soldiers laughed at the poor soil and the valley, each carried a rifle slung over his shoulder, polished and oiled, their uniforms sweat-soaked and dusty.

José crouched behind laurels before they saw him, and from his hiding place, he observed the tall one pointing to a passion fruit vine growing over a lintel. The heavy-set man urged the talkative one to hurry as they must reach the church before vespers. Within a few feet, José stood up and smiled at the fat soldier.

"An angel smiles upon us," said Direito, the heavy one. "We must be in Campanário."

"This doesn't feel like heaven. Move along. The sun's hot and I'm thirsty," said the slender one, Mandado.

"The dark eyes are friendly. He knows where cold water is. Give us water before we perish in this god-forsaken desert," said Direito.

Mandado hit the rump of the pack animal with a willow switch. He moved beyond José with an anxious expression as if he avoided a devil.

"What're you doing in the middle of nowhere?" said Mandado.

"I work these gardens for my family," said José.

"I see. You're a peasant. Who do you belong to?"

Before José could answer, Direito, tanned by the sun and wearing a cap with a strange visor, his long mustache drooping below his jaw line said, "I don't see enough land to survive on. You have soil down on the river. This is poor land."

Mandado leaned on the rump of the beast, an annoyed look on his face.

"Senhor António Abreu owns this land. It is the land of our ancestors, stolen by him when he duped my great grandmother."

"How long have you worked?" Direito said.

"Since I was six I worked, sir! The *Senhorio* taxes us. We've nothing left. We have no *reis* to buy land."

"What are you called?" said Mandado.

"I'm José Abreu of the valley of the melons."

"We are Mandado and Direito," said the round one, and he winked and pointed at the tall one leaning on the mule's hind quarter. This land is divided in the manner of the *Minho*. It's much the same in Bragança. No land for the young and no food in the villages and no place for King Carlos to send the ones that run away from the Army and live in South America, South Africa, Mozambique."

"Where're you going, this afternoon?" said José.

"To meet our Captain, the people refuse to stop using bad water. We'll confiscate the well."

Mandado wiped his sweat-covered brow. His shirt and trousers darkened. He yearned for refreshment and followed José to the spring concealed in the underbrush. After filling his clay jug with fresh water, José handed it to him. He let water swirl over his hands and drank a palm full of shining water.

The soldiers sat in the shade. José gave the mule cool draughts of water from his hat. The men forgot their Captain. They asked about the village. They were curious about the Festival of Saint Blaise. After dunking his bandanna in water, Mandado mopped his face. Direito rolled himself a cigarette and offered one to José. José shook his head and held up the jug.

"Who's first?"

"Direito will drink. Direito is first," said Mandado.

"No, Mandado must precede Direito."

José raised the jug to his lips and drank long. "Who's first?"

Direito took the jug and raised it to his lips and splashed water along his tanned cheeks, beads of water shining on his mustache. He smiled at the jug, opened his mouth and swallowed the cold silver rush of water.

"We're on a mission. The water in their well is bad and we're going to keep them from drinking it. We seek young men that hide from King Carlos. Keep it quiet"

"I drink from that well. It tastes fine. You make a difficulty for the villagers," said José.

"The people that drink die and the others disobey the order of the governor. The commander in Funchal sent a message posted by the well and they kept drinking the water."

"I can't read. Only the women read," said José.

Mandado wiped his sweat on his sleeve. He whistled. He let the jug slip from his hands and José caught it.

"I can't read like my sisters," said José.

"The lad doesn't read," said Mandado.

"I know a few letters!"

"Why don't you learn? You're a native." Direito dipped his bandanna in the cool water and wiped his head.

"You understand obligation," he said. "I work the gardens and have little time for reading. The priest owns books and gives lessons to my sisters. He refuses to teach boys."

"Learn to read, you'll do well in the army. I learned by looking in a book. Before tattoo, in the hot barracks, I'd read," said Mandado.

"The Captain sent his favorites to school. They became sergeants. They received more *reis* than us," said Direito.

"Once, I couldn't read and worked in the onion fields in *Costa da Caparica*. Food was scarce and we owned no land. We belonged to the men that owned the onion harvest. You pulled onions for them or you didn't eat. We went from house to house with a burlap bag. I went into the army at sixteen. I wanted to run but there was no place to hide. The neighbors told the priest when they saw me in the village."

"Did you learn to read in the army?" said José.

"No. My old Aunt taught me. The army taught me to sweep floors and wash with strong soap. I learned to make a bed and shoot a rifle. I learned to drink wine and find a woman when I wanted one," said Direito.

"Where do you stay?" said José.

"We live in the old Fort of St. James since we arrived from Lisbon, a stinking hole with small rooms and damp beds. I wish the pirates destroyed it when they set it afire during their raids."

"The army was as boring as my village in the *Minho*. The officers worked us from reveille until tattoo."

Mandado led the mule up the slope and onto the path. "We stayed in *Porto Moniz*, on a bivouac and swam in the lava pools with British soldiers. I had never been in salt water." He offered a cigarette.

"I'd like to leave my village," said José.

"Are you old enough for the army?" said Direito.

"I'm fifteen going to be sixteen."

"You've time to run away," said Mandado.

"Not time enough. I want to live in the mountains with my brother and be free of the land."

"Freedom to follow the wind," said Direito.

Direito slapped the mule, and the mortar clanked as the two soldiers and their mule climbed to the top of the ridge. From there, they saw a crowd of peasants down in the village. "Our captain will be furious. We were to meet at noon."

They made a great show, stood tall and marched into the village. Old men whistled and boys ran to greet them. José lingered to hear about the well. He looked over his shoulder for spies sent by the *Senhorio*. He rubbed his hands clean on his trousers and mingled with the villagers.

"There's an Englishman over there, he's speaking Portuguese, tall with blue eyes," said Mandado.

"That's Senhor Talbot. He's stands with my friend, Pistola," said José.

The square filled with soldiers and José wondered where they'd concealed themselves. No signals came from Ribeira Brava or from Câmara de Lobos! He waved to Pistola and Senhor Talbot. A bugle sounded and the soldiers stood in formation.

The rising dust obscured their ranks and an officer spoke to them with cold, unmoving eyes. The soldiers marched toward the church and they wheeled around and faced the *praça*. A rooster strutted between them and the crowd.

Father Segundo, the chief of police and Pistola gathered to greet the captain. He strode up and saluted them and shook each man's hand and snapped his cap in a salute. They were indifferent to the crowd. The small group talked for a long time about the well.

After tying up their mule, Direito and Mandado slipped into the rear rank. They smiled when José walked by them but didn't move, eyeing their commander's resplendent uniform.

The captain listened to the priest. He leaned into prelate's face, unbending and remote, scratching his left hand and keeping his eye on the crowd.

José scanned the eyes of his friends and neighbors. Mariazinha made the sign of the cross. She raised her eyes toward Heaven and fingered her rosary beads. Carlos of the Church, five years old this month, pissed into the poinsettias growing along the wall at Castagna's. His father, the cobbler, chased him away. The three Brazão sisters cried. Their cousin Jaime had died after he had drunk from the well. José moved into the crowd to better hear the captain. The priest told the captain to respect the people. At parade rest, the military stood silently and were amused by the irate peasants.

"I don't know those that died or drank the water," said the captain. "My orders are to seal the well. My men guarded it but the people drank the water. The orders were posted. They were warned. No one is to drink from this well."

"Five deaths are nothing. We lost a dozen folks last spring from influenza," said the chief of police.

Father Segundo listened. His unhappiness showed in his eyes. "Our water is forbidden. The people have to haul water. They have a right to this water. The Church is saddened by the deaths and understands the wishes of the Commander, but to require our friends to haul their daily water is unreasonable."

"Understand I am under orders from the King. Please assist the competent Portuguese authorities, calm the villains so we can do our duty," the Captain said.

Pistola remained silent. He waved to acquaintances, smiled at the boys. One boy beat his dog with a piece of rope. Pistola encouraged Talbot to speak to the Captain. The chief of police threatened the crowd with his sword, and touched the officer's arm. The officer was surprised and lowered his revolver.

The girl, Rosa Castagna, ran over to José and congratulated him on Maria's marriage to Joachim Silva. "My father can't afford to haul water. He needs us to repair shoes. We use this well many times a day."

Old man Castagna swore at the police chief for yelling at the crowd.

"I'm following orders," said the officer.

"Whose?"

"The *freguesia*, the parish, gave me orders."

"The priest knows nothing of orders. Ribeira Brava can't tell Campanário where to drink water."

"Funchal sent us a message."

"Funchal sent them a message! Did you hear him, gentlemen? They know nothing of us in Funchal. Why would they send a message for Campanário?" Senhor Castagna laughed.

"To save lives, stupid," said the sergeant.

The old man swung on the officer.

"Gentlemen calm yourselves wait a moment. This matter of water can be settled," said Father Segundo.

The neighbors flitted like rock sparrows, delicate and alert. They chattered their rage inflicted on those who'd listen. There was a shrug of shoulders, an elbow nudged, hands swept the air as if by magic to change the soldiers into lizards and chase them away from the well.

Rosa heard José's account of Henrique. She rubbed her toe on the cobbles. Tatara the imp of *Calçada* caught their attention. He grinned into the captain's face, cursed and threw his hat into the dust, stomped on it, picked it up and cleaned it off and shaking his fist in the air, threw the hat down and stomped on it again.

The sun beat down on the crowd. Waves of heat and dust engulfed the square. The soldiers were tired and ready to fall out. José and Rosa and Senhor Talbot looked from the balcony in front of the church. The square was as large as a *praça* and paved with cobble stones.

"Something must be done. The people need help," said José.

"It's a matter of patience. A few days and the well waters clean themselves," said Pistola.

"The anger of the peasants is great. The peasants look to you Pistola," said Talbot.

Direito and Mandado ran to assemble the mortar on orders of their captain. This mortar impressed the villagers and they watched the mule and the third man who aided the strange pair. The rest of the soldiers stacked rifles and fled into the shadows of the square out of the sun and into the wine shop. The mortar was unpacked and fitted together.

Pistola spoke for the first time. "My well in Calçada is excellent and all of you are welcome to draw water."

"They can drink from the *levada*," said Father Segundo.

"Father we do not drink dirty warm water. Since the earliest days, we drank from springs and wells."

Talbot listened. "The mortar frightens and fascinates. It's a show of force."

The captain unrolled a copy of the gold-sealed orders with red ribbon and signaled the bugler. The bugler played a lively call and the captain read the official words. He took a new document from his tunic.

"By order of his royal majesty King Carlos, a draft of men to fill the seventh cavalry in Algarve dispatched from Madeira. Every able-bodied male that is the age of sixteen years must enroll beginning Wednesday, April 23rd, 1901. This is an obligation of loyalty to his majesty and faith in Mother Portugal. Signed, this sixth day of January in the year of Our Lord, nineteen hundred and one. The signature is Joaquim Soares Mendes, Commandante, Guarda Fiscal, Funchal, Island of Madeira."

The crowd was silent. Manuel Reis, the assistant in Pistola's shop, ran to José.

"They'll want me this time. I'll hide in the mountains and run until I drop dead. I hope Henrique will help."

"Henrique never went with the army. I'll send him word," said José.

"Your Father owns enough chestnut trees to send you to Brazil," said Pistola. Manuel grimaced.

His family couldn't buy off his military duty. He'd flee. He saw the shiny metal and the precise gear of the mortar.

As he turned to leave, the villagers parted and Aunt Augusta carried her jugs toward the well. Her black dress caught the eye of the enlisted men guarding the well. She'd drawn water here for over eighty years. One soldier advanced on her.

"No water here, today, Auntie. No water for a long time."

She didn't speak. She set down her jugs and peered into the well. She spit into the dust at the feet of the soldier. Taking the well-rope, she made a bowline to lower her jug.

"I've tasted this water many times. It's good water."

The enlisted man shouted to his captain. "The old one draws water." He said. The captain had been scolding the priest and he ran toward the old woman.

"Didn't you hear the order from Funchal? The paper nailed to this board says this water is not fit to drink. The water is forbidden."

Squinting at the captain, Augusta said, "You shut your mouth. I live here and I drink this water." She shook her fist at him.

Rosa went to the Aunt and held her by the elbow. "Come, Aunt, we can find water down by the schoolhouse."

"No dear. This water's fine. It's better for me. I've drunk it since childhood."

Two enlisted men summoned by the captain stood before the aunt with their rifles at port arms. The crowd was silent. The priest bowed his head. The Aunt raised her fist in the air. "*Basta*! Enough! *Bastardo*!"

José felt the sun hot on his head. His tongue tasted of metal. José put his arm around her and Rosa took her arms and pulled her away from the well.

"Never," shouted the Aunt. The soldiers swung the butts of their rifles at her. The bystanders frightened by the soldiers hurried through Castagna's gate and down the steps into the garden.

Talbot said, "The priest should stand up for the old lady." Pistola told the priest to keep the soldiers away from the aunt but Father Segundo urged the crowd to go home and gave the soldiers his blessing.

Talbot shook his head and told Pistola this was no way to govern the people. In the square, he heard the names of the young men wanted for service read from the roll.

"José, come and stay with me in Funchal. It is best you are absent from this place now," said Talbot.

José smiled and shrugged. "I'm under the authority of the *Senhorio* and have no permission to leave the land," said José.

Father Segundo hopped down the path to see José. "You're an Abreu," he said.

"Yes, Father, José Santos de Abreu." José removed his cap. He lowered his eyes and he tried to focus, but they were so dry he couldn't open them.

"You belong to the Abreu. You seldom attend Mass."

"I work long days, Father."

"We don't work on the Sabbath."

The *Senhorio* ordered work on the first day of the week, Senhor."

"He has no authority to work you on the Sabbath."

"We work seven days to live, Senhor. We know nothing else."

"I'll speak to him. He comes to Mass with his women. I was not aware... I had no idea."

"Sire, please don't speak to the Senhorio. He'll make trouble. We have to work."

José rolled his eyes and his knees weakened. The sun was inside his head. He pulled his biretta down over his eyes to shut out the light. Spots appeared before his eyes, floating green coins. He waved to Talbot and Pistola. They quieted the old aunt. He smiled at Rosa. A sweet voice said over and over that he must go to Mass, go to Mass. He fell and his knees hit the cobbles, the bright sunlight falling around him.

CHAPTER IX

The priest, cobbler and policeman hovered over José lying on the cobbles in the street in front of the home and shoeshop of Senhor Duro Castagna, Rosa's father. They mumbled to one another and did nothing but look down on him and shaking their heads let the Castagna women tend to him. The women carried him into the house. He lay on the floor with a pillow to support his head. Rosa and her mother put cloths of cold water to his forehead and lips.

"The sun strips us naked," he heard Rosa's mother say. Her voice echoed along red corridors dancing with sunlight. He heard Pistola and the Captain talk of the well. The men moved around and beyond him, gargoyle silhouettes dark and forbidding. The women wept and peered into his face.

Rosa picked up a green bottle and pour wine for the priest and the captain and her father.

"How long will you stay in the town, Senhor Captain?" said Father Segundo.

"The villagers must stop drinking from the well."

The priest closed his eyes and nodded. "It will be difficult to keep them from drawing water from it."

"They may water their animals and gardens but not drink it. They disobey the King's order if they drink it," said the captain.

"I can't assure you they'll obey. They've listened to me preach for twenty-five years. Their minds are secretive. They are independent and do what they wish."

"I'll seal the well. We filled a spring in Funchal. The people kept drinking the bad water. We sealed their spring and they regained health. There were many deaths, Padre!"

"They say Funchal has a new three inch pipe to carry water from Monte to the Chafariz market," said the Priest.

"The pipe follows the railroad track and there is a new hotel at *Campo da Barca*. Do you want a hotel on the village square?"

The priest laughed and raised his wine glass. "We'd need young men for a hotel. You draft them and take them away from us."

"We'll read the roll. New recruits serve King Carlos on the mainland. If they don't appear, I find them and arrest them."

61

Lying on the kitchen floor José opened his eyes and smelled cigarette smoke. Senhor Castagna winked at him and said to the Captain, "We need young men on the land. Six years is too long."

"We know the law, Senhor. It has no heart," said Father Segundo

Pistola and Talbot arrived from the street and greeted the men. Pistola leaned over him and shook his hand and said good morning. . "We heard you had sunstroke and came to see you. Talbot is sailing to Funchal today and wanted to say good-bye."

José raised his head and drank from an old cup. "Good-bye, Senhor. I hope to see you soon." Talbot shook his hand and he and Pistola nodded to the men and left.

Home seemed distant in his mind. Senhora Castagna and Rosa got him to his feet and led him upstairs to a bed and covered him with blankets.

"I must work. Give me my hat. They need me at home," he said.

"You've been hit by the sun," *Dona* Castagna said. "You'll sleep here tonight."

Rosa brought him another blanket. The Priest came into the room and blessed him saying, "Don't worry, little one. Don't fret. The *Senhorio* will pay for his sins in eternity. He can't work his men on the Sabbath."

Rosa dressed in a white blouse, red and white skirt, red skull cap, her long black hair hanging to her hips. She stood at the foot of his bed. He pretended to sleep.

"They carried you into the house, cold as a mackerel and pale only worse. You opened your eyes and were as limp as a *lapa*, a limpet" she said.

"I'm fine. I'll soon get up and feed my goats. I'll tell Maria the soldiers have arrived to take away the young men."

"She'll hear about them. Rest until you feel better." she said.

He tried to rise. His head was heavy and he lay on the pillow and closed his eyes.

The next thing he knew the Captain was in the room looking down at him and asking him questions.

He told the captain his name.

"There is a rumor I heard someone wants to hold Talbot for ransom," said the captain.

"I know nothing, Senhor. You'd best speak with the *Senhorio*."

"The army is steady work for young men. They live in Funchal and are sent to the metropolis during their third year. Those that refuse we send to prison, working under guards, little food and no freedom."

"Come along," said the Priest. "He 's not well and he is not yet sixteen."

José looked out the window of bedroom. The western ridges of the island were pink and the valley below blue then purple descending into shadow with a red stripe on the horizon.

"I'll sleep in your Mother's house," he said to Rosa. It's an honor until I'm well enough to return home. Send word to my Mother and sisters in Ribeira Melões." Rosa smiled and went off.

He curled up in the bed. Images of sunlight and soldiers rose in his head and he heard in his dream the voice of Maria. It was time to climb the ladder into the loft. He followed her up into the darkness and they settled into the straw and in each other's arms fell asleep.

Much later in the dark, the smell of soup awakened him. The church bells rang and pigs grunted outside his window. He became aware that he was not home but lying in a strange bed.

He climbed out the window over the cool tiles of the shed roof and tiptoeing across the patio, pissed into the blackberry bushes. He crawled back through the window and into bed. Rosa's mother called to someone. He pulled up the blanket and went back to sleep.

In the morning, Rosa leaned over the bed and kissed him. She pulled off his blanket and led him to the kitchen. Senhor Castagna set down his basket of broad beans and washed his hands at the trough. A streak of white hair enlivened his sideburns. He was a strong silent man, known for his skill making shoes. He nodded at José and said prayers before they ate.

Senhora Castagna spoke rapidly and crossed herself when saying the word sunstroke and her husband raised his eyebrows. Rosa brought more soup and bread. He ate in silence. He had never eaten in a home away from home.

Rosa looked down at her soup. Her father observed every glance she gave him. She smiled and left the room to eat her fish and rice in the kitchen. José enjoyed the vegetables and fish. He tasted each morsel. Each tasted new and different from the way mother cooked them.

Rosa's mother led him back to the narrow chamber with one bed, a fine bureau and chairs, the sun illuminated the ceiling. A window overlooked the churchyard. She covered him with a coarse blanket like the one Henrique gave him in the mountain hut. He dozed after his meal and saw bright metal disks. He drew himself into a ball and made a warm place in the damp sheets and blankets. He spent the whole day in bed only getting up for soup and bread and a trip to the outhouse.

That night, the clock in the church-tower struck the hour and he heard someone. He listened. Rosa leaned against the wall by the window in the moonlight.

"You shouldn't have come," he said. "Your father will find out."

Rosa touched his hand. "Maria sent word. The *Senhorio* is angry and wants to see you. She spoke to the priest about giving you reading lessons."

She stood in silence. He knew she wanted him. He closed his eyes and pretended to sleep.

"I'm sorry to be in this room," he said. I wish I were at home. I'm a burden."

"I've watched you in the fields. I wanted to speak with you. You are hidden from the eyes of the neighbors in my house and I can kiss you," she said.

"You're beautiful Rosa but I've given my heart to Maria."

"She's your sister. You can love both of us."

"I want to be free. In the army, I'd be free of the *Senhorio* and a slave to King Carlos. The church may be the way for me to be free."

"I see myself serving communion, wearing the surplice and offering the cup with my right hand and wiping the rim with white linen after it touches your lips."

She was surprised to hear him talk this way. He believed that one day he would read and write and sign his name.

Rosa pouted and pursed her lips. He kissed her and told her about nights in the mountains, the way mists hang along the ridges in the moonlight, sheep lie in the pasture amidst the rocks, shepherds and dogs sleeping close by.

"Speak with father," Rosa said. "Tomorrow make arrangements. He'll offer you a place in his shop. My brothers work in Funchal. They'll not object."

"They'll return during bad times. I'll be turned out. We'd depend on your family. I want to be able to read and write and make my own living."

"We could flee to Brazil. My brothers talk of sailing to Rio."

"They've saved and have money for passage. We have no *reis*. They have served the military and can return without fear. We could never return."

Rosa covered her ears with her hands and shook her head. She lay down beside him. He jumped out of bed and stood in the cool air by the window, the church bright in the moonlight. Black triangular shadows crossed the streets and cottages, and stone facades shown like ice and the night wind blew down from the sierra.

"I may become a priest and go into the church," he said.

"You'd marry Christ! You'd be running away. You're a man, not a black skirt listening to confessions of old women."

"Maria spoke to Father Segundo. That doesn't mean I'll become a priest. Your brothers ran off to Funchal after their military service. You learned to cobble shoes from your father. No women do that. I work the land and grow a few vegetables. There's never enough to eat and pay the *Senhorio*. I must be free."

"Maria wants you in school and you wants you working on the land! You can't do both."

"She's marrying Joachim Silva and leaving our home. She reads, writes and embroiders beautiful linens. João, Silvino, and I work the land. Why should she care what I do?"

"You love Maria. She'd help you and I'd teach you."

He pulled the blankets over his head. Rosa reached in a grasped his shoulder. He held her away. "Don't make a sound," he said.

She looked him in the eye. She held him.

"I can't marry you. Father would throw me off the land," he said. "He'd beat me."

"Your father doesn't beat you! I don't believe it. My father doesn't touch me." Rosa said. "I swear by the virgin."

"Father sees the land ready for harvest. The fruits of the land are ripe. The *Senhorio* demands his portion. Father worries about paying his share and beats us."

"Promise me your heart," she said.

"I've given it to Maria."

"You love me a little," she said.

She cried and stroked his hair. She went to the door and turning, kissed her fingers tips. "I'll return," she said and disappeared down the stairs.

The dog growled in the yard during the night. Senhor Castagna cleared his throat the sound distinct in another part of the house. José saw Maria and Rosa, Rosa and Maria, in his dream. He loved Maria and couldn't bear the thought of her leaving home and seldom seeing her. Rosa was beautiful radiant dark hair large eyes and he felt a great attraction for her but he had to be true to himself. He had to be free of the feudal authority that was grinding him and his family into the earth. His dreams were frightening. He fought the priest who refused to teach him to be literate. Wild scenes arose in his mind. He ran away into the mountains taking Maria with him and they lived in a cave. The soldiers came looking for him when he was of age and he had to flee to the summits and he lay huddled in the lea of a huge rock with the snow driving across the sierra and his feelings slow and his hands and feet numb. He crawled along the edge of the precipice and slipped. He was falling and suddenly he felt the pillow and he awoke shaking to find himself in bed and he was relieved to be alive and worried that Rosa might come to the bedroom to see him again. The whole night he slept fitfully and he got up from the bed about three o' clock. He stood by the window. The church tower dominated the square, a dark hulk ands a sentry walked across the cobbles in the moonlight. He shivered and returned to bed.

In the morning the sunlight off the cobbles of the churchyard dazzled him. On the square, a line of soldiers aimed their rifles at the peasants.

CHAPTER X

The widow of Paulo Pereira dressed in black walked through the front entrance of the church with its massive oak panels and moved as in a dream down the aisle. The morning sunlight from the high dome windows illuminated her head and shoulders. José saluted her, the Aunt he'd known since childhood.

"It's a beautiful morning," he said. She ignored him. He removed his biretta and stooped before the basin of holy water and crossed himself with damp fingers.

Where were Rosa and her mother? The gold nave was warm and brilliant, candles burned on the altar their glow reflected off the censer and the eagle and the cross, golden light. He went to the right pews where the men sat on Sunday. On the other side of the sanctuary, the women whispered. A young woman in black entered from the porch, moved into the silence in the sanctuary and the murmuring of prayers echoed along the tracery, this young beauty genuflected and rose from her knees raising her eyes to Christ on the cross.

José closed his eyes and listened to the rise and the fall of voices in prayer. Where were Rosa and her mother? The women used their prayer beads while waiting for confession. Maria sat with the women from Ribeira Melões. He wanted to kiss her cheek. The priest called, "Enter," and another woman in black went up to the curtain and knelt at the shuttered window.

He wondered what Maria confessed. She was a young woman and lived a quiet life. She stood and walked to the booth and he wished he were the priest. He'd nod his head and tell her to never fret and to pray Our Father every morning when she opened her eyes. Must he confess Rosa's visit that other night? Working in the fields, he had dreamed of women. He'd confess his dreams. The more he thought about Rosa, the less he wanted to take confession. Could the priest see into his head? He waited his turn.

Maria on her way to the confessional didn't speak on her way by him. She smiled. Her eyes were sweet, dark and calm. After the priest spoke to her, the priest beckoned him to the window. He knelt and waited. The voice asked him to confess.

"I can't," he said.

"Why can't you?"

"I'm not a Catholic."

"You speak with the accent of this village. I see you attend Mass and you are not baptized. Confess my son and become a Catholic."

He stood and turned to leave. Something in the voice its tone soothed him like a freshly-cut melon. He felt peaceful and he knelt and said, "I don't believe."

The words surprised him. The shutter banged back and the priest's head appeared. "How is it possible for one so young? You suffered sunstroke and God saved your life."

"My life is misery, Father."

"Without God's love life is Hell on earth."

"I need my own land. I want wood to build a house."

"Things never make us happy, my son. Land is not love. Come and confess your sins and gain eternal life."

"I don't sin," he said.

"We're all sinners."

"I kicked the Senhorio's knife away during his fight with Talbot. I didn't feed my goats while I stayed at Castagna's. I didn't help João haul carrots. Desire burns my heart."

"Wonderful. What is your desire?" said the priest.

"I want to read and write, Father."

"That's not a sin! Why reading and writing?"

"My sisters write letters to family in Lisbon and read aloud while making embroideries."

He shut his mouth to keep from shouting at the priest. Holy orders would free him of family and feudal obligations. Priests sat in the darkness and listened to dreams. They gave men and women magic words to recite and sad imagery to ease pain, shame and poverty.

"You asked to attend school once before. Your first duty is to your father. We need one or two readers in each family. Your sisters have the time. They attend church and confess themselves. Go with your father and do what he commands you. Listen to the *Senhorio* and carry out your obligations to the demesne. Our Lord showed patience on the cross."

The priest patted his fat belly under the black surplice and smiled. He reached through the grill and touched the slender fingers.

"I can work my whole life. Now, I want to learn," said José.

"Your father can't write. He works the land and is a patient man."

He looked into the face of the priest. The old crow pecked at his eyes. This large black bird in a cassock had a long sharp beaky nose ready to jab him in the eyes.

He bit his lip and swore to himself. He left the cubicle and stood before the altar and kneeling said Our Fathers and Hail Mary.

The young woman in black moved ahead and into a side aisle, her skirt swayed back and forth and her bare feet whispered over the tiles. He examined the carvings and plaques erected by wealthy families to preserve their names. The woman disappeared and he went along the passage looking for her.

He found the door to the crypt and opening it, peered down into the gloom. He sought Rosa and her mother. A flight of stone steps led down and the damp earth rose on mildew air issuing from the depths, a strange dry dusty odor. He descended three steps and listened for footsteps with a heavy heart. Had Rosa gone into the crypt? Footsteps barely audible lured him into the darkness; suddenly light hit his eyes and he closed them. His eyes adjusted and he saw the doorway that opened into the cemetery north of the sanctuary. In the light from the door, he saw the piles of bones on shelves. He ran over the cobbles and up the stairs and back into the Sanctuary and rested until his heart was calm.

Maybe Rosa was in the loft. He walked up the steps going into the choir loft. In the loft, he opened the door to the belfry. He lingered at the balcony window until he saw the square was empty, except for the soldiers guarding the well. On the steps of the vestibule, Father Segundo talked with the widow Pereira in black.

José hurried down from the window in the choir loft and went over to the priest.

"Senhora Castagna and her daughter asked for you." said the priest.

"My mother worked in the rectory and learned to read and write under Father Domingo," he said.

"It's best for you to work for your father."

"It pays nothing and I have no money for lessons."

"Go and see Pistola. He'll find you a place in his shop."

"The *Senhorio* wouldn't give me permission."

"Pistola will speak for you."

"They can't agree those two. I wish to work for Jesus. My mother did."

The priest shrugged and leaned forward. "You're too old to be an altar boy. God loves us whether or not we know how to read or write. He wants us to live in families. Do your father's work."

"I wish to serve Jesus, Father."

69

"Let me see you after Mass on Sunday and bring your father. Jesus loves sons who are faithful to their fathers." The priest skipped away.

José shook his fist at the fleeting figure of the priest. In the square, the sunlight blinded his eyes and he squinted. He reached Castagna's house and felt his way through their gate and into the doorway like a blind man.

There were four slices of fine bread on his plate. Rosa's mother winked and poured coffee into his cup. At home, he ate plain bread. He spread marmalade on the bread and tasted its bitterness.

"You went to the church! I looked for you in the bedroom but you were not there."

"I wanted to speak with the Priest." He fondled his cup and avoided her eyes.

"You were foolish to go outside. Sunlight weakens the eyes. Your eyes are still weak from your spell."

"Where's Rosa? I looked for her in church and could not find her."

"She feeds the chickens and the pigs. Do you want to marry her?"

He fussed with his marmalade and bread.

She poured him more coffee. She knew her daughter's dream. He must not sleep another night in that room. Rosa went to him while she and Duro slept.

He slipped out of the kitchen when her mother shook down the fire. He hid in the banana grove and saw Talbot's sloop tied up to the quay. He lay down and closed his eyes and planned to go home and feed his goats. .

Rosa's father startled him. The old man walked through the bananas with a load of weeds in the bright sunlight. José listened to women calling back and forth between their cottages. He heard the soldiers in the square and he followed Senhor Castagna to the pig house. The soldiers quiet during the *sesta* now drilled in the late afternoon square. The rooster scratched the cobbles and Rosa cut spinach for the goats. He bent over the trough after the old man washed and doused his face. The cool water soothed his face.

"Where did you go?" said Rosa "Maria came looking for you. My mother thought you'd gone home."

"I went to church looking for you. I saw the priest and he refused to help me. I'll see Pistola about work in his shop. I rested in the banana grove instead of up in the bedroom."

When her father entered the house, Rosa offered him her cheek and then her lips. They held hands and went into the kitchen together.

"You'd better go home. Your mother will defend your leaving the land without permission. If your father catches you, he'll beat you," said Senhor Castagna. . ªI'm so hungry I could eat a whole chicken," he said to his wife.

José seldom ate chicken and he sat down with the Castagna family beside Senhor Duro. They ate bread at home after they paid the taxes. Most of the year, they ate *milho*, cold strips of corn meal.

"You want to marry my Rosa?" said Senhor Duro.

The tone of the voice chilled him. He didn't put his spoon into his soup. José hesitated. Chicken soup with bread to dunk in it and the old man staring at him! Young men slept with neighbor's daughters when they wished to marry them.

"She's a fine girl, my Rosa," said Senhor Duro. He grinned.

"I don't have the money to support a wife," said José.

"She cooks and grows fine vegetables. She hauled water from the well before the army sealed it. Her embroidery is the finest. She has the best needle in Campanário. You came to ask for her hand, didn't you?"

The Senhora said, "He suffered sunstroke and the priest and Pistola carried him to our doorstep. He needed rest before going back to work."

José wanted Rosa to like him. Words didn't come and he sat quietly and ate his chicken soup.

"He wants her or he wouldn't stay here. I saw his eye on her," said Senhor Duro.

José stood up. "I can leave, sir."

"No, stay," said Rosa.

"He stood in the sun, let him stand in darkness," said Senhor Duro.

"He isn't well. You can see for yourself. Be pleasant or I'll go and stay with my Aunt Amelia," said Senhora Castagna.

"We speak for his health," said Rosa.

"He sleeps one more night under this roof, no more. Tomorrow, he goes home to his family." He turned to José.

"If you wish to mend boots and learn how to make shoes, I have a place for you. You can live here and for seven years work leather. Marry my daughter. She's a good girl."

"It's impossible, Senhor. I'm going into the church. I can't marry her. She's a fine girl. You're fortunate to have such a daughter."

"Tomorrow, you leave my house."

The old man ate his chicken and rice smacking his lips and wiping them with his sleeve. He ordered Rosa to serve him more chicken. He wanted her to make José her man.

"It's settled. You sleep in the little room. Tomorrow, you leave."

CHAPTER XI

Stars across the heavens shone in the dark sky, the church silhouetted against them. From his pillow in the bedroom of Rosa's family, he heard the sentries pace back and forth across the square. The hours marked by the clock dragged by. After midnight, he fell into a long sleep and awakened to shouts before dawn when the stars faded and sounds of birds and rivulets carried from the slopes of Quinta Grande. In dream his ancestor Abreu said, "The King can't keep you from this well. The water belongs to the people." More shouting at the well and the sounds of boots running across the square aroused him from his bed and he looked out the window. The church was built thirty feet above the square on a platform of granite blocks and to reach its doors two flights of stone stairs wound up to the terrace before its great white stucco façade. From his window at the Castagna's, José saw the gardens and cottages of Campanário and the magnificent fields of sugar cane and the groves of bananas. The church was a citadel built during the last century of stout walls unadorned with decoration and a tall campanile with a clutch of bells and a flock of pigeons that inhabited the square in the daylight and roosted in the tower at night. Above the Sanctuary in the church a three quarters balcony housed the organ and the choir loft. Down in the square at this moment, the peasants and the soldiers fought over the well whose caused typhoid fever.

The land, people and water belonged to the King. Since the beginning, the Senhorio had authority over every thing. José had to leave the land or he would be enslaved and suffer the Senhorio for the rest of his life. He heard twigs crackle in the kitchen fireplace and smelled smoke. In the bedroom he pulled on his trousers and walked down the hallway toward the kitchen. Before the church-bell tolled Morning Prayer, he had heard Rosa feed dry chips into the flames, their snap and crackling and the sound of the pots set on the stove and he smelled coffee brewing.

"I heard the soldiers leave on Thursday for Ribeira Brava. Do you think the well has bad water?" Rosa said.

"Rosa, don't drink the water until we get the captain's order. I don't know the water is bad. The army knows. We don't." Mother sighed.

Rosa's father, Senhor Duro, fed his hunting dog bits of codfish. Rosa poured his coffee. José said good morning. Senhor Duro smiled and carved a lath with a jackknife.

"I spoke with Father Segundo about going to school. He's a wise priest. School is for the women. What good are books to you and me? You work the land and I make shoes. We harvest grapes. We cut sugar cane and timber for market. That's our work, not writing letters and books."

"There's no land here for me, Senhor. My land is in Brazil."

"Your father needs you. Forget school. You can read the stars. Split wood for your mother's fire. Forget Brazil."

"I can't promise to forget, Senhor," he said.

Dona Castagna sat in the corner and sorted *nêsperas,* Chinese loquat, picked from her favorite tree. The small apricot-like fruit tasted of apple and plum. She offered him fruit for his breakfast.

Senhor Duro felt his knife's blade with his thumb. He drew a line across his neck with back of the blade and scowled.

"The army makes men slaves. They ship them to Lisbon. Many leave the island and never return. Yesterday, two soldiers asked me to mend their boots. They carried water for my pig and goats to pay me. The land is ruined by taking away the young men. I hate the sight of soldiers." He said the King's name and slammed the palm of his hand on the table.

José thanked Rosa's mother and father for their hospitality and left for home. He promised himself to return their kindness. Rosa walked out with him and unlocked the gate. He pulled on his biretta and wrapped the burlap around his shoulders.

"Where're you off to?" she said.

"I go to find Maria."

Rosa pushed his shoulder. "You're cruel. You're in love with yourself. You can't read and write your name." She slammed the gate. He rang the bell and yelled for her. Her face never appeared on the terrace. He walked into the square. It was the day the captain was to read the roll of those required to join the militia, their obligation under the law.

Soldiers drank their coffee around a fire in the square. Ana Fernandes walked across the square on her way to Mass. The soldiers watched her swaying skirt. They were silent and unmoving except for drying their capes and holding their hands toward the fire. A rooster scratched debris from between the cobbles and beat his wings and crowed, his crown bright in the glare of the fire.

"Good morning, young man," said Direito. "You're up early. To see us call the men named on the King's roll, no doubt."

"I had sunstroke, Senhor. I'm ill. I've missed work. My family misses my work on the land."

"How is the head, my boy? The old sun hits hard," said Mandado.

A soldier by the name of Algoz played an Algarve tune on his *machete.* The enlisted men cleaned their rifles and boots. The eldest wore a beard. He scolded Direito and spat tobacco juice into the fire. His snare drum hung from a hook attached to his belt. With a steady beat of the drum, tap, tap, tap, the soldiers formed and marched in single file into the square. The adjutant and bugler stood at attention. The adjutant read names off the roll. The first name was José Bernardo, José's cousin from *Calçada.* No one came forward. The square was silent. After reading the roll and taking into custody two young men, the captain led his troops up the slope by the church to search for Bernardo, the old soldier beating the drum, and the daylong search for reluctant conscripts began.

The street dogs howled and a black shepherd dog at Casa Camacho ripped the drummer's trouser. The captain beat the dog off with his quarter-staff.

José followed Direito and Mandado along the ridge.

The troop halted at the Bernardo gate. It was locked. Anita Bernardo the old grandmother stood up over a row of potted geraniums and looked down at the soldiers.

"Who are you? What do you want?" she said.

"The King's officer, Senhora, with a message for the family."

"Yes sir, with whom do you wish to speak?"

"Is this the Bernardo estate? I have a summons for José Bernardo. He's to proceed with me to Funchal to do his honorable service for king and country. Open the door, Senhora."

"Nobody home today, sorry Sir Captain. You come another day." The soldiers smiled at one another and nodded and leaned against the wall.

"Where's the family?"

"They work the gardens on the top, sir."

"Thank you, madam. Please notify José Bernardo he's to report immediately to me in the square by tomorrow morning. Good day."

The captain strode toward the ridge. The men complained and a youth about three hundred meters ahead of the patrol dropped his firewood and fled into a low canopy of grapevines.

Direito pointed his rifle into the vines. "I know you're in there. Come out or I'll fire." There was silence.

The sun rose hotter than the previous three days. The *leste* was blowing.

The captain leaned against the shaded wall, beads of sweat dripping down his cheeks. He was tired from the heat of the march. He waited for a reply from the vineyard.

The young man stood up and raised his hand, revealing a somber face.

"Where's José Bernardo?" said the captain.

"I don't know anyone by that name, Senhor."

"You know his name. Why did you run when you saw my patrol?"

"I thought the soldiers came for me, sir."

"You live on this land! You know this guy Bernardo," said Mandado.

"I don't understand, sir."

"José Bernardo. That's his family cottage in the cabbage patch over on the ridge," said Direito.

"He's not with me, Senhor. You'd see him."

"These peasants never tell us anything. Bernardo hides in the banana grove or the sugar cane and laughs at us," said Mandado.

"If you know where he's hiding and don't tell us, you break the law," yelled the captain.

The youth apologized and disappeared from view and the patrol moved on. The search along the ridge was long and hot and fruitless.

"Someone hides him. It happens in the villages. We arrive at night, in the morning, or at noon. It's the same. The men are hidden," said the captain.

"When warned they flee to the mountains. You can wait for them in the village," said José.

They returned to the Bernardo house. The captain rang the bell. The gate was open and the old woman sat in the yard embroidering a piece of linen. The captain walked up the steps and the old woman followed him along the terrace as if to put him under her spell.

The wily José Bernardo had slipped into the kitchen for a piece of tuna. He fled through the back garden and into the vineyard. The captain yelled to his men and with shouting and whistling they ran through the alley and into the vineyard. One stood at the gate. They went both sides of the house. Two of them leapt onto the back wall. They jumped into the vineyard and ran down the slope beneath the lattices, flushing José Bernardo into the open. The chase continued along the well-cultivated terraces and onto the square. The patrol surrounded the church.

The peasants in the gardens saw José Bernardo run into the church, soon after the clock struck eleven.

The captain fired his pistol into the air. He was far away, but it alerted two men and they fired their rifles after the fleeing man. The soldiers guarding the well ran to assist them. José walked the last hundred meters into the square, his feet bruised from the run down the slope and hurt from the hot cobblestones.

The captain ordered guards at the doors of the church. "Call the good Father," said the captain. Two soldiers ran to the priest's house. Three soldiers went into the market behind the church to search in the stalls along the warren of alleys and rundown shops.

The soldiers whistled to one another happy for a chase with promise of capturing their man. Their reward would be a *sesta* in the wine shops. The priest refused them entry to the Sanctuary with rifles. They could search and grab the villain, but they must arrest him on the porch. Father Segundo went inside to talk with José Bernardo before they captured him.

"You'll hide Bernardo, Father. We'll never find him," said the captain.

The priest looked grim and folded his arms across his cassock and listened to the captain.

"I'll talk with him. He can't escape and he'll walk out of the church with me," said the priest.

"Please help him, father," said José. "He doesn't want to serve. He wants to stay with his family."

"He can't hide in the church. God bless him. He's obliged to serve. It's the law of the land."

José glared at the priest. The soldiers' eagerness and laughter made him angry and he wanted to run into the church. The priest went in by the church door and slammed it after him.

The captain paced back and forth in front of the closed door. The men complained they wanted to eat and take *sesta*. The priest called to the captain. They entered the gloom and the captain genuflected at the head of the aisle.

"The rascal won't come and we'll drag him on his knees," said Mandado.

José Bernardo's sisters appeared and held him until the priest commanded them to kneel and pray. They knelt and José looked up at the cross and prayed for his cousin Bernardo. The soldiers moved up the aisle and stood on either side of the kneeling figure and took him when he stood up from the blessing. The priest kissed him on both cheeks and said good-bye. They carried Bernardo by the elbows to the door and tossed him on the pavement.

He screamed and they paid no attention. They shackled his wrists and led him off to the well where he refused the meal the soldiers offered him made earlier on the fire. The soldiers talked about the obscene words the villagers had yelled at them that morning fighting over the village well.

Again the women of the village returned to the square. While the soldiers surrounded the church, the women rushed to the well and drew water. One soldier blew his whistle. The women screamed at him. Dozens of soldiers ran to the well and with their rifles pushed the women away, grabbed their buckets and poured the water onto the cobblestones. The women chased the soldiers and spit on them. They screamed obscenities, their tongues darted like snakes and their words flew like angry bats. The small boys threw stones and the soldiers went after them. The women drew more water from the well. The soldiers confiscated their buckets and dumped water onto the cobbles amidst screaming, laughter and swearing. Aunt Maria of *Fajã Velha* grabbed a rifle and pointed it at the captain.

"No water from this well," said the captain. "Arrest that woman." The Aunt struggled with the adjutant to keep possession of the rifle. "You were born from the tail of a pig," she screamed.

The priest opened the door of the church and walked across the square and stood by the bound Bernardo. The attention of the women and the soldiers moved to the captain accepting the young man for military service. For the moment the fight over the well quieted down except for swearing and fingers making foul signs of defiance. José moved close to his cousin. "How do you feel, Bernardo?" he said.

"Can't you see? Father Segundo promised the soldiers wouldn't bind me." He raised his manacled hands above his head. "Don't believe priests. The soldiers shackled me."

CHAPTER XII

Maria and José snuggled under the blankets in the cave where the goats lived. She was teaching him to write. He now wrote his name and copied the penitential psalms. From the cave, they observed Talbot's sloop tied up at the quay. Writing his name in the dust was over and José deciphered sentences in the religious papers his Maria brought him from church.

They lay in the warm blankets and he was half-awake when she asked him about Rosa. He told her of Rosa's coming to him in the bedroom. Maria said, "Men are to meet virgins with a family member present."

"Widows and old maids say so and their gossip ruins good names and reputations," he said.

"You blackened her name," said Maria.

"I want to sail with Talbot," he said. She was surprised.

He closed his eyes and saw the sloop, its sail on the horizon. He imagined himself on the deck and waving good-bye to Campanário.

"The priest refused to let me join the brotherhood. I have no way to leave the land."

"You're staying on the land," said Maria. "Our family needs you. You have no patience. Priests favor us women. We have patience." She watched him staring at the sloop tied up at the quay. "Talbot leaves soon, thank goodness. You haven't worked many hours and father's angry."

"I'm soon sixteen and the military will come after me."

She touched his forehead and his ears, studied his eyes. "You've the land and our family."

"You'll marry and leave the land and our family. I'm slave to the land. I dreamt last night the soldiers knocked at the door and Father took them to the goats' cave and they tied me up. The guards carried me to the pebbled beach and I saw Talbot sail away without me. I jumped into the water and the soldiers fired their rifles. I couldn't swim to the sloop."

"It was a bad dream. The sloop is tied up at the quay."

"The dream was real."

"Speak with Talbot," she said. She kissed him. The wind blew through the banana grove along the slope. Wind-driven clouds covered the western sky, vapor from a cauldron, disappearing into space like witch's brew.

Maria wandered down the grove wearing her school clothes, white blouse and black skirt with a straw hat under which she wore a bright blue kerchief that covered her ears. She brought his lunch to the edge of the sugar cane and they ate under the grape arbor.

He'd weeded carrots, wiped his brow with his sleeve and saw her coming toward him in the sun's glare. The drum cadence drifted across the valley. The soldiers searched for another recruit. They moved in single file along *Fajã Velha*. Her shadow covered his face and Maria threw her arms around him. "I can't see the soldiers," he said.

"Never mind them."

"The women throw rocks at them!"

"Rosa wants to see you. I saw her at school."

"She's troubled," he said. "The more you speak to her, the more she'll want to marry me and worse to go away with me."

"She knows I'm to be married. She's jealous."

José ate the bread and goat's cheese she brought him for lunch and listened to her gossip about the women in the square arguing with the soldiers.

"Father Segundo told me to follow in my father's footsteps. My father never served in the army! My life is different than my father's," he said.

"Forget the army. Let's enjoy lunch."

"Is the *Senhorio* sending men for me?"

"The women were talking of the knife you kicked on the pebbled beach. They're sorry you had sunstroke The *Senhorio* sent men out to spy on you."

"What did Pistola say?"

"To come and visit him. He'll talk with the priest."

"Evil comes in threes--the *Senhorio*, the priest, the army. Are you going to marry Silva?"

"I'll marry him when he asks Father for my hand."

She poured goat's milk into a cup, humming to herself, a *festa* tune with old fashioned words. The kestrels hovered at the top of the valley and searched for prey.

"I'll leave home once you marry," he said. "The house is happy with you there. My heart will be broken when you leave."

She held his hand and closed her eyes. "You can visit me in Calçada," she said.

"At night, I'll be without you and see you in my dreams."

"Rosa wants to sleep with you."

He laughed. "Rosa dreams of me! She asked me to marry her and I didn't ask her father Senhor Duro for her hand."

"You have a future with her. Her family has work for you. You'll have a trade."

"I'll never work for the Castagna family."

"The army will snare you when you reach sixteen. I wanted you happy before I left home and married."

"My name is not on the baptismal roll. I'll have to work the land with Silvino and João and father."

"You can live with Henrique."

"He didn't want me in the mountains. He's alone and life's hard there. He is jealous of his freedom and wants no government officials roaming the mountains looking for him. It's better for now to live in the family."

He heard the snare drum and bugle in the village. The soldiers searched for those men resisting conscription. Every time he had gone to visit Pistola, spies had reported his leaving the land to the *Senhorio*. Even his trips to the quay were known throughout the village. From the cave while eating his lunch he watched the wherrymen on the waterfront loading Talbot's sloop. Fishing boats sailed west toward Ribeira Brava.

After their lunch, Maria climbed back up to the school house and he worked in the fields below the village. He cut hay for the goats, tied a bundle of cuttings and carried it to the cave. They nickered and nuzzled his hand.

He met father at the gate to his cottage and knelt. "Father, give me your blessing," he said. He kissed his father's hand.

The old man smiled. "Have you worked today?"

"I cut hay for my goats."

"Soldiers wander the land! The *Senhorio* approved of your stone work. He doesn't trust you. You left the land without his permission. He hates you for kicking his knife. You continue to disobey his authority. It's better to smile on a serpent and receive its affections than suffer its bite."

"Give him my compliments," said José.

"Where are João and Silvino?"

"They haul baskets to the pebbled beach and carrying up goods for Pistola's shop. This morning the wherrymen loaded Talbot's sloop."

"Good, the foreigner embarks."

"I wish to sail with him."

"You belong to this land. There is much work to do."

"I'm sick, not feeling well."

Father walked away.

José found a grassy slope and cradled his sickle in his hand and ran the whetstone along its blade in short circular movements and felt for dull spots. He ran the stone along the blade, first one edge and then the other. He cut a bundle of hay and lifted it onto his head and shoulders. The load shaded him from the sun and he walked over the dusty soil in his bare feet toward the goats' cave in the slope above the cottage.

On the way he stopped for a drink of water. His mother kissed him. "My boy struck down by the sun. Bed is a better place for you than out in the sun."

Maria embroidered and gossiped. Luisa and Julia smiled and nodded. The cousins, Eulalia and Augusta, wielded their needles through their linens, unconcerned.

He lifted his bundle of hay and went to the cave. His goats were happy to see him. He fed them and talked to them. Preto licked his hand, tickling his palm with his rough tongue. Gringo spoke softly and stared, her eyes almond-slits.

He closed his eyes and leaned back against the cool basalt. Talbot appeared in his mind, Talbot with tanned face and his arm in the sling. The Senhorio yelled. The knife fell on the beach pebbles in the sunlight. He opened his eyes. Who would feed his goats when he left the island? There was no grass and water in their cave! He'd lead them into the mountains. They'd be free. They'd be wild on the plateau at Rabaçal.

João's sharp whistle signaled alarm. José dropped hay into the goat's trough and ran along the ridge and down the slope into the yard in front of his house.

Maria and Luisa saw him run and followed him out the gate of their cottage. "Hurry, Hurry," said João. José warned Maria and Luisa to turn back. They paid him no heed and ran to see the soldiers.

CHAPTER XIII

The angry voices of soldiers rising and falling like wild bees tormented in their hive drew the attention of the villagers. José and his family ran from the cottage and climbed the steep path to the square. It took them fifteen minutes to reach the square about a kilometer via the trail. From the terrace of the church, Direito shouted and waved to the soldiers on the pebbled beach. He dressed in sweat-soaked khaki and leather, his rifle held against his cartridge belt, hot, oily, its brass green from sweat. His fellow Mandado pointed to the sugar cane field below.

Silvino lay on his back with his leg twisted underneath him. Direito tried to lift him. Silvino's basket lay on the ground with its packets, embroidery thread, tops, linens and fish-line spilled out over the ground. Silvino had lost his footing when hurrying along the narrow path while delivering goods to Pistola's shop.

"It's going to feel better," said Direito.

"Get my wife. I'm dying!" Silvino had not served militia duty and lived some of the time at home with his family and some of the time with his Natalia.

"He's broken his leg. I can't bear his screams and swearing," Direito said.

"Mandado will calm him. Soldiers swear oaths," said José.

Mandado examined Silvino and said, "Cut two poles and we'll carry him to the landlord."

Maria and Luisa ran to Silvino and kissed and fussed over him. A third soldier appeared. He led Joachim Gonçalves of Fajã Sul, tied with a rope, and last of all and out of breath the old Aunt, Tia Nita, scurried up.

Silvino heard the singsong voice of the old Aunt and whispered to Maria. "He wants to speak with the old Aunt," she said.

"What for?" said Direito.

"To ease the pain," said Luisa.

Direito shook his head and spit on his boot, rubbed it off and swore. "She can't heal it."

João grinned. He climbed along the upper path and whistled for Jaime and Manuel Abreu, cousins of the *Senhorio*. Each carried a pole.

The soldiers made a carry-all from jackets and poles. Calls and whistles spread the news. Silvino closed his eyes and the soldiers lifted him, legs spread out and limp. The makeshift stretcher was raised and moved up the embankment, Silvino was silent amidst the swearing. The soldiers set him down on the village path. Direito lit a cigarette and puffed on it and set it between the injured man's lips. The soldiers passed around a goatskin of wine and each took a swig.

João ran ahead of the entourage and retrieved his bail of willows. José heard the click of a hammer.

"If you flee, you'll be shot," said Direito to Joachim.

"Help me pick up the linens and goods off the ground," said José.

At the bridge, the clan rested by the stream, and Little Manuel of the Chapel yelled to his Uncle to hurry home before the retinue crossed the bridge. News traveled from peasant to peasant through the gardens of the village. Two peasants ran to the top of the ridge and signaled their cousins in Maçapez.

Father cursed Silvino and the soldiers. He threw his biretta on the ground. Mother wept and prayed. "It's the end of the world." Father blamed Silvino.

"Without Silvino, the produce won't be ready for the trip to Funchal."

The *Senhorio* swore at them for standing on the bridge doing nothing. He ordered them back to work.

"Who's going to set my leg?" said Silvino

The old Aunt walked with a slight tilt of head and a quick scuffle of her bare feet in the dust over to him and said, "I'll heal it."

The peasants laughed. They eyed the old lady and waited to hear what the Senhorio said to her who paid nothing for her land, and knew its history and whose land belonged to António and Beatris Abreu from Arco da Calheta in ancient times.

The Senhorio enjoyed the crowd. They owed him their allegiance. They awaited his command, hated him, but their ties to the land kept them obedient. Without his land they'd perish. The *Senhorio* looked in their faces for signs of disobedience. He whipped his trouser leg with a stick of sugar cane. He glared at the old Aunt.

He said, "Senhora Aldeia, fetch Pistola from Maçapez. I must speak with him."

"It's an honor your grace," said his oldest granddaughter. He nodded. Aldeia trotted over the bridge. The peasants waited in silence.

Direito said, "Carry Silvino to the quay and put him on the Blandy Brothers' boat. Good doctors in Funchal."

"They have three doctors and they're expensive. It'd cost too much. We'd have to carry him to the pebbled beach and hurt him," said Father.

"He could sail with Talbot," said João.

The *Senhorio* said to the old Aunt, "No, you'll not. Don't touch him." The onlookers left when they saw she wasn't about to heal the leg. They said nothing to the *Senhorio*.

"Talbot does not sail today. He dines with me," said the *Senhorio*. "This matter of the leg is urgent."

Pistola examined the leg and went home to his shop and talked it over with Talbot. There in Maçapez, Pistola was mother and father, doctor and dentist, lawyer and judge. He held no hereditary rank and owned little land during this period. The Senhorio was irked that this outlander, Pistola, whose family controlled Funchal in the early days of discovery, was judge of Campanário. Pistola found it a pleasure and a privilege to have Talbot as his guest.

"I see you've caught our Joachim," Pistola said.

"Yes, Senhor," said Direito. "He was wily, but his cousins needed water and we let them use the well and they told us to his hiding place."

"You were under orders to seal the well," said José.

Mandado and Direito shrugged and winked at the *Senhorio*. "We obey orders and arrest men on the roll that refuse to serve. A little bad water won't kill them. They only made soup."

"Where'd you find Joachim?"

"We caught the rascal in the cave near the pebbled beach. He waited to sail on *Falcon*."

"The Blandys are our friends and they'd tell us. You needn't take him."

"Senhor, we capture the men whose names were read off the roll before we return to the city. The King's order requires our obedience."

Silvino, forgotten on the ground, his eyes closed, lay like a dead man and Mother wiped his forehead with a cloth and prayed over him.

"I need Silvino for carrying vegetables to the boat. I'll sell no produce," said Father. "Surely, you'll allow José to haul baskets to the pebbled beach."

The *Senhorio* swore and blew snot from his nose.

"If I see him on the beach, I'll have him beaten until he can't walk."

"Senhor, I send things to the market. Silvino is ready for the grave. João cannot work day and night. Two strong men are fit for the job, Senhor."

Father argued and wheedled with him. The *Senhorio* hit flies off Silvino's trouser. "Carry him to my quinta and lay him on the patio," he said to the soldiers.

"The taxes come from selling vegetables, Senhor. *Onde não há dinheiro nada el reis o seu quinhão.* Without money, I've nothing to pay the Senhorio."

"Shut up," said the Senhorio.

Father cursed the Senhorio when he worked alone on the land, but stopped swearing and followed the Senhorio up the slope, hat in hand. He waved away Mother and Maria, Julia, Luisa with a slap of his hat. Mother rolled her eyes and followed him and left Silvino with the soldiers.

José vowed to haul loads to assist João, though he was banned from the beach. He waited and the soldiers carried Silvino toward the quinta, hitched up his trousers, retied the knot and fled into the sugar cane field.

He heard wheezing and coughing and spitting in the lower end of the field. He whittled a stick into dagger-like shape. The stout man in the white shirt and black trousers wore braces and a shepherd's hat. It was Henrique.

"How's my beach fighter? I hear Silvino broke his leg!" The voice never broke and his bright even teeth showed in a shy smile. José jumped down off the wall and shook Henrique's hand.

Henrique said, "I heard you had sunstroke, you slept at Castagna's and you want to take holy orders!"

"You know all the gossip in Campanário, Henrique. Dona Castagna's soup was excellent."

"How's your Talbot?"

"Fine, I'm going to visit him in Funchal. He dines with Pistola this evening."

"That Rosa spied me coming down the mountain. She's a beauty. I've known her since she was a baby. She'd make you a good wife."

"Have you come to take me off to the mountains?"

"No, I want no excuse for the militia or anyone else to invade the heights. If you joined me as soon as you were of age the militia would come after me. I came to buy salt, coffee, sugar and a little flour and return to the heights alone."

"Will you help us a few days to bear the harvest to the pebbled beach?"

"No, I'll only be in the village long enough to buy provisions."

"I must be off to see how Silvino will fare," said José Henrique waved him good and turned off down the slope toward Maçapez and Pistola's shop.

The servants and neighbors crowded around the Senhorio's quinta. Pistola moved up the path and examined the herb garden. He knew more about crops and animals and wild life than any man or woman in the village.

He was a difficult man to cheat when you sold sugar cane or wine. He bought the best wine during the harvest and stored it in his cave at the beach.

The Senhorio swore at the soldiers. After much argument and cursing, they nodded their heads and agreed to set the leg. Silvino screamed when they applied hot cloths. They drank brandy in quick sips as they worked on him. The men held his leg and they pulled when the lever was set. The soldiers drank dollops of wine to their success. They eyed the straightened leg. Silvino fainted. Pistola stayed for dinner.

José hid in the Flame of the Forest tree and waited for Pistola to leave the quinta. Two hours later, Pistola having calmed the Senhorio said good-bye. In the twilight, his raspy breath marked his progress along the path. José met him on the ridge above Maçapez. They sat and talked about the best way for José to leave home. "How'd you learn French?" said José.

"My Uncle sent me to Funchal and the Christian Brothers had a school. Their policy changed to teach girls and in a few years they no longer taught young men. Women spend their days cooking, embroidering and counting money. Father Segundo has nothing against you. It's church policy. Women do not threaten their authority."

"You were lucky to learn to read and write, Senhor."

"I managed my Uncle's shop on the holidays. We worked from dawn to dark and into the night using primitive lamps with laurel oil for fuel."

"Maria teaches me a little to write and read," said José.

"The shop was better in those days. The accounts were kept in good order. . I sell and deal and make peace with neighbors, but I can't stay awake at night to mark the books."

They walked down the path into Maçapez and listened to the soldiers calling to one another in the darkness. They sat on the steps of the shop. Pistola took down the key from its hiding place behind the shutter and opened the door.

He lit a lamp. The shop was a mountain of jumble. Lines in trade -- hoes, pickaxes, trowels, wine casks, canned food, cloth, beeswax, needles, salt cod, hats, boots, harmonicas, beans, lentils, cayenne pepper.

"I want to work for you," said José

"Your Father needs you. Silvino can't work for at least eight months!"

"Senhor, I want to count goods and weight flour, salt and sugar. The land's poor and I'm the youngest. The land has nothing for me."

"I promised the shop to Manuel Joachim when he returns from the militia. My Uncle had eight brothers. He'll not support them. The land in Maçapez is rich but can't feed and clothe his family. They're poor and by saving tiny bits over time they'll buy passage to Brazil!"

"They take on apprentices in Funchal."

"Work is scarce. Many men sail to Minas Gerais where the gold is and the land spreads out as far as the eye can see."

"Senhor Talbot may help me. I ask him again in Funchal."

"Don't cry, my friend. I'll talk with him. He'll reward you for kicking the knife."

"Please give me a place in the shop, Senhor."

"I'll do what I can," said Pistola from the dark gallery. A whistle rose from the hills. They listened to it. José replied. No sound. The village and church tower were lit by the streetlamps and the stars shown above the silhouettes of the mountains. Bare feet in the dust, João walked through the lamplight, grinning like a circus bear and joined José at Pistola's.

"Silvino's sleeping. The Senhorio sent thanks and obligations to Senhor Pistola. Will Silvino be down long?"

"It'll be eight careful weeks! When the doctor comes on Wednesday, he'll examine the leg and put it in a cast. Silvino shouldn't be moved."

"Father received permission for you to haul vegetables to the boat. The Senhorio reversed his order."

José tossed straw in the rain barrel and the ripples broke up the reflections of the stars.

"It's late," said Pistola.

"You'll see Talbot in the morning, Senhor?" said José

"Yes. The Talbots are wine merchants and own land in Funchal and may know of something. Off to bed. Beware of soldiers."

"José caused our family trouble by helping Talbot," João said to Pistola.

"He'll learn."

"He led soldiers into the village and to the well. Tongues are wagging."

"The well is in the square. The blame lies with me. Those villagers are mad," said José. He bade Pistola goodnight.

Pistola called after them, "Work every day and don't listen to gossip. Give Silvino my blessing, good night and good luck."

At sea, the lanterns of the fishing boats glowed like stars floating in the cavern of space. José and João pissed on the posts that marked the Senhorio's demesne and laughed. They climbed *Fajã Velha* and hiked into the valley of the melons. Maria heard them singing in the darkness and drew a jug of wine and set it on the table. She kissed José when he came into the kitchen. She blew out the lamp and climbed up the ladder into the loft. The brothers drank their wine and followed her and they fell asleep together. Early in the dawn, mother hit the trough as she dipped for water. José opened his eyes. He listened to mother washing the steps and the pathway. Maria slept. Dawn lighted the valley and a new day of labor hauling baskets down the path and down the steps to the quay.

CHAPTER XIV

The morning sky blue as dyer's woad, a magnificent dome with sunlight over the grapevines and the fruit trees bought tears to his eyes. It gave him courage to rise up and work. He drank his brew made from rubbing a chicory bean against a coffee bean and saved the coffee bean for tomorrow's cup.

He watered and fed the goats pampering and hugging them. Without Silvino's wages the family couldn't pay their portion of the Senhorio's tax. Father hired no men from Quinta Grande to cut the sugar cane. Silvino's land was small and low in the valley by the cliff near Tia Nita's cottage and next to nowhere.

Father called him from the backdoor. He bid goodbye to his goats and hurried down to the house. The onions curing in the sun on the roof of the pigs' pen were ready to braid and hang in the kitchen. The cabbage seedlings behind the house were to be transplanted today. Father was unshaven, mean-looking and blinking his eyes.

"Oh God, Silvino can't work," Father said. "You must work for two of you, no daydreaming of sails. The baskets to the cave, the pig manure spread on the upper garden and beetles picked off the vines." The old man rubbed the stubble on his chin. His high cheek bones gave him the look of a devil.

"João works. The cousins lend a hand. Playing in the sun causes sunstroke. Do your work and be proud." Father examined the cracked stonework where the wall hung over the path.

José wanted permission to visit Pistola that evening but didn't ask father, worried about work, land and taxes.

"I'm able, father. I'll work early and haul the vegetables to the boat. This wall can wait. It hasn't fallen down!"

"I'll die soon. You'll try to do my work, but you won't be able to do it. You know too little."

José waited by father's knee and asked his blessing and kissed his hand.

"Promise to work this land after I die," said father.

"I'll pay off the debt to the Senhorio. I can't promise you to work the land. The land is poor."

The old man closed his eyes, shutting out José's words.

João scratched his back against an arbor post.

"Are you ready?" said José.

"It's best to haul early in the day," said João. "Father is going to transplant the cabbages."

José prayed for luck and kissed mother on her cheeks and Maria on the lips. He whistled. He picked up his burlap and followed João.

Tia Nita whose real name was Luisa de Jesus and called witch-woman by the villagers, hailed them on the height of land overlooking the sea. They borrowed her key to Pistola's cave at the beach where they stored vegetables to be taken by tugboat to Funchal. She reached down between her breasts and pulled out the key. Her stone hut with the straw roof was dilapidated and ancient-looking. "Be sure to return my key," she said. She waved them off and huddled before her fire. In the twilight on their way home, she offered them wine. José felt he was a man of the slopes.

"I'm sorry," he said to her. "You wanted to heal Silvino. The Senhorio turned you away. You'd have cured him."

She shrugged. "The Senhorio's a flea. I blow him away with a puff of smoke."

"He's one mean bastard, that guy," said João.

They had hauled vegetables until twilight and made their last trip down in darkness. Great wicker baskets balanced on the shoulder one at a time. José grunted under the load. The trail wound through prickly pear. The volcanic soil was sun-dried with a loose crust and its carpet of sand surprised others and hurtled down the steep. The basket's weight shifted and he turned. At the brink, he eased the basket against the side-hill and rested. The air moved up the slope cooling his face and shoulders. Below him, on the surface of the ocean, waves crashed against the shore, forcing themselves between crevices and dashing high and black. Silent from this distance, the grey crests were silent and shining white in the darkness, hundreds of meters below. The sounds moved on the night-wind softly increasing with the roar.

His arms were numb as he shouldered the basket. Shards of light shattered through clouds parting in the sky. The wind tore at the stone huts and whipped across the sugar cane fields. It whipped wild branches in the orchards, twisted vines, raced through the village paths, and sang in the belfry of the chapel-on-the- cliff.

The basket tipped. He righted it and moved down the long slope. This stretch ended in a sharp turn. The path zigzagged down the cliff. By standing straight it was possible to balance and ease the feet one at a time.

The wind hit with force as he rounded the turn on the promontory and in the fading glow he saw the steps cut into the lava rock, going down into darkness.

The high tide smashed against the rocks at the base of the cliff, hit with force and sent waves running up the rocks. The wind sang and moaned in the holes and crevices, like voices in Hell.

His shoulder hurt and he moved under the load, holding his breath, for from this point he saw nothing but the ocean down below him. The rough slope of broken rocks was one hundred and eighty-five meters and he saw fierce waves breaking on the rocks. Without a railing or wall, the path gave no protection, and once he fell, the loose rocks would hasten his fall.

One misstep and he'd slide down the slope to be smashed to bits. The waves would toss him on the rocks. He saw himself as a lizard crawling up a vertical wall. He saw his basket of vegetables spilling down the rocky slope buffeted by the surge of wind, by the evil of the world, a great force moving it down into the ocean. He saw his ancestors. From the dead they spoke to him. Their voices echoed in the caves along the cliff and their faces peered at him out of the darkness.

He moved his foot ahead of him with caution and he lost his footing on the slope. His left foot slipped forward and he regained balance. The pebbled beach below was outlined by white foam. The backwash loomed closer. The dark mouths of the caves appeared.

The sea had made a dike of pebbles deposited in layers during winter storms. Behind this, the villagers had built stone cottages.

While José hurried along the shore toward Pistola's cave he saw the glow of a fire. Soldiers warmed themselves by the fire and guarded the conscripts to be shipped by boat in the morning to Funchal. He smelled their coffee and broiled fish. José heaved down his load.

"Abreu of the sunstroke!" said one soldier.

"Yes Senhor."

"How's Silvino?" said Manuel Reis beyond the fire in the shadows.

"I haven't seen him. Mother says he's better. He doesn't sleep well."

"We'll miss him," said José Bernardo.

Joachim Gonçalves greeted José with a smile and sad eyes. Two soldiers threw off blankets and gathered around the fire.

"When will I see you again?" said José.

Manuel shrugged. "We sail to Funchal and then who knows where..."

Mandado cradled his rifle in his arms. He saw the sad faces and winked at Direito.

"You should be proud to serve your King," said Direito. He yawned. The late hour patrolling the village ruined his sleep and he missed the *sestas* at Fort Saint James in Funchal.

"The tide and wind are high," said a wherryman.

"Where's your family?" said José.

"They'll be here to see me off. I'll die in Angola or Goa," said José Bernardo. "My mother cried and cursed the King."

José grabbed Mandado's rifle.

"*Bastardo* give it back."

José pointed the rifle at his chest. Mandado jumped. "Don't be foolish, boy. These fellows are conscripts. You can't help them."

"Run quickly. I'll follow you." said José.

Direito pointed his rifle at José "Run and see what happens."

"The day we pick you up for the King, we'll cross your name off the roll. But you'll never reach the fort," yelled Mandado. "The captain will hear of you, *bastardo*."

"Run, I tell you. Run for the slopes. Direito can shoot me. Run into the dark."

The three conscripts stared at José. They didn't move until Direito raised his rifle.

"If José fires on me, I'll blow away the three of you."

"Please, lower your gun, José. You can't save us. Forget the damn army and run off to the heights. You have troubles with the Senhorio."

José Bernardo pled with him. Roberto Camacho, a fisherman from Ribeira Brava, reached for the rifle. José jumped away and pulled the hammer back.

"Please, give it up," said Joachim Gonçalves. "You'll regret it when the Army takes you."

José saw the soldiers wouldn't fire on him. The urgings of his friends weakened his gesture. Direito and Mandado blamed one another. They cursed the captain for giving them the duty and not sending two more men to relieve them and for guarding a poisoned well in an ignorant village.

They laughed at him. He relaxed and smelled the coffee and the broiled fish. He enjoyed the warmth of the fire. He listened to his friends. They laughed and joked even though they were leaving home for six years.

He handed the rifle to Mandado. Direito swore at him, threatening him with his fist.

He knelt before the fire and pulled down his biretta so the soldiers couldn't see his face. He had work tomorrow. He had to haul Tia Nita's baskets.

João arrived with a basket, scornful at seeing José by the fire. José Bernardo wrapped his arms around José's shoulders and offered him a piece of fish. José had lost precious time and he carried his basket to the cave and set it down.

On his return to the fire, Manuel said to him, "Never mind, José, the soldiers can't harm us. My God! They could've shot you."

José stared into the fire and ate his piece of fish.

"Say something. Speak man," said Joachim Gonçalves.

José ate the delicate piece of broiled fish and turned away. João led him to the way up the path. José looked back as darkness covered the beach. He held his head up and stared at the great stone *campanário* rising from the sea. He crossed himself and listened to the rattle of the pebbles in the tide sucked down the stony shingle. He wished with his heart to be as free as the sea. He turned and followed João up the steep slope without looking back.

CHAPTER XV

The next morning, the ocean lay before his eyes as he walked along the pebbled beach with his basket of vegetables on his shoulder. The ocean was a great flat plain. He wished he could walk on its desert surface and journey to the continent. Pistola's cook waved at him and João. They spent most of the day hauling baskets of vegetables to the cave. Alvaro Rodrigues, called the dreamer by the villagers, talked of leaving Madeira. He never went further away from Campanário than Ribeira Brava. José sensed he could walk on the sea if he believed with all his heart and walk away to be free of the land and its lord.

In the afternoon, José watched the wherrymen steer their green skiffs up to the quay. Alvaro stood by the fire on the beach. The soldiers guarded the conscripts and waited for Blandy's boat. Alvaro offered João and José a drink. The wind from the Desertas stiffened.

"Let's have a taste of wine, yes, yes, yes," Alvaro said.

In the restaurant, four villagers played cards and drank wine, the air suffused with cigarette smoke. Alvaro lit a half-butt rolled earlier that morning. He spit into the brass cuspidor and pushed glasses of red wine across the counter.

"I've worked twenty years. It's enough. I want to live in the mountains with Henrique." He sipped from his glass and gazed at the shining sea.

"Why not pack up and go to the Paúl da Serra?"

"Enough of that!" said the Tatara, the agent of the Senhorio who urged him to confront Talbot.

"Henrique is the lucky one. He lives by himself without landlords and priests. He's free as a kestrel," said José

"You don't know the mountains in winter, young man," said Tatara.

"Henrique and Gold Tooth know about ice and snow. The King's men hunt the mountaineers and warn others against fleeing there, said José

"Lisbon controls Madeira with a general and his militia. Freedom is in the mountains," said Tatara.

"I sing melodies to the ocean. I watch folks going to Funchal and listen to their gossip. I've been to church and Maçapez twice this year. I know nothing of snow and ice," said Alvaro.

"I saw you at *festa*," said Twenty-Seven. "You'd quit the mountains after a few days."

"The soldiers would hunt you down, José. They came to drink beer and they'll not forget you took Mandado's rifle," said Alvaro.

"I'll run away. The young men serve six years for nothing."

"They fight for the King and the country," said Tatara.

"For love of the land and our flag," said Twenty-Seven.

"You served. Do you love the mountains?" said José.

"The Army was big. I couldn't breathe. I ran away and they caught me in Ribeira Brava," said Alvaro.

"Why'd you stay in Campanário? The landlords destroyed the land by cutting down the Spanish chestnuts and pines," said José.

"I dreamed of running away. That Gonçalves the millionaire from Uruguay made millions of *reis* selling our timber."

"Henrique sells a little timber. He couldn't support a family."

"I can't support a family on what Pistola pays me to cook lunch and serve wine. Who needs a woman? Freedom is serious." said Alvaro.

"You could jump a ship and sail to Tenerife," said José.

"Alvaro hasn't money for papers," said Tatara.

"What papers?"

"You need gold seals and official names to leave the island," said Twenty-Seven.

"I'd never be able to return to see my family without papers. I'd miss attending the Festa of Saint Blaise."

"We need freedom, Alvaro. We dream and this pebbled beach remains when we're gone," said José

José drank his thimbleful of wine.

"You're too young to remember. The Army collected taxes for the King during the famine," said Twenty-Seven. "Your brother has the best world. He comes down for festivals and lives alone on the heights. He never served in the Army."

"Alvaro and José are mad. So shut up!" said Tatara.

"Henrique nearly froze one winter. He was forced down by the snow and wind. He obeyed God," said Twenty-Seven.

"I don't know what God has to do with snow and wind," said Alvaro. "I've never seen God."

Alvaro rubbed his nose. His cheeks were ruddy from the wine. José felt the heat of the sun on his head. His eyes hurt. Alvaro faced the sea, forlorn, his face wrinkled.

One fisherman built up the fire and another broiled fish. *Falcon* blew its whistle. The wherrymen stirred. José poured milk into the mugs and Alvaro followed with the pail of hot coffee.

"God's in church," said Rui the fisherman.

"The priest's not God," said Alvaro.

"He's dresses like God," said Twenty-Seven.

"He wears women's clothes and lives with women. The village could fall into the sea and the priest wouldn't care," said Alvaro. He spit into the fire.

"The priest won't let me go to school," said José.

"He'll do nothing for us. He teaches women. Go and live with Henrique." Alvaro sipped his coffee.

The winds died in the late afternoon. On the pebbled beach, the men mended nets and spread them out. They tied lines together for catching *espada*. They sharpened the barbs of their fishing hooks. The Blandy tug rested five hundred meters off the quay. The wherrymen loaded her, swearing and whistling. Jorge Bonito, the half-wit, spittle oozing from his mouth, played with his knife and laughed to himself.

The tug's whistle blew ready to sail for Ribeira Brava. Jorge pocketed his knife and dragged himself toward the fishermen. The wheels of his cart were shiny and worn.

"You going to Maçapez?" he whined.

José gazed into the fire. Jorge reached for a broiled fish and cried out when he burned his fingers. He cursed the virgin.

Rui jumped. "Watch your tongue. God listens." He crossed himself and fingered the cross hanging on its golden chain on his chest, a treasure won betting a cockfight.

Roberto, the cask-maker, lifted a fish off the fire and blew on it. He handed it to the whimpering boy. "Leave him alone. He's heard something and may talk. He can't work and he hears all the gossip."

The half-wit Jorge Bonito known for his black curly hair bit chunks of fish and swallowed them, sucking at his fingers and licking off the juice. Bones and scales, head and tail, went into his mouth. His eyes popped out and cheeks bulged. He coughed. Ruy raised his hand and the lad continued chewing. The men smoked cigarettes and drank coffee. After a night on the ocean they rested and took out playing cards and a bottle of *aguardente.*

"What did you see, today, my friend?" said Roberto.

"The priest said Mass. The soldiers came to pour cement," said Jorge.

"What did he say? Where pour cement?"

"In the well, the Priest said that soldiers came to seal the well."

"What Sons-of-a-Bitches! My grandfather drank from that well. He met my grandmother there drawing water," said Alvaro.

"The sign says not to drink the water or the Army will imprison us," said Jorge, "José was the one showed two soldiers into the village and led them to the well. They didn't know where the village was and thought it was the Valley of the Melons."

"Direito and Mandado would've found the village without him."

"José didn't poison the well," said Rui.

"He leaves the land without the lord's permission," said Roberto.

"I finished my work, Senhor," said José.

"You kicked the knife. Why did you kick the knife?"

"I don't know." José braided a fish-line he found by the fire. "The stranger had a bruised arm."

"You kicked the knife. What an insult! You'll suffer for it!" said Rui.

Jorge crossed his eyes and shivered. He looked around at the men and crawled behind Roberto.

"I kicked the knife. The Senhorio punished me for it with a day in his high field hauling stone," said José.

"You don't help strangers and forget your own," said Roberto.

The fishermen listened in silence. Roberto stirred the fire and stared into the coals. Jorge Bonito born with paralyzed legs pointed his knife at José. He took it from his rags, only the net mender at the water's edge saw the blade. Jorge drew signs in the air with his finger and across his neck.

"Enough, enough," said Rui. "Save your signs for church."

"I love church," said Jorge the wanderer who reported gossip and watched comings and goings in the village square.

"The church teaches not to kill," said Alvaro.

"The devil must die," Jorge said, grinning and winking.

Ferdinando, the wherryman, heard the insult and rubbed his ear. The fishermen swore. "God listens and remembers."

"Praise God!" said the wanderer, lowering his knife.

"You should love God more than men," said José.

Jorge pointed the knife at José. "You're a Bastard!"

Marcelo grabbed his wrist. "Go away. Crawl into your hole."

"Go to the women," said Zino, the one cooking the fish.

"Go! Up the trail," said Alvaro.

When they saw Jorge draw his knife, Vasco, Alberto, and Justino ran up from the quay. Men knitting nets jumped. Porters yelled. The wherrymen joyously left their routine.

"What's up?" said Justino. "He wants to cut?" Roberto said the first wherryman up from the beach.

"Have a bit of fish," said Alvaro.

"A drink?" asked Zino.

"Nothing but a squabble," said Ferdinando.

José turned away. Zino caught his arm and swung him into the group of fishermen. The fishermen demanded news.

"The church, the church, always the church," shouted Alvaro.

Jorge punched Marcelo. He returned them with jabs to the gut. Jorge dropped his knife in the sand. He swore at José and made obscene signs. The fishermen laughed.

"If you need strong arms, whistle," said Alberto the wherryman.

José touched him on the shoulder and grinned. Jorge stared with grim eyes. He made a sign with his finger. The drool dropped off his chin. His dark eyes were hard as pebbles.

José waved to the fishermen and wherrymen. "See you later. I'm off."

He ran across the pebbled beach and climbing the steps he rested at the top of the cliff. The pebbled beach shone in the setting sun and the dark figures of fishermen worked the nets and lines. The stunted figure of Jorge on his wheeled platform set by the fire listening to the men talk about leaving Madeira. .

José shivered and turned to climb higher. He vowed he'd leave if it was his last living act. The only sounds came from the village square soldiers sealing the well with cement, their loud voices and hammering echoing off the surrounding heights.

CHAPTER XVI

"The melon plants are dying," José said. He climbed through the shrubs and undergrowth. He felt the soil dry as dust. No water diverted from the *levada* into the sluice. Three days before, João was to open the gate in the night to irrigate the garden according to *água de giro,* the monthly schedule. The hullabaloo with the soldiers and Silvino's broken leg had distracted João. Father's curse watered no melons.

José turned the gear and raised the crossed bars opening the sluice gate and water flowed into the irrigation trough.

When he met João at the goat's cave, he said, "I've let water into the melons."

João said, "We're not entitled to water now."

"You neglected to open the sluice."

"The Senhorio will receive a report. Father will hear of the violation. They're talking about the open sluice over in *Amoreira*. So you opened the sluice and let water into the melons? Vasco Araujo discovered it. You're in trouble!"

"I wanted to save the melons. The vines were dying. You'd forgotten to release the water on the *água de giro,*" said José.

"And you opened the sluice. You're the one to be punished for it."

"Who forgot the irrigation?" said José.

"We'll guard the patch for the rest of the summer. Someone turned off the water in the night." said João. "I opened it on schedule. I swear I did. Either Jorge the half-wit, or someone in his family sent by the Senhorio closed it and destroyed the melons."

"João forgot to give the melons their watering on the *água de giro;* I turned the water into them so they'll ripen for market. The family will have melons to sell," said José.

His father's whistle caught his ear. The old man appeared with a rabbit slung over his shoulder. Father skinned out the rabbit. Seeing the water irrigating the melons, father said, "The Lord is angry at me."

"I saved your vines. They were dying. I did my best."

"I'll have to give up a night's water to pay back." The old man's voice broke. The vein in his temple darkened and his Adam's apple wobbled. He spit.

Father swore at God Almighty, the priests and his good-for-nothing sons. He cursed everyone and hit José.

José's shoulder smarted from repeated blows with the strap. He jumped and ran toward the kitchen. Father cursed and pushed Maria aside and went after José. Mother grabbed the strap. "Let me alone, woman," said Father. The old man hit José hard.

The sisters screamed, "Stop Father, You're mad." He cursed them all and the girls laughed.

"José is a criminal. He deserves to be thrown from the cliff," said father.

The chase continued and José climbed into the loft and escaped father's wrath.

Thinking of his son's death quieted father. He sat on the bench and cried. "Come down, coward. You're ungrateful. Why can't you be faithful to the family?"

José listened from the dark under the eaves. He heard the sound of the strap whipping the ladder. What if the old man climbed the ladder? Had he beaten Henrique? He counted the number of blows on the ladder. He heard a whack on the iron stove and closed his eyes. The sound of water poured into a glass. He listened in the silence.

Before daylight the next morning, José whispered to mother he was leaving. He ate a breakfast of corn meal and coffee. She cried and wanted him home. She cut his corn meal in strips and fried it. She hummed to herself as she stirred up the coals in the ashes and added hard wood to freshen the fire and made his breakfast.

She said, "The women gossip about the day you took the rifle. They say you were a coward. You didn't fire the rifle that day on the beach. Their sons lost an opportunity to escape from the soldiers. Your name was sent to the commandant in Funchal."

"I'm off. I can escape their tongues. These women will still be talking about me the day I'm buried."

Dawn moved over the villages--Arrieiro, Encumeada Alta, Poco de Neve, São António, Torrinhas de Boa Ventura. Sunlight touched the peaks of Torres and Ruivo. Bright bands of clouds spread across the eastern horizon. José gathered his things-- dried cod, corn meal, biretta, knife, burlap bag. In the yard, he turned and held Mother's hand and kissed her on both cheeks. Her tears fell and she wiped her cheek with her apron.

"I'll see you at the Festival of Saint Blaise," he said.

Wisps of smoke rose from the chimneys of the cottages in the Valley of the Melons as he climbed the ridge. Two ghost-like figures, women on their way to Mass, walked across the bridge. A cry arose across the valley and curled into his ear, an eerie sound almost bird-like, unearthly. Though he was anxious to set off, he listened to the weird sound, almost human, a child-like cry. He looked off toward the mountain and the trail leading to the height and hesitated. He turned back and walked down the path toward the strange sounds.

CHAPTER XVII

The wind rustled the grass along the cliff's edge. José cocked his ear and listened to the cries from the dark house. Women were keening for the dead.

As he walked through the garden he felt each bare foot pick up the fine dust. He saw two shadows in the Old Aunt's garden. Two women were keening, hands wrapped up in their shawls.

"She doesn't move," said the dark one.

José climbed the steep bank beyond the old Aunt's garden. The cries of the women raised the hairs on the back of his neck. As he moved toward the house, the women stopped keening.

The door gave, swinging wide, dry and soft to his touch, it swung open and beyond he saw light across the stone floor. The silence touched his ear, pitiful and long, like a bird sitting still on a branch.

He whispered, "Tia Nita."

He leaned against the doorjamb and examined the room. An odor of vinegar tickled his nose, rotting cloth, decayed fish. He pinched his nose and stepped inside. Her bed was empty. The curtains moved in the parlor, the morning air filling them and they moved gently in the sunlight. He saw her in her chair, not rocking as was her wont tilted forward.

"Tia?" He moved toward where she sat.

Her eyes stared at him, and he lost balance and slid to the floor. He coughed.

He inched forward on his hands and knees. Her hand was solid and cold. He knew she went to bed at sunset. Many evenings he had seen her looking out her bedroom window and he had waved to her. She had signed the air with her finger and drawing her shawl close to her shoulders waved and disappeared from the window. Tia Nita knew the folk ways of her ancestors. He remembered the time she healed Maria Fernandes. Silvino had carried the basket of herbs for her. Tia Nita hunched over her crooked walking stick and staggered along the pebbled pavement.

His sisters called the potion, spider soup, and Maria Fernandes drank it. That herbal mess saved her from a miscarriage. Young women delivered their babies with the assistance of Tia Nita. He wiped away his tears.

She looked alive. The clock sounded the six. He looked for Medo, her cat. The cat spit at him when he offered it a piece of fish. Nita's eyes were dark and her hair white as the curtains of daylight through the window.

He ran outdoors. He shivered and regretted he had entered the house. He spit on his hand and danced three circles dragging his toe in the dust. That would drive away the evil eye. The old crones had stopped keening and ate their dried cod. He raised his eyes to the hills and levadas. God watches over Tia Nita, he thought.

The keening had attracted a swarm of villagers; they wound down the trail toward the solitary cottage on the edge of the cliff. José whistled three long staccato notes and two whipping long ones, loud to soft, his João whistle.

João never answered his signal that night, and José found him the next day in mid-morning, carrying a load of firewood. João yawned, set down his bundle and stretched out under the anona tree. "Tia Nita haunted the valley. I'm happy she's gone."

"She nursed the sick and cured our Maria of bronchitis," said José. "Tia Nita was descended from the old Abreu clan. She knew of the kidnapping of women for ransom, the rapes, the Evil Eye."

"She's dead," said João. "I heard the keening. Forget her. Let some one else bury her."

João refused to assist him. José returned to the cottage alone to watch over her. The spectators and mourners stood outside and prayed. They eyed him with curiosity and shook their heads when he entered the cottage.

He fell asleep on the floor while keeping an eye on her corpse. In his dream Tia Nita chanted over the waters in a strange language and beat the surface of the stream with olive branches. When he awoke, the villagers had left for their cottages and he left for home.

His mother served him bread and cabbage soup. She scolded him for leaving the land without permission from the landlord.

"I'll leave the land whenever I wish to. I am a free man. When the Senhorio heard I left the land, he sent me to the stone-yard. He won't send me there again."

She begged him to stay away from the cottage of Tia Nita.

"I know nothing of her death."

"They say you were seen leaving the cottage by two women keening in her yard!" Mother cried. "Tia Nita was a plague on our family. She's gone. Please keep away from her cottage or rumors will follow you."

He and father went to the *Quinta* of the Senhorio. Father said, "My son will tell you what he knows about Tia Nita."

"I heard you were in her presence," said the Senhorio. He smelled of sour his breath, unwashed shirt and trousers. He had been drinking for three days. "What did you see there?"

José looked up at the Senhorio. *A Deus poderas mentir, mas não podes enganar a Deus,* you may lie to God but you cannot deceive Him. "I found her sitting in her chair by the window, dead!"

"Why didn't you call for help?"

"I whistled for João. Two women were keening."

"Maybe she was alive," said the Senhorio.

"I touched her hand. It was cold."

The Senhorio said, "You heard him say he touched the hand of a witch. I want you to remember his words."

The neighbors grimaced. Vasco covered his eyes with his hands. Izidro and Marcelo crossed their arms and stood together for comfort. The women shook their heads and remained silent. They knew the landlord hated José and he was out to threaten him and punish him and drive him into submission.

José returned to the cottage with the Senhorio. The dead woman lay on her bed, a crucifix clutched in her hands, prayer beads wound between her fingers. The women had shut her eyes and placed a coin on each lid. She was dressed in black and not the traditional white smock.

"Why is she dressed in black?" said José.

"She wasn't a Christian."

"She's holding the cross and prayer beads."

"That's to save her soul," said the Senhorio.

"I've nothing to say," said José.

Father Segundo arrived and questioned him. "You must answer. You must know something, some words to calm her neighbors."

The women whispered among themselves in the yard. Their patter and gossip was more alive than the official questioning of Father Segundo and the Senhorio.

"The body will be thrown on the rocks," said the eldest of the black crows. "She surely was a witch. Truly she was a daughter of the evil eye."

José watched Father Segundo and looked for am excuse to flee, but the old eyes of the priest watched him.

"I'll ask this young man further questions."

"That won't be necessary, Father. He belongs to these lands. I want him to stay until he has worked his obligation. He lives under my authority."

"The Senhorio knows Lent. The Church must squelch rumors and gossip before we celebrate Lent. By Shrove Tuesday and the Festival of Saint Blaise, this business must be settled. I will make a decision tonight on how to dispose of her corpse."

José struggled up the path of Fajã Velha with the Priest. Along the way, he assured Father Segundo that he'd nothing to do with the death of Tia Nita.

"The women say you were her friend. They say you've spoken with her for many years and you had messages from her, messages from the dead."

"No sir, I know nothing, Senhor."

"This woman cursed our well. Don't lie about her. I shall pursue this and know everything. You arrived with soldiers the day they came to seek the well. The women saw you. You came from the cottage where the Tai Nita died. They say, these women, that the army will destroy the well, and that the dead woman set the evil eye on us. You must tell me what she told you. We want to live in peace and safe from evil spirits." The priest crossed himself.

"Tia Nita delivered babies and cured the sick. I never heard her curse the neighbors."

"If you spread the word that she cured others, you do the work of the devil," hissed Father Segundo, the old beetle.

Father Segundo stopped asking questions. José said, "When may I learn to read, Father?"

"Reading and writing are not for you. Forget lessons and work for your father. The family needs you in the gardens on the land. Your father will tell you what to do."

"Will you say Mass for Tia Nita?"

"My son, she cursed the church and put spells on the innocent."

"I'll break her spell by learning to read and write," said José.

"The old Aunt was under the evil eye. She failed God. God throws evil out of his house. You are one of His but she is not one of God's." The priest hurried off to the rectory. Alone standing on the cobbles, José looked up and shook his fist at the church tower with the shadow of its great cross darkening the square.

CHAPTER XVIII

Flies rose in a cloud from the sun-bleached steak bones thrown by the wayside after the autumn festival as José stepped into the shade and wiped the sweat from his forehead. Pistola's shop lay quiet in the fierce sunlight and Maçapez was deserted except for Araujo the cripple that reported news to the neighbors during sesta by dragging himself by his arms over the cobbles on a platform with wooden wheels. Pistola lay in his hammock slung between the shop and the terrace post outside the taberna where he served drinks and lunch. He fanned himself with a newspaper and greeted José. The news of Tia Nita's death moved on the tips of the villagers' tongues, fresh gossip, and Pistola eagerly wanted to hear José's report.

Pistola rolled his eyes and laughed when he spoke of Father Segundo. "Yes, he controls burial. Nothing said to him will open a grave." He laughed. "He'll not lay Tia Nita in her grave."

"She deserves better," said José.

"You held up those soldiers with their own rifle on the beach! Your word will fall on deaf ears"

"I wanted the conscripts to run off. I didn't fire the rifle. I want to live in the mountains with my brother," said José.

He scuffed his toe along the cobbled edge and stared at Pistola.

"The conscripts refused to run, crazy bastards," José said.

"Where could they hide in the village? It meant running away and hiding with soldiers hunting them day after day. No place to return to and no safe cave."

Pistola sent for lemonade. José admired the fruit trees growing along Pistola's garden wall—guavas, loquats, avocado pears, custard apples.

"Father Segundo wants her corpse thrown on the rocks. He'll wait for public opinion to support him."

"The corpse will rot. It's too late."

Pistola patted his shoulder. "God's man must weigh and balance. He'd like to say the water in the well will turn sweet. He doesn't know if her death will release the curse. He wants her death to cure the sick. He'll follow custom. He'll wait until rumor and gossip cease."

"Father Segundo won't allow her burial. I'll bury her corpse. She can't hear the Mass." José told Pistola how much he hated the priest for not giving Tia Nita a funeral Mass. She'd helped women during childbirth. She held Ana Margarida in her arms until the woman died, and old António Gomes after his excommunication was healed by her medicine.

"I liked her. She was an old crone and she deserved better. Her house will be shut and become derelict. I'll need a house some day. I'm youngest and there'll never be a house for me."

Pistola closed his eyes and dreamed of a perfect village in the sunlight free of the feudal way of life.

"Time has a way of changing things. Unhappiness fades. The village will remain. I'll speak to Father Segundo about you."

"You waste your time. He didn't listen and sent me to my father. He won't teach me to read and write," said José.

"I understand priests. I'll speak with Father Segundo."

"Talking will change nothing," said José.

"That may be," said Pistola, "You'll need time, and talking with Father Segundo may give you enough time to find a place to hide—maybe Funchal-town."

"I don't know the town. I want to be in the mountains. I need time to find the shepherd Gold Tooth. Henrique refused to take me in."

"The mountains are bare and remote. The only work is cutting lumber at Fontes do Cedro. You'd meet sailors in Funchal—foreigners in the streets. Talbot can find you a bed with his family."

They knew sesta ended when the women arrived with baskets. Rock sparrows hopped along the alley picking out grains from the cobbles. Pistola closed his eyes and wiped his forehead. José followed him into the shop to resume working.

In the shop, José measured out flour and ground coffee. The women filled their clay jugs with molasses. They made cookies for the Festival of Saint Blaise. Olive oil cost three *reis.* Women bought olive oil and cotton cloth sent from Lisbon. His family couldn't afford these things. They'd get by with salt and sugar, some corn and oatmeal.

Dona Ana cooked with pork fat instead of olive oil. Outside José heard the whine of insects. Two boys played with wooden tops. A new top cost one *real.* They'd whittled theirs from Spanish pine.

José worked in the shop late. In the twilight, Pistola swept the patio and listened to the men drinking wine on the terrace. Off in the shadows, sounds of women hurrying home. They shut their gates, slammed shutters. Mist settled into the valley and Aunt Julia called her cat with whistles and hand-clapping.

The wherrymen appeared at the top of the cliff carrying cases of goods for the shop. They ordered glasses of wine and stepped up to the bar with Pistola and Izidro.

Blackeye rounded the corner and headed for the terrace. José slipped off the steps and ran into the sugar cane field. His face flushed when he saw this friend of the Senhorio.

One of the wherrymen called out to him softly, "João will meet you at the river of the lilies. I see you're working for Pistola. Good!"

Pistola barricaded the doors for the night. He mopped his brow and gained back his breath. He weighed so much that when he walked it sounded as if he were going to suffocate. The men admired his girth and his reputation for telling the truth.

"Alzira said it's decided. The old Aunt will be thrown into the sea. Blackeye heard on his way into the village," said Pistola.

"I'll find João."

"I'll speak with the priest. See me before you run off into the mountains," said Pistola. "The soldiers are coming back to demand the priest's roll of young men. They'll seal up the well. I'll talk with the priest. I urge you to stay a little while."

Pistola waved to him as José reached the ridge. Then, he went through the passageway leading from the bar into the shop where he would figure accounts until dinner.

José whistled for João in the dense growth of lilies below Fajã Velha. The sound of the thin stream of water falling into the pool masked João's footsteps. The image of a bright sail appeared in his mind. He remembered seeing the sloop move gracefully up to the quay. He'd hidden in the caves from his father with no boat to sail himself away. João's high shrill whistle sounded and José jumped out of the thicket. There was his brother hauling a sack. João displayed the amber in his sack.

"Where did you get it?" said José.

"Senhor Mendes found it on the beach and sent me there. In Calçada, they'll cut and clean it."

"You left the land without permission?"

"Yes, and on the pebbled beach, I collected the hampers and locked them in the cave. Old Senhor Mendes whistled. He'll give me three bottles of wine and three laurel sticks of *espatada* during the festival.

José and João walked along the valley toward home, darkness settling around them and only their shirts visible through the mist.

"Tia Nita's corpse will be thrown into the sea," said José.

"Yes, I heard."

"The family wants her buried. Father Segundo could order it, but he can't because he fears the curse of a dead witch," said José.

"She'll end up on the rocks," said João.

"Not this time," said José. "We'll carry her out and bury her tonight."

João shook his head. He walked away and avoided Jose's talk by hurrying toward home and looking for his mother who would be ladling out the soup, hot and steaming. "We'll be seen." He dropped his sack beside the trough and plunged his hands into the water.

"Tonight," said José, "before the priest makes up his mind. We can sleep in the cave with the goats."

After the evening meal with their sisters, the two slipped away.

The few bright stars in the sky above the mists were soon covered by clouds. They worked their way down the steep slope and cut along the cliff to the old Aunt's cottage. The night-wind blew from the sea and they saw Deserta Grande, dark against the northeast sea. José grabbed João so he wouldn't run. No corpse could be buried without the priest. She'd been lying on her bed two days. The women that loved her had paid their respects. Her cottage was stripped bare. Things disappeared, taken by strangers.

"I think we'd better wait. She's lies in the dark and I don't want to see her," said João.

"Her face won't be visible. Tomorrow is too late," said José.

"Father Segundo won't confirm me if he hears about this."

"Tia Nita was the midwife and brought you into this world. Her herbs cured mother when she was dying of influenza. You owe her a decent burial."

"Where can we bury her?"

"In the smuggler's cave," said José.

"They'll never look for her in that cave."

"I can't think of a better grave."

"She's too heavy and the opening too high on the cliff," said João.

Their luck soured, the moon rose over Chão. They waited on the edge of the cliff hoping that the cottage would remain in the mists, but moonlight illuminated the cactus and rocks, pale and snowy, their rigid shapes like frost-covered plants on the summit of Pico Ruivo.

"The priest has asked the soldiers to throw her body off the cliff, so we must take her away tonight," said José.

João worried about the men working on the quay. They'd see the body being hauled into the cave. He scanned the beach for fishermen.

He stared at the surf and the moonlit objects on the pebbled beach. He hugged himself with his arms to keep warm and followed José to where they saw her cottage. Where the trail ended in the pine-covered steep, he saw silhouettes but no movement. No lights along the shore or in her cottage.

They crawled into the garden a few yards and then into the bright moonlight where pepper and tomato plants were dark against the soil. The ground was soft. She had cultivated her garden the day she died.

José felt her presence in the garden, and waited to see if Tia Nita would appear and walk in the garden. She was laid out on her bed. The wind touched the curtains and they gently moved back and forth on the silent air. He listened for the sound of footsteps in the dust. He and João crouched outside and waited for the wind to die down. A figure appeared on the ridge.

A whistle blew and its sound echoed off the rocks across the valley. They waited for its answer. Another whistle blew higher up the slope near the chapel. José raised his finger to his lips. João did not whistle an answer.

A rabbit surprised by them in the garden hopped out of the shadows and into the yard. João giggled. The rabbit leapt in the air and landed facing José, one ear bent, nose sniffing the air.

"He wants a companion," said José.

João laughed. The rabbit ran toward the house and toward the doorway. "He wants to visit the old Aunt," said João.

Outside the moonlit door, they hesitated, the silence overwhelmed them, and they did not speak. The cool sea breeze touched their brows and cheeks and they feared touching her.

Tia Nita's corpse lay on the bed where José had last seen her when the priest questioned him. Her kerchief was missing. They moved silently through the gloom. In the moonlight, she was smaller than José remembered. The crucifix and beads were gone. The arms were cement-like and rigid. Their dryness and lifelessness shocked him. He held her under the shoulders and João lifted the back of her heels, but they couldn't lift her. João spread her legs and took an ankle under each arm.

They carried her corpse through the door and down the path toward the ocean. They moved slowly, less they stumbled or fell.

"It's too bright. We picked a poor night. I'm being crushed," said João. He swore.

"Move quicker. I can smell her. We should have carried her last night," said José.

A cry sounded from the ridge above the cottage. They set the corpse on the gravel path and hid themselves in the rocks. The cry was answered by a tenor voice, "*Si,*" followed by reverberating cries, unintelligible at this distance. The slopes returned to silence and they crept out of the thicket and picked up the corpse. They carried the corpse toward the steepest part of the trail.

José bit on his lip and gripped her by the armpits. He saw the pebbled beach and the surf below shining in the moonlight. He knew how to move so that fishermen returning from their night's trip wouldn't see them. He shifted his weight and tried to support João who was bearing the brunt of the corpse. He couldn't see where he was stepping.

The cave's mouth was a black opening in the cliff overlooking the great stone campanário, rock spire, in the sea. The sandstone cliffs were dry and safe for the tons of produce shipped to Funchal or received on shore and carried on men's shoulders to the village high above the cliff.

The corpse farted, a living sound, long and distinct. João heaved it forward and away with sudden energy. José grabbed for the body but lost his grip and was fortunate to save himself from falling head first over the cliff onto the rocks below. The body fell headfirst, rolled three times end-over-end and landed on the rocks. João watched in silence and listened for sounds from the corpse.

"God help me." he said, making the sign of the cross, "I didn't drop her. My foot slipped and it was either her or me!"

"Why did you throw her?" said José.

"I thought she was alive. Didn't you?"

José swore at him. "Maybe she's alive and will rise like Our Lord."

"Halloo, Halloo!" shouted someone at the top of the cliff.

João ducked back down into the shadows cast by the prickly pear. "Who's that?"

"I can't see them. If they see us, they'll know we carried her off."

They waited in the darkness. Three figures emerged from the trail at the top by the old Aunt's cottage. The last man yelled to his companions and urged them on. The men stopped at the precipice and spying the body on the rocks waited for the third man. "Some bastard threw her corpse off the cliff."

"We were charged with it."

José itched himself and held Joao's arm so he would not move, not to look up, not to breathe.

"Father Segundo sent us too late." It was Salamão, the Senhorio's steward. The three men stood in the moonlight smoking cigarettes. They searched the slopes for the villains, José and João. The Senhorio's nephew, Araujo, walked toward José's hiding place. He stopped to piss and lighting another cigarette, called to his comrades. They'd sighted something on the beach. The three hurried to investigate, forgetting the corpse.

José and João sat until they were limber. They listened to the night-wind and the surf. When the night was silent, they climbed down onto the rocks.

They carried her up through the debris of a rock fall.

"We'll not get into the cave before daylight. Some fisherman is sure to awaken and come to check on his boat and see us."

They struggled to carry her corpse but it exhausted them.

"Where'd the men go?"

"To tell Father Segundo she's been fed to the fish of the sea. They saw her corpse lying above the tidemark."

José ran to the beach and took a rope from an old dory.

They hauled her corpse up the cliff-side and into the cave. Bats flew out screaming. João handled her gingerly worried that she'd speak. They placed the body far back in the cave, and they hurried off. The dark and the bats frightened them.

"This cave is too high above the trail for them to see her. Tomorrow, we'll come at sunset when the cave is light and drag the body farther to the back. The bat shit's stifling," said José.

As they climbed back down to the trail, they saw fishermen returning from their night's trip. They bathed in the *cisterna* and arrived home and daylight streaked the eastern sky with bands of red. They bedded down with their goats in the cave on the slope above the cottage. Maria found them asleep when she went to feed and water the goats.

CHAPTER XIX

José opened his eyes and looked into the sky. The kestrel hovered on the morning air, rose on the current swiftly rising above the sea cliff, the rays of sunlight coloring its reddish brown plumage on top and revealing the gray beneath its wings and along its body. The bird was intent on looking for mice, beetles, grasshoppers, and chicks. Slowly, the bird drifted away and suddenly sailed out of sight on an updraft of air.

Maria's footsteps sounded on the path. Before daylight she heard the news at Mass. Tia Nita's body was gone from her cottage.

"Come down for breakfast!" said Maria, "I met Aunt Georgina on the high ridge after church."

José and João went out to feed their goats. They stopped at the trough beside the door of the cottage and washed their faces and hands. Aunt Georgina sat at the table snapping string beans. She greeted them and kissed João.

"Will you work in my garden? My husband has another woman. What am I to do?"

"How can that be? He's a Grandfather," said João.

"Letters come from Africa. He sends money. He doesn't write. She writes for him, letters I can't read myself!"

"I wish I lived in Africa," said José. "He married another woman when he's married to you! How can he do that?"

José and Maria embarrassed by his question turned to one another.

"Father Segundo ordered the village men to search for Tia Nita's corpse," said Maria.

"My Aunt deserves a decent burial," said Mother.

119

"Father Segundo blames us for her death," said Aunt Georgina.

José winked at João. He stuffed another chunk of cold cornmeal into his mouth.

"What others news in the village?" said João.

"The soldiers returned. They know we're been drinking the well water." Georgina snuffled. She untied and redid her kerchief.

"They're coming for conscripts. They have papers to carry out the royal orders. We must keep an eye on them," said José.

José teased Aunt Georgina. She hid food and never shared it. She wouldn't offer him wine and he knew she had a cellar full of wine barrels.

"The wife shouldn't be separated from the husband. I've heard the priest read those words from the Book. The wife should be where the husband goes, to the new country. The priest makes him return, not to see his wife, but to bring money to Madeira from foreign lands. The priest told you years ago to remain in the village until your husband sent for you," said José.

"You should respect me. I'm your Aunt," said Georgina.

"Thank you, Aunt. Thank you for the news," said João. "I give you honor and respect, dear Auntie. We're off on our Sunday walk."

Aunt Georgina pursed her lips and spit out the doorway. She gathered up her basket before the family left. Julia danced ahead of them on the pathway, laughing and pointing out birds and interesting clouds on the summits of the mountains.

"*Com El Reis, e com a Inquisicão psiu!*" Julia said. With the King and the Inquisition--hush!

Maria told her to lower her voice. "Pistola's on the porch with his family and they will hear you from the shade where they're eating *favas*, peas."

120

"The men can't find the corpse of Tia Nita," said Pistola. He fiddled in his right ear with his finger.

The Gonçalves's sat playing cards and drinking passion fruit juice. Luisa kissed José. She had married Manuel Fernandes, the dark-eyed one with olive brow and bright lips.

"Good afternoon," she said to the Abreus and embraced mother and Julia and Maria, giving João, her favorite, a hug.

"Father Segundo spoke to me about José's going to school and it is more difficult than I first knew... There is more to the arrangement," said Pistola.

"I don't understand," said José.

"Your family's never been close to the Church. Father Segundo believes you practice Jewish rituals in secret."

"As peredes tem ouvidos, walls have ears. Please be careful what you say, Senhor," said Mother. "I belong to Christ's Church and my daughters are baptized Christians. My husband attends Mass on festival days but he does work on the Sabbath when ordered to work by the landlord. José is not baptized. My husband baptized at age sixteen."

"Father Segundo wants his folk baptized," said Pistola.

"We have faith in the land. We love the church more than we love Father Segundo," said Mother. "We can't afford a church wedding but Maria will be married in church. That's our faith. We marry in church."

"Father Segundo knew Tia Nita practiced the Hebrew beliefs. He called her a pig, and he forbids Abreu men to take communion," said Pistola.

Mother grew quiet. "We say special words at home. They are family words we cannot say to others. Tia Nita practiced the faith our ancestors had when they sailed to Madeira."

"Are you Jews now?" asked Pistola.

"No, Senhor, we don't call ourselves New Christians," said Maria. "Our family may have been Jews in the earliest days and baptized to escape burning at the stake but we have no way of knowing if it is true or not."

José was surprised. His mother and sisters understood the past. They concealed these practices. He accepted them as old customs.

"My whole family is Christian. I'm not a Marrano," said José.

"You want to read and to write. You want to be free of serving in the army. The first step is baptism and acceptance by the church and you become a student, later," said Pistola.

"I am owned by the landlord. It would be switching from one owner to another," said José.

"*Asno de muitos, lobos o comem.*" said Luisa. The ass owned by all is eaten by the wolves. Why should José join the church?"

"Father Segundo is dishonest," said José. He knows where Tia Nita's corpse is hidden and isn't telling us. He won't give me lessons and he is a liar."

Pistola stood up. "He will give you lessons but you must first belong to his church. You'll be safe in another way. I'll give you a new name. With a new name you'll be written on the baptismal list but with a girl's name. The Army can't take an underage recruit. It's a matter of birth-date. They can't recruit a man until he's sixteen. The army uses the list. You will not be on the list because it is a list of the men. The ones on the list belong to the King and can be taken in service. Think of baptizing as a girl and allow the font water to touch your head."

José cursed the land, the church, and the people. "My Father was a fool to serve the Senhorio. I'll go into the mountains and live with Henrique. I want to be free of the Church and the army."

Pistola grew tired of José's yammering and took him off into the banana grove, away from the others.

"You'll be baptized in disguise as a girl."

José laughed. "Why?"

"The priest can send you to the army by giving them your name even though you are not on the roll. After baptism, your name will be entered on the roll but with a girl's name."

"How can he write my name on the roll?"

"You'll be dressed as a girl," said the storekeeper. "The point is that you will be baptized and eligible for holy orders and not on the roll with your real name and thus not available for military service."

José laughed. "No, that's impossible. My sisters will know it's me. I can't do it."

"Father Segundo wants you baptized. He knows you'll never become a priest if you spend six years in the militia. This way, you join the church. You'll study and learn their ways. He'll accept you with a girl's name. He only teaches women to read and write."

"He'll teach with a girl's name even when he knows I'm a boy!" José was confused.

"Yes, the church has ways that are not the ways of our village," said Pistola.

"Who'll dress me? I can't dress myself."

"Rosa, the cobbler's daughter agreed to help. She's sworn to secrecy."

José sighed.

"You'll be ready on Shrove Tuesday. The disappearance of the corpse makes trouble for Father Segundo. He accuses many of the deed and demands names of those that took the corpse away."

"I thought he'd be happy to know the corpse had disappeared. He's rid of the witch of Campanário."

"He was happy until the corpse went missing. He sent men to her cottage. They examined the rocks and the beach. The men claim they saw her corpse in the moonlight. Now, Father Segundo wants to know who threw the corpse onto the rocks."

"The priest wouldn't have buried her," said José.

"Burial's burial, whether it's at sea or in the earth. What happens to us when we're dead is nothing. What happens in life is everything. Come along. We'll join the others. You'll see Rosa. By the Festival of Saint Blaise, you'll be free of the army."

Maria and Rosa argued over the way to make up José disguise, cross and sharp-witted. "You need a blouse to cover his breasts," said Maria. "He needs bows to give him the look of the wealthy daughters of the sugar mill owners in Calheta."

The mothers sat in the pews on the right side of the church, and whispered when Pistola walked through the door with a strange girl. José clung to the shopkeeper's arm and closed his eyes, and Pistola led him down the aisle.

He wobbled a little on his heels, and when seated, he folded his arms under his veil, feeling peculiar in gloves that reached to his elbows. Maria and Rosa had combed his hair over his ears and shaped it a little. His sister Luisa didn't recognize him, for he heard her whispering. "Who is she?"

"I heard she's an Abreu cousin from Porto Moniz," said Maria.

"I never saw her at festivals. She's stout enough to be one of the Flemish from Calheta," said Luisa.

"She should baptize in her own parish," said Rosa, agreeing with her. She winked at Maria.

"Pistola is an angel. He arranged the baptism by writing to the priest. She should kneel before Christ whatever village she lives in," said Maria.

José was seated at the rear of the class to be baptized. They'd marched down the aisle hand in hand and were seated in the front pew.

The priest entered. "At the prayers of our Holy Fathers, O Lord Jesus Christ our God has mercy upon us. Amen."

The Deacon began saying: "O heavenly King, the Comforter, the Spirit of Truth, who art of all places and fillest all things, the treasure of blessings and the giver of life, descend and rest upon us, and cleanse us from all impurity, and save our souls, O gracious God."

José's forearm burned where the girls had shaved him, and now he froze with goose bumps along his arms. Though covered with layers, he felt bare, and he lowered his eyes which gave him a look of shyness and doubt. He dreamed of the sea where he'd feel the sun and the wind touching him and never see young girls. The girls turned and listened to the mesmerizing voice of the Deacon vesting.

"O God, cleanse me a sinner, and you have mercy upon me."

The Deacon walked across the sanctuary and put on his tunic, praying aloud, and kissing the stole and putting it on his left shoulder. He placed the cuffs over his hands, saying magic words over each hand. He returned to the offertory table and set out the sacred vessels: the paten on the left, the chalice the holiest of cups, on the right hand.

The priests marched back and forth before the girls in procession. The young women knelt together before sitting to watch the ordering of the Holy and Divine Liturgy.

José crossed himself and prayed that his face was not visible to his sisters, especially Maria. He couldn't remember if João and Silvino worked today. Almost covered though he was, the urge to throw off the dress kept rising within him, and he prayed not to give in and flee. The face of Tia Nita appeared in his mind, her body lying in the cave, the smell of the bat dung.

125

She looked peaceful, sleeping amidst the sound of the sea-wind through the openings and crevices of the cave.

The priest whispered the *Quicunque Vult.* "So there is One Father, not three Fathers, one son, not three sons: one Holy Ghost, not three Holy Ghosts..."

His sponsors were Rosa, Maria, and Pistola the enviable shopkeeper, Manuel Joachim Gonçalves. When asked, they each answered, "No, she's not baptized."

The priest told the girls they'd been conceived and born in Sin. Flesh couldn't please God. He prayed for the saving grace that came to Noah and the children of Israel at the Red Sea, so grace would come to these young women.

When he finished praying, the whole parish stood for the reading of Saint John in the third chapter, the first verse. The priest's voice increased in volume and rising high above their heads echoed off the ceiling of the church.

José moved his hip a little to ease the itch gnawing at him while he sat cramped in the dress and about ready to faint from the incense and the heat. The candles, the sweaty bodies, the incensed air sickened him and he rocked on his heels and bent his knees. The dress clung to his *traseiros.*

"Do you renounce the devil and all his works, the vain pomp and glory of the world, and the carnal desires of the flesh?"

José thought the children of Israel cursed him in outer darkness for saying these words. After three more questions where they'd been told to answer yes, each girl walked up to the piscine. José waited for the priest to ask his name. Pistola answered for him. "Amália Gonçalves Rodrigues."

José trembled. He reached out and clung to the edge of the piscine. The stonework cooled his hand and standing near the priest frightened him. The water touched his forehead in the sign of the cross. He closed his eyes. He knelt with the others and said the Our Father.

They stood up on signal and the priest exhorted the Godparents to rise for Christ, to proceed in all virtues, to live Godliness.

As soon as he reached the steps of the church, José hitched up his skirt and ran down the path to Maçapez, ribbons and bows flying about his hips. Laughter bubbled out of his mouth. Tears streaked down his cheeks. He jumped over wine barrels. He skipped, shrieking and whistling. One of the girls, Vitória, asked him to walk home with her so she could show her 'hope chest'. He told her not today, sorry.

"You have a beautiful voice," said Vitória Capelinha.

Carlos da Sousa, a retired sweetshop owner from Funchal, hailed Pistola on the steps of the church.

"The soldiers marched from Ribeira Brava, militia headquarters for the parish district. They embarked off Blandys' boat. Old Santos saw them."

"They march to the high levada to surprise the bandits in Estreito da Câmara De Lobos. The rumors say they come to seal the well," said Pistola. "Tell those you see, the soldiers are coming."

José changed in the upper chamber over the shop. He wore his Sunday clothes--clean white shirt, black wool trousers, and straw hat.

"Your name is now on the roll, Amália Rodrigues," said Pistola.

"Thank you, Senhor. The army's coming and I'll run and tell João. They'll hunt for Tia Nita's corpse."

Pistola waved to José. The young man's slight figure hurried away over the cobble stones and up the path to home. The army had arrived to search for new recruits and impress them into the militia. No matter that José was baptized with a girl's name and though still not sixteen, he worried the soldiers would come after him.

CHAPTER XX

To the beat of a snare drum, the militia marched in the afternoon breeze. Boys and dogs followed the patrol as they went along the curving roadway through Ribeira Melões. José and João ran from their vegetable garden and caught up with the angry mob the last half mile before they marched into the village square. The neighbors lined up and blocked the soldiers from sealing their well. The crowd huddled in the cold February gusts off the sierras and watched the platoon as it snaked its way from Fajã Velha with a bugle fanfare and full cadence.

The captain's hat was pulled down over his forehead. His curls hung over his ears. His heels stamped in the dust, the breeze snatching the dust from his heels. The drummer hit staccato beats, a handkerchief over his mouth giving him the appearance of a pirate.

Carlos Gomes ran into the square. "The captain's going to arrest those who drank from the well."

"What foolishness! My neighbors drink to quench their thirst. Death comes from the curse of the witch woman," said Duro Castagna.

"The army punishes those who disobey the King. Those who drink spread typhoid," said Blackeye.

"The priest said it's the curse, but my family's used this water since they landed at Campanário, four hundred years ago," said Maria Gonçalves.

The soldiers marched within ten meters of the peasants and strutted in quick time. They passed the well and followed their captain into the square and lined up in front of the gate to the church. The captain called rear march and halted them facing the crowd. He said, "Company, halt, parade rest." The troops stared at the crowd. Having gone from attention to rest without Order arms! They grimaced and rested at order arms, placing their rifles forward.

The adjutant ran up the steps of the priest's house and rang the bell. Alzira peered out through the gate. She locked the gate and went inside the house. The bell rang and she didn't answer. The Captain ordered the sergeant to present himself before the gate. The old lady unlocked the door. The sergeant pushed the iron grillwork against the wall, angry over Alzira's disrespect.

José signaled João and they moved out of the wind and dust. After the crowd waited a long time, Father Segundo and the captain appeared on the terrace. They watched the crowd milling around the well. The captain's lips moved and José couldn't read them. The captain stepped one pace forward and saluted. "He honors the church," murmured Blackeye.

The captain returned to his men and called them to attention. "Fall out and prepare to stack rifles," he said.

Three soldiers made a tripod by attaching their swivels together, and when they knelt, three others stacked their rifles against the tripod. One trooper remained to guard the weapons. The others marched in single file into Father Segundo's storehouse. They returned carrying bags of cement and shovels. Before the astonished crowd, they mixed cement. The captain directed half the platoon in building a wooden box to form a cement cover, to seal the well.

"We can't carry water from the *levada*. We need it close by at our elbows," said Rosa's mother.

"You can haul water while your old man makes shoes," said Twenty-seven.

José saw the Captain's eye, alert and curious, and he hid behind Senhor Bonito, the Senhorio's yardman. Bonito spoke to the Captain. "You can be sure Father Segundo had a hand in this. You stored your cement in his storehouse. The priest can exorcise the curse on this well with the Cross."

"Please stop capping the well. I beg you in the name of Mother Mary," said Rosa's mother.

"I'm sorry Senhora," said the captain. "I have orders. They are to cover it with cement. Dig yourself a new well."

The captain turned on José, pointing his finger. "You're the one that took the rifle from one of my men and attempted to free the conscripts."

José closed his eyes and wished himself in the mountains above the cliffs and ridges, hovering over the island and the sea like the kestrel. He eyed the square. He ran his hand over his thigh determined to run.

"I'll recognize your name on the roll. Father Segundo told me you were José Abreu and when I see it on the roll, I'll send for you."

José pretended not to hear and the captain raised his voice. "I have four names and I need a fifth. If your name is not on the list, I'll demand to know why."

"I'm not sixteen, Senhor," said José. He scowled. The captain would enlist him if his name appeared on the list.

"No man endangers my men and escapes scot-free."

Father Domingo sent out two jugs of wine at that moment. The soldiers clapped their hands and saluted Alzira. She gathered her shawl about her shoulders. She spit and saliva landed on the captain's boot. The captain shook his fist at the crowd and they jeered at him. He retired to a table in the rear of Father Segundo's storehouse and tried to catch flies. The flies landed on the table and crawled toward him, but never within his reach. When the sunlight moved, darkness cooled their wings, and the flies drifted in a cloud. During *sesta,* the square darkened and the soldiers settled down to play cards and drink.

Pistola met João and José on the steps. "I tell you, the captain's going to ask Father Segundo add my name to the roll," said José.

Pistola hitched up his suspenders and returned to unpacking hand tools and hanging them on hooks along the shop wall. His neck itched along the edge of his rumpled collar.

"The well is on the villagers' mind. Father Segundo can't forbid them to haul water. He knows the soldiers will cap and seal the well. They'll remain for the enlistment. Be patient and don't run away to the mountains."

"Father Segundo knew the soldiers were coming and he hid the shovels and cement in his storehouse," said José.

"I know he did. In the early days of Madeira, we needed water and more land for gardens. We fought the pirates and the army and one another, and the church stood by and said nothing and it won. We have strange quilted holdings of land. Water is gold."

"The captain invited José and Joãoto coffee. Father Segundo will add my name to the list, Senhor."

Pistola sat with his elbows on the table and remained long over each sip of coffee as if he'd forgotten them. He moved his spoon across a crack. The afternoon breeze caught the leaves of the bananas and the bleat of a goat sounded from off on the hillside. Pistola sat and wrote on a piece of paper.

José said, "Senhor, send a message to your friend Talbot in wonderful words that conceal magic. Find a place for me in Funchal."

"I'm thinking," said Pistola. "You can't run into the mountains because the militia will put a price on your head. Men have sailed from Madeira without papers. It's been done for years and years and the men returned old and gray. It may be worse than death to run away."

"I can live with the shepherds on the Paúl da Serra and I've never seen the waterfalls at Rabaçal."

"The priest hasn't given them your name."

João said, "José is crazy, Senhor."

"He's frightened by the militia. Wait until spring, José. The mountains warm up and the rains cease."

"José, we must run," said João.

"The shepherds won't take him in. Rumors spread. The villagers say José showed Direito and Mandado the well," said Pistola.

"I see years of labor and toil, a hard life," said José.

Pistola scratched his stomach and went into the shop. "I'll send you to Talbot with a bushel of custard apples. He sent me gifts and I wish to return his favor."

"I need the Senhorio's permission to leave the land," said José.

"I'll speak with that devil. He's avoided me since that day on the beach when you kicked his knife. Father Segundo will speak with him for me. Go to him and ask his permission and look on the bright side," said Pistola.

"Father Segundo sent men to search the rocks for Tia Nita's corpse," said João.

"Once a corpse disappears, it never returns," said Pistola. "Paulo Neto saw the corpse on the rocks in the moonlight."

"Father Segundo wanted her corpse thrown into the sea," said José.

"Forget it, I tell you."

"The soldiers know her corpse was on the rocks. They heard the gossip in the square."

"The military district of Ribeira Brava knows about her death and the business of the polluted well. The enlistment comes at a bad time. If you flee, you rebel against the King," said Pistola.

"I'll ask permission to go to Funchal. Talbot of the beautiful sloop will find me a place."

On the way to see the *Senhorio*, Tia Nita's face appeared before them in the twilight. José and João broke into a run. João fretted. "You knew Father Segundo ordered her corpse thrown into the sea. We had bad luck. The men saw her in the moonlight. Curse the lizards! Why'd I touch the corpse?"

"They don't know the smuggler's cave. They'll never find her corpse," said José.

"You're crazy to go to Funchal. The villagers say you were Tia Nita's friend and know where her corpse is."

José and João fed their goats and carried down wood for the cook-fire. In the kitchen, Mother stirred the cabbage soup and sliced corn meal. Later, in darkness, they heard the last bugle call for the soldiers to return to their bivouac.

In the morning, Maria laughed as she applied red to José's lips. He dressed in his grandfather's costume for Shrove Tuesday.

"I don't like *masquerados*. They're ghosts."

At breakfast, Julia said, "Their buzzing sounds of the masquerados frighten me. They run through our gardens and trample on the cabbage plants and throw cobblestones."

"Cover your ears," said João.

"I like the candy they throw for the children," said mother.

José looked like a ghost in his costume. His face was covered with ashes and his nose, eyebrows and chin painted white. He had circles painted around his eyes and black soot on his ears. He wore a dress and a *carapuça*, knitted cap, about thirty centimeters high with a tassel on it.

José peered at the red lipstick dots on his cheeks, the appearance of disease. He looked as if he had emerged from the grave and as he pulled on his gloves left by an Italian stonecutter, Richelli of Canhas, he whistled and old fold tune, to himself.

"Please stop. I'm reminded of Tia Nita's flute and her playing that song and I see her walking the heights," said Maria.

"I'm a ghost and I don't want to be one, dear Maria. I go to Funchal-town in disguise."

"Your Grandfather put rose dots on his cheeks and put them on his face to celebrate his dead ancestors," said Father.

José waved good-bye and turned down the path. On the pebbled beach, the soldiers searched passengers. Pistola waited for him with the crate of Custard Apples for Talbot to be taken to Funchal.

"Father Segundo didn't give your name to the Captain yet. Never fear," Pistola said.

José disgusted the soldiers. They met him at the tugboat and hated his outlandish costume and did not recognize him...

"Pagan make-believe," said the lean soldier with a black mustache. A surge in the tide rocked the wherry as it moved through the sea toward the tarred and smoky stern of *Falcon*. José slipped one real into the wherryman's hand, given to him by Pistola. He stared at the old wrecked dory on the beach. The sailors yelled for him to climb aboard. The village men carrying boxes from Pistola's cave waved to him.

José leaned on the sooty rail and watched Campanário grow smaller until it was a white blur on the steep slopes of the island. The mountains rose up and dominated the horizon. As the tug rounded the highest sea cliff he looked back and saw the spire in the sea, like God's finger and kept his eye on it until it disappeared from his view.

CHAPTER XXI

Garth Talbot spread out *The Times* and read the headlines while the boy in the white jacket set the pot of morning coffee on the table covered with a fresh linen cloth. His chair gave him a view of Funchal harbor and the Brazen Head. Flocks of terns flew off the cape and over the dark blue sea. *Falcon*, Blandy's tug, steamed into the bay and anchored by the mole. Garth sipped his coffee and mused over the view -—the yacht club and the historic chapel of Saint Catherine built by Constanza the wife of Zarco in the 15th century. On the hill beyond Saint Peter's, the tower of Santa Clara convent church, its elegant tiles gleamed in the sunlight. Along the shore, bullocks dragged sledges and donkeys hauled cargo from the beach to near-by warehouses. The blue and gold Madeiran flags and the national flag few from the turrets of Fort Saint James. He loved reading his morning paper, sitting on the terrace overlooking the town. He felt at home in town, the bright flowers and shrubs in the gardens below and the wherrymen, like water bugs, rowing passengers out to vessels at anchor. He seldom wanted the bustle of London.

José stepped ashore and asked the direction to Blandy's office. The clerk pointed to Zarco Avenue toward the English Rooms where yes, Senhor Talbot ate breakfast around ten o' clock.

A crippled boy dragged himself over the cobbles on a homemade cart and directed José to Avenida Arriaga. José thanked him and lingered by the public gardens to examine the exotic flowers. Beyond the garden, he saw the entrance to the English Rooms, and in the dark, cool entry, he climbed the ornate mahogany stairway and asked for Senhor Talbot.

He saw Talbot on the terrace, under the lace-like shadows of the bougainvillea. Talbot read his newspaper, "Delivered off the steamship, *Zweena*, piloted by Captain Zadok Taylor."

"May I help you, O little one with death mask over his face," said António, the waiter. "You mask well for Shrove Tuesday." The waiter raised his eyebrows and shrugged when José asked to speak with Senhor

Talbot. António moved toward a couple seated at a round table dismissing José.

Talbot seeing the dress and mask beckoned the waiter. "You Lusitanians make much of Lent," he said.

"It's our pleasure, sir. We sing and dance and when meeting our friends, we try to identify them. This lad wishes to speak with you. I told him you didn't speak with strangers."

"Do I know him?"

"He said so. He arrived on *Falcon.* He says something about custard apples and a pistol."

"Yes, yes. Send him over," said Talbot, folding his paper. José set down his hamper and untied his *carapuça.* He saluted and smiled.

"I'm José of Ribeira Melões, Senhor. I kicked the knife of the Senhorio."

"Yes, of course, please sit down. I recognized your voice. I stayed in Maçapez after landing my sloop. How is Senhor Gonçalves?"

"Pistola is fine and sends you greetings and wishes for good health and sends you these custard apples," said José.

He told Talbot about the trouble between the army and the villagers over the capping of the well. The cry of the sledge men with the oxen drifted up from the street, "*Ça para mim boi! Ca-ca-ca-ca.*"

Strangers on the sidewalk stopped and seeing José on the terrace stared at his mask. Talbot understood country words and in halting Portuguese conversed with him.

"I've wanted to visit Pistola soon. Either I go by water or I spend two days walking over the mountains."

"Pistola wishes to see you, Senhor." José lowered his eyes and stared at the chipped stone of the terrace, unable to look Talbot in the eye.

"Would you like coffee?"

"Yes, I would Senhor, very much." His mouth watered. He'd been an hour on the boat and thirsty.

"I've read about gold mining in Brazil. My family owns land in Minas Gerais. I'll help you in a small way for your kindness on the beach. "

"It was bad luck, Senhor."

"Was it?"

"The Senhorio punished me for leaving without his permission. The priest won't teach me to read and write. When I'm sixteen, I'll be taken into the army for six years. I've had bad luck." He lapsed into silence, surprised by his words. He prayed for a job in Funchal.

A boy came and stood by the table. Talbot nodded and the boy said, "Senhor Talbot, your mother wishes to see you at tea, today."

"How is my dear mother, this morning?"

"Very well, Senhor. She reads in the garden at the Vila Camacho and plans to see you at tea-time. She sends compliments to her friends at the English Rooms."

"Did she dine out last evening, Ruy?"

"She went to Reid's Hotel in her carriage, attended the band concert in the city garden and took a ride over the newly-built road to Câmara de Lobos."

"Your English is fine, my friend. Tell Mother, I'll meet her at Reid's for tea."

Before Camacho turned away, Talbot introduced him. "This is the fellow that saved me during that fight on the beach," said Talbot.

Camacho said, "I heard that Campanário cannot use their village well."

"More trouble, Senhor," said José. "It's the worst of times."

"You'll return to Campanário, this evening!" said Talbot.

José knitted his eyebrows. "Yes or the Senhorio will send his men looking for me."

"I have a message for Pistola. I can send men to Brazil, if they're willing to leave Madeira for two years. They'll make good money in the gold fields."

"I wish to go to Brazil, Senhor."

"That may be. I'd advance your fare. They need pick and shovel men in Minas Gerais."

"Senhor, the land is hard here and produces little. I work every day." José said. Tears filled his eyes.

"You need a chance," said Talbot.

"I must serve the army. I've no choice. If not, I'm still a slave of the *Senhorio* and the priest won't teach me."

"I'll help if I can."

"I've no money, Senhor, nothing, only the clothes you see. Money helps. It never did me any harm."

Rising from his chair and taking his newspaper, Talbot said, "Come with me. I know Captain Taylor. He can set you up with a passage. He sails to Brazil and can arrange something."

José much relieved to leave the linen-covered tables, the hovering waiters and the Victorian gentility, followed Talbot to the front desk, where Talbot exchanged greetings with the clerk and collected his mail and gave instructions as to his whereabouts. They moved down the stairway and through the mahogany door and out into the rush of Shrove Tuesday merrymakers.

"I can't leave without the landlord's permission. I'd face death on return."

"Don't be grim. Pistola can work it out. He knows the ropes."

Two strangers walked by the terrace. José turned his face away. "We're vassals to the Senhorio. We live on his land. If it doesn't provide, we can't live. We owe him our lives."

"You'll send your family money. The men send money home to Madeira. Money will pay for laborers and taxes," said Talbot.

"I can't leave without the landlord's permission. Mother wants me home. My brothers and sisters don't want me to leave."

José held his elbows close to his body and looked for likely spies from the village in the folk passing the English Club. Talbot told him to wait and went into the Blandy steamship office to inquire about the sailing dates for the *Zweena.*

The street was crowded: donkey carts, drivers shouting, tourists chatting in English, French and German. No one, he thought, would find him in his masquerade outfit and along these cobbled streets. Talbot hurried down the steps from Blandys.

"Come to dinner. Manuel Pestana cooks on the *Zweena* and is ashore for Lent. His captain assured me."

"When would I sail?"

"The boat leaves once a month. It'll take time to arrange it."

The masqueraders buzzed in the street and asked for money. José had no money and avoided them.

"I've no other clothes, Senhor."

"You're fine in costume. My friends want to see how you dressed for Shrove Tuesday. I'll meet you on the Rua das pretas at seven o' clock," Talbot said.

"I must return tomorrow before the Senhorio learns from his spies I'm in Funchal. I don't want to be a soldier at São Martinho."

Talbot startled, said, "Don't worry. I'll speak with Pistola. I'm going to attend the Festival of Saint Blaise."

"Life moves with the cunning of a lizard," José said.

"I know the officials." Talbot said "This knowing of clerks--endless papers and signatures and stamps and seals. The island imprisons its citizens with documents. Those with cash pay the fees."

He waved Talbot goodbye and moved into the jostling crowd. Two young ladies, about Maria's age, laughed at his mask. Dark shining eyes stared at him. They wore white blouses, long braided hair and dressed in Sunday skirts and holiday shoes. Under a bright awning, they sold embroideries in the street.

Though he would not speak with unfamiliar women, he moved toward them. Young men didn't greet or nod to women for fear of being reported to the women's fathers and brothers. When gossip caught up with a man, he was ruined.

"We're from Machico," they said. "Ten *reis*," said the dark one.

"It's beautiful work. Who refused it?"

"Barratt Limited, rua liberdade. We can't tell, Senhor, how much he pays."

"Ten *reis* are not enough."

"We know, we know—seven and more hours a day with needlework, and then washing and ironing."

José admired their linens. Their bright skirts delighted him, blouses, spotless and bright in the sunlight. Drum beats sounded from the heights and he turned to the taller of the women.

"We sing and play to celebrate our victory over the Spanish, at the Pico Fort." She folded and packed her cloths. "Come along."

José hesitated and the smiling women beckoned him. He winked at the short one and lent his hand to carry bails into their friend's shop.

Would he return for dinner? He didn't mind if he missed the boat, forgotten were his troubles and his appointment with Talbot and he followed the ladies along the pavement through the crowds and masquerados.

CHAPTER XXII

José watched the familiar black hat move through the crowded pavement, recognized the Abreu nose and mouth of the man eyeing the faces. He was a distant cousin, an agent of the Senhorio. José covered his face and hid behind a column until the man passed by. The girls led him through the exotic park. Dark branches of Australian evergreens, cool flowers, each of the trees labeled with a metal tag and names he couldn't read, tall trees, smelling of mountain berries. The white blouses of the girls shined in the gloom. He'd forgotten dinner and he smelled cabbage soup. He embraced each girl as he would his sisters wishing them good-bye and hurrying off to his appointment.

I was to dine with Senhor Talbot. I'm meeting with him, he thought. He had been to Funchal few times and enjoyed wandering through the town to view the buildings, parks and the crowds of people walking on the pavements.

In the market on the Praça Chafariz, he looked over his shoulder for the agent and moved in and out of buyers and shoppers. He drank from the fountain and watched the clouds in the sunset, bright colors reflecting off the sea, the sky on the water, yellow, pink and orange cloud-banks. The sea breezes moved through the twilit trees.

Lights appeared in windows. The lamplighter walked into the praça and with his pole raised the glass. He adjusted the flame. José watched him raising the glass with one thrust of his arm touched off brilliant flame. Together he and the lamplighter strolled along the pavement of the Rua Santa Maria. José asked, "Where is the adega on Rua da cadeia velha?" The adega was set up in the old jail from the days of empire. A drunken sailor sat at one of the tables set out on the pavement.

Talbot ordered tomato and onion soup, one course of whitefish, broiled instead of boiled as in Campanário. The fried rice with carrots tasted like his mother's. Talbot urged him to eat. The first meat he'd had since the Christmas festival brought a smile to José's face.

He wiped his mouth with the linen napkin. The man from the Pico Fort stood by the door and watched them eating dinner. Talbot signed the *conta* and gave a tip to the boy. He saw a man in a black hat leaning against the doorjamb, the face indistinct in the gloom. This man rushed forward and pushed José out into the cobbled street.

Talbot said, "Stop that, Senhor. Wait a minute, sir!"

The tall skinny companion of the spy in the black hat said, "Tell the Englishman to shut up. What does he know?"

"New Christian, new Christian," said the laughing woman in the lurid yellow and red mask. She pulled at the sleeve of José's shirt.

"Leave him alone," said Talbot.

The man in the black hat hit José. "Monkey of the world!" he said.

"One of the pigs that plague the earth," said the tall skinny one.

"Stay away from me. I don't know you," said José.

He and Talbot ran away down the street. The men ran after them, buzzing and taunting. The masqueraders gathered and shouted, "He's the Marrano, the pig."

A man hidden in a doorway threw José to the pavement. When José got to his knees, the woman kicked him in the stomach.

"Go home. Police, help police!" said Talbot. To José he said, "Run to the harbor and once on the waterfront you'll get away from these animals. I'll see you in the village during the Festival of Saint Blaise."

An English couple asked Talbot, "What's wrong?"

"Those men hate Jews. They recognized the disguise of this young man in the Lenten costume and will beat him if they catch him."

Talbot's speaking English distracted the vicious mob. José ran through the crowd of holiday-seekers. The gang of masquerados swore and chased him, laughing and screaming at him.

"Death to the red-spotted devil, kill the evil eye," Their yelling grew louder as they raced after him.

His side hurt and he hid in an alley. He ran in the direction of the cathedral in a burst of speed. The sounds of feet on the cobbles neared and the gang ran beyond the doorway of the Apolo Restaurant.

He closed his eyes and the image of the man in the black hat that followed him during the afternoon arose in his mind. At the bottom of the alley, he ran out onto the esplanade by the fish market. He hid behind the columns of the customs house. The avenue was broad and fewer tourists were on the pavement. The masquerados continued along the sidewalks under the twilit trees and turned up Avenida Zarco.

Three men searched the alleys. José ran across the cobbled street and jumped on the sea wall. The gang didn't observe him until he made his jump onto the beach and ran toward a beached dory. His pursuers ran along the sea wall.

José crouched and skirted the edge of the water. He reached the boats moored at the yacht club and hid among them. The men searched among the boats.

Spying a skiff with oars, sandwiched between two smaller boats pulled up on the shore, José leapt aboard and pushed it into the sea, and rowed toward the larger boats out in the dark harbor.

He heard the strains of Fayal folksongs over the water and rowed toward the lighted fantail of a large ship. The singers saw him and threw down a rope ladder. Aboard the steamer he met the captain, Julian Simon, and found he was going to sail for the Azores in the morning. The name of the ship was *Wazzan*. He sat and listened to their singing. From the bulkhead, he peered at the shore where the men searched for him at the yacht club.

"Where is the tugboat for Ribeira Brava?" he asked the cook.

"You want *Falcon*," said Pedro. "She returns from Machico early in the morning when she takes on sugar and grain before sailing west."

After talking over the sailings for Brazil with Pedro, José fell into a deep sleep on the deck under a lifeboat and the whistle of a tugboat awakened him at midnight.

Pedro said, "That's Blandy's other tugboat, *Hawk*, arriving from Porto Santo. She'll dock by the buoy for the African Steamship Line."

Pedro told him the *S. S. Wazzan* sailed to Brazil. Young men signed on and they returned to Madeira old men come back to look for wives and settled down in the remote villages of the island. Pedro knew the cook on the Wazzan's sister-ship, *Zweena*.

"Masqueraders chased me through the streets. I did nothing to them. Do you think my mask offended them?" he said.

"I don't know," said Pedro. "I stay away from the cities and crowds. A small village is better for me. Ask us sailors about villagers. We spend only a little time on the streets to buy a few things. Funchal lives off tourists and sailors."

José slept the rest of the night on a stack of canvas. In the morning, Pedro served him coffee with cream and sugar and store bread. José enjoyed breakfast and thanked him.

"Come aboard anytime you see us off the mole," said Pedro. "Be sure to give my best to my friend the cook on the *Zweena*."

An Angolan deckhand rowed José over to *Falcon*. He promised José to return the skiff to the Yacht club.

From a lighter approaching the Blandy tug, Talbot yelled at José. "Halloo, halloo you there!" Talbot held up a box. With him was his guest from London William Jenkins. They swung over the rail and climbed from the gangway onto the tugboat. "I knew you'd take *Falcon* home. Where'd you spend the night?"

"I spent it on the *Wazzan*," said José.

"That street gang was out to beat you up and might have killed you. I went to the police and they were not impressed."

"What a lovely box, Senhor Talbot!"

"It has fresh chocolates for Pistola, British, brought from England by Jenkins here. He'll join me for the Festival of Saint Blaise."

"I'll give your compliments to Pistola," said José, "and tell him to look for you at the festival."

"I'd forgotten that Jews once wore costumes on Shrove Tuesday and painted their faces. That custom was observed more than a century ago," said Talbot.

"I painted my face the way my Grandfather did when he went to the masquerade."

"Thank Pistola for the custard apples. There is a note in the bag," said Talbot.

Talbot and Jenkins disembarked. José waved. The mountains dominated the harbor, clouds hovering over them. He wished he were leaving for Brazil. He wished the two girls he'd met in the street were going off to Brazil with him.

When *Falcon* docked at Campanário Soldiers guarded the quay and met José as he stepped out of the wherry and asked him questions. "Where've you been? Who gave you permission?"

"I'm going to Maçapez to deliver this box to Pistola."

They paid no attention when he said, "from the Englishman, Talbot."

146

Blandy's tug moved offshore into the mists. The soldiers allowed him to land and the officer dispatched one man to accompany him to the village.

Over the cliffs two kestrels soared on the currents of air, hovering above the valley, peering down on crevices and shrubs. Pistola stood in the doorway of his shop and waved to José.

"I was chased by masqueraders through the streets of Funchal," he said.

"Welcome home. We looked for you last evening," said Pistola.

"I spent the night in the harbor after I was chased by a street gang. The ship *Wazzan* was going to Brazil."

"They mistook you for a Jew," said Pistola.

"How did they do that? I'm Catholic."

"Your Grandfather painted his face in that manner. It was an old custom of the Jews to paint their faces and join the masqueraders and still practiced here in the village."

"Senhor Talbot will visit you during the Festival of Saint Blaise. He brings a guest. The man Jenkins has studied beetles at Rabaçal. They'll spend the first night with Mr. Veitch at Jardim da Serra."

"And this box?" said Pistola.

"It's from your Talbot, with a note inside."

"What else did he say?"

"He wanted me to go to Brazil for gold mining."

"They have snakes there, queer animals, and birds that fly backwards. Gold in Brazil! We have rainbows in the valley of the melons and pots of gold," said Pistola.

Pistola measured out sugar for a young woman with two children. He limped around the counter and leaned on it to support himself. "My Uncle ran away to Brazil without papers and the soldiers shot him."

"Senhor Talbot said he'll get papers."

"It's easier said than done. The *Senhorio* sent his men looking for you." He shrugged his shoulders.

"Senhor Talbot thanked you for the *anona,* custard apples, and sends you greetings. I met a man on the *Wazzan* who will pay my passage across the great sea," said José. "I'd love a sweet."

Pistola beckoned to Paulo, his helper, and they walked out onto the terrace where they could talk without eavesdropping by the men at the bar. Pistola took the box of chocolates with him.

"That man you met was an agent and you'd pay back the expense of your passage to him with interest."

Pistola opened the box and offered them chocolates. He slit open the envelope from Talbot and read the letter.

"I don't read," said José. "If I could write, I'd send you a letter from Brazil."

"It's expensive to obtain papers."

"The cook Pedro said I could ship without papers."

"You'd never return home. *El Reis* would publish your name in official notices. Every village in Madeira would recognize your name. The mailman, the priest, the police officers would ask folks if they had seen you and your name would be on everyone's lips."

"Life is living death. I've no land, no inheritance. My family has no wealth."

"I understand my friend. The competent authorities won't sign your passport."

José felt the old dread the smell of rotting cabbages, the cackle of the old Aunt, the hot sun beating on his head when he worked in the gardens. "Speak with your friend Talbot. I beg you." He raised his arm and itched at his elbow.

"Brazil is far away and a dangerous land," said Pistola.

"No worse than Funchal. The masqueraders wanted to kill me."

"You need your family. Father Segundo hasn't forgotten you and neither has the militia Captain. The men in the Valley of the Melons have the reputation of not attending church and they don't drink Christ's blood. The church remembers them, remembers every sin."

"Where can I go?" said José.

"You can live with the fishermen in Ribeira Brava," said Pistola.

"I know nothing about Jews. Those fishermen are wild. I'll go to live with my brother Henrique in the mountains."

"The *Senhorio* sent his men out after you, little one. Go and hide. I told your father you were in Funchal. He is mad at you. You must disappear into the countryside. I'll deny you were here." Pistola stood up and shook his hand.

"I'll work. That's all I know," said José

At that moment, the *Senhorio's* men walked into the shop for their afternoon glasses of wine. They eyed José and whispered. They looked over their shoulders at him and swore. He waved good-bye to Pistola and Paulo eating the fine chocolates from Talbot.

At the goats' cave, he washed off his make-up and threw aside his costume. He smelled soup cooking down in the kitchen. He knelt and said the words he had heard chanted by Tia Nita.

"Hear, O Israel. The Lord is our God, one Lord, and you must love Him with all your heart and soul and strength. These commandments I give you this day are to be kept in your heart; you shall repeat them to your sons, and speak them in the fields..."

José ran his fingers through his hair and rubbed the back of his neck. He saw steamships and dreamed they were sailing to Brazil and he sailed on one of them.

The waves broke over the rocks below the smuggler's cave. Surf churned white, and sunlight on its crest broke into fiery jewels.

CHAPTER XXIII

Regret, sorrow, longing, *saudade*, nostalgia, the thought of leaving home pursued José after his return from Funchal. He walked alone through the family vineyard. Light caught the dewdrops along the dark and leafless vines. He thought about the times he danced at the festival, carried the banner of Christ with its bright red crusader cross, and sat with Julia and Maria enjoying the sunset colors on the clouds and the sea and the listened to the fine band music.

He walked on through Sítio de Furnas e Amoreiras, the Place of the Caverns and Mulberry Trees. The gulf of the Valley of the Melons spread out before him, the sun shining on the grape vines and the kestrel hovering on the wind at the head of the gulf. He climbed the ridge through gardens, row on row of red soil terraces, cultivated and hilled with sweet potatoes, cabbages and melons. João's whistled to him.

"You promised not to tell," said José. "You told the authorities about Tia Nita.

"Julia and Maria promised and crossed their hearts, but told"

"Yes and word spread quicker than a kestrel seizes a sparrow." He hit João on the sleeve.

"I know Julia and Maria kept quiet. The Senhorio sent his men looking for you."

"Where can I hide?" said José.

"Go to the mountains. Henrique knows the distant trails and caves to hide in."

João was gleeful and hopped from one bare foot to the other. "You'll go with me," said José.

"Not me. I'm staying home."

151

"You carried her corpse with me."

"I've forgotten that. I didn't tell the authorities. I'm sorry for your troubles but you must leave before these men catch you."

José spit and wiped his mouth. "You're no help to me at all."

On his return home, he saw three men climbing up the pathway to his house. He hurried up into the loft and found his boots and wool stockings. He found his sweater hidden in João's sack. He pulled on his knitted cap and listened for footsteps outside. He didn't want to flee to the mountains. He'd miss the festival. He'd not hear the rockets, the morning of the first day. He climbed down the ladder to the kitchen. Mother had instinctively understood his rush to leave and she handed him a sack with bread and a chunk of goat's cheese. He quickly climbed across the kitchen gardens and the yard before the goat's cave all the while listening for the men approaching his cottage.

He heard the men speaking to mother and caught a glimpse of angry faces in the yard below and turned away and rapidly climbed the slope toward the summit in the bright sunshine until he ran out of breath.

He rested on the crest of the slope and ate his bread and cheese and walked the rest of the day along the trails northwest and into the high country. In the twilight he entered the high forest with its moss and great squat oak trees. The sea breeze was cold and he pulled down the flap of his *carapuça*. He sat in a sheltered grove and peeled a banana. He listened to the green finches singing. The trail below him was quiet. He scanned the slope to see if the men followed him up the ridge in the twilight. He closed his eyes and slept.

Two hours later, he awoke. He walked until he was tired and halted in the laurel wood. He heard no voices, nor sounds of sheep. The dark silhouette of Henrique's hut showed against the sky and he searched for Henrique. He opened the door and finding the room empty dropped down on Henrique's bunk exhausted and slept.

At dawn, he brewed coffee and ate a few dried chestnuts. In the sunrise he stood on the highest elevation and surveyed the landscape. He sat down in the light to rest from his hike to the summit and looked across the peaks and rising mists from the valley below. Across the way, a shepherd with his flock huddled in his cape, awaiting the warmth of the sun. A horn sounded and a man with a moustache hiked up through the glen, wearing a beret and carrying a walking stick. José counted the sheep until he forgot the number. An hour later, a voice said, "Good morning, Senhor."

The sun-wrinkled face smiled. The old man dropped his food bag and threw off the wineskin slung over his shoulder.

"Where are your sheep?" said José.

"They're coming the long way around. Where are yours?"

"I'm no shepherd. I'm José, looking for Henrique the Abreu. You know him? Have you seen him in these mountains?"

"I know an Henrique of the Fairies!"

"He cuts timber hunts rabbits and lives off the land."

"Each of us lives off the land." Vincent Nobrega of Caldeirão Verde leaned into the wind and smiled. "When Henrique wanders during winter storms he sleeps in my hut. We speak little enjoying the fire and the stars after the winter storm when snow has fallen and lies bright on the slopes."

José whittled a stick and nodded at the eighty-five year old shepherd.

"I walk and eat a morsel and whistle for my dogs. I follow the sheep to see they don't fall into sink holes or lose their way."

He'd seen Henrique two weeks before. Henrique had cut willows along the river above Boa Ventura. The bundles were floated down to Arco de St. Jorge during high water.

"I've nowhere to sleep tonight," said José.

"My corral lies in the rocks on the way to Serra De Agua. The sheep sleep there. Come along and meet my companion, Gold Tooth."

"Your friend may have seen Henrique."

"He may have. I don't remember, the world fades from me and I see the festivals at Camacha in my mind, the apples and cider and broiled beef," said Vincent.

The old man opened his food sack and offered goat cheese. José ate bits of cheese as the knife pared them off the chunk. They crumbled in his mouth, rich, milky, pungent. He seldom ate cheese at home. His mother sent it off to market. The peasants sent it to the market and saved none to use for themselves.

After drinking from his wine skin and packing his cheese, Vincent whistled for his dogs. The dogs sensed home and rounded up the sheep. They ran ahead until signaled. José yelled obscene words, and imitating the old man, made new sounds, sucking through his teeth, blowing with full cheeks, laughing and moving the sheep toward Pico Grande.

In the mists, he saw a corral built by using natural rock. The mouth of the narrow crevice had been sealed with a high dry-wall. A gate of rough-hewn timber closed the entry to keep the animals from wandering out. José climbed up the barrier to watch the sheep in the corral. He held the gate while the old man locked it.

"Why are goats in with sheep?" said José. The old man gathering the goats hadn't heard him. The mists thickened and darkness fell, the sheep-dogs whined for their meal.

"The goats climb out of here when I don't tie them for the night, and they've gone off by morning."

Once the sheep and goats were bedded down for the night and the dogs fed, José followed Vincent into the maze, out of the pen and up through the rocky passage to the stone hut built into the side of the mountain.

"My Caramajo friend calls himself Gold Tooth, a name given to him by his villagers. He may know the whereabouts of Henrique. He's roamed these mountain pastures for many years."

The only light inside the hut was a fire, kindled by the old man. He set a metal pot on the flames and sliced thin a few potatoes for soup. The room smelled of mildew and leather and dung.

Outside the dogs barked, and footsteps signaled Gold Tooth's arrival. A short man with brown eyes and dressed in brown stepped through the door and laughed when José. "You must be the fellow that fled Campanário." He laughed again. "I told those gardeners looking for you to turn back. They'd lose themselves and die here. They know nothing about mountains. There were three of them"

"Come have some coffee and soup," said Vincent. José pulled out his cup from his sack

"You're welcome to stay." His chewing slurred his words. "You know better than to run from a *senhorio*. They're the King's chosen men and pledged to uphold the feudal law."

The coffee tasted of chicory. The liquid greased José's lip. He thought of refusing the soup, but its odor of cabbage and onions convinced him to accept a mug. Gold Tooth passed him chunks of bread. "What brings you to God's world?" he said.

"I beg your pardon, Senhor!"

"Those garden men didn't say much. They were eager to speak with you. We meet all kinds of men here murderers, thieves, rapists, adulterers. The heights are cold and windy and God lives here waiting for us. The animals graze off the weeds and grasses. The southern slopes look more like a desert than pasture. Can you live in this desert?"

"I'm seeking my brother, Henrique de Abreu."

Both men laughed. Gold Tooth licked his spoon and shoved it into his soup. He ate bread, and chestnuts he dug from the ashes at the fire's edge. He peeled one and asked José why he'd run away.

"My brother and I hid Tia Nita's corpse. The priest refused to bury her. I've no rights in the valley. I live on the feudal land with my large family and we barely survive."

"Those that come here have the devil on their heels," said Vincent.

"What is the news from Hell?" said Gold Tooth.

José cradled his cup and soothed his hands. He didn't feel at home with these two before the smoking fire. The old man leaned onto his robe enjoying the cigarette he'd rolled after drinking his cabbage soup. Vincent smiled and remained silent.

"The soldiers sealed the village well. It was contaminated. Women now carry water a great distance. The men are angry with the priest for siding with the soldiers."

"The old ways die slowly. They love their old well. Always, there's suffering. I'm sad," said Gold Tooth.

"The land is poor. We sell as much as we can. Our family once owned it long ago. Our António our cousin born from the pig's tail is the *senhorio* and owns everything."

"I've heard talk of this *senhorio* in the *cantinas* of Canhas and Ponta Do Sol. They say he's hungry for land, like the mad landlords during the olden times," said Vincent.

"I remember the *senhorios* when I was a boy," said Gold tooth. "They ruled with an iron fist. They were the gods of the land."

"We do everything under his authority. We pay him taxes every year, the best animals, the best fruits of the land."

"Life is suffering. We live in its cauldron of gossip and intrigue," said Vincent.

"You're corrupted. Hell is too good for you. This lad has years yet to live and lonely wandering ahead of him." Gold Tooth kept silent. The dogs barked. "Too many us die alone in the mountains," said Gold Tooth.

"I must find my brother. The *Senhorio* ordered his men to capture me."

"Alberto from Saint Vincent saw your brother cutting timber for Manuel Soares from his village," said Gold Tooth. "I believe Henrique hates company. He lives alone and far away from the authorities. He hates those violate who intrude on his independence."

"I'll walk to Saint Vincent in the morning," said José.

"Stay with us until your legs are strong. The trails are steep and long beyond here and will take hours to climb."

"If Henrique works beyond Vinhaticos, I want to go there and seek him. Thank you sirs for supper," he said.

"It's nothing," said Vincent, wrapping himself into his blanket.

José warmed his feet and lay back, the fire flickered and a ghost-like figure shone in the darkness. He prayed. When he awoke in the morning, the shepherds had eaten and left to release their sheep from the pen. The fire burned brightly.

CHAPTER XXIV

The old man pointed to the northwest and the mountain ridge and said, "The last day I saw him Henrique worked over there." He pointed to a distant plain to the west. The sheep spread out over the sunlit ridge, the dogs wandering the slope explored holes for rabbits. Vincent huddled out of the wind and called for his coffee.

"Over in that district you'll find your brother. It's a wild place."

José shivered and gathered firewood from the underbrush. He set the wood in a heap. Gold Tooth poured more coffee.

"Will I find the place?"

"You follow the ridge and cross the Brava into the Vinhaticos," said Gold Tooth.

"They know his name. He's a reputation with the people on the heights. He cuts timber there. The natives say he's an odd one, stays alone by himself. He buys salt pork in the village. He's a devil for work," said Vincent.

"How'd they know of him?"

"Word travels, my friend. We wander the heights and see ghosts, and we go into the valley to buy tobacco and a little sugar and tea. The peasants know us and whenever they see a climber or inspector of *levadas* they tell us."

Gold Tooth rolled a cigarette, closing the sack of tobacco by holding one string with his teeth and pulling it shut. "Henrique buys from us. The valley folk know the rainbows."

"I live by rainbows," said Vincent. "What do I see while tending sheep?"

"I like the kestrels. They fly over the valley of the melons high in the blue and the currents of air carry them through the rainbows," said José.

Gold Tooth laughed. Old Vincent closed his eyes and waited.

"How old are you, my son?"

"I am going on sixteen years in May, Senhor. I've worked since I learned to walk. I have two goats. I love the sea. My sheep live in the clouds over the sea." He leaned against the bed-rock and pulled off his knitted cap, he closed his eyes and forgot the shepherds. He saw a white sail moving on the horizon toward the island. "I hate the Senhorio," he said.

The shepherds laughed and shook their fists. They understood landlords. "You're old enough to be a slave," said Gold Tooth.

"You've years ahead of you and the way is narrow and long. Look at these slopes." He pointed out the region below. "These lands give little. They demand hours of climbing, labor and faith." Vincent interrupted.

"Once you're broken in, work is invisible. Enjoy each quick day before night falls."

"I'll be fine after I talk with Henrique."

Gold Tooth pointed to the tract. "You must go, or night will overtake you on the trail. Make your way through Bica da Canja during daylight."

José embraced the old shepherd. Each time he stopped on the trail to rest, he saw the lone figure standing on the mountain. He wished to spend his life with the shepherds. The fire burning in the hut, the friendly voices, coffee, the smell of chestnuts, lingered with him. Clouds streamed across the sky from the north coast, great caravels and seamen from the days of Empire--sailing across the sky, free and curious, discovering worlds, new peoples--great clouds moved like the poetry he memorized and sang as a child, that made him feel *saudade,* moved through his mind as he hiked the ridge leading southwest toward Grande Ribeira.

The trail led into a river valley with streams of water rushing over the rocks. Birds hopped along the bank. The vegetation was dense. He lost track of the trail. The trees were tall and dark, sounds of insects cushioned by the green hedges. The world of the heights and even Campanário were distant. He listened for chopping, for whistling, for the barking for a dog. The quiet of the forest calmed his mind. He sat at the top of the bank and listened.

After many hours walking, he saw the church spire of Rosário. Avenues of green, mimosa and eucalyptus saplings in files crowded each side of the valley and the trail opened into a track made by wild goats.

A crone with kerchief hiding her face waved him away from her. She gave reluctantly a few directions into the wild. He met a priest on a bicycle. "Henrique de Abreu works that way," said the priest. "Where're you from, young man?"

"From the summit of the mountain, Father, I hope to find Henrique by nightfall," said José.

"Follow the tributary track, you'll see him. They say he works in the pass. God bless."

The priest hopped on his bicycle and peddled off, his crow-like shoulders hunched over the handle bars. An hour later, chopping sounds on the breeze sent José walking toward the sound. He whistled. The chopping ceased and a reply touched the ear. José waited and whistled again.

A man bare-chested was cutting down a great tree with a hand axe. He saw him when light reflected off the sweating torso. He saw a cloth band tied around the dark head.

"Henrique, Henrique, is it you?"

"Yes, Senhor, I'm the Abreu."

"It's me, José. God be with you, Senhor. Give me your blessing."

The brothers embraced. "What sadness brings you to this place? Has your our mother died? Has the Senhorio taken more land from my father? "

"No evil news. Mother and father are in good health. The sisters send best wishes. Silvino broke his leg, you may have heard and it heals."

"Are you traveling to St. Vincent?"

"I'm running away from home. It's a long story," said José.

They rested in the shade of a Madeiran heath tree. Henrique, small as a gnome and wrinkled from constant exposure to the sun, listened. Deep set lines curved around his mouth, and his chin was square with a cleft.

"This is fine timber. The Senhorio that lives in St. Vincent paid me to cut the tall ones and haul them to the village. This is the best work I've found," said Henrique.

José told him about hiding the corpse in the smuggler's cave. Henrique swore when he heard The Senhorio's men were looking for José.

"I can hide you. After a few days, you must go home."

"No, I shan't." I won't be the slave of the Senhorio. Pistola and Maria couldn't advise me. João refused to help."

"The Senhorio had the right to lock you up. Here, work is scarce for those that leave their villages. We survive and we don't want newcomers. I'd never return to Campanário. You must get papers. The Senhorio has the authority."

José held up his hand. Henrique kept talking. "Once you tell your story to the authorities, they'll believe you and give you papers."

"The old Aunt followed the practices of the Jews. She memorized and said the prayers taught to her as a child. I learned them. I didn't know they were forbidden."

"No matter, we've Christian. They can't hold the old religion against us," said Henrique.

"The priest hated the old Aunt. She was never free to live. She suffered for her beliefs?"

"It may be as you say. I can't know for sure." Henrique chopped and felled the tree. José found the old kettle and filled it with spring water and set it on the coals, adding more wood chips to the fire.

Henrique and José slipped into camp in the twilight that night and they ate cabbage soup. José washed up in the stream and carried a bucket of water up to the camp. They were silent and spoke little.

"The land grows little most seasons. You want to live in the mountains. The mountain men talk of Brazil. More leave the heights. In Estreito de Câmara de Lobos, I've seen a hundred men cutting stone in the quarry for bread and soup, and wine on Sunday. The fleet at Câmara de Lobos has more fishermen than boats. Life is bad for those on the land. The peasants don't run into the mountains.

ªWe live like the sheep and the goats. The nights are long and lonely, and our guts growl on the soup we eat to make it through the day."

"It's better than priests and landlords," said José.

The next day, he and Henrique had felled trees, and they had moved logs with a long pole and had piled them on the roadway for oxen to drag off.

With the morning star shining brightly, the birds sang in the forest, and as they sang in the violet twilight. His brother's axe echoed across the stream. José's hands blistered and toughened from using the crow bar. He learned to lever with his body and eased his arms. That day Henrique killed a rabbit with his shot gun. The soups of rice and onion and chestnut gave way to rabbit stew.

Between spoonfuls of soup, Henrique said, "You must return to The *Senhorio* and tell the truth. He'll listen to you and make a judgment."

"It's impossible. The man is a thief and a liar."

"I agree. He stole our land. He divided it so we work for nothing. We fight over small plots not worth a thousand *reis*. Remain loyal to the family."

"I love my brothers and sisters," said José. "But I won't return to the land."

Henrique raised his wooden bowl and drank off the last of the stew, and ripped a chunk of bread off the loaf. He frowned. "You won't go back?"

"I can't be a slave to the land. I refuse the authority of the *Senhorio.* The church offered me nothing. It's ignorance to live in slavery."

"What is your obligation to father?"

"What do I owe him?"

"Life, he gave you breath."

"Must I ransom my life to pay him for it? It'd be better to throw myself into the sea, or work at the bottom of the devil's pit, to be chained in a cave and never see the sun."

"To live and die alone is foolish. You can't live without your family. You envy me. I have no wife, no children, and no evenings at the wine-shop with friends."

"You have Vincent and Gold Tooth. I can live alone."

Henrique laughed. "You haven't paid for your birth."

They argued honor and their place in the world. José said he was going to Brazil when Pistola and Talbot found a passage for him. Henrique stared and said nothing.

The Madeiran pigeons called in the twilight. He dreamed of the sloop sailing away with him. Henrique returned from Rosário and brought the gossip of the village. He had bought fresh sardines. They broiled sardines, a welcome addition to their meal. José boiled up a soup of rice, tomato, and onions.

The green wine from Seixal was dry and sweet. They drank to health. Henrique tapped the ends of his fingers in an attitude of prayer. The wine went to Jose's head and he chatted like a magpie.

"Who do I owe?"

"You owe our family for your life. Loyalty to mother and father is a duty. And the youngest son must serve, no matter what he thinks or feels. You work and obey the landlord. That's the way it's always been."

Henrique drank another glass of wine and wiped his bright lips. "Ungrateful son," he said.

There was silence and crickets sang on the plain and night birds. They collected their belongings scattered on the ground around the campfire and prepared for sleeping in the tent. José wanted to obey his brother and to believe in the old Truths. "If the land provided a living, it might be possible to live with the family but with António as Senhorio, never," said José.

"Church and family, country and King," Henrique said. He himself had rejected them by living in the mountains. "They make life worth living. How can you question them? They act on your behalf. Without them, you'd be nothing."

José built up the fire with bits of hard wood. The blankets were dry and warm, and he slid himself between them shivering from the evening air. "I'm going to Brazil, no matter what you say. You ran to the mountains. You should understand more about these things."

"You're mistaken," said Henrique.

"You were the eldest. You never married or worked the land. I'm youngest. I'm free of Father. He has our sisters to care for him when he's old and feeble."

"You've no right to run away," said Henrique.

"I'm going to sail to Brazil and freedom."

His brother rolled out of the blankets and crawled out of the tent. José was half asleep when he heard him return. "I'll show you my cache, where I hide my coins," said Henrique. "Should I die, you'll need gold."

"I don't need gold. I have Brazil," said José.

"You see through the eyes of the kestrel and feel life through your heart and you can't see the great distance to truth."

Henrique slept and breathed heavily.

José settled himself in his blanket and closed his eyes. He listened to the night, leaves like falling water, magical and soft. Nothing Henrique said would keep him in Madeira. The whispers of Maria saying her prayers before she lay down beside him rose in his mind. He heard Henrique say, "Bastard," in his sleep.

CHAPTER XXV

Before dawn, Henrique crouched over the gray bed of the fire and blew into the feathery ashes and the coals glowed and ignited the kindling. The air felt damp and a stiff breeze blew southeast from the sea. José shivered and buttoned his shirt. The coffee and pan-bread tasted good. He stuffed a few chestnuts into his pocket. Henrique led him to the ridge. The land fell away on the sides of the path, chasms hundreds of meters below. José carried a climber's rope and Henrique cradled an earthen jug under one arm.

Mist blew by them and vistas of stars faded and daylight bleached away the blue sky. The path wound through a forest of stunted trees. An expanse of dried up, wind-blown ghosts of plateau trees spread out to the horizon. In brighter light, the flat grass tableland appeared out of the mists. White and black sheep dotted the plain. In old stories told to him as a child, this plain was called the Paúl da Serra.

They walked across the plain to the edge of a cliff and below he saw a canyon surrounded by high cliffs about forty-five hectares.

"I must let you down by rope. You can't climb down. You'll kill yourself," said Henrique. "I'll let you down. The cave is on the north of the canyon. My cache is under the wicker mats. The sunlight's reflections off the pool of spring water light up the cave."

He indicated the handholds in the rock. "Take your time. I want you to remember the place until the day you die. You'll need this jug."

"You've shown me the canyon. I'll stay and you go down. I'll return another day," he said.

"I want you to see the cache. I may never see you again. The fairies live by that spring. Offer them a drink from your jug."

"They live in the cave, I suppose. When will you fetch me?"

"Later on, I'll pray you sail to Brazil." Henrique let out the rope. He saw José's knitted cap disappear over the side.

José swung out into space and steadied his descent by grasping a heath shrub growing from a crevice in the cliff.

"I'll meet you at sunset," he yelled up to Henrique.

The valley had trees along the edge of grassland. The walls in vertical lines rose to the sky and trees grew around the spring. He stood in a great natural pit. He stretched his neck to see the top of the cliff. The climb out was straight up.

He slipped out of the sling and waved his hand. The rope disappeared up the cliff side. He took a deep breath and walked toward the pasture on the north side. He looked for wild goats and sheep. The walls of the canyon rose vertical to the rim. Water stained the rocks with red and yellow and plants grew from the precipice, bright green, primitive, desert-looking.

At the far end of the pasture, he saw a dark opening in the canyon wall. Sunlight shone the fine grasses before it. He walked slowly across the pasture, amazed by the silence, no birds and no lizards. He felt the heat of the sun on him and sought the trees at the spring of water. The shade cooled him and outside the grove the meadow gleamed in the sunlight. Steep ledges made a series of vertical lips around the rim of the canyon over hangings of cacti, streams of water, smooth as glass.

The cave was dry and dark. He lay on the cool floor and sunlight reflected off the pool. The light moved along the ceiling of the cave. In a dream, Pistola handed him papers. He signed his name and Pistola applied a wax seal with red and green ribbons, the colors of King Carlos. He stood on the deck and shook the hand of the *Zweena's* captain. On the fantail he waved good-bye. Maria had kissed his cheek.

He was thirsty and drank from the jug. He left the cave and went out in the pasture. A shepherd moved far off to the southwest on the southwest rim. He whistled and waved. The man saw him and walked away. Was it Henrique?

Doves landed in the grass and flew off when they saw him. He found no leather sack, no chest, and no cache if it were there.

He hiked along the floor of the canyon. He touched the rock with his fingertips He'd climbed cliffs above the pebbled beach. He hunted for rabbits on them with João and Silvino. Henrique was not coming back for him!

He ran his fingertips over the surface of the walls. He stared up the rock-face and slowly examined the promontory from the base to the rim. Sunlight obliterated detail.

Hundreds of rock faces surrounded him. He had to discover a way out before dark. Sunlight brightened the surfaces and they darkened from passing clouds covering the sun. The grasses of the pasture were green. They had water. Where did water go when it rained? He leapt up and ran across the meadow. He found shallow pools and they flowed into a stream with high shrubs and trees. In the wood along the north wall was a pond.

From the sediment of the pond he retrieved a cup and cleaned it out with sand. The handle made a beautiful loop. The cup had a blue glaze over white clay. On the bottom of the cup were the letters, ZARCO. He had heard the family name of the blue-eyed explorer named Gonçalves Zarco. Men had explored the canyon. He wandered along the edge of the canyon in the late afternoon sunlight and searched for a way to the rim and the plateau.

"Henrique, Henrique," he called. His whistle echoed off the canyon walls. He laughed at his brother's joke. He swore to the Virgin, to her Son, and to Our Father. He prayed for deliverance.

Inhuman rock, lifeless volcanic rubble, smooth veins amidst porous moonstone; green rocks, fern and wort, mists through the seasons of the year coming in with the northeast winds; bright growth, red and yellow; ghost-like lizards with patches of dark rock. The trees were tall enough to launch him onto a high ledge. He needed a slender perch, like ones found by the Madeiran pigeons in the deep shrubs above the *levadas*.

Had he left word with Maria? When he didn't return she'd look for him. She'd meet Gold Tooth. João wouldn't listen and assist her to find him. He'd say the family was better off without him. He wept.

At sunset, spider-like, webbed-lines appeared in the rock face along the canyon. The angle of failing light revealed cracks with possible handholds for ascent.

He braced his knee against the rock and pushed with his foot. He felt a slight indentation and wedged his big toe into position.

He reached overhead and his fingertips held and he pulled himself up. He balanced with his right knee and found a hold and grasped it with his free hand.

The flat, dish-like surface allowed him to move higher and with his left hand he patted the rock and felt a crevice for leverage.

His weight held and he pushed his toe into the crevice. A bird sang, beautiful, clear, and calm.

He rubbed his hand on his trouser and felt for a firm handhold. The rock ahead was warm from the day's sun and dry and he slowly crept up a few meters. The expanse ahead glistened in the setting sun. He couldn't see a way around a patch of wet lichens.

Down on the pasture-land, Madeiran sparrows cheerful and lively chirped and fed on grass seeds. Climbing back down, he thanked god for the small ascent. Before he descended, he observed the weathered rock face and their colors.

He went to the spring and pushed his face into the water distorting the leafy silhouettes on the silver surface. He doused his head and drank a long cold draught. He lay in the cave and watched the light fading. He wanted to climb to the top where vermilion clouds brightened the sky over the plateau. He traced his route, his eye sort a new turn, a better way up. He considered other spots along the base of the cliff. He wanted to discover a new way. He knew the faults of the one he had climbed.

He patted his stomach. He would eat bilberries at the top. They grew along the *levada* under the lily-of-the-valley trees. He drank more water. Black Caps flew through pink clouds over the canyon. He envied their freedom. He thought he heard a whistle on a far-off ridge and he whistled. He ran to the middle of the pasture and whistled, no answer, only echoes.

He thought of blowing a signal with the jug and rushed back to the cave and poured water out of the jug and blew a loud note across its mouth with a puff of air and adjusted its sound. He blew a long loud note. He repeated this until he felt weak and listened for a reply. The time for Henrique to return had passed and the black line of the ridge showed against the stars. He shivered in the dampness and turned toward the cave, tossing the jug on the ground.

Though the cave was warm and dry, gusts of night wind blew mist. He rested by sitting up with his arms supported by his knees and his cheek resting on his jacket. The night was long and damp and uncomfortable. First, he lay on his side and then sat up. He walked to warm up.

The morning sun glorious and warm awoke him, and he stretched and walked to the western side of the canyon and let the sun warm him. He drank two cupfuls of water and searched the trees and the edge of the scrub and grassland and there were no berries. He scanned the rim of the canyon for shepherds.

He pulled at his right ear and thought. If he climbed out of this Hell, he'd be lucky. He sucked in his gut and the taste of coffee rose into his nose. He spit it out and it returned, and he yawned and stared into the sky. It must never cloud over at this altitude.

The walls looked higher in the bright morning light and he was determined to climb them, the way he scaled the cliffs at home.

The overhang at the top made a shadow which concealed the surface he had to cross and move along the rock-face. Tomorrow, he would be weaker for not having eaten and he would not have the strength to crawl across that space.

He went back to the beautiful spring and drank two more cups of water, a toast to himself, whispering to his health, and may God be with you, Senhor, as you fly out of this desert place. He marched to the spot, his head high like the men marched into the village in the opening procession of the Festival of Saint Blaise. He saw the red and white flags emblazoned with the cross of the knights templar, the women and children laughing and clapping their hands, the men silent and *saudade*. Where he climbed yesterday, his fingers touched the ledge and the feeling returned, and he leapt up and placed his knee in the dish-like surface.

Balancing himself with his left hand alone, he reached up with his right hand and pulled himself higher. His ascent to the overhang was rapid this time and he examined the rock face to the right. It looked strange in the light, the web of dark and light, new and unexplored. He stared and closed his eyes and saw the image of the rock face ahead. He touched the surface to right side with his toe and moved out where he knew the horizontal crack gave him a good hold.

He edged across the expanse of porous rock, like a spider on his bedroom wall. He prayed and spread himself out. His hands slid lower on the dry surface, and his foot, first his left, then his right, touched the smooth surface.

CHAPTER XXVI

The rough texture of the rock-face rubbed and numbed his finger-tips. He reached above his head and touched a hole and his finger-tips fit. He held himself against the cliff to keep from sliding and rested a moment before swinging into space. He pulled up.

His progress up and over the rim of the canyon exhausted him. Above the overhang, he stretched out on a narrow shelf.

The ledge from the pit was steep and rough and the distance short. Henrique had picked the location for descent where the ridge was low, forty meters to the canyon floor, good for lowering a rope, vertical with few handholds.

He traversed a section of crumbling, sandy volcanic waste. The sun beat on his back. Dark impressions were handholds and led upward to the crest. He pulled himself up and moved toward the top.

The cacti spines of a prickly pear hung over a ledge twenty meters above him. A lizard climbed across the rock's surface and paused to doze in the sunlight and scurried away.

Grains of sand trickled down. He changed direction and crossed over. Climbing was worse. He rested until his heart beat slowly.

His foot fell asleep and he wiggled his toe, massaged his thigh and rid it of cramp. He moved higher and examined the stretch of rock ahead.

Pale shadows dappled the smooth-looking slope. Gravel bits crumbled and pieces fell beneath his palm, rain-like bits down the ravine side. He blew through his nose.

When he closed his eyes, bubbling water appeared and he tasted spruce, and he touched cool leaves, mirrored in the spring.

He heard the breeze through the trees in the canyon below. The trees would break his fall and he'd crawl to the spring and bathe his face, maybe his arm would be broken.

He pressed his palm against the ledge and crawled along its surface.

The next formation was easier and he climbed twenty meters. In minutes, he stood on the precipice, the Paúl da Serra, a great plain spread for kilometers before him. Beyond the sheep scattered on the plain, the trail east wound through dry brush. He crawled into the shade of a boulder and slept.

The way back to Henrique's tent took a long time. He lost his way in the maze of a dense growth of mimosa he heard the trickling waters much like those that had lulled him to sleep during the night he spent with Henrique. The tent door was tied shut and he pulled the bows loose and peered inside. His sack and burlap cape were there. He ate chestnuts and peeled an orange. He listened for the sound of axes and wood cutting. No echoes of the axe. Henrique was away in the forest.

He left the flap of the tent open. He took goat's cheese and bread. From the top of the ridge he waved good-bye.

He reached Lombo do Mouro at sunset. Below, the valley of Ribeira da Furna dropped toward Serra De Agua. He surveyed the Paúl da Serra to the west and the dark green hills beyond. The blue sky before evening's haze covered the dome of sky. The land lay beautiful and quiet. How long before he'd sleep in peace?

A shepherd named Paulo near Serra Da Agua joined him for the night. By morning he was walking the dusty track toward the sea. The track went along the river and he stared at the fierce current, the wind from the mountains blowing off the waves, pressing the water toward the sea. He turned and faced the mountains. The wind pressed against his eyelids and he leaned into it. He passed the church in Ribeira Brava. On the beach he talked with fishermen mending nets. They asked him to fish for tuna at sunset.

"I have to see a friend in Campanário," he said.

He lay down next to a boat painted with bright blue eyes and fell asleep. The air smelled of salty mist and he listened to calls of the fishermen as they launched their boats through the surf.

When Pedro Oliveira shook him awake, José touched the fisherman's pock-marked nose and blinked.

"Good morning, lad. You stayed the night."

The tired face leaned over him. The old man rubbed his whiskered chin with his thumb.

A soft rain fell and the fishermen waded into the surf. "Thank you, Senhor. I go to Campanário, today," he said.

"We'll sail by the great spire. You can swim to the pebbled beach." Oliveira poured coffee.

"The horizon clears enough to sail," said the old man.

José waved good-bye and watched them sail and then climbed the steep cliff east of the village. He slipped in mud and fell on his knees, water dripping off his nose and chin, rivers of water raced by him. At the top of the mountains to the north, a thunderstorm broke, its fury ripped leaves off shrubs and trees. His shirt clung to his chest and he shivered. He wanted hot soup and as he continued into his valley, the waters churned by him, dyed red, and his boots squished through mud.

He came upon Monkey-face who worked for the *Senhorio* and Blackeye. He slowed and smiled. They squinted from beneath their burlap sacks. They looked like monks. He laughed.

"Where're you going?" said Monkey-face.

"Home to a dry bed," he said.

"You'd better come with us. The *Senhorio* has a dry bed for you," said Blackeye.

He ran down the flooded pathway, slipped and fell. The men tied his wrists with rope and led him through the storm by the *quinta* of the *Senhorio*. They locked him into the slave quarters above the onion field.

He yelled for help and searched the walls. They were covered with dentals and drawings. He huddled under a blanket, hungry and cold and dreamed of sailing ships. They came for him in the morning.

The Senhorio ate muskmelon with a silver spoon while sitting on the patio, his favorites waiting on him. "More sugar, Senhora Antónia? Drink hot coffee!" The woman wiped away crumbs and shooed flies from the spotless linen. The servant at the *Senhorio's* elbow poured spring water into a crystal goblet.

The Senhorio spat into the mud at the edge of the patio and eyed the slender figure at the table. The *Senhorio* smacked his lips and spooned great chunks of melon into his mouth. José stared at him. The eyes said, I'm looking at a pig, it's nothing to me.

The Senhorio stared, said nothing and ate his melon, a piece of bread, and sipped his coffee. He asked for more coffee. He admired the rainbow over the valley.

"You've been away," he said. José said nothing. "You ran away when I sent for you. Hours of work were lost. I will lose you to the militia."

He paused and nodded to the servants and with his child-like hand, motioned them to clear the table.

"You left without my permission. You've disobeyed me. What do you say for yourself?"

"Nothing," said José.

"Your sister told me you know something about the disappearance of Tia Nita's corpse."

"I saw nothing. The corpse was swept away by the sea," said José.

"Lies, you saw her alive. You spoke with her. You worked in my stone quarry and she gathered herbs in the nearby field."

"*O Senhor*, I'm wet and tired. I visited with Henrique and have hiked from beyond Bica da Canja. I wish to go to my father's."

"Not yet, tell me about the Tia Nita's death."

"I went to her house after collecting Silvino's baskets. I had carried produce to the cave at the beach. Two women saw me. They keened outside. I went in and saw the dead Aunt in her chair."

"Father Segundo ordered her thrown into the sea. My men didn't find her body. Removing a body is against the law. The unfaithful deserve their fate."

"I've nothing to say," said José.

To Monkey-Face and Blackeye, the Senhorio said, "Lock him in the slave quarters. I won't wait for the tongue-tied to speak." Pointing his finger he said, "You and João buried her corpse. You deny it?"

"I'm hungry. I want my mother's soup."

"Send word to Senhora Abreu. We hold her son. He'll stay until he talks."

From his cell window, José watched the women in the fields harvest the onions. The crickets sang along the Ribeira Melões. João brought bread and soup for his supper.

"Your gossip got me here. Why'd you talk, loud mouth?" said José.

"I'm sorry. I wanted nothing to do with that stinking corpse. You should've stayed in the mountains."

"Henrique double-crossed me. He cast me into a pit."

176

The next morning, the kestrel hovered in the wind. The ocean spread out beneath the bird. Green leaves in the valley reflected the sunlight. João brought breakfast early, bread, cheese and coffee from Pistola.

"What does the Pistola say?"

"Be patient until the festival of Saint Blaise. Your friend Talbot from Funchal will visit. You'll be freed," said João. "We need you to plant potatoes."

Each day the women came to harvest the onions. Rosa Castagna among them and he whistled at her.

"You're more beautiful each morning. Your loving care healed me of the sunstroke."

She smiled. "The *Senhorio* wants to know where the Tia Nita is buried."

"I don't know," he said. "I've nothing to tell him."

"I want you freed," she said.

She brought him figs and oranges from the Senhorio's own trees. She whispered, "I love you."

The women embroidered under the chestnut trees and laughed together. Each wore a straw hat and a kerchief, to keep away the sunlight.

"The Senhorio wants you to confess. The priest wants your confession. He believes you threw her body into the sea," said Rosa.

"Why do you work for the *Senhorio*?" José said.

"We pay for the things we buy from Pistola--leather, nails, tallow, thread, needles. We owe much *reis*. Father sent me to work at the *quinta* for the *Senhorio* until the debts are paid."

"It's shameful. You shouldn't work outside your father's house until you marry."

The next morning she said to him, "The *Senhorio* took me into his bed the first night I stayed in his house." She burst into tears. "After a week he tired of me and I work with his other women."

He hid his face in his hands. Once a week, Blackeye came to ask if he were ready to speak with the *Senhorio*. José shook his head.

That day, Rosa smiled at his tears. Looking across the sea to the Desertas, she told him she wanted to go away with him to a new land. The women worked on the far side of the onion field, and Rosa unbuttoned her blouse. Her breasts swung free in the sunlight. "Go away, you temptress," said José.

Her beautiful breasts appeared in his dreams. She laughed and stuck out her tongue at him.

"I'll tell your father. You should be kept at home."

She covered her breasts, her eyes shining and defiant. She reached through the bars and pulling him toward her, she kissed him.

"I'm bonded to the Senhorio until my father's debts are paid. On the day I'm free, I belong to you," she said.

CHAPTER XXVII

In the morning, Rosa came to his cell window, radiant like Our Lady, eyelids lowered, lips demure. Her figure was radiant and he wanted to feel her breasts, visible and soft.

José said, "Blackeye and Monkey-face took me to see Father Segundo and he wished me to confess my sins. He called me ignorant. I didn't confess. Blackeye locked me back in this cell."

"The square is decorated with flowers and flags. I'm sorry you'll miss the beauty of Saint Blaise," she said.

"I've searched this cell. I'm caught here like an ant in a bottle. I can't bear it."

"The Senhorio has the key. I've seen it."

"You can open this door with the key."

"I can't get the key. The Senhorio keeps it on a nail behind the kitchen door. I looked for it but it was gone. He hung it from the crucifix above his bed."

"Fetch it and return it before he knows."

"Where will you hide?" she said.

"I'll go to the smuggler's cave!"

"Take me to Brazil," she said.

"The voyage is dangerous and I've nobody there, no family. Rosa bring the key. He'll never miss it."

"He sits on the patio and directs the household. I'll talk with mother," she said.

"She'll talk you out of it."

"You'll run and I'll never find you. I'm afraid."

"Get the key. I'll take you with me," he said.

"I can't. The captain visits the Senhorio. The militia returned to the village. They search for those that refused to serve."

"I must leave today."

"They've brought Hell on their heads."

José threw his pillow on the cell floor and seized the bars. "Get the key. I'll be turned over to the militia."

"I can't steal the key. The Senhorio sleeps there!"

He crossed himself and held her hand. He promised to take her with him and crossed his fingers.

"We'll hide in the mountains," he said.

Tears ran down her face. She held his hand. "The Senhorio will beat me if they catch me with the key." She kissed his hand, frowned and said, "As god is my judge, I'll free you. Father promised me to the Senhorio's nephew. I can't live with Alberto. He'll ruin me."

"You don't steal," he said. "I'll fight from this cell and I'll rot here. God does justice in Heaven," he said.

She waved to him from across the onion field. She blew him kisses and disappeared into the sugar cane.

The dew in the grass wet her feet. As she walked along, she waved to the servants. She walked up the stone steps and into the great front hall. The clock ticked on the high-boy. She listened to its beautiful melody when it struck the hour. The tiles cooled her feet. She watched for the servants and crept down the hallway toward the patio.

On the patio, the Senhorio sat at the linen-covered table admiring his old china, a cup of steaming coffee sat before him. She asked for his blessing and arranged the apples and oranges in the bowl. She avoided his eyes. He stared at her breasts with his big brown eyes and smiled. She covered her navel.

"Have you come to see me?" he said.

"Yes, Senhor, I come unto the house of my lord."

"Will you take a nap with me, Senhora?"

"I can't. I'll work here and live at home with my father and mother."

"Stay here at the *quinta* with me while I arrange your marriage."

"I can't, Senhor."

"You won't sleep with me. Have you visited with José?"

"Yes, I have. I have refused the hand of Alberto in marriage."

"She likes me this morning but can't live in my *quinta* or accept my nephew Alberto in marriage." He laughed.

He finished drinking his coffee and beckoned her into the bedroom. She followed about six paces behind him and the draught blew down the hallway and she shivered.

He pointed to the bed with a sigh, slammed the door and shoved the bolt home. He unfastened his belt and dropped his trousers. She lay back on the bed and turned her head away.

As she raised her knees, she saw the key. It hung from the crucifix and she prayed to the man on the cross. The Senhorio mounted her and heaved until he tired himself. She felt a pain and her pelvis hurt. He relaxed and rolled off. He lit a cigarette and smoked it and stared at the ceiling. She looked at the blue sky outside and prayed he wouldn't ever look at her again. She was going to take the key. His eyelids drooped. She prayed to the Virgin. He closed his eyes.

The cock crowed and she heard the women washing clothes in the stream beyond the fig trees. A spider crossed the ceiling, stopped at a crack in the corner and went across and into the crucifix. She shivered. She had to touch the key. It was antique and cumbersome. Her leg went to sleep and she wriggled her toes and listened. His breathing was smooth. She sat up and buttoned her blouse. She touched his ankle and he didn't move.

Outside the window she saw women kneeling on the rocks in the middle of the stream, their thin faded dresses revealed their slender figures. Their kerchiefs protected their faces from the sunlight. No servants worked in the garden.

The Senhorio rolled to the middle of the bed and sighed. She stood up and tiptoed to the chair. She picked up the chair and set it by the bed. The body of Christ had a lean smooth tummy and long slender thighs. She stood on the chair and looked on the Senhor and at Christ. The man on the bed had only to open his eyes and he'd see her standing on the chair. She looked for the spider and reached for the key. Her hand touched the leather ring. She jumped down and stuck the key in her waistband. She covered it with her blouse. She ran to the door and grabbed the bolt. It stuck. She gave it another heave.

The Senhorio mumbled something about kisses.

She ran to the window. The ground was a half-story below. Vines covered the patio. She tried the bolt again. It didn't give.

Oh Christ, help me! A servant might call the Senhorio from the patio. Ana the housekeeper might knock at the door.

She hung her leg over the windowsill and looked back at the sleeping old man on the bed. She felt bitter. He slept contented as a child. She lowered herself along the stucco wall and felt for the lintel with her toes.

The key dropped from her waistband. She let go of the sill and fell to the flagstones. She lay with eyes closed. Did she break a bone?

"Who's there?" said Alzira the cook.

"Rosa of the church," she said.

"Are you working, you slut?"

"Please forgive me, Alzira. I needed *reis* for my dowry, or Alberto won't accept me."

"The Senhorio is a beast. He's a glutton. You should've stayed home."

"Roll up your tongue, Alzira."

The key bent during the fall. The cook glared at her and turned to her kettle to taste the soup. Rosa hid the key in her waistband and ran out. She paused in the stream and squatted and splashed herself until she felt cold. She arrived at the slave quarters out of breath.

"Hurry, no time for tears," José said. The key wouldn't turn in the lock. No matter how she tried, the door remained locked.

"What are you waiting for?" he said.

"I dropped the key when I jumped out of the window and it won't turn in he lock."

"Try again. He'll send his men when he sees the key is missing."

She sobbed. The Senhorio would see she'd gone through the window. She wedged the key against the side of the jamb.

"Take the key to the forge."

"I've no money for the blacksmith."

"Old Ferreiro's a friend of your father's."

She cried on the way to the blacksmith shop. The gossipy villagers heard the anvil. They asked old Ferreiro, "How did she bend the key?"

She held out the key and gripped it with both hands and squeezed until her fingers turned pale. Three men couldn't bend it. How was she to pay? An old pain moved in her head. The nap with the Senhorio hurt her back and she wished she were dead. "I'm not feeling well," she said to her mother. "I'll be in bed."

The hammer striking the anvil awakened her and she covered her head with her pillow. The square was bright and the interior of the shop a black rectangle. Ferreiro gave her a familiar greeting. He winked and patted her skirt.

Did he know she'd come from the bed of the Senhorio?

"Come after *sesta*," he said. He folded his apron and left to eat at home.

She waited under the custard apple tree until he entered his garden and she went through the yard with its metal objects lying about.

She looked over the rack of tongs and pliers. She'd seen him reduce hot bars and bend them like sugar cane.

She set the key on the anvil and stopped to listen for Ferreiro's footsteps—stretchers and points, men's tools. She picked up a kilo-hammer with a leather strap through the hole in the handle. The bent key rolled on the scarred anvil.

She tapped gently. He lived near-by and he'd hear it. She hit a few more blows with no effect. Her hand hurt. She stopped and rubbed feeling back into her palm.

She closed her eyes. The bend in the key turned and slipped over many times. Her hand was black. The next blow caught her fingers and the hammer fell to the earthen floor.

Holding the key up to the light from the cob-webbed window, she saw the straighter angle. She went to the anvil and by tapping she worked the key until it looked perfect to her eye.

"Who's there?" said old Ferreiro.

"You're dreaming, old man," she said. He grabbed her and hugged her. She pulled away from his embrace. He caught her at the doorway. She pushed him away, laughing. She washed the key in the trough first, then lathered her hands and arms and rinsed them until they were clean. He kissed her good-bye.

CHAPTER XXVIII

Rosa didn't return that day. José looked for her across the onion fields and on the path to the village and caught no glimpse of her. Yesterday, she'd run into the village with the key and he waited for her until sleep overtook him. Early this morning preparations continued for the festival of Saint Blaise. Women and children carried bundles of boughs gathered in the laurel wood and burlap bags packed full with evergreens. The children wove the roping and women decorated the church in garlands. The men set flagpoles along the roadway to the church and around the square. Flags with the cross of the Knights Templar waved in the breeze and red and white banners marked the route of the procession on opening day.

Men carried metal cylinders to Fajã Velha and set them up for rocket-launchers along the ridge west of the church. Juca carried a long pole on his shoulders. He rolled it on top of the stone wall near José's prison cell. He rested and wiped the sweat from his brow and frowned.

"Juca let me haul the pole. I'll dig the hole and help you raise it," José said.

"The Senhorio won't let you out of this cell. You're a trouble-maker."

"Have you seen Rosa?"

Juca scowled and didn't want to answer him, looked uneasy and wiped his forehead.

"I haven't seen her. I'll walk by the Senhorio's *quinta* and look for Rosa."

José teased Juca. "I might run away. The Senhorio doesn't trust me. We worked together in the onions, remember?"

Juca grinned and left through the thicket toward the *quinta.* He met Rosa and ran toward her.

"I'm going to the Senhorio so José can help me with poles," Juca said.

"Wait," said Rosa. "José doesn't want to work today."

"I need him to carry poles for the festival stalls." He shrugged and ran up the pathway to the *quinta.*

Rosa rushed across the onion field with the key concealed in her embroidery basket. She took it out and unlocked the cell door. José kissed her on the cheek and skipped across the onion field and waved.

"Wait. I'll lock the door," she said.

"Juca's gone to get the key. Go home and hide in the wine cellar. See you later."

"José, I brought you lunch—cornmeal, fish and oranges, for two." She locked the door and ran after him. He shook his head and held up his hand.

"I'll hide and send word by Pistola. Juca won't be back with the key. You have it. Return it. No one will miss it. They'll think Juca's mad when he tells them I'm going to work with him."

He ran to the banana grove and waved once more before he lost sight of her.

Rosa hid her face in her skirt and cried during her long walk back to the *quinta* and hung the key from the crucifix. In the kitchen she said to the cook, "José isn't in his cell." The words surprised her. "Juca helped him," she said and ran out the door. The Senhorio swore at Juca. "I've had nothing to do with José," he said. No one believed Juca. By the time Rosa reached home, the villagers knew of José's escape from his cell.

The next morning before daylight, he came down from the heights and crept behind João and tapped him on the shoulder. He'd slept in the goats' hut. João jumped up and swung at him.

"It's you. The villagers hunted for you. Juca and Alberto combed the ridge above the valley. They forgot the goat's cave. Rosa told us of your escape. Maria and Julia comforted her but Rosa wouldn't spend the night and ran home in the twilight."

"I need help," José said.

"The Senhorio's ordered your capture. I won't assist you. He gave Manuel of the Flowers his whip to beat you with when they catch you before the villagers in the square."

"Father Domingo won't allow it."

João laughed. "Father Domingo told Father Segundo you hid Tia Nita's corpse in the caves above the pebbled beach. Father Segundo promises to make you confess.

João fetched José's knitted cap and burlap cape. "Mother sent you chestnuts and salt cod. Henrique left you in a pit. He had good sense." João had wanted José whipped and sent back to the land.

"Henrique was jealous. Don't forget it. You're no friend," said José.

João cursed him. José said good-bye and left for the goats' cave.

Light mists blew around the mouth of the cave and he fed handfuls of New Zealand spinach to his goats. He climbed the trail into the mountains and heard the signals of his pursuers along the slopes. The mists on the heights that afternoon were heavy and rains forced him down into the Jardim da Serra. The heights were thick with fog and he was tired and hungry and lost his way. After a long search he caught a glimpse of the great *quinta* owned by Henry Veitch, the British consul and once on the estate he rested in the orchard kept a watch over the fields for the gardeners.

The clouds moved in and he took refuge in the old storage barn. Mists obscured the thatched cottages along the edge of the orchard. He went out and picked a few apples off the ground and listened to the brook trickling through the meadow. If the weather broke by morning, he'd look for Gold Tooth and his flock. Should he see out Henrique?

He spent the next day wandering east into the stone quarries of Estreito de Câmara de Lobos. He rubbed his arms. With nightfall, he walked under falling rain and he climbed down to the *levada*. He moved west into the rain and early in the evening he found a shelter used for sheep during foul weather. He hid among the sheep and their warmth lulled him to sleep.

Morning brought worse weather and high winds with tropical torrents pouring down the slopes and swelling streams. He huddled in the straw with the goats and ate carrots from his sack. The sweet smelling grasses covered him while he listened to the wind whine.

He stayed in the cave until twilight. He enjoyed the sleepy chewing sound of the sheep and he relaxed in the straw knowing his pursuers wouldn't search during the storm.

He took a pan from the cupboard with the milking pans to boil his salt cod. After eating dried chestnuts and boiled fish, he walked toward Campanário. Fog swirled around the church tower and he turned down the slope listening for sounds. He worked his way behind the schoolhouse. Three women passed the outhouses behind the cottages in Maçapez. He hid in the shrubbery until Pistola closed his shop's doorway for the night. Water dripped into the gutters and no sound issued from the house. A figure in the twilight moved down the path carrying a heavy load of sugar cane.

José slipped off the porch and around the corner out of sight. Another man trudged by with a bale of sugar cane, the tip of his cigarette an orange glow. He heard no footsteps and knocked on the door.

"Who's there?" said Pistola.

"José."

The bolt scraped and the door swung open.

"You're a brave lad to come here when you know men are hunting for you."

"It's nothing. I have no place to go. João sent them to look in the goats' cave."

"Come in, we have soup and bread."

He followed Pistola through the dark passage and up the narrow stairway.

"The whole village knows about your escape. You'll have to hide until Talbot and Jenkins arrive for the festival. He's made arrangements I'm sure."

"I can't wait in the village. Henrique won't take me in so I've no place in the mountains. He left me in a canyon to die. The shepherds refuse to take in wanderers. They fear the government authorities."

"Go to the fisherman on the beach."

"The fishermen at Ribeira Brava are cutthroats and gamblers."

"You can sleep here. In the daytime you must hide. Many folk come to shop and enjoy at drink here in Maçapez."

"I need to hide nearby."

"Tia Nita's cottage is on the path to the beach. You can work in my cave during the daylight. My men say they lose crates and things. You can keep an eye on them."

"The cottage lies in full view of the valley. I could see everyone coming and going," said José.

Ana, the servant, set a steaming pot of cabbage soup on the bare table and ladled it out into bowls. Amália, Pistola's faithful neighbor, helped his wife with housework. His daughter, little Maria, gazed over at José with her dark eyes and admired him as if he'd come from the mountains of the moon. She had tiny hands and wrote on sheets of wrapping paper on a desk her father had made for her. José asked if she'd write for him after the meal and she squealed with delight.

"The men at the beach are indifferent. They make their living by their wits and won't interfere with the militia. If you don't like Tia Nita's cottage, there's a room in the rear of my cave. It's safe. It puts you near the quay and close to the beach. You can light a fire but the peasants will see its smoke and know the cave has a resident.

"Let me know when Talbot is here?"

"You can count on it. I'll give you a few days work. I can pay in silver," said Pistola. There was a knock on the door.

"Tatara, Tatara is here. Open up."

Pistola pushed away from the table and headed down the dark passageway. José hid himself in the bedroom closet where Pistola stored oranges. Tatara accepted a bowl of soup, unaware of Pistola's scowl.

"Young Abreu escaped. The Senhorio said he has a knife. The weather will drive him off the heights and into the village."

"Only gossip," said Pistola. "He's young and he escaped from the slave quarters. He's not insane. He wants to be free of the land. He wants to be happy."

"The Senhorio is angry, Senhor. With respect to your honor, he has rights."

José crawled out from the closet and admired the determination in Pistola's face. The shopkeeper resisted the arguments for feudal authority. Tatara drank his soup, unaware of José or Pistola's guarded words. Pistola measured his words and spoke gently and his beliefs were hidden from Tatara.

"We've seen your master's anger before. We've not been threatened by him."

"You'll not help in the search!" said Tatara. "We look for the scoundrel in the morning."

"You're wasting time. It's better to cut the cane in cool weather and men can haul off bails all day."

Tatara said, "The Abreu family is frightened. The old man might kill him given the chance. I like José. He's wild and unpredictable. He acts crazy at times. I'd like him better if he obeyed and worked with his brothers."

Pistola sat in silence. He waited until Tatara .finished his soup

"The Abreu were Jews in the time of King John. This José is a good lad. Forget about chasing him down like a wild animal. Only Tia Nita practiced the Jewish religion. Forgive and forget," said Pistola.

"She taught others magic and believed in the evil eye. The dead live in the blood, hidden and waiting to undermine the church." said Tatara.

Pistola talked with Tatara for three hours. By the time the man stood up to leave he was calm. Pistola sent him off into the night, softly slid the bolt on the door and dropped the bar across it.

In morning light, José climbed down to the pebbled beach and found the bed in Pistola's cave. He opened the mold-covered door leading into the rear of the cavern. It had a window overlooking the sea and a bed made of straw, wool rugs and blankets.

He sat alone at the worn table with two candles. He ate sea-weed and limpets he collected from the rocks along the shore. He boiled rice in a pot he found there along with a wooden bowl and spoons and empty wine bottles. He went to the pool at the foot of the waterfall and filled the wine bottles with fresh water. And he cleaned the refuse off the table.

He went into the storage area and arranged boxes and crates while Pistola's men napped. He listened to the gossip and observed the wherrymen hauling goods and marking the tally. The wherrymen yelled and the mountaineers argued with them about the slips of paper they used to buy supplies from Pistola. They received receipts for their produce. *Falcon,* Blandy's tugboat arrived with the mail from Funchal. The men loaded the tugboat with bundles of sugar cane from the caves.

On the third day, Pistola appeared in his cave and examined the storage. He checked the numbers and counted the copies of receipts given out by his men. He sat and fanned himself with a black hat.

José worried about leaving Campanário for Funchal. "When will I go aboard? When will Talbot arrive with his friend Jenkins?"

"Never worry. I'll send you cut willow from my storehouse on the mountain and you can weave baskets, more *r*eis for your trip. My men will remain silent when asked if they have seen you. The soldiers will never look in this cave. I've sent Talbot a message by telegraph to Funchal to the Casino & Stranger's Club. When Senhor Talbot collects his mail, he will get the message and wire me the sailing date of the *Wazzan*."

"How long will it take?"

"Be patient. I don't know. You'll leave soon. Remember, not everyone escapes."

"If the Senhorio catches me he will turn me over to the militia. The priest won't protect me."

Pistola nodded, his dark brown eyes saddened. "Rosa came to see me."

"Rosa wants to go to Brazil with me," José said.

"It's possible for her. Life's going to be Hell. She helped you escape from the Senhorio."

"What good is a woman in the goldfields? She'd die from heat or loneliness."

"I'm sorry to tell that I wasn't able to buy the stamps and seal for your passport. You'll have to leave without them. I couldn't arrange them."

"Can I board the ship without them?"

"You'll sail to Brazil. If you don't like it, go to British Guiana. Returning to Madeira is forbidden, once you sail."

José said nothing.

"You'll not have enough work and my men may talk. One may tell the priest, so you must run off on Saturday. You can sail with my friends, the fishermen at Ponta Do Sol to Calheta where your ancestors lived."

"I spent a night with Pedro on the beach at Ribeira Brava. He'll feed me. Tell them to land me there. The telegraph station is near the beach."

"You'll get my message but remember, tell no one where you're going. You talk too much. The sugar harvest goes well. Soon the Festival of Saint Blaise begins."

They shook hands. "I'll return for the festival if I don't receive your message. It'll be my last celebration," José said.

"The villages along this coast have heard of your escape from confinement. The King's agents will be asking for you. They have ears in every wine shop from Quinta Grande to Calheta. Good luck."

José dreamed that agents of the King captured him. They took him in Pistola's vineyard where the laughing witches, the sisters of Tia Nita, bound him with vines. The spirit of Tia Nita appeared during the night and poured a potent into his mouth. Words from the kabala appeared in gold and the eyes of the evil one stared at him, yellow and green out of a blue face. He was tempted to run and hurl himself into the sea. He prayed to Our Lady and she gave him patience. He waited for the fishermen and their boats at the pebbled beach. He looked out at the horizon and carved tops from hard wood.

CHAPTER XXIX

The cry of fishwives greeted the boats off the campanário. The two fishing boats rode low in the water and sailed in through the glare of the afternoon sunlight. Four fishermen launched a skiff and rowed themselves into the backwater and off-loaded pallets of fish. Four men waded into the surf to greet the larger vessel.

The fishermen wore patched pants and shirts, a merry disguise that concealed their fortunes. Both boats beached and the women tossed their baskets up to the waiting hands aboard, their eyes bright and alert. Each stood still when her basket filled with fish was set on her shoulder.

The women walked slowly up the pebbled beach and climbed the steps to that led to the village with their baskets of fish on their heads while the fishermen hurried into the Pistola's wine shop. In the shade of the old sail, wherrymen played cards. The pebbled beach was quiet and lulled by the rhythmic sound of the tide.

The beach was deserted and the Senhorio's men nowhere in sight. José had watched the unloading of the fish and he inched across the beach toward the weather-beaten sail where the fishermen lay, taking care not to attract their attention. The captain snored and the hairs of his moustache that grew over his lips moved with each breath. These fishermen were descended from Greeks and Italians that had sailed to Madeira in the 15th century. They fought for honor with knives.

José preferred the fishermen of Ribeira Brava. They were more honest than the fishermen of Ponta da Sol and his own village. Ponta da Sol was isolated without a militia barracks or a telegraph. The short one with the bushy black eyebrows woke and grimaced.

Once José sought refuge with the fishermen and without them he'd be on his own with only a few reis. The smuggler's cave was close to the pebbled beach. That was its advantage and weakness. The fisherman Aldo seeing José kicked the captain's foot and awakened him. The captain hand reached for his knife. He said to José, "Who are you?"

"Friend of Pistola, you've seen me on the beach."

"You drank with us, didn't you?"

"No, I work in Pistola's cave tallying cargo," said José

"Pistola sells good wine. Not as fine as the grape made by the monks at Fajã dos Padres."

The fishermen sat up and played a game of cards using for a table the bottom of their dory. The captain's eyes lightened. The wood gatherers worked across the beach retrieving bits and pieces of wood from the windrow of seaweed. The captain yelled a greeting and cursed them. "How much for wood?" said the Captain.

The oldest peasant said, "Two *real* for these *queima.*"

The fishermen ate *bacalhau* cooked on the fire and the wine loosened their tongues and the wood gatherers joined them. "Only eighteen bundles!"

"Yes, Senhor captain."

"You make me a fool. I need wood and you want gold, my good man, accept what I'm willing to give."

"It's not enough," said the peasant.

"I'll give a dozen *espada,* scabbard fish."

After a silence, the peasant went to the fire and tossed on a stick of wood and shook his head. The crippled one son of Alzira who spent his days at Pistola's bar asked the captain about the wood.

"The bastards want too much. I'll buy half and give two baskets of fish. They'll accept drinks," said the captain.

"I'll stack your wood in the long boat. I want to go with you to Ribeira Brava with your permission." said José.

"I need coins. How can I pay for a few bundles of wood? You better find yourself another boat."

José haggled and the captain of the *Anho Branco* agreed to land him at Ribeira Brava if he went fishing with him. Worn hands dealt cards. Jacinto rolled a cigarette. The men swore when they were dealt a bad hand. Coins passed from hand to dory-bottom, to hand to pocket. The sailor-in-blue won a pile of coins by his right hand. From the cave of the wood gatherers José loaded two bundles of pinewood aboard the *Anho Branco*.

The captain with the black mustache hissed. The men looked up. Rosa walked on the beach. José set his bundle of wood and watched her coming toward the boat. .

The sailors were silent. They narrowed their eyes and stared at their cards pretending they did not see Rosa.

"Hello, little girl," said the captain. "You better run home before your father hears you are alone on the beach."

José walked to the wherry and leaned against its bow as the dock-boys did. Why did she want to run away with him? There was no reason. The sailors would gladly take her when she smiled at them and they saw she wanted to be on her own.

She walked up to José. "You weren't at Pistola's cave. I looked for you. He sent me to warn you. The *Senhorio* heard you had slept in the cave and sent his men searching for you."

"Your mother heard and the priest and King Carlos. What does Pistola say?"

"José, be kind. I want to be with you."

"I'm sailing with these fishermen. Your place is with family. These strangers have their eyes on you. Run now, back home before Senhor Duro your father misses you."

One minute he was calm and the next he lashed out at her. She fell on her knee and hid her face in her kerchief.

"*Basta*, enough," he said. "*Vai para casa*, go home."

The captain grinned and the fishermen clapped.

"Bravo! You tell her, like a man."

Rosa turned and walked away. Her bare feet left prints in the wet sand. She climbed the steps up the cliff her back straight and stiff as if she carried a basket on her head. He waved as she disappeared from view. He slammed his hand against the spar of the wherry.

The card playing resumed. He finished loading and lay down in the shade of the dory and waited for the fishermen to repair their nets.

In the late afternoon the fishermen men threw down their cards, dozed, drank more wine, rolled up their trousers and waded into the surf alongside their boat. The captain in his bare feet swore at the pebbles.

"How far out do we sail?" José asked Bem Brazão.

"About eight leagues, more or less. I never judge distance when I'm at sea."

"Do you see steamships from Funchal?"

Brazão pointed to the streams where boats went off to the Canaries, Argentina and South Africa.

"Where is the direction for Brazil?"

"Off there. We see the regular Rio boats."

"Some steamships buy fish in the Bay of Funchal. We lay by and their cooks yell to us. We sell without tax. It's better than the market, no fishwives and no tax men."

"How many *reis* do they want to go to Rio?" said José.

"I don't know. In Ribeira Brava passengers pay big money for stamps and seals, and the papers are good for immigration," said the dark one.

The fishermen pulled their oars hard through the waves and the sea air filled their lungs. José spat. The setting sun glowed and the huts and the church with tall pines on the mountainsides were bathed in orange light. The sea was dark and waves moved against the rock-bound shore. Each sailor went to his dory and hauled his ragged lateen and the small craft heaved into the southwest.

José baited small hooks for *espada*, the black scabbard fish that lived at twenty dekameters. The long-level fields of Bugio Island lay off the starboard.

"We take blacks and whites," said Bem. "They've eyes like witches."

"They've rows of sharp teeth, like barracuda. *Espada* are longer than eels and tastier," said José.

"You'll haul the long lines," said the captain. "Life ashore is dull. You slave for nothing and live in bondage. The sea gives you freedom and courage but she kills you in the end."

They baited hundreds of hooks in strings of twenty and lowered them down, attached an anchor-line to a buoy, running a cable from buoy to buoy. José rowed the long-boat toward the island. Bem paid out the cable until they scrambled through the surf and attached it to an iron ring in the rocks off Bugio.

The first haul brought thirty fish from buoy number one. They sharpened their knives and talked about clouds, friends and enemies in the sky. They swore at storm clouds using the words reserved for hated cousins.

"Some day I'm going to follow the clouds over the sea to the other side," said José. The swaying motion of the deck ended in a quick chop. His stomach felt dull, his mouth tasted coppery, acidic and felt greasy. The crew jabbered a mixture of Spanish, French, and Italian—sea words, from their ancestors along with their Madeiran dialect.

"Brazil is faraway, my friend. You'd never return. The gold fields do something to your head. You go *loco*. You'll die there," said Bem.

By morning, the fishermen hauled their *espada* and the captain headed for the Funchal market. Off Fort St. James, the fishermen jumped into the shallow water and waded into the beach. Women in dark shawls and kerchiefs waited with baskets. José waded in from the boat with a pallet of fish on his shoulder and threw espada onto the beach for the women. He heard the buzz and chatter of the fish market further up the shore. With their haul displayed, the fishermen left for the cantina and ate fried potatoes, eggs, and sausage. They untangled lines and mended rips in their nets splicing and knotting. José fell down from fatigue on the sands.

One after the other, the sailors curled up in the shade cast by *Goddess Diana*, her unblinking eyes stared over them, her lips painted red, honoring them and loving them while they slept. José smelled broiled fish. Rolling up on his shoulder, he saw Bem dabbing olive oil and vinegar on fillets of mackerel and setting them on the brazier. He looked into the blue sky. He dreamed of the goddess during the storm.

Bem said, "An old guy left a message. You're to land at Ribeira Brava or it's into the army you go."

"I'm going to Brazil."

Bem laughed. "You're too poor. You can't afford the papers. I don't believe you."

"They sell the papers at R.B. They ask for coins to make it sweet," said Pedro. He rubbed his hands together.

"I tell you, it'll be two hundred *reis* with the passport," said Bem.

José whistled. "My father doesn't make that much in the whole year."

"If you go to sea, you'll make one-half real a day."

"I'd drown in the storms beyond the Desertas," said José. "My father works from daylight to dark and pays for things we can't grow--olive oil, salt and pepper, sugar and dried salt cod. He saved the bristle of the pig's chin. He seldom has *reis*. His life is one of pay, pay, and pay—even for the land and the water. He pays the priest to keep his soul from Hell."

"Go to sea with us." said the captain.

"Do you know the Valley of the Melons? It's the poorest land in Campanário, narrow and rocky the sun bakes the soil and winds dry out the vegetables and plants. We haul everything by hand. We receive the *levada* water last and pay first. The *água de giro* water appears when the plants are dead."

"No *reis* made there," said Bem.

"I'd steal from the *Senhorio* to get money for my papers. The *Senhorio* eats up the profits of the land and the people. He takes every barrel of wine and every stalk of bananas .I'll make him pay up. He'd cut off my balls if he heard me talking like a freeman."

"Close your mouth. The wind carries words to listening ears."

"What does gossip matter? The priest cuts off my head, the family scalds my heart and the *Senhorio* enslaves my body."

"Sorrow never made a life," said Bem.

"I asked Maria to write a letter to Sintra to the King pleading for justice."

"Your life is here on the beach. Eat your fish before the wild dogs grab it." Old Pedro offered José wine from a skin.

Heading back to sea, the lights of old Funchal shone in the black velvet of the Torrinhas. The wine cleared his throat. The old beach man shook his hand and his farewell brought tears to José's eyes.

"If the King knew you were going to leave without papers, he'd send the militia and toss you in jail," said the one called the gnome.

"Go beat on your old lady," one said to the captain. "She sells your shares, cheap."

For two hours, the boat sailed into the wide sea and José ate slices of pork cooked with carrots, garlic and parsley. The sun had set and they let out their lines for squid, using a dead one tied to a line to attract the live ones.

Gatto, the old man of the beach whom they brought along for this trip, delighted them with a squid that weighed two kilos. Gatto's son, Melo, cut the bait into bits. He and his father rowed off into the dark with a paraffin lamp to guide them. Like stars in the sky, the tiny lights of the skiffs bobbed on the moving waters. José watched the long boats moving into line for the night's work. The fishermen were free and, if José fished with them, he'd arrive free at Campanário in the morning light.

Pedro cast off five fathoms of line and coiled the remaining three hundred meters on the deck. "Pray for a blue marlin or a grandfather tuna," he said.

José poured himself a cup of water and tossed a drop into the ocean for luck. Smoke appeared on the horizon. One moment the expanse of water was dark and empty, and then like a ghost ship, a steamer moved into the space of darkness. "Will they see us?" said José.

"Yes. She sails close enough for us to see the decks and we salute her seamen."

Pedro held the line against the rail, his welted hands silent and waiting. José watched the steamer hove into view and imagined swimming to her side. The immensity of her frightened him. He saw himself being hauled aboard by her deckhands and questioned about his climbing her side with only the assistance of a rope they had carelessly hung over the bow.

"She looks like one of those ships from the Africa Steamship Line. They pass through here every two or three weeks," said Bem. He swore to the virgin and the devil and then Pedro yelled. The rope spun through Pedro's hands and he grasped it. The electric movement of the fish surprised him and with one hand Pedro grabbed a gunny sack to assure his grip but it didn't work.

José yelled, "Hold the bastard!" He saw the powerful gnarled hands in the light of the swinging lantern. They held the line, and Pedro clenched his teeth and sang to the fish, "O mystery, I know you want to leave me... but you son of a bitch, I've got you now... come... Goddamn devil... I'm going to hold you by the tail."

The line rose up and the old man kept pressure on the fish. José forgot the lights of the steamer and concentrated on the fish. Bem spit into the water and cursed the fish and prayed over the blood rising in Pedro's hands. Pedro held on and said nothing.

CHAPTER XXX

The line felt as solid as the handle of a hoe and as smooth and taut. The glow of the lantern revealed the dead eyes of Pedro staring into the darkness. Pedro held the line in both hands in silence. José rolled and lit him a cigarette and placed it between Pedro's lips. Pedro took a long drag and wiggled the cigarette. The wet burlap reduced friction on his hands smelling of sweat and blood. Jose's hands hurt for Pedro's swollen flesh, fierce with the pain from the pressure of the fish.

Pedro directed them by nodding his head and rolling his eyes. His mouth was dry and he wetted his lips with his tongue. Bem poured water into his mouth. He signaled he couldn't hold the line. José grabbed the line and gave the old man a chance to wrap burlap around his hand.

Minutes passed into an hour, and little by little Pedro pulled the rope over the rail. José saw enough line to make a coil and he looped it on the deck. His bare feet slipped.

Pedro slammed his feet on the deck and yelled, "Pa Epah!" The fish yanked a few centimeters of line into the deep and the old man held him and urged him up and closer to the boat.

Bem and José hauled their lines and coiled them and moved them away. Pedro jumped and whirled across the deck. He stamped the gunwale with his foot, and his dancing sent messages to the fish, for its strange leaps gave Pedro joy. He knew the fish was tired and the struggle was nearly ended.

The white belly of the fish showed in the dark water, its ghostly shape luminous in the deep. Bem gaffed the tuna behind the dorsal fin, and with a rope tied around its tail, tried to heave it aboard. They were tired hauling it and waited for Melo and Gatto.

"It weighs at least one hundred and seventy-five kilos," said Pedro. He kissed his hands and danced around the deck, hugging them to lessen the pain. Gatto laughed, "This one is the baby of the one we lost."

"Where is your fish, you son of the pig? You lie in your teeth." Over the water, José heard rowing in the darkness, even during the thrashing of the tuna and swearing and laughing, he heard a boat moving toward the *Goddess Diana.*

Melo told of sadness. "This tuna moved the deck boat over the water like a steamer. The fleet grew small in the distance and I saw fireflies over the water. Luckily, the bitch turned back, or we'd be half-way to the Salvage Islands."

Gatto said, "She weighed over two hundred kilos, as God is my judge. I saw her rise out of the water like the veil of the Virgin."

"Yeh, and she jumped into the boat with you and kissed your ass, so you'd free her and she leaped back into the deep," said Pedro.

"The gaffing threw us off, and I heaved forward and tried to plunge the point home, but it bit flesh and hit bone. My second jab, I hit her in the meat and tore a hole. It didn't hold and she dived into the darkness and I couldn't see her no more. I'm lucky to be alive. The lines tangled around my feet, flew in the air and took me by the neck. I fought for breath. The she devil herself was choking me," said Gatto.

A pale gray cloud in the crown of the sky grew and covered the stars from view. The breeze dropped, and a cool calm fell.

Bem caught a sword fish in the early light and they sailed to Bugio to haul their *espada* settings before heading for Funchal market. Pedro sawed off the horn of the fish to protect them from thrashings. Hung up and ashore, she weighed twenty-five kilos.

Pedro laughed, after looking in the long boat. "You're empty, you bastards," he said. "You never saw a tuna."

They fished south of Cabo Girâo when an ocean-going steamer sailed out of Funchal Bay. "That's the *Wazzan.* She'll turn about and sail southeast toward the Canaries where she'll pick up passengers for South Africa. Next voyage she'll make a run to Brazil."

José stared at the plume of smoke boiling from her stack, the mysterious gleam of her port-holes over the waters, and he wanted his mother. He lay in the loft opening his eyes and hearing the movements of his mother in the kitchen as she made the fire and he heard boiling water and clatter of coffee mugs.

Fishing made him happy. The twigs burning and the coffee smell of Brazil lured him back home. The liner disappeared from view and he sighed. The rest of the way in, he tied knots. Bem tested them and showed him how to secure a bowline. Gatto and Melo sharpened their knives. They gutted the fish and threw entrails to gulls. The maddening flock cried and the air was a cloud of beating wings moving over the deck and around the bow.

The air freshened and the current moved the fishing boats swiftly toward the breakwater. Funchal appeared in sunlight, green forest and sheer cliffs, gray and red and black, gulls drifting off the water and crying after the *Goddess Diana*. And the angry birds beat at them with their wings and cried to one another. There were the rumors and whispers in the village urging him to run away to sea.

He jumped into the surf and helped guide the prow through the racing flood until the keel wedged into the sand. He saw the oxen-men moving their animals around to hitch the hauling line. He smelled the beach fires and coffee. He hurried across the sands for a hot cup.

That was a good thing, for police officers arrived asking for him and where they could find him. The fishermen shrugged. When asked questions, they'd never seen anything. They knew nothing.

A ladybug landed on José's hand.

"Joaninha-joaninha, vai lavar os pés do Nosso Senhor, ladybug, ladybug, go wash the feet of Our Father, " he said. He tossed her into the air.

He was tired from the night of fishing. The fishwives haggled and fought over prices and fish and the voices of tourists hurrying along the sea front frightened him. He closed his eyes and wished he were back in his bed of straw with Maria beside him, warm and sleepy-eyed.

The old card-player from the Fort said, "Soldiers came looking for you. They wanted to know the name of your boat and when it returned. I sent them to the customs house. I said we didn't know you."

The old man spit and shrugged. He returned to his bottle and urged his comrades to drink with him.

The harbor boys dragged the tuna up the beach and into the market, their lean leg muscles taut, their tanned shoulders sunlit, they sang with glee.

He thought of six years in the militia. Those that returned from service to the village were hollow men, listless and wouldn't work the land. He needed the money to buy documents and the fees for sailing away. It took families eight years to buy a passage. He opened his eyes.

"You don't look well."

Pedro swigged wine from a wicker-covered bottle. José grabbed it and drank the *water-with-teeth*. It burned his lips and down in his gut.

"You've been up too long. Sleep. I'll keep a watch for the soldiers," Pedro said.

"I'm going back to the Valley of the Melons."

"You're crazy. They're after you. The peasants will see you and the Senhorio will lock you up. You want to kill yourself?"

"I need my sisters and my mother. I haven't got word from Pistola on the sailing of the steamship. I'm not in Ponta do Sol or Ribeira Brava. There are soldiers and policemen in old Funchal."

"You liked fishing. Stay with us and wait for the old shopkeeper to send word. He'll send you to Brazil."

"I want to see the Festival of Saint Blaise. You go to Camacha for the apple festival. This is my church's festival. João carried my bundles of sugar cane to the beach. With his broken leg, Silvino can't help. Father is too old to carry sixty kilos."

"How can I make you go to sea? You work hard and fast. You remember... you'd make a good fisherman. You have the head and the legs for boat work," said Pedro.

"Thank you, Senhor. Talbot returns to Campanário for the festival. He'll find me a way to Brazil. He has money. I'll send him gold from Brazil as soon as I have worked and have some."

"We'll land at Ribeira Brava, tomorrow night."

"The soldiers know I'm with you. They have spies in every village." He put two mackerel into his sack. Pedro walked the beach with him and they shook hands by the pier. José made his way through boats at the yacht club and the boat repair and up the steep path that led to Reid's.

The sun beat down on his shoulders as he walked to Câmara De Lobos. The ox-sledges moved over the new cobbled road with loads of British residents, out for their ride in the sunshine and sea air. He hurried through the alleys by the *camara,* city hall, where strangers had their throats cut. The climb to the *estreito,* narrow strait, was steep and long. In the cool breeze at the top, he pulled his burlap around him and rested. He went into the dark nave of the church and prayed for his mother and for the soul of Tia Nita. He dozed in the pew and felt the cheek of his sister when she kissed him goodnight.

Along the slope of Quinta Grande, he saw soldiers questioning peasants. While he hid in a vineyard, the militia marched along the path to Campanário. He hid behind the rocks and observed them.

Direito and Esquerda questioned a man with a pole who escorted his pig to market. These two mopped their brows and complained about the heat. More soldiers came along the track. These new ones were official-looking in polished belts and straps over the shoulders, like the men that lived in the *São Martinho* barracks.

Direito led the way, his rifle slung over his shoulders and behind his neck so it supported his arms, like Christ hanging from the cross. Esquerda dragged his rifle by the stacking swivel. They stopped a peasant carrying a sack of flour. Esquerda retrieved his rifle and brushed off the dust, looking nervously. He spit on his hands and rubbed the stock with grease from his nose.

"The pig man doesn't eat pig," said Esquerda. He thumbed his nose at the old man.

"May he live the way of the *Marranos*, a pig that won't eat pig," laughed Direito.

They joked and laughed as they moved further on. It was too late to rush on ahead. There were other patrols. These marauders knew him.

Esquerda stopped to piss on the cactus beside the trail. Direito was disgusted and rested his rifle under his armpit like he was hunting rabbits. He climbed close. His canister reflected the sunlight, his bandoliers dark with sweat flapped against his damp shirt. He gazed over the trail and the slope with care. They searched slowly with great care for fugitives.

"Come along, we'll never get to the festival, if you piss your life away," said Direito. He opened his canteen and swilled water letting it run down his chin and neck.

Any second now he'll see me, thought José. In his heart, he knew they were friends, but he wasn't sure. They liked to rest and talk with the women doing embroidery and to cadge fruit from horsemen and listen to peasant-gossip along the way. Esquerda hadn't seen him.

He jumped up and hopped down through the cactus toward them. It surprised Direito and he raised his rifle.

"Don't shoot. I'm not a baby rabbit. It's me," said José.

"Hello there, hello," shouted Esquerda. He straightened himself up and made it look like an official piss. José rushed up laughing. Esquerda urged his pal not to shoot, his lips severe.

"You know him, the shepherd working in the stone field, he showed us the way into the village," said Esquerda.

"Have a drink of water, holy shepherd," said Direito. He lowered his rifle and scratched his chin. He wanted to know who in hell José was, jumping out of the cactus like a rabbit.

"He could've been a drunk and on his way home from the festival and ready to knife someone," said Esquerda. "Better luck next time, fast gun."

Direito shrugged off Esquerda's wild words and said, "Come along or we'll miss the procession at the festival."

"Your captain sends you to the festival? Do you dance?" said José.

"We're sent to guard the well. The natives are angry. The captain had trouble since the day we capped it. Father Domingo helped us and on Sunday he told the folk to cooperate. Later, they tore off the cap and drank water from the well."

"We'll capture the young men that ran away from the militia. We know their names and they'll attend the festival of Saint Blaise."

"Son of a bitching roll of names," said Direito. "We missed a couple of recruits last March in Camacha. We were sent back to the district and they fought like tigers."

"They knew King Carlos demands six years and the pay is the lowest in Christendom," said Esquerda.

"How is money in the militia?" said José.

"They pay less than pruning vines or quarrying stone.

"You know cut cabbage, cut chard, cut vines, cut cane, cut pigs, cut fish... cut off your balls... work, work, work."

Esquerda mopped his brow. "They pay in food and uniforms, and once a month you get paid ten *reis*."

"The azure-winged magpie has more gold in her nest in the beautiful green tree of Monchique than King Carlos," said Direito. "I cut flowers for the market in Portimão. I made more in a week than a soldier in a month."

"The recruits you hunt here know hoe to hide well," said José. "I'm sorry I can't help you."

"You'd like the army, money or not," said Esquerda. "We drink a little wine, eat meals and we have cigarettes. What more can a man ask?"

They paused by the giant chestnut known throughout Madeira. From the height, they saw the church and the banners of Christ, red and white, fluttering in the breeze.

"Were you in Funchal long?" said Esquerda.

"Visiting a friend," said José.

"You stayed away without permission of your landlord?"

"You're coming from Funchal, aren't you?" Direito opened his eyes wide.

"I fished with my friend, Oliveira and Pedro the fisherman."

"He lives on the beach at Ribeira Brava. You are freer than the boys in my native village. What will the *Senhorio* say?"

"I've nothing to say to him. I ran away."

"You left the land? You didn't get permission. The only way to leave the land is with the word of the landlord." said Esquerda.

"The *Senhorio* locked me up and I unlocked the cell door and ran."

Direito raised his rifle and pointed it at José's nose.

"You'd better come with us. We know about runaway peasants."

"Up on your feet, march—one, two three..."

"You're friends," said José. Esquerda laughed at them. "I led you to my village."

"They reward us for runaways. We need money for wine. The *negramola*, 'Black Spring' wine they sell in your village is expensive. We like its flavor. The folk make us pay through the nose. They hate us for sealing their precious well."

"Good sirs, let me see my mother before you take me to see the Senhorio, please."

"Young men always ask for their mothers. Come along, march, and step lively. We'll tell the Senhorio what a fine young man you are." Direito laughed and cocked the hammer of his rifle.

Down the slopes of Calçada along the eastern ridge, the two soldiers led José, each with his rifle at the ready lest he run. José saw his brother João stand up in the cane field and the soldiers didn't see him. João had heard the soldiers and raised his head and saw José.

Estreito tired of holding up his rifle and slung it over his shoulder and gave Direito the honor. Taking out his flute, he played a bright festival tune as they marched down the steep under the bright sun, the dust billowing around them, the lizards scurrying over the rocks.

CHAPTER XXXI

The crickets sang in the dark of the sugar cane thicket. Direito ceased playing his flute. José limped along and slowed the pace of the two soldiers and he slipped off and listened to the crickets. Direito and Esquerda paid him no attention. They talked about the Senhoras dancing in the square, drinking their wine and listening to festival music.

"I've a splinter in my toe," said José.

He sat down and rubbed his foot and stared at his toe.

"The crickets are singing. We are late to report to our captain. On your feet," said Direito, raising his rifle.

"Evening comes. I feel the dew. Keep moving. No, rest a bit. I'll keep my eye on you," said Esquerda.

"The ants chew red spots on your ass. They smell bread crumbs in your pocket," said José.

"Ha. Ha! The sun melted your brains. I'll take you straight to the Senhorio," said Esquerda.

The trail skirted along the edge of the precipice overlooking the church square. From the thicket along the path, João whistled. It startled Direito and he bent over the wall listened for the sound. João groaned like a wounded soldier.

"Someone fell and he's hurting!" Esquerda said.

"It's a soldier," said José.

Esquerda searched in the gloom.

"It's slippery. I know that slope. You better let me look," said José.

Dreadful sounds came from the underbrush. Another groan, Direito and Esquerda prayed to the Virgin.

"I've my rifle aimed at you," said Direito.

"José stays with me. You go and find the poor chap," said Esquerda. "The captain punishes stragglers."

"It's coming from that thicket. I've a bearing on it," said Direito.

João screamed. The soldier's attention turned to the landscape below the trail.

José leaped off the wall and ducked under the banana leaves and slid to his knees. He jumped up and zigzagged to avoid rifle slugs, fell into the grass near where João lay in the grass with his palm over his lips, laughing.

The soldiers didn't fire their rifles. "Come out, wherever you are, bastards," said Direito. He swore in the name of the Virgin and what devils were going to do to José.

"Good-by, see you later," said João.

João and José scurried down the slope, jumped off the wall and ran along the *levada*. At the foot-bridge, they shouted and called to the soldiers. They jumped into the deep water of the *levada*, and waded along its course.

Direito heard their shouts and remembering his rifle, ordered them to stop in the name of the King and fired off a round.

"They can't shoot straight," said José.

"Those drunks deserve to fall off a cliff. They drink until they can't stand up, and leer at the women in the square," said João. "I thought you sailed for Brazil!"

"I needed papers to return. It's a long way to sail."

José and João slid down the mountainside until the water in the *levada* dropped and became a waterfall. They were wet and shivering. They hid in the sugar cane and waited for the soldiers. They saw Direito and Esquerda groping down the trail, whistling and swearing and blaming one another for the escape.

João and José thumbed their noses at them and hurried off to the Valley of the Melons.

"I saw Talbot and his friend Jenkins. You know him the stranger that sails the beautiful boat with the white sail," said João.

"Where was he?" said José.

"He's at Maçapez with Pistola staying above the shop and takes meals on the patio."

"How is the family?"

"The *Senhorio* threatened Father. At dinner Father waved his knife, and cursed your name, slashing and spitting... shaking his fist."

"He thought me dead! Did he think I'd return?"

"The soldiers searched Pistol's cave and soldiers questioned the wherrymen about you. You had sailed for Ponta Do Sol they said. No one saw you embark. The captain telegraphed Ribeira Brava to arrest you on arrival."

"I'm here."

"Yes, and Henrique appeared for the festival. He said you were dead. We said you returned from the mountains. He wept and said he'd thrown you into a pit."

"When love is lost, little can be done in this world to regain it," said José.

João fluttered his eyelashes. José couldn't see his eyes. "Maria marries Joachim in June," he said.

José said, "I love her myself."

"Silvino's leg mends. There is too much work for me alone. I hate the *Senhorio*. I want to own my land."

"Once he's heard I'm in the valley, he'll send his men. I'll be off," said José.

Mother stood by the kitchen door. Her hair was white except for one strand, the wing of a raven, black as a limpet's shell. She smiled at him. He felt her soft cheek and smelled her olive sweetness.

"Are you my José?"

She kissed him on both cheeks. He kissed her hand and asked her blessing.

"Have you eaten?"

She stirred the soup and dished a steaming ladle of cabbage and potatoes, steaming hot and peppery with sausage bits.

"I'm full. The sailors in old Funchal fed me fish."

He drank his bowl of soup. Dried onions and garlic and herbs hung in braids about the stove. The hens settled for the night. Mother cut strips of cold cornmeal and fried them. João fed the goats.

"I chased the pig from the garden while João looked for you on the beach. Father went to set up the rockets. He'd not help me with the pig," said mother. "I filled the bucket. The pig followed me part of the way to the hutch, but she's huge. I twisted her tail. She lay down and smiled. I sang her a song, and cried while she ate the peelings in the bucket and she followed me like a good woman. The rest of the day I washed clothes in the river and dried them on the rocks."

"Have you seen the Senhorio?"

"Blackeye came from the quinta and demanded cash for the sugar cane. We don't have *reis*. We owe for cutters and laborers now."

Mother wished herself back in Calçada and her girlhood. She felt abandoned.

"The Senhorio will send men to search. I'll hide at sunset," José said

Maria laughed in the passageway and rushed into the kitchen. She kissed him. Julia pulled his hair and said, "You're handsome. Running around the countryside does it."

"Two soldiers ran into the square. They said something about an escaped recruit. Their captain wrote words on paper," Maria said.

"Two soldiers called Direito and Esquerda. They followed us," said Julia.

"They took me prisoner and I ran away. The soldiers will arrest for me."

Maria wanted him to sleep at home. João laughed about his hiding in the caves and swore at soldiers for chasing village women. They ate without father, laughing and telling old stories about the Festival of Saint Blaise.

After *sesta*, Maria followed him to the doorway and kissed him goodbye. With his pitch fork, he lifted a stack of hay over his head like an umbrella and walked underneath it into the valley. The neighbors working in the last of the daylight in their gardens didn't recognize him under the load of hay.

At the cow shed he dropped the load of hay and kissed the old cow's ears and cried. He'd carried her food and water since she was a calf. "You're locked into this hut for life. We own you like the *Senhorio* owns us. You'll never know the freedom of a pasture. With luck, I'll escape and sail to freedom."

The cow chewed her cud and stared. "You eat the sweetest grasses and give the best milk and you're tied in this hut. You belong on green pastures." He lay down in the sweet-smelling hay.

The rockets of Saint Blaise signaled the opening of the festival at daylight. Silvino fed the cow.

"Where're you working?" he said.

"I can't work. I'm hiding from the soldiers," said José.

"We need you for planting the onions and garlic. Forget the militia and the church. Work the land. Soon the cherry, the loquat, the passion fruit vine will blossom."

"I'm like Henrique, no wife, no children. I go wherever I please. If I stay on the land, I'll be captured and thrown into prison."

"You know the Senhorio and his madness."

"I try to forget him. He'll die someday. I can't wait for him to die."

"Other men avoided the militia, *destacamento,* detachment."

"The priest knows I'm sixteen soon. The King demands obedience. There's not enough land. The promise of the land is lost. Honor is dead."

Silvino's eyes filled with tears. He rested his hand on José's shoulder. "Don't say it. You want happiness, not madness. Wherever you go, always remember me."

"The gardens grow lush. We are their slaves—digging, planting, and watering. I'll remember you, Silvino. You'd dream if you were me. There is nothing left for the youngest."

Eulalia, Silvino's wife, whistled from the cottage. Silvino shook his hand. José waved. His brother's eyes, his unhappiness, angered him and he wanted to kill the *Senhorio* and free the land for Silvino.

"I hope to see you again," said Silvino.

"I'll return."

"The old bastard landlord said he'd lock you up and you'd rot in Hell."

"Yes he would. He's a bastard. I'll see you again soon."

On the pebbled beach waves broke on the rocks and mists blew from the sea and drifted around José. Blandy's boat arrived and Tristão threw off the mail. The wherrymen piled wicker chairs and packed them in pallets. They worked in the mouth of Pistola's cave! José waited in the rocks until they finished. The men joked and laughed about the women at the festival. The sugar cane was piled high on the quay and José looked for a place to hide.

José returned to the smuggler's cave. The corpse of Tia Nita buried there, made it difficult for him to sleep. It was now the cave of the dead.

The wherrymen yelled to a patrol of soldiers coming along the pebbled beach. The soldiers questioned them. They waved their arms and pointed toward the village.

During the afternoon the sun beat on the pebbles and heated them like chestnuts roasted for the festival. José climbed back to the cave. The smell of bat dung was intense. I'll suffocate in there, he thought. He boosted himself up over the parapet and crawled into the mouth of the cave.

From the entrance of the cave, he had a view of the beach and the *campanário* rising from the sea and the quay with its bundles of sugar cane piled and waiting transport to Funchal. He'd climb down after dark to find water and spend the night in Pistola's storage cave.

That afternoon, a band of soldiers patrolled the sea-front. They climbed to the pool at the foot of the waterfall and examined the cliffs with a telescope. They signaled their patrol on the height with flags. Advance men went on the quay and inspected the bundles. They spoke with the fishermen.

The soldiers sat in the wine shop and drank until sun set. In groups of two and three, the soldiers climbed the steps to the top of the cliff and crossed through the fields that led to the village square.

José saw them leave and whistled the festival march. He dreamed of favas and listening to the band play in the square. Talbot and Jenkins would be at the festival and he wanted to ask them about his passage to Brazil.

The cave floor was hard and a draught of air blew across it. The sounds in the wind blowing through the cave were the whispers of the spirit of Tia Nita.

CHAPTER XXXII

The wind blowing through the cave awakened him, the whispers of a dark voice, a low-pitched hum rising and falling on the night air. Its notes rose to a scream and ceased altogether only to create a new cry. A spectral figure appeared in the darkness and stared at him and José pulled the blanket over his head and wrapped himself tightly in his robe.

The figure leaned over him and he leapt from his blanket and ran to the opening of the cave and looked out, the white foam along the shore visible in the gloom. The sea air was chilly and he looked for living figures on the desolate beach. He rubbed his arms and took his knitted rug and pulled it over him. Though he pulled his knees up and rubbed his ankles, he was cold.

His stomach gurgled and he rolled over and stretched his right leg and farted. He thought of visiting the Senhorio and asking his permission to leave the island. The militia searched for him and if they captured him, he'd serve six years and be returned to the land and in bondage forever.

The cool breezes through the cave increased and he rubbed his arms and legs in the darkness and warmed himself. He'd go into the sea and swim out until he couldn't swim. He'd be free with no worry of return. He was sore from sleeping on basalt. The stars faded in the sky and the restless sea, the rising daylight failed to cheer him. The wind lulled him to sleep, and waves broke on the rocks below the smuggler's cave.

On the day of the Festival of Saint Blaise rockets burst over the sleepy village, startling the roosters that heralded the dawn with steely eyes. The old cock in Rosa's yard flapped his wings and crowed, wattles red. A string of firecrackers popped off, flung into the square by the soldier that guarded the well on the night watch by the church. Rockets exploded in the air and echoed off the mountains.

Laurel roping, poinsettias, and banners with the Crusader's cross decorated the square and the church filled and early Mass was sung. Jaime, Joachim, Aldo, Henrique, and Manuel, who had paid the ten thousand *reis* to pay for the festival, pulled on their gray calf-skin gloves and hoisted their scabbards and hung their swords from gold-embroidered straps. They presented themselves before the hall mirror and inspected their proper uniforms and adjusted their hats at the correct angle. Out in the cobbled street, they assembled for the procession to the church.

José emerged from the cave into the sunlight and scouted the beach, no soldiers. He climbed the ridge and in twenty minutes was in the crowded square. Saint Blaise cured children of throat infections and lung diseases. He felt lost in the crowd, strangers from the continent and South America. The smell of broiled beef on a skewer and the taste of candied almonds made his mouth water. The peasants spent their seed money. They bought broad beans, *bacalhau,* salt cod, and beef on a skewer. Children ran laughing along the booths that sold wine and brandy to the men-folk.

Another rocket burst in the air. Mass was over and the parishioners streamed together down the steps of the church. José rushed ahead of them and into Pistola's shop for dried chestnuts. He took a glass of water from the bar. He hid himself behind the wine casks and listened. Some one entered the shop. Rosa looked into the bar. He whistled. She saw him.

"Are you looking for someone?" he said.

"I've a message from Pistola. He wants to meet you here after dark," she said. "He heard of your escape from the soldiers. He said you have no place to hide but the caves. The soldiers will search for you after the festival. I brought you bananas and oranges."

"You should've stayed in the square. Your family will miss you."

"I had to see you. They caught me with the key and my engagement to Alberto's broken off. I'm free."

"You can't live in a cave."

"Please let me go with you."

"It's dangerous. I know nothing about Brazil and can't even buy passage."

"I can't live here. The Senhorio slept with me. Albert was a paid man. I'd have served two masters."

"The *Senhorio* bedded you? I don't believe it. You're lying."

"To get the key, I slept with him."

"You didn't. You didn't."

She grabbed his wrists and yanked his hands from his ears. "I gave him my body and he knows I helped you escape from the cell. He beat me. I told him I unlocked the cell door."

"I'll kill the bastard."

He opened his knife and swore. He'd find the Senhorio and cut his throat. He'd go after the militia captain and Father Segundo and God himself.

José swore and cried.

Rosa held him. "Hide until nightfall. Don't be foolish. You can send for me and I sail to Brazil. The Senhorio swore you were my lover!

"You're not a whore," he said.

"Father forced me to tell why I refused to marry Alberto. He was angry. I told him, I loved you."

"I love my mother and my sisters," he said.

"You love them and pretend to love me."

"I'm not a free man. How can I love? My pockets are empty."

"We'll run away." Rosa said.

"I love Maria. Stay with your family and find a husband."

Rosa stared at him. He peeled an orange, divided the sweet edible pulp and offered her half. She shook her head.

"I love you like a sister loves a brother. You can love me," she said.

"If I loved you, I'd make the *Senhorio* suffer,"

Rosa laughed. "You don't love me. If you give me your word, you'll murder the Senhorio! What foolishness! Run away from Madeira and take madness with you."

"A girl wants a marriage into a good family. Your mother dreams of your wedding day."

Her lips trembled and she cried, wiping the tears away with her skirt. "I want to be yours." He touched her hand.

"I didn't ask for your hand. Alberto did. I can't."

She lowered her eyes. "You live the life of a lizard and the soldiers can't take you to serve in the King's army. You talk of dreams and can't love." She looked him in the eye and said, "Love."

"Senhora, I love the land and own none. I live in my father's house. I've no house of my own. I'm a slave on the land, a slave of the *Senhorio*."

Her face was stone-like. She raised her hand and touched her temple as if she were wiping away fear. She withdrew, sitting alone, her back straight and her eyes shut.

José ate his orange. He went to the door of the shop and checked the patio for soldiers and she followed him.

"I want to go with you. What do I care about this place? I want a new life."

"The difficulties are great and the dangers unknown."

"You've never been to Brazil," she said.

"The fishermen know. Their friends went to Brazil. Life is hard there. Without passports, they can't return to Madeira. I can't take you with me."

"You don't want me."

"You stole the key and you'll suffer for it. I owe you more than I can pay."

"Take me with you."

"I can't."

She covered her mouth with her hand and tears fell down her cheek and there was no sound from her.

A puff of smoke on the heights and a rocket barrage signaled the official opening of the Festival of Saint Blaise.

"Go dancing and singing, it's festival," he said. "Men from all over the island are in the square."

"What do I care? I can't go with you?" she said.

He took her hand. "We'll talk with Pistola. He is the sage of Maçapez. He knows about Brazil. We can't live in Madeira."

He walked her to the top of the cliff in view of the beach and the hillsides. Lizards darted into hiding. The water fell off the cliff and into the pool where it overflowed into the blue sea.

Off the pebbled beach an old dory covered with weed and kelp moved on the tide, its paint worn and bleached to shades of gray and green, blended with the rocks, ghostly and water-logged, worn oars lying across its centerboard.

At the festival, peasants wore their Sunday best. Men in black trousers and white shirts with *Zé Povinho* black hats. The women wore their red and white folk-dancing skirts, white embroidered blouses and light calf-skin boots. The shop at Maçapez bustled with holiday folk. Pistola was nowhere in sight. He'd taken Talbot and Jenkins to the square to see the procession.

José and Rosa hid in the field owned by João Gonçalves. She talked about Brazil and how happy she'd be in a country where they spoke Portuguese.

The day of the festival dawned. The neighbors chatted about dancing, eating broad beans and drinking wine. The merrymaking grew louder. Soldiers arrived and ordered glasses of wine, sat on Pistola's patio and sang rowdy songs.

"We can see Pistola when his shop closes. Please sit near the door and tell him I'll come at dark," José said.

"You promised to see him with me," Rosa said.

"The soldiers will arrest me on sight."

"You can wear my kerchief and talk in a high voice like you did when you were baptized." She winked.

"Pistola entertains Talbot and Jenkins. Until he closes the shop for the night, I can't linger."

José hid in the sugar cane. More rockets exploded high on the mountain.

"Where're you going?" he said.

"I'm with you," said Rosa.

"I'll come for you during the band concert. The square is crowded and the dancing attracts everyone's attention."

"Every time I close my eyes, I see you." Rosa said.

Tears rose in her eyes and she kissed him and ran off to join her family at the festival. The church bells rang for evening Mass. Josés went to Manuel Cabral's garden and hid in the banana grove.

The sun had set and a veil of mist spread over the twilight. The Deserta Islands were salmon pink as the sun bathed them one last time before it sank below the western horizon and darkness fell over the islands. José waited for darkness and slipped away from the thicket and climbed up path to Pistola's shop. The soldiers on the patio were drunk and singing and swearing. The young men of the village wagered over the harvest of the grapes in August and their card games.

CHAPTER XXXIII

Fireworks burst in the evening sky and folk-dances in the square brought the festival to life. Last minute items were bought at the shop from Pistola in Maçapez, matches, kerosene, coffee, sugar. Tristão Andrade and Manuel Batista smoked cigarettes on the patio. The village girls ate *broas*, cookies, and drank *bicas*, coffees, and José lay in Pistola's garden among loquat and guava trees concealed from the shoppers and card players on the patio waiting to speak with Pistola.

"They won't find José," said Tristão.

Cigarette smoke drifted from Manuel's nose and into his eyes. "Maybe he's dead. The soldiers escorted him into the village. Soldiers lie. The *Senhorio's* men searched the district for José and returned empty-handed."

"Rosa released him from the slave quarters. José spoke with Direito and Esquerda," Manuel said.

"His escape gave the Senhorio a black eye. There was trouble enough with soldiers and the well." said Tristão.

"Tia Nita once said that the spirits would take the young men of the village away. A spirit took Abreu."

"She's dead herself. I haven't seen her."

"She's missing. She walked off and hid in the mountains with shepherds," Tristão said.

"The Brazâo sisters found her. Their keening was dreadful. Maybe José will show up. The spirits may free him."

"That's hocus-pocus for the priests. Rosa stole the Senhorio's key and José hid either in the caves or the mountains."

Manuel and Tristão walked off the patio and climbed the path up to the square toward the sound of band music.

Sebastão-of-the-chapel slapped Manuel on the back. "Come and dance. The girls want to watch you."

"Not while the soldiers keep watch. I don't like soldiers. They're mean. They guard that well as if it were the opening to Hell and I say let them go to Hell," said Manuel.

José saw the old men drift across the patio and buy glasses of wine at the bar. They toasted the health of the soldiers that were drunker and louder, swearing and calling for more brandy. The soldiers told filthy stories about the prostitutes of old Funchal.

Children ran out of the shop and into the old peasant's shop. "Olive oil," shouted a woman in an aquamarine shawl. Two boys ate candy and giggled and flopped down on the cobbles imitating the drunken soldiers. The African soldier drank home-made brandy and did fall onto the cobbles and lay in a stupor.

When the patio was deserted and quiet the shop shuttered for the night, José crept out of the garden and across the cobbles. By the front gate, he listened for voices. He hurried to Pistola's door, knocked and held his breath. Was he at home?

The door swung open. Pistola smiled and beckoned him into the dining room. Garth Talbot and William Jenkins sat in chairs at the table, dressed in knickers and cardigans.

José spoke in a rush he was so relieved to see Talbot. He smiled though the Englishmen couldn't understand the mercurial Madeiran tongue. The Englishmen drank cups of tea and admired Pistola's orchids. Pistola poured José a cup of coffee and Nina, his wife, brought *Bola de Berlim.* The house smelled of sweets and garlic and biscuits. Fireworks burst and reverberated off the cliffs above the village.

"A most enjoyable evening, I must say," said Jenkins. "I'm going to tell my London friends about this splendid festival. What a shame you don't do bed-and-breakfast."

"Yes Sir," said Pistola. "We need business. Our friend's on-the-lam, as you say. The soldiers want him for the army. Father Segundo gave his name to the captain."

Both me men turned toward him.

"Did Rosa see you, Senhor?"

"Yes, the *Senhorio* is mad over the affair. Stay away from him," said Pistola.

"Yes, by all means," said Talbot. "José better hear my arrangements."

"Yes, tell him so I can hear the details," said Pistola.

"I tell them once. No rumors. Do I make myself clear?"

"Yes, Senhor, we swear."

"Blandy Brothers has a passage weekly out of London calling at Funchal. Steamship *Zweena*, twenty-eight hundred ton, Captain Taylor in command, runs into Johannesburg. This trip she calls at Rio. Her cook João Morales helps Madeirans cross the water."

"Senhor, I met him on the *S. S. Wazzan*. He knew the *Zweena's* crew," said José.

"Exactly, you'll board with Morales tomorrow evening before the *Zweena* sails for Rio."

José didn't understand.

"He'll miss it. The soldiers guard the beach. The festival delayed their departure. Rumor and gossip spread to Quinta Grande and Câmara De Lobos. They know he's wanted. His family can't keep him. He doesn't understand appointments, especially in Funchal, tomorrow evening." Pistola pulled his ear.

"I'll row out to meet her," José said.

Jenkins whistled. "Too risky lad, they'd never see you."

"If they knew, they'd look for him," said Pistola.

"We'll telegraph. You've had a telegraph wire for ten years, I believe," said Talbot.

"Yes Senhor, I know the man that sends the messages. He's a friend and will keep it confidential. But this way is uncertain."

"The whole business is chancy, a ramshackle affair," said Jenkins.

"Can you guarantee a secret message?" said Talbot.

"I can send a request to Captain Taylor asking him to swing by Campanário on his way south. He's bunked in the Casino & Stranger's Club. He knows Cossart's daughter. She's the one that served us old brandy during your last visit. The odds are great but it's worth a try."

"What scheme you dreaming up, old chap?" said Jenkins.

"We'll sail out and keep an eye out for José. We'll distract the militia. The wherrymen know my sloop. I blew in here, so I can blow in again."

"You won't have to sail. José knows fishermen at Ribeira Brava. Knowing the *Zweena's* time of departure, these fishermen can sail to meet it."

"Too many mouths to spread the word and endanger the scheme," said Talbot.

"I'll be there. The weather may change. I don't trust the rogues along the coast."

"Whatever you wish, Senhor," said Pistola.

Jenkins cracked his knuckles and hopped up from his rocking chair. "Let's go up to the square and watch the folk-dancing before I fall asleep."

José shook hands. "Thank you, Senhor Talbot. I'll sleep in the smuggler's cave. I'm ready to sail."

"I'm pleased to help. You've no papers. Don't fret, Morales is honest."

"Good luck and sail like Hell if the authorities come after you," said Jenkins.

"I'll send Rosa with a message," said Pistola.

"Please send someone else. She wants to run away and join me."

Pistola smiled. "I know. She told me, my friend."

"Two passengers are awkward. Wait and I'll arrange something for Rosa," Talbot said.

The door banged with the blows of a solid object. Pistola hurried to open the door. José ran and hid himself in the bedroom. Jenkins and Talbot stared into the entryway.

"Good evening, gentlemen," said Pistola. "What brings you to my door on the evening of the festival?"

"José Abreu was seen entering your house, Senhor." said Esquerda.

"I'm sorry, honored soldier, you are mistaken."

"Don't give me *linguiça,* baloney, old fellow. This José entered your gate and ran up the stairway."

"He's nowhere in sight. He went elsewhere."

Direito and Esquerda pressed themselves into the entryway. They saw the Englishmen. "Who are these strangers?" said Direito. "They saw him!"

"Friends of mind from Funchal, they saw nothing, they are my guests for the festival. Come in and meet them, good sirs."

Pistola offered the drunken Direito a bottle of his best Maçapez wine. "We've a dish of delicious broad beans. Taste some."

"No, no, we seek the runaway. Thank you, Senhor. Come along Esquerda."

"Don't lie to us old Grandfather. We know this fellow's here," said Esquerda.

"You can see for yourselves," said Pistola. He led them from the dining room into the sitting room. He opened the wardrobe where he collected the clothing he sold at Sunday market.

His cupboard overflowed with dry goods for the store. The soldiers rummaged through the rooms interested in the inventory. Their search carried them toward the bedroom where José stood by the window trying to make up his mind whether to jump out onto the porch or hide in the room. The soldiers rushed into the bedroom and saw him climb through the window.

They shouted: "Halt in the name of the King."

José jumped and startled two more soldiers below. "He's on the roof," yelled Esquerda.

Esquerda hopped out the window in pursuit of José. Direito ran down the stairway, aimed his rifle at the roof and fired.

A great cry rose up. "You are son of a bitch, you son of a bitch."

Pistola, Talbot and Jenkins ran out of the house. Direito fired two rounds into the darkness. "What are you firing at?" said Pistola. He squinted out of his good eye.

"You hid him in your house," said Direito.

"I don't shut and lock my windows at night. I breathe fresh air. He came off the roof and through the open window. He's a climber."

"Your man's wounded," said Talbot.

"Why'd you shoot your partner?" Pistola made a face at Direito. "Come and help him."

"I didn't shoot him. The runaway did."

Pistola shook his head. The soldiers believed José had fired on Esquerda. Word was sent to the soldiers bivouacked around the village square. Pistola tied a tourniquet onto Esquerda's leg. He held a lamp over the leg and Talbot cut the trouser with shears and exposed the wound. The bone was not broken.

"Dispatch one of your men to the captain," said Talbot.

"The men are dancing," said Direito, much peeved.

"Never mind, we'll carry your comrade to the church. He can't sleep here. I won't have it," said Pistola.

Jenkins held the leg while Pistola poured iodine into the wound and dressed it.

Pistola smoothed the feelings of the soldiers with shot glasses of his best brandy. Talbot and Jenkins hoisted Esquerda into a hammock. He swore at them. The arrival of a wounded soldier in a hammock created great interest in the square.

"This leg hurts like hell," said Esquerda, "Tell the *Senhorio* and his peasants, this means war and we'll hunt down his peasant."

José fled across the valley under the cover of darkness to the Place of Caves and Mulberry Trees. He lay flat on his stomach on the floor of the Smuggler's cave. At daybreak, sky rockets signaled the second day of the festival. He rubbed his eyes. From the ridge top of Fajã Velha he saw the soldiers in the square like angry bees and he remembered the fireworks the evening before, wild stars in the dark sky.

CHAPTER XXXIV

The band played lively folk tunes and the dancers in brightly colored costumes leaped into the air and ended their circular pattern of intricate steps. The festival goers clapped their hands. Red and yellow lanterns lighted the cobbles and bars in the decorated booths along the square sold beer, brandy and wine. The militia settled down and enjoyed itself drinking and dancing with no thought of guard duty or pursuing draftees.

José stood on the volcanic ridge and looked on the festivities and wished he were in the square with his brothers and sisters. Darkness fell and the stars showed in the night sky and crickets sang as he climbed through the prickly pear and under the banana plants. He didn't know what to do with himself. He missed the festivities and music made it difficult to keep out of the square. His wandering brought him down into the schoolyard. He went in over the worn marble doorstep and to the classroom where his sisters learned to read and write. The room smelled of chalk and oiled wood mingled with the odor of gall from ink drying in the wells of the desks. He ran his fingers over the blackboard, cool and dry, and made letters in the chalk dust with his finger. He felt the letdown of too many hours keeping out of the way of soldiers and those spies of the *Senhorio.* He lay behind the teacher's desk on the cool floor and pulled his burlap around himself.

Morning light awakened him. Bright haze covered the schoolyard. Birds sang on the edge of the watering trough. He rubbed his eyes and scooped up handfuls of water from the fountain. He sat at a desk and ate bananas and a custard apple. He found a telescope in the drawer of the teacher's desk and slipped it into his pocket. He climbed to the ledge above the school house and looked out over the square.

One lone soldier with a rifle guarded the square, walking its perimeter. He took the telescope from his pocket and scanned the pebbled beach where an armed guard paced back and forth across the quay. A squad hiked in single file down through the fields. The first soldier stopped on the cliff-top and surveyed the beach. The patrol searched every hiding place as it swept the ridge, men leaving the trail and going through the sugar cane and into the banana groves. They were determined to find him.

235

Smoke rose from the white Arabic chimney at his house. It was the time of the morning mother cooked breakfast, boiling up the coffee, cutting the bread and setting out custard apples. He walked to his cousin's potato patch in the early sunlight. He reached between the dew-covered green leaves and dug into the soil and found a large tuber. He polished soil off the potato and dug his teeth into the crisp round flesh and chewed slowly and savored its raw flavor. He cut down a sugar cane stalk and split its thick tough stem and sucked its marrow.

The village was fretful after its outburst of carnival. The presence of the soldiers aroused the neighborhood. They feared for their daughters. The festival erupted, with its marching and singing and drinking. The peasants celebrated their feudal burdens forgotten.

The sea looked solid and calm across to the island of *Deserta Grande*. Men lived there and survived, maybe he'd sail there and live on rabbits, goats and fish. In winter, he'd kill a goat and salt down the flesh and store it in the cave. In the earliest days soon after its discovery, the island had wheat fields. Through his telescope he saw wild grasses on a treeless plain surrounded by rocks carved from bedrock and eroded by the sea winds.

He adjusted the borrowed telescope the school teacher used for viewing incoming boats on the sea. He peered at the shoreline of the deserted island for a good place to land a dory. How long would it take to row to the island? He'd seen the cave during the fishing trip before they laid out their nets off Bugio. Now it appeared a dark shadow.

He moved the glass down to see the pebbled beach. More soldiers were posted along the seafront. He trained the scope on the village square. The market was busy and soldiers kept a watch over the sealed well. He spied the vineyard on the edge of the cliff where the old Aunt collected herbs. He called her Tia Nita, but her family name was Sousa. The vines were bathed in sunlight, leafy green, church tower shining, pigeons swooping out and fluttering back to their perches in the bell-loft. The street was an aisle of flags, white cotton emblazoned with red crosses. The crowds gathered in the square. He peered through the brass scope at the joyous festival and he wished more than ever to be in the happy throng.

The Holy Ghost Association lined up for the grand procession down the only street of Campanário. First, the men of Saint Blaise arranged themselves at attention in their black suits, white shirts with maroon ties, bright maroon sashes over their right shoulders. They drew their swords and saluted their commander, the oldest Abreu of the clan in the valley of the melons. God is proud of them, José thought. They are ready to defend the church to the death if necessary.

Behind the village-men, the band, dressed in bright red jackets and wearing black British helmets, played a spirited tune. The soldiers assembled, their colors at the front, and their captain strutted around giving orders to his sergeants. The school children gathered at the rear of the parade with their masks, noise makers and wooden carts specially decorated for the festival.

The parade moved forward when the clock in the belfry rang ten o' clock. The band reached the square first and in single file moved into the bandstand built for the holiday concerts. The procession marched into church for the Mass. When they emerged from the church after the Mass hungry and thirsty they rushed to the stalls for their wine, bowls of soup, bits of beef and codfish cooked over bright coals in braziers set on the cobbled street.

Where was João in this crowd? He spied Maria wearing her beautiful black veil. His sisters, Julia and Luisa, walked arm in arm nodding and smiling at the soldiers. The soldiers on the quay covered the approach to Pistola's cave. He wanted to return there to see whatever message was sent to him about his going aboard the *Zweena*. He searched with the telescope for a long time and didn't see João in the crowd.

He moved to the other side of the promontory and through the telescope viewed the valley to the west. Few soldiers patrolled the valley. One soldier leaned against the parapet of the bridge on the route home. His stomach gurgled. He was famished and ran down the slope, tripped and fell and landed at the bottom close to the *levada*. He moved toward the sentry and smelled his cigarette smoke, drifting on the air from the bridge over the stream. He left the path and waded through the stream. The guard still smoked and looked toward the festival.

He went into his mother's kitchen and dined on leftover boiled cornmeal cut into strips, sweet potatoes, and chestnuts. He filled his bundle with bananas, oranges, figs and two large apples.

He whistled a long shrill note and listened for soldiers and climbed toward the cliff and his outlook from where he'd seen Talbot and his sloop that summer's day long ago. A whistle returned his from the goat's cave.

"It's you," said João, "You caused us trouble."

"I came for a little food and a favor, I didn't see you at Saint Blaise," he said.

"I was sent home to work. I do my work and yours. And you ask a favor!"

"I want you to find Pistola."

"I'm under orders. I can't go again to the festival. You have no authority. The soldiers will capture you. You'll rot in prison."

"João, I'm leaving. I've no money for papers. My friends found me passage. I need to know when the ship sails by Campanário."

"You'll run away! You were the one who led the two drunken soldiers to the village square and pointed out the well to them."

"Everyone hates me. I'm sorry you have to do my share of the work. I'll miss grapevines, orange trees and this anona tree. Henrique dreams always of these valley gardens."

"I'll look for Pistola. You caused us trouble. I won't listen to you."

"I've sadness in my heart. You can't see it. Say nothing to anyone and get the word from Pistola," he said.

He stared at his brother. João was a stranger like the soldiers.

The wind off the sierra blew João's hair onto his forehead, shading his eyes. João picked up a few pebbles and tossed them one at a time at his bare feet.

"Father Domingo asked for you."

"I've seen too much of him."

"His housekeeper told mother for you to see him."

"I'm not seeing the priest."

João whacked off the tops of a few sprouts with his knife. He fed the goats and cursed.

"You know the old dory on the beach, the one Tia Nita used to gather her limpets. I'll hide in the rocks back from the beach," he said.

"The one with the rotten hull, the dory we hunted with for limpets by the black rock, the one only good for firewood?"

"I'll be there at *sesta*. If you see Rosa, tell her I'm in the smuggler's cave. She's to see Pistola if she has questions."

"You've forgotten your duty to the family," said João.

"Not the way you think. Grandfather worried on his death bed. Who's going to feed the animals, water the garden, cut the wood? My god, he was dying and he only talked about work. Day labor is always with us. You owe your life to the Senhorio. I don't."

José handed João his Saint Blaise medal, the medallion given to him by his Grandfather. He wouldn't carry medals to Brazil.

He covered his mouth with his hand, "Soldiers come."

"I told them I saw you very early this morning," said João. He grinned.

Soldiers moved through the cane field. They splashed through irrigation ditches to inspect tunnels and abandoned medieval buildings from the time of the Abreu governors. They sent patrols up the beach looking for José.

José heard soldiers talking with João. He edged down the ridge keeping out of sight yet moving toward the cliff's edge. He waited for the pebbled beach to be clear of soldiers and climbed down into the cave. He'd worried João wouldn't see Pistola and Rosa would seek him out.

A heavy mist moved down the valley obscuring the beach, muffling sound. He pulled his woolen cap down over his eyes. February was influenza month. Death carried off those weakened by age. His move from the smuggler's cave down and into Pistola's cave was impossible with soldiers guarding the quay.

In the cave the smell of bat dung and sea weed was strong. He spread out burlap bags to lie on. The steady rise and fall, the roll and click of pebbles, in their unending rush and rhythm of the tide up the beach and back into the luminous surf lulled him to sleep.

In the darkness of his dream, fireworks flashed, and he stood in the square under the flare of torches surrounded by the peasants. The glare made their faces orange. He danced with Rosa.

In his sleep Father Segundo yelled, "Grab him. He disobeyed the *Senhorio*. He refused to serve his King." The dancers ran after him, grabbing at his shirt and swung him onto the cobblestones. They hurled stones. He raised his hands to his face and cried out. His cries enraged them and they threw larger stones.

He saw his blood on the cobblestones. A cry rose from his throat and his scream awoke him from his nightmare.

João had said, "You're dreaming and mad in the bargain."

José listened. The surf pounded on the rocks. He saw a figure in the gloom. "João?" he said.

"This ain't the rocks beyond the dory," said João.

"The pebbled beach was too dangerous?"

"No one saw me climb here."

"I've had a bad dream," said José.

"Pistola's message is strange. '*Zweena* delayed in Funchal roads! Taylor sails in daylight, sorry.'"

"It's a bad message for me. I must sail in darkness," said José.

"Rosa's angry. I told her nothing. You didn't meet her at Pistola's. She arrived in the midst of soldiers firing at you. I told her you hid in the smuggler's cave. You went to Pistola's cave. I'm off home. Good-bye, A*deus*, Henrique will be happy in the mountains without you."

"Tell him, good luck and thanks for nothing."

José found the old dory in darkness of his dream and his eyes adjusted to the light over the ocean and he judged the distance. The *Zweena* made an arc along this shore and moved southwest. The old dory rode low in the waves. He heard the surf pounding the rocks at high tide.

The tide moved up the rocks and the small pebbles on the beach rattled and rolled down over the large pebbles and made a clicking sound. He heard Tia Nita's slippers moving over the ground, the hush of their leather imprinting the volcanic soil, her figure in the garden, in a long black shawl, beckoning him with her hand and disappearing into her cottage, a black kerchief covering her face. She arose from the sea, her wrinkled face expressionless and her sad brown eyes staring with affection at plants and flowers, her hand touched their green leaves. She tied a tomato vine and whispered to the yellow blossoming stars on the green tendrils. She bent over and cut a cabbage with one swift movement of the knife she concealed in her shawl. José followed her into the house. She sliced the cabbage into fine threads with the knife held tightly in her bloated hand.

She dropped the cuttings into a pot of boiling water. She poked at the fire with a pine faggot. Heat and ash filled his nose and the odor of sliced potato for the soup, on the sideboard.

Tia Nita's spirit hummed softly and danced back and forth, sat in her rocking chair and rocked with the wind blowing through the cave. An ancient tune emerged from her lips and she sang over her knitting, humming under her breath. José opened his eyes and he couldn't see. The cave was dark and cold. He hungered for hot cabbage soup and chilled to the bone, pulled up his woolen robe.

CHAPTER XXXV

Under a sky of bright stars, festival lamps illuminated the dark streets of Campanário. The church with candles and lanterns blazed with light, and large bonfires burned along the cobbled streets in the square and churchyard. He made his way through a maze of alley ways and into the middle of the festivities.

Band members dressed in black seated themselves for the evening concert, giving the bandstand a formal, somber touch in the midst of moving colors, flames and flowers. Three peasants brought their own beef to broil over the fire. They trotted to the wine shop to join the brisk trade in large tumblers of dark red, and the *estrangeiros*, strangers, drank *vinho verde*.

He disguised himself by pulling his knitted cap over his ears and tying his scarf over his mouth. The dancers and diners were happy and laughing, and distracted by drunken soldiers. He moved unnoticed by Castagna's house, Rosa poured water from a crock of broad beans in the light of her father's celebration fire. He dismissed speaking to her and hurried toward the front gate of the Priest's house.

The front gate was lit by braziers of oil hanging from chains, a tripod set on either side of the entrance. The servant girls swept the walk clean, and trimmed the fine hedge. Pots of geraniums decorated the walkway. The stairs to the door had caladium lilies and orchids on each step, their pots scrubbed clean, white clay, shining in the firelight. He moved along the back wall and around the corner where he pushed at the iron bars and swung the gate. The housekeeper sat slicing fruit at the kitchen table.

Looking up at him, she said, "Good evening. Father is eating his dinner."

"I can't linger, Senhora," he said.

She led him into the dining room. Father Domingo sat at the head of a large mahogany table covered with white linen on which platters of food were arranged so he could easily reach them. The silver service gleamed in

243

the candlelight and the flowers in the center of the table as fresh-looking as morning dew. A large linen cloth pinned to his collar covered his surplice. He blew air through his nose and glared.

"Please enter and be seated while I finish," said the Priest.

It was too late. Over and over nothing, visions of the ocean appeared and spread out in his mind and he was swimming away from the pebbled beach.

The priest rang his silver bell for the girls to clear the plates and platters of leftover food. The girls hesitated wanting to offer him a taste, but the priest waved them away. He hadn't eaten since morning and he wanted a potato. The broiled beef and the marinade tuna and the chicken with tomatoes went off to the kitchen. A plain potato would taste fine. The priest wiped his fingers with his linen napkin. He folded it and slid it back into the silver ring and rested his hands on the tablecloth.

"I know you defy the Senhorio. You broke the law and left without his authority. Not long ago we killed those that fled the land and broke their bond. You ran into the mountains."

"I was beaten and locked up, Father. The King freed the slaves. I'm not a slave."

"A man has a sacred bond. He owes the *Senhorio* his life. He pays taxes and works on the great harvests. You did not cut sugar cane and carry the bundles to the pebbled beach."

"I wanted to live with Henrique. I went to the mountains where he cuts timber and he threw me into a ravine to die."

"He's a bad man. I don't listen to outlaws. You ran away from the *Senhorio*."

The priest stood and beckoned him into the sitting room. He continued. "I have a proposition. I've found a place. You are a child of God and a sinner. The church will teach you obedience. You'll join us. The militia searches for you. I gave them your name. When you enter holy orders, I'll tell the captain I was mistaken. The Senhorio demands satisfaction but he recognizes the King's right. Either you freely choose to join us or the militia takes you for six years. You'll go to Funchal for the first year and later to the great cities of Porto and Coimbra. A life devoted to God is happier than one in the army. You wanted to read and write. This is your chance to prove it. We have fine training. We spend years perfecting the mind. You'd be assigned to a parish in your eighth year of study."

"I want to be freed of the Senhorio so I can live a free life," he said.

"You belong to the Abreu clan. You believe in God, young man. Before I go to my bed, tell me what you desire."

"I want land and a home without The Senhorio," he said.

The priest curled his lip. "And you want to read and write, too. Give up the world and live in the church. Learn about the living spirit. The land offers you little. Accept a life with God and you gain much."

He shrugged and lowered his eyes.

"And you've seen Rosa Castagna without her father's blessing. She wants to marry you. When you join the order, you'll give her up. I've arranged a suitable husband for her."

"No thank you, Father. I want to live my life."

"You'll marry her and satisfy honor," said the priest.

"Never she's a child. I love another."

"She loves you and wants you for her husband. You've been seen alone talking with her!"

"I say never. She can choose from the young men that come to the festival. With another, she'll be happy. Say nothing more of marriage."

The priest rubbed his nose. "Well, you are free to choose the way of penance. It offers you life without women, without family. You'll do well with us. Your mind is strong and we can train it."

"I can't, Senhor. Your offer is generous."

The tone of the priest's voice changed. "Then kneel and confess. You need to confess your sins before the militia takes you. I'll call the captain. The soldiers won't search further and they can enjoy the festival. They'll celebrate Saint Blaise."

He knelt before the priest. He thought of nothing to say. He trembled and dropped his knitted biretta.

"I'm not on the roll. I was never baptized. You deceived Pistola turning my name over to the captain. You broke your promise to him. You lied." That he said these last words surprised him.

The priest coughed and pushed him to the floor. "You lizard, you deserve your fate. It's the militia for you. No one calls me a liar and escapes the justice of the church. You're crazy!"

The priest's voice rose until it sounded like a scream. The housekeeper heard it and ran into the room. He shouted for her to leave. He changed his mind and ran into the hallway. "Run out to the patio and call the soldiers. I have their man. Quickly, quickly before I change my mind."

He didn't wait to hear the priest's tirade. He dashed through the passageway and into the kitchen. On the patio, he leapt up on the wall and looked down onto the square. Three soldiers ran toward the rectory. He heard the priest's footsteps running onto the patio.

"Traitor, stop the traitor. Stop him!"

The housekeeper, as fleet as a deer, appeared with Direito and Esquerda behind her, laughing and merry-eyed.

Hundreds of revelers heard the outcry. They spread the word around the square. More soldiers ran into the square. Esquerda knelt in the street and swung his rifle down to check its breech. He loosened the strap and blew into the chamber.

The old blacksmith ran after Direito, bellowing like a bull. "Captain, capture the swine." And then, "Officer, officer, this way, the priest's house, hurry."

They passed the front gate and went around the back. He jumped and ran into the square. The band played a familiar march tune, oblivious to the commotion. A few eyes spied him as he ran up the steps of the church. He ran down the aisle and stopped to catch his breath. Outside, soldiers converged on the terrace below the bandstand, awaited orders. The crowd stopped dancing, startled by the appearance of the priest and his household. The priest without his jacket or biretta or his impressive cape ran into the square.

Quiet settled on the square. The band stopped playing. The dancers gathered around the priest. A few mumbles and shouts died away. "Your truant is within your grasp," said the priest to the soldiers.

The crowd rushed up the steps, pushing children aside and paying no attention to the soldiers who loaded their rifles. At the church door, the peasants halted. The captain spoke to the priest about entering the sacred precinct.

"Go on, go on in. He went into the basilica," said the priest.

"We can't raid a church," said Direito.

"The scoundrel ran in there. Yes, we saw him," said the old crone who loved soldiers.

"Yes, we can. Father says so. Open the door, Senhor," said Esquerda.

"Who is it?" said Mandado.

"That crazy son of a bitch, The *Senhorio's* runaway from the tail of the pig," said Blackeye.

"Who is right? Move forward," said the priest.

The captain refused to storm the building. The soldiers swore and demanded the order to pursue their quarry.

"I am right," said Direito.

"Then open the door, stupid," said Esquerdo. Direito shook his head and refused to touch the door. The crowd now pushed them against the door. "Open the door, Father," said the peasants.

The priest drew himself up to his full height and looked at the faces of his people. "Remember it is the house of God." He whispered something and crossed himself slowly to catch every sympathetic eye. He swung the door open and three men fought for the ring on the left side of the door and swung it half open. The crowd surged forward, the soldiers raced into the church.

He ran through the basilica and around back of the altar and listened in the *bema* when the crowd roared into the narthex. He retreated into the darkest corner of the apse and searched for a way out through the transepts. He saw nothing and felt the walls, trying to remember where the assistants moved as they assisted the priest in communion. His confusion lost him the time gained during the conversations at the church door. He ran to the stairs leading to the organ and choir loft, not quickly enough to pass unseen. The soldiers reached the altar and tried to genuflect while holding their rifles.

From the choir master's stall, he saw them run down the aisles and around the columns through the darkness. The glow of the candles on the altar illuminated the figures running into the church from the firelight of the square, screaming and grotesque.

The only way was the bell ringer's loft. He climbed it last in childhood. His friends once dared him to climb it during Easter when he was five. He climbed into the bell tower and dropped an egg on his friends and swore by Our Lady he was sorry. The ascent made him dizzy and sweaty, but he let the egg go and it splat on the cobblestones, a bright yellow star. Sounds below, told him the soldiers were at the stairway to the loft.

He climbed the narrow passage way, it was almost vertical, higher into the darkness and the smell of dust and pigeon droppings.

"He's not here," yelled one soldier and a voice yelled back, "The bell tower, the top stair, Senhor."

Immediately, the soldiers remaining at the main door raced into the square and craned their necks at the steeple. They refused to enter the church, and they made a bold display of aiming their weapons at the clock face.

The captain gave orders in a strident voice. It rose in the basilica, echoing off the chamber walls. Every door was manned and the building surrounded.

He climbed a timber with pegs higher into the bell ringer's loft. This led up and into the tower room itself where the bells hung. He was breathless and not thinking and heard the heavy breathing of a soldier climbing the steps below him.

The night wind moved through the arches of the bell tower and cooled him. A reverberating pulse of air moved him closer to the edge of the sill. The wind made a sound through the bells like sleeping pigeons, feathers ruffled and then smoothed by an invisible hand. He placed one foot on the walkway, no wider than his foot, and touched the cold basalt covering the bell-window sashes. The light from the festival below covered the stonework with a warm glow.

The band remained silent. He heard men shouting, their voices blurred and indistinct on the night wind. Far below, the pigeons lined up on the roof of the nave, flew up and away, frightened by his presence in the tower. They flew back and pushed off again, in twos and threes until they found safe roosts on roofs around the square. His pursuers were silent, below in the darkness of the loft.

He peered into the black well below the bell wheels. He heard nothing and saw only the gloomy curves of gears and wheels, the antique machinery that made the mysterious tolling. The church's bell tower high above the square gave him a view of the festival, the cliffs, the cane fields, the restless ocean beyond, and no visible way, no path to escape his perch.

CHAPTER XXXVI

He crawled along the sill of the bell tower window on his hands and knees hidden from the figures in the square and caused no alarm. He squeezed into the arch out of the wind with a view of the square. Soldiers ran into the square and peered up at the tower. The captain himself walked into the square and examined the portal to the basilica and his men dashed forward and saluted. He wished to hear their words, and they were faint and indistinct. Direito and Esquerda spoke with the priest. Mandado cornered Pistola in front of Castagna's to question him about the foreigners and pointed his finger at the Englishmen dressed in dark blue and black. Their caps drew the attention of the festival goers who wore their best finery-- white shirts and blouses, red vests and brightly colored skirts. One soldier reported to the captain near Talbot and Jenkins. The captain dismissed the soldiers and they went to the nearest wine stall. More soldiers appeared in the square. They guarded the church and he knew other soldiers were posted at the rear of the building, though he couldn't see them.

They knew he was perched in the belfry and could wait the rest of the night and the morrow, changing sentries and waiting for him to climb down and arrest him as he tried to leave the church. The natives continued their dancing and merriment. The band resumed its concert as if nothing had disrupted its program. The soldiers assembled with lanterns and in groups of three went off. He saw one unit move into the cemetery. When they failed to appear, he knew they'd gone into the crypt to search for him.

He laughed thinking of their anxiety in the crypt with its odor of earth and darkness and spirits. He feared hiding in the smuggler's cave with the body of the old Aunt. He listened for the soldier who climbed after him up the stairs but there was no sound of crawling or climbing below him in the belfry.

The captain joined the priest for a drink. They leaned on their elbows against the plank bar of the stall. Soldiers returned to the square confused by the brightness of the fires and dancing. More soldiers returned to enjoy the music and toss down tumblers of wine. Rosa's father served them drams of

251

brandy from the small barrel at his festival stall. It appeared that many soldiers gave up the search and joined the festival.

He wormed himself into a comfortable position. The wind and the dampness were cold. He watched the evening progress, the goodnights of Pistola and the Englishmen, the priest walking back to his gate with his housekeeper and her girls. He had no view of the doors of the church where soldiers were on guard duty. He inched along the outer wall of the tower and examined its columns, the scene over forty meters below now brightening in the light of the risen moon.

His eye scanned the horizon for the steamship from Funchal. Before long, one moved into view. He thought it might be the *Zweena*. The glow of lights in the pale sea was beyond a man's rowing out to them.

Rosa and her friends joined the folk dancing. They made a joyous group in their white blouses with red and white pleated skirts. Their white boots made by their fathers especially for festivals were bright against the cobbles. He remembered his father said the red caps with the silver tassels didn't originate in Calheta. They were a custom brought from the Minho.

The Senhorio strolled down the avenue and into the dance arena accompanied by his loyal attendants and hangers-on. He danced with his cousin Julia, and took Rosa to be his partner.

The crowd stared and listened with curiosity trying to discern the least trace of passion between The Senhorio and Rosa. The men leaning with their elbows on the serving boards of the stalls set their wines glasses down and turned to watch the swirling skirt of the young girl with admiring eyes. The women noted the tongue of the *Senhorio* and glanced at the priest and his faithful to see what the Pharisees said when they saw the couple dancing.

"Bastard, I'll cut his tongue out," said the Senhorio.

José pounded his fist into his palm. He cursed family, land and the mother of the mad son of a bitch.

The Senhorio smiled and moved in easy circles around the formation of dancers. The music increased in tempo and the dancers leapt in the air. With a crescendo in the finale, the band played faster and ended on one triumphant note. The landlord swung her about and lifted her high and setting her down, he doffed his cap and kneeled on one leg before her. Rosa was pale and silent, her black eyes shining. She curtsied and fled to her mother and sisters where they watched her from the balcony.

He wanted to jump from the tower into their midst and tear the hair off the *Senhorio's* head. He wished he danced with Rosa. He saw the old thatched roofs of the poor, their cottages built of whitewashed stone, and the sea itself spread beyond the shore. The moonlight shining on the vineyards and the tiled roofs of the cottages calmed him. He was ready to climb down and make his way to the dory on the pebbled beach and row out to the *Zweena* before daylight.

He concentrated on the figures in the square and yawned. The perimeter of the church was guarded. The night wind blew with greater force, rustling through the banana groves and tearing at the flags on their poles. The banners lashed against their staffs and decorations were ripped away, flowers and laurel leaves blowing along the cobbles.

He backed along the narrow parapet and edged around toward the south face and avoided the wind a little. His teeth chattered and he massaged his legs and ran-in-place. Each hour the clock's bell struck and sent a deep resonating tone through the belfry marking the appointed number and the loss of darkness. The fatigue from running through the church and up the stairs and climbing the tower and the fear of the soldiers were gone and he pondered fleeing the church and climbing down over the cliff and onto the pebbled beach.

He loved the stars. They were brighter now with the moon obscured by clouds. His eyes closed. He opened them, surprised he'd been sleeping and he traced the Southern Cross, thankful Pedro and his friends named the formations and told him stories of the stars.

The sea to the southeast glowed with a faint light off Cabo Girão. He stood up and stretched while the portholes of the steamship grew distinct. What looked like the movement of a snail in the sea grew into a pack of dolphins. The steamer caught his attention before he thought of signaling it on the starlit sea.

The captain dismissed the soldiers at the close of the festival and left a contingent to guard the basilica. The dancing ended for the night and the band members went off to the cottages where they were guests. A rooster crowed and a fire-cracker exploded.

One soldier guarded the deserted praça. His rifle hung from his shoulder, his hat pulled over his eyes and his face and uniform one shadow. He halted by the bandstand and listened. He stood silent for minutes, straight and tall with his hand held in a fist around the strap, the rifle sling, as if he saluted God and the church. His hand moved to his side and he turned back. The rifle hung down his back, and when he reached the far end of the square, he leaned against the wall and rested.

José counted the number of passes made by the sentry; they were fewer and slower. He crawled to the edge of parapet to see the walls of the steeple in the dim lighting. The rough stone afforded few handholds. He couldn't climb down on the side away from the night watch. He must go back into the basilica and its silent darkness.

If the soldiers were inside the basilica, they'd hear his footsteps in the loft. The vault magnified the sound of footsteps on the stairway. The wind made sounds and each sound echoed off the high stone vault. At the top of the bell ringer's loft, he held his breath and listened. No sound from the sentry. He stepped down one step at a time on the rungs pegged into the rough timber. Each step down to the organ loft creaked. He counted each one two three. Light came from a series of tiny windows at the top of the nave and the vigil lamp near the altar.

Halfway down, he stopped and prayed, Jacob and Moses and Christ. A sound arose from the pews. A soldier in the vestibule cleared his throat and spit. The distinct footsteps faded as the man marched across the square to speak with his counterpart.

José shifted his weight on the step and the tread creaked. He balanced on one foot in the dark and listened for a response to his presence in the loft. He moved as a ghost which amused him and he put his weight on the other foot and slipped down one more step. He felt the cold flagstones of the pavement.

The guards were silent. The flagstones were damp and he pinched his nose to prevent a sneeze. He moved down the center aisle toward the door, and looking through the keyhole, he saw moonlight on the square. It was as bright as day and made it impossible to creep out and pass unseen through the sentries.

Other soldiers were posted on the market side of the church and along the stalls leading toward the priest's house. He turned back into the gloom and the frail light from the altar. The only escape was through the graveyard and out onto the slope above the square. The cypress trees concealed the graveyard from the square and the guards on duty.

He tried the doors of the nave to the portico but they were locked.

He wanted to rest and wait for the sexton to open the doors for Matins. Women would be on their way to Mass. At the door in the transept, he heard boots moving in slow cadence back and forth guarding the door.

The cupboard in the sacristy was locked and he was hungry and could not get out a loaf of bread. He pulled on a deacon's vestment and ran in the eastern transept to warm up. He ran along the transept to warm his legs. He tried the altar door. The village boys had smoked behind the altar told jokes and stories during the Mass. Earlier, he'd listened to the soldiers yelling to one another as they moved into position and surrounded the church. "Go into the bone house. Come here and check the gate, Albino," yelled one.

He went to the cemetery with his mother when she left flowers on his grandparent's grave and they passed the stairwell down into the crypt.

The narrow passageway between two columns curved down into darkness. The dust clung to his bare feet. What if he saw his grandfather? The old man's remains were dug up and placed in a chamber below the altar. A ghost at the foot of the stairs!

Grandfather was as wrinkled as a sun-dried fig when he last saw him alive. He sat on the settee built of grapevine wood rolling his own cigarette and spitting gobs of mucus into a clay pot.

He seldom spoke to grandfather; the old man was rough with him and smelled. His mother taught him to say, "Give me your blessing, grandfather." The words came back to him and whispered them. The memory was dry and as powdery as the dust.

In the darkness, the old man wouldn't be able to see him. He'd say, "Good morning, Grandfather. Do you want a coffee? I haven't seen you for a long time."

The spirit said, "What are you doing in the land of the dead, my boy? A bone house is not a good place for a boy. You should be in the gardens of the Valley of the Melons where I worked the land for the *Senhorio* until the day I died. Work, now, before you die."

The spirit moved ahead of him in the gloom and he followed it through the crypt. A shining host moved over the piles of bone. God knew the path through the darkness and beyond the closed door that led out of the crypt.

He stopped at the bottom of the steps and the silence overwhelmed him. No passing of the guards their footsteps ringing on the cobblestones penetrated the cell. He turned his head, moving it slightly to catch light but his eye caught no light.

If grandfather spoke he'd ask for light. With light he'd walk through the storehouse of bones without fear.

He heard a sound.

"Who's there?" he whispered.

His voice startled him. It was the voice of a stranger to him. He shouldn't have spoken and his lips moved before he heard the sound of his voice, his ears had tricked him.

He hit his head on the lintel and touched dried bone with his fingertips. He backed off and turned toward the apse. He was too far into dark of the crypt to turn back.

CHAPTER XXXVII

Darkness surrounded José and he couldn't see when he opened his eyes. He blinked and no flashes of grid-like rays appeared. He heard a sound and listened in darkness, poised over silence, a rising, his senses straining for the edge. A draft of cool air curled over his toes and ankles. He moved toward it. His eyes tested the darkness, his hands in front of him reached to touch familiar substance. The night air seeped in through a barred opening or under the threshold of the cemetery door where he and the village boys entered on hot summer afternoons and lay hidden in darkness.

The floor smoothed and slightly inclined and he moved slowly and listened for the rustle of air over dusty pavements. He saw light and an outline of a door opened a crack. It appeared in the corner of his eye and he raised his chin to see its glimmer. The door was not pulled shut and opened less than a decimeter and nightlight illuminated the threshold and jamb. He breathed easier.

The wind blew through the cypress and crickets sang. The crypt was silent and nothing greeted him. He pulled open the door. Tall dark trees and stars etched the sky. The fresh air smelled of resin and dew. The trees towered over the luminous marble headstones.

He hurried along the sunken passageway leading up into the graveyard. The dark cypresses were a good place for the soldiers to set up an ambush. He risked a run into the cypresses and buried himself amidst their branches; the needles cut into his face and scratched his arms. He heard a sound and held his breath.

A hand touched his shoulder in the darkness. It was Rosa. He grabbed her in his arms. She kissed him on the cheek and he wanted Maria and his sisters at home. "What are you doing here?"

"The soldiers guarded the church. They forgot the cemetery gate. I thought you'd never come out." She hugged him.

"I saw you dancing in the square. I'd kill the Senhorio if I could get my hands on him. How could you dance with him?"

"I had no choice. I was in front of the crowd."

"Did Pistola give you a message for me?"

"Pistola said nothing. His English friends sailed to Funchal on *Falcon*. I stayed in the square waiting for you. The soldiers drank their wine and wandered off and fell asleep. A few remained to guard the church. One walked along the praça. Two guarded the market side and another patrolled the priest's house."

"You unlocked the gate to the crypt!" he said.

"Maria Augusta gave me the key. I opened the gate. I didn't go inside. I was afraid."

He saw the early glimmer of dawn and said, "I must go to the pebbled beach while it is still covered in darkness."

"A soldier is in the square. We'll go around the square."

José ran softly through the graveyard and pulled himself to the top of the wall. He pulled Rosa up. Not a sound rose from the cypress trees.

"I'm going with you," she said.

They cut through Calçada the mists rising along the valley. He held her hand. He'd never held her hand before.

"We can hide in the smuggler's cave," she said.

"No, they know it well. I have nothing to eat there. Go home. Your bed is empty."

"I always go to early Mass. I'm standing before the altar by at this hour."

"The captain believes I'm in the loft or belfry and will send the soldiers to search the basilica in daylight. Your father wouldn't allow you to be with soldiers."

"He knows I'm safe at church."

"You aren't. It's better for you to go home."

"I want to go with you."

"You can join me later. It's safer. Hurry home before the militia forms in the square."

Rosa lowered her head. He looked at her bare feet.

"Please leave for my sake. They'll take me and you'll be miserable. I'll serve in the army six years."

"Must I leave you?"

"Yes. Go now, there's time. You can speak later this morning with Pistola. I have his word. Talbot arranged one passage. We can't go together."

"You promised me to meet me. You never met me at Pistola's. Promise me this time and mean it. Now meet me at the smuggler's cave."

"I can't. Once the soldiers search the church, they'll sound an alarm. I may be taken. Go, before it's too late."

Rosa turned away from him. The morning mists rose in the breeze. Through them he caught a glimpse of the pebbled beach. She came back and kissed him. She walked away through the mist toward the church her head down.

"See you later," she said.

"Hurry, you're not in your bed."

Rosa moved away through a corridor of mists and was swallowed by its vapor, as white as a snow bank in the mountains. He waved and she disappeared in the mist. He listened for soldiers hailing her. He prayed she'd pass unchallenged by the sentries.

The mist thickened and the clock struck four when his bare feet touched the pebbles. The water slapped the rocks and the pebbles forced up the shingle rolled back down into the sea. The sound guided him through the mists and he found the old dory at the end of the beach where landslides had left rocky debris. The dory was fastened to an iron ring belayed in the rock. It was long with oars still a-float in the water in it. The topside was bleached and dried out its paint flaking off, faded blue and chalk white, the wood split from weather and age.

In the mist he heard the water against the quay and the sounds of the wherrymen loading up their skiffs for the arrival of the tug boat. He smelled a fire. The soldiers stood by it, warming themselves and talked about the girls at the festival.

José bailed out the dory. The mists were thick and gray. He felt so tired. He smelled fried pork from the soldiers' fire. He was tempted to join them and warm himself by the bright coals.

He had planned to eat supper with Pistola. The dash into the church from the soldiers prevented him from Pistola's. There was chestnuts and cod fish in the cupboard at Pistola's cave. He walked slowly along the beach toward it.

The mouth of the cave was close to the quay and smooth going. He risked the sentries firing on him. The wind came in off the water and the mists rose enough for him to see the waves and they were calmer than yesterday.

In Pistola's cave the air was warm and made him drowsy. He ate dried chestnuts and pieces of bacalhau. The shouting of the wherrymen awakened him, and he hurried to the mouth of the cave. It was daylight. He prayed the *Zweena* had set sail from Funchal and would this morning steam close by the campanário.

CHAPTER XXXVIII

Rosa glimpsed José bent forward hurrying away when the mists swallowed him. Mists obliterated the landscape from the pebbled beach to the mountains. Trees disappeared and in the early light the valley lay in sheets of vapor in shades of gray.

José moved swiftly through the village and climbed down over the cliff to the pebbled beach. He heard the voices of soldiers muffled in the gloom and across the beach closer he heard one say something about drinking and dancing.

"He'll walk by. We won't see him," said another.

Rosa went across the square and through the street gate into her yard. Her mother had left the inner gate unlocked and ajar and waited for her in the kitchen.

"You weren't in your bed. You were with Abreu!"

"I was at the cemetery. I'm going to Brazil."

"You'll marry first, my daughter."

"There's no time."

"Stay with me. Daughters of mine don't cause me great sadness. You went home with your cousins after the *festa*!"

"I love him. I want him for my husband."

"He's an outlaw like his brother. José refuses to obey the *Senhorio*. He's a wanted man. The priest damned his soul."

"I want him more than anything in the world."

Mother stuck a finger in her ear and swore by the virgin.

Rosa cried. She knelt at the foot of her bed and raised her eyes to the virgin. "Please *Nossa Senhora* give me strength." She put on a dry skirt and blouse. Her eyes were dark in the hall mirror.

The first strands of sunlight glowed through the mists as she rushed across the square. Soldiers stood at the entrance of the church and as she

261

passed and went in to the Mass they inspected her. Father Segundo announced the soldiers had searched the sanctuary. José Abreu was not arrested yet and anyone that saw him was to report it to the captain of the militia.

Father Domingo spoke to the early worshippers from the pulpit, "Yes, the soldiers sealed up our well for the community water. They followed the order of the Governor of Madeira in Funchal who knew nothing of Campanário."

She pulled her kerchief around her face. She went down on her knees and prayed.

The chief of police and the captain knocked on her father's door. Father smiled and nodded. "I'm a poor cobbler. I'll try to help you, gentlemen," he said.

"We've come about Abreu. We cornered him in the church and he slipped by the guards in the mist. He may be here," said the captain.

"Father Segundo said your daughter knows him. We have questions."

Rosa waited for her father's call. He shouted on his way to her room.

"Did you go to the cemetery this morning?"

"Yes, I went to my grandparents' grave." She dared not lie.

"Why did you go there? Why go in the night, daughter?"

The captain held his fancy cap in his hand and stared at her breasts.

"I prayed for our family. I've done it since childhood."

The chief of police said, "In the middle of the night! Mass isn't until four-thirty, and you went in darkness. I don't believe you."

Rosa shook her head and lowered her eyes.

"You saw Abreu. You had to. The crypt was the only passage unguarded," said the captain.

Father's eyes narrowed. "Extraordinary. You had gone to him when he was locked in the slave quarters. I remember you picked onions in the field.

You fed him when he suffered sunstroke. You were nearby when he left the crypt."

The chief of police said. "She knows and won't tell."

"The Senhorio told us she stole his key and the young man escaped," said the captain.

"The door into the crypt is locked at sunset when the gardener finishes his work. If she went into the cemetery, she unlocked that door," said the chief.

"Senhor, my daughter will tell the truth." Duro Castagna turned and asked, "Rosa, did you open the gate for José?"

"No, I found it ajar when I went to the cemetery. I saw no one."

"Lies, the gardener locked the gate," said the captain.

Father didn't like officials. "I'll make her tell." He said to her: "Are you going to tell me or am I going to make you?"

She lowered her eyes. The first blow hit her face with the back of his hand. It sent her off-balance and she reached for the wall. She covered her ear and bit her lip. Her defiance enraged him.

He hit her on the shoulders and back. Her mind went black and she screamed.

He whipped off his belt and beat her in front of strangers! She ran. She didn't care where as long as she got away from him. He swung after her and missed. He cursed the devil. She fled from the stairs toward her room where she'd been cornered before and she turned away and ran out to the patio and jumped into the garden. She heard them swearing and their boots on the pavement. She hid behind the outhouse.

"Come out, ungrateful child. I give you a home and you disgrace my name. God damn you and your children and Abreu that bastard."

He coughed, cleared his throat and spat into the cabbages, gagging, blowing and rasping. He regained breath and cursed. She covered her ears and waited. They searched the yard. She heard the captain soothing father. "We meant no harm, Senhor. She'll return. We'll learn the story, one way or another."

"She knows something or she'd not run. Believe me, gentlemen."

"I know you're there," Duro Castagna yelled.

"My men searched your yard. Father Segundo wanted to question Abreu before I took him to Funchal," said the captain.

"I'll arrest her," said the chief of police.

The sunlight was bright now and she hid in the cane fields and avoided the soldiers who had discovered the hidden path into Maçapez. Each time a soldier signaled, she hid and waited to see the way the patrol went and searched. This succeeded until she ran into the soldier smoking the cigarette as lazy as a sow in *sesta*. Smoke drifted from his nostrils and mouth, drifted off cheeks and hair. His eyelids lowered like a lizard dozing in sunshine.

Rosa threw a rock. He raised his head and looked into the vines. He fussed with his rifle. He listened for another sound in the vineyard and she ran into the schoolyard. She thought the mists concealed her when the soldier who was now below her turned and spoke. "Where are going, my pretty one?"

She ducked around the corner of the school house. Esquerda leaned on the parapet and watched her. He dozed. The sound of a rock awakened him. The search for Abreu made him nervous. When Rosa dashed up the steps to avoid Direito, Esquerda turned his head. He saw her appear at the same instant she saw him. What a joy to see her. He smiled at the thought of his captain's praise.

"Halt and don't move." His voice was sharper and clearer than she remembered. She'd seen him on the square, an overfed drunken regular, eyes leering at the women, mouth dry and drinking wine at breakfast. She didn't wait for him. His companion aimed his rifle at her. Esquerda chased after her, though his weight slowed him down and he was stiff from carousing. His patrols kept him fit and he was quicker on his feet than it appeared. He caught her arm and swung her toward his Direito. She spun like a top and fell on hands and knees.

The other sentry blew his whistle, revealing his dirty, green, food-encrusted teeth. Esquerda called for Direito, the one that pissed in the square and watched women on their way from Mass.

"Good work. The captain will be pleased we caught her."

"Don't tie them," she said, curling up and concealing her hands.

She cried. The three men pulled her to her feet and tied a rope around her arms. She scratched Esquerda on the cheek. He laughed and kissed her neck and held her hands while the others secured the rope.

"Take your hands off me filthy lizard."

Her mother ran to meet them and swore at the soldiers. Maria das Almas heaped threats on the soldiers. "You come near me and you die like a stuck pig."

The soldiers lifted Rosa by the elbows and presented her to the sergeant at the guard house. A private ran for the captain. He was drinking with her father, Duro Castagna and the chief of police at the *pastelaria.* The three of them walked across the square and glared at Rosa.
After a long wait, the captain said, "Where is José Abreu?"

She closed her eyes and pretended she didn't hear. The women sneered at the captain.

"We have no time for stubbornness."

She opened her eyes. Esquerda leered at her. She covered her breasts with her kerchief.

"We'll make you talk," said the captain.

Father threatened her with his fist. "I'll send you to the nuns. You're a disgrace."

Mother pled with the captain. "She'll tell." Mother wanted her home.

"Speak, or we'll make you," said the chief.

Rosa sobbed. She saw no escape. Daylight was on them. The church and the cottages appeared and the poinsettias in full bloom were bright along the square.

"I'll never tell. I'll speak with Pistola. He's a gentleman," she said.

"Who is Pistola?" said the captain.

"The man from Maçapez," said the chief of police.

"Manuel Joachim Gonçalves, he rules without land, the one that knows strangers and speaks foreign tongues," said Father. "She'll answer him, I know. I believe her. She'll tell."

"Esquerda, fetch Father Segundo," said the captain.

He ordered Mandado to Maçapez. "He's the one that hid the lad and let him go," said Esquerda.

"Tell him we demand his presence. I know it's early."

"We act on the orders of His Majesty King Carlos," said the captain.

"King Carlos is a tyrant. Madeira is a free land," said Rosa.

"Rosa, please help these men. It's for the best," said Mother. "José has an obligation to the King. Others serve the six years and more. The captain wants to know where José ran when he left the cemetery."

Rosa couldn't be truthful. The Senhorio had made her his whore. Father had beaten her and would now send her to Saint Catherine's in Funchal. She told when the soldiers humiliated her.

"He hides in the smuggler's cave," she said.

"We know many caves above the beach," said the captain.
"Which one is the smuggler's cave?"
"Let King Carlos find it. You want José, look for yourself."

"Watch your tongue young lady. Slander against his royal majesty is punishable under the law," said the chief of police.

She looked to Pistola to save her. Father gave them directions to the cave. Rosa had betrayed José and she cried.

"When did you last see him, or meet him?"

The questioners surrounded her where she sat on the cobbles. They untied her arms and she rubbed them. She remained silent. The enlisted men tired of it and hit her.

"We can open her mouth, sir," said Esquerda.

He ran his finger down her arm and gave her a look. He'd whip her close to death given the chance.

When he walked into the circle of soldiers, Father Segundo looked angry. The soldier had interrupted his nap. He was angry when he saw Rosa struggling against Esquerda's grip and her tormented face.

"You're wasting your time. She won't talk until Senhor Gonçalves comes from his shop in Maçapez. She'll tell him and you'll hear it."

"But Father, we've lost the pursuit of the young man. I've sent men to the cave. News travels swiftly in these villages. The whole populace knows the story and even Abreu himself. The mists make it difficult. The cliffs are steep and unfamiliar and the folk were born to this land," said the captain.

"I know, I know," said Father Segundo. "The mists rise with the sun. This February air is heavy with moisture. The sun covers the mountains in light and dries the air and mists drift along the ridges and up the heights. You'll see."

The priest secured her release and she went into the kitchen with mother. They served coffee and bread to the soldiers. Direito grumbled and swore. The captain conversed with the priest. The men lounged outside and looked down the path for Pistola. The captain sent word to his patrol on the beach to search the smuggler's cave and to post a sentry at its entrance. Rosa cried in her mother's arms.

CHAPTER XXXIX

Pistola wiped off the bar with a damp cloth and laughed at the soldier repeating over and over, "I have orders. I'm to escort you to Castagna's."

"I'm sorry, my good man. I've accounting to finish before my inventory. I've lost two days with friends. Festival or no festival I'll put my books in order."

"The captain demands your presence, Senhor, to speak with the girl. She knows where the rebel is," said Mandado.

"You tell your captain he's welcome to come to Maçapez with the girl. I'll speak to Rosa. I'm staying in the shop."

Pistola was anxious for the telegraph message from Talbot. Talbot and Jenkins had enjoyed their evening visit with him and returned to Funchal to meet Captain Taylor of the *Zweena*. He was to meet the early Blandy boat.

After the disgruntled soldier ran off to seek the captain, Senhora Castagna appeared on the porch and implored Pistola to defend Rosa.

"The captain threatens her. Please Senhor, come with me."

"Where is Rosa?"

"They've taken her to the priests' house. The soldiers molested her, Senhor."

"Not at the priest's. They know she helped José escape. They've failed to catch him."

"Please come." Her eyes filled with tears.

"Wait a little and they'll arrive with her. Don't fuss. I'll hear them out. I'll speak for you."

"My husband, Senhor Castagna beat her. She wanted to run off with Abreu. They're crazy these soldiers. She has no common sense."

Senhora Castagna moaned and tore at her sweater with her hand. He patted her shoulder and handed her a cup of coffee.

"Your Rosa will speak. You say nothing. I'll deal with the Father Segundo and the chief of police and the captain. No crying."

Pistola sent Jaime to the telegraph office. "I want a message from Talbot. The agent must have received it from Funchal."

The soldiers appeared at his shop with rifles and bloodshot eyes after a night of drinking and dancing. They were vain, seeking the admiration of the peasants as servants of the King and demanded favors as they marched through the countryside—a glass of wine, a cigarette, a custard apple. The morning mists concealed their antics with women on the way to Mass.

The soldier with the limp, the stupid one who shot himself in the leg the night before when they chased José led the troopers onto the patio. The captain and his retinue milled outside the shop until Father Domingo and Father Segundo arrived and pushed their way through the gathering. Esquerda and Direito bowed and fought over opening the door for the two priests. Rosa, her arm held by her father, spit at the clown-like Esquerda as she passed by him on her entrance into the shop and hurried inside.

Pistola smiled and greeted Father Domingo. He moved out from behind the bar and sat in his old chair to hear the evidence.

"You need some flour and salt, dear Rosa! A piece of Cod!" He winked. "Here is tobacco for your men, good captain. I hope there'll be no discharge of rifles on my property like we experienced the last time your men were in residence, and if you will be good enough to remove your caps, gentlemen."

The neighbors wanted to hear his court. They stood on the porch and peered in the windows. Direito and Mandado took off their caps after the captain uncovered.

Pistola offered his chair to Father Segundo and the priest refused it. The captain leaned forward, the smell of goat's cheese, the bright lettering on the sardine cans, the canaries silent and nervous in wooden cages hanging above the counter, made Pistola eager to get on with the proceeding.

"Senhora Castagna tells me of your misfortune, good captain. I received your kind message earlier. I wasn't free to leave my business on a moment's notice. I'm sure you appreciate my position being a man under orders yourself."

"The women in this village refused to cooperate with the competent Portuguese authorities. And this young woman won't answer my questions. Even the good Father can't get the facts so I can capture and arrest the rebellious draftee," said the captain.

"Yes, so I'm told."

"She told us he hid in the smuggler's cave. My men searched for it. Senhor Castagna's directions led us nowhere. My advanced party found it with great difficulty."

"You wish to learn who helped him escape from the church, if I'm not mistaken."

"Correct. Whoever cooperated with the runaway must be exposed and punished."

"You mustn't forget that José Abreu is a native of our village and belongs to this land. We may appear to dismiss the law without fully weighing the King's will in these matters, but let me assure you, Sir, we are free to defend our neighbors while we examine the law that may appear to be unyielding and possibly unjust."

"Question the girl yourself to ascertain the facts. I must carry out my charge from the Governor of Madeira and answer to him for missing conscripts."

The gathered folk stirred and turned their heads at a newcomer. The Senhorio, landlord of the fief in the Valley of the Melons, born from the pig's tail, glanced over the crowd with disdain and moved to the front of the session, his right and his honor. Blackeye and Twenty-Seven pushed away those close enough to touch his landlord. The women shied and covered their eyes with their kerchiefs and tightened their shawls.

"Good morning, *O Senhor*, Welcome to Maçapez and my humble establishment."

The Senhorio said, with eyes as metallic as *reis*, "I seek my rebellious tenant, José, whom I understand was not captured by the militia, though they were armed with the authority of the King." Father Domingo turned pale.

Pistola glanced at the clock whose ticking was muffled by the bodies packed into his shop and overflowing onto the steps. He said, "This is serious business. To settle it will take months, and it is complicated by the fact that this young lady loves José Abreu, and wishes to be his woman. The young man has no property in this world. He can't read or write our tongue. He's nothing to offer her, nor does she have a dowry, her father having arranged her marriage to Alberto Gonçalves."

"I want Abreu captured and returned to me. I don't need her word," said the *Senhorio*.

"You have the right. Abreu belongs to you and his capture is necessary under orders to compel him to fulfill his obligation to the King. This woman, this Rosa, helped him to escape your domain and her questioning is necessary, Senhor," said Father Segundo.

"The Senhorio has a right to question her. Rosa Castagna enjoyed his company, lived in his household and owes him allegiance," said Twenty-Seven.

"She's involved with Abreu," said Father Segundo.

"Abreu belongs to the Senhorio. Let him question her about the rebel's escape after the militia trapped him in the church," said Blackeye.

"I'll question Rosa in private. She'll not speak before this mob," said Pistola.

Two young boys, Leonel and Arnaldo, laughed and slapped one another. The captain ordered them taken from the shop, and Mandado chased them from behind the flour barrels where they hid and listened to the gossip of the women.

"Now, quickly," said the Captain, "I must know Abreu's hiding place."

Rosa drew her shawl around her, hands clasped over her breasts, and glared at the soldiers.

Pistola gently grasped her elbow and moved her around the bar and through the curtain into the back room and beyond into his office. He cautioned her, his finger to his lips. Her eyes brightened. In the shop, Paulo and Jaime sold goods and served drinks to the soldiers.

"I know you helped him. You can't help José now. He's leaving on a boat off this coast this morning."

Rosa cried.

"I want you to show the captain the cave. There is no time to think of your self. They'll shoot if they catch sight of him."

"I want to go to Brazil."

"I'm sorry he goes alone. You can go later. He'll make money in the new land and send for you."

"I can't go home. Father beats me. I disobeyed the Senhorio. The villagers spit on me."

"Take the soldiers to the hiding place and confess you helped him escape from the church."

"You knew José was running away to Brazil and didn't tell me."

"You have no choice. You can live in Funchal. I'll arrange it with Talbot."

272

"I want to go with José."

"Go now with the soldiers and lead them to the smuggler's cave. If they arrive at the cave and find him he will be arrested. He owes six years to the King and obedience to the Senhorio."

"What do you want me to do?"

"Go and tell them. Say you helped him and you'll show them the cave."

"I can't."

"You can, and you can move to Funchal and cook for the Talbot family and learn English and have one free day a week."

"José's going into the army or to Brazil. I'll never marry Alberto. The Senhorio won't leave me alone. He knows I love José."

"The sisters of Saint Catherine's on the Rua Das Cruzes will take you in to teach children. The Senhorio can't visit you there. Men are not admitted. The sisters teach about fourteen hundred children and can use your help. You can live with the Talbot family."

Rosa hid her face in her hands.

"I'll make arrangements," he said. "Don't cry. We have to face them."

He led her back into the shop.

Senhor Castagna refused to give his consent as a matter of principle. "I'll beat sense into her."

"She agreed to lead your men to the cave," Pistola said to the Captain.

Father Domingo arranged for her confession. He was patient with her father and mother and smoothed over the role of the church in these matters and worked out the affair. He called in her father and mother and told them Rosa was going to Funchal to work and live with a proper British family.

The captain stood his men at attention outside the shop, eager to leave for the beach. He knocked on the bar and asked if the girl was ready to escort him to the smuggler's cave. He thanked Pistola for his sagacity and ordered the troops to re-assemble on the pebbled beach.

Pistola emerged from the shop wearing his best black hat, a clean white shirt and new boots. Under his arm he held his account book and a packet of letters for the Blandy boat. The villagers were silent and waiting for him. He waved to them and stood up on the top step.

In his quiet voice he said, "You should know that Rosa whom we love in our hearts helped Abreu escape from the church. She loved him and went into the cemetery where she unlocked the crypt door. She will help the militia in their search. Rosa won't live in Campanário because of these events. She'll be taken to Funchal and work with the nuns and live with the Talbot family."

The captain said, "Yes Sir! Thank you, Senhor." He ordered his men to proceed to the beach and to keep their eyes open for the villain. The captain and the chief of police led them toward the beach with the Senhorio and his bodyguards following and they argued about a man's bond, Father Segundo, on the side of letting the King have the rebel for six years and returning him to the Senhorio for hard labor, shrugged his shoulders and climbed up to the square and in his dining room sat in his comfortable antique chair and rang the bell for breakfast.

Pistola stopped about twenty-five meters from the top of the cliff and talked with Rosa. Her parents leaned forward listening to every word he said.

"The captain and the Senhorio want to question you about the escape from the slave quarters. I urged them to forget this whole affair once they have captured José. Remain close by me and let me do the talking when they search the cave."

The village boys ran ahead and stumbled over rocks and whistled at the soldier beating on his drum. The men in the fields heard the commotion and joined the entourage. The goat-boys that tendered the flocks climbed down to view the ruckus.

Last of all, the hammock bearers carrying an English family that attended the Festival of Saint Blaise joined the throng.

Pistola listened for the whistle of the Blandy boat. He heard drum beats and marching in the mist. He took out his pocket watch and checked arrival time. *Falcon* arrived at nine o' clock, off the quay. Talbot and Jenkins had made connections with Captain Taylor, yet he could not be certain until he received a telegraph message. The sun heated the land and the mists blew away. He scanned the sea for signs of the *Zweena*.

Rosa shivered and imagined herself in white entering the cool interior of the great cathedral in Funchal and kneeling before the Virgin to thank her. She wished she were in church. Her long night vigil with José tired her out and she dreaded further questioning by the Captain.

The peasants gathered along the pebbled beach. They argued with the advanced party of soldiers.

As Pistola walked Rosa onto the beach word passed out of the cave that the soldiers didn't find the rebel.

"He slept there," said one soldier.

"And we found garbage and a basket with food," said the Mandado.

The captain not satisfied with the first search of the cave and sent in six more men. The soldiers swore bats wouldn't keep them from the depths of the cave to search it. They prepared torches of pine faggots given to them by Armando at the shop.

Pistola had never seen so many villagers on the pebbled beach this early on a working day. Most of them never went to the seaside without produce or a hamper of embroidery for shipping. They hired boys to haul firewood and vegetables.

The captain called Rosa to the front of the crowd. She pointed out the marks in the rock where hand and foot holds were used to climb up to the mouth of the smuggler's cave.

The six soldiers handed over their rifles to their companions and two of them strapped the pine faggots to their backs. They volunteered to scale the wall and search. They disappeared into the cave and the eyes of the onlookers strained to see a glimpse of their heads when they shouted to the captain. The village boys kept climbing up part-way in a hail of cat-calls lost their courage and slid down and ran from the soldiers.

Rosa prayed for José and forgiveness. "Holy Mother, give me strength to love him. Help me to leave my family whom I love with all my heart. Look down with kindness on José and keep his love for me in his heart. Open his heart toward me, and loving me more each day, make him send money for my passage."

Out in the mist, *Falcon* blew its whistle. The soldiers turned their attention toward the sea. The villagers moved onto the quay to see the landing of the tug, curious about the soldiers and their search in the smuggler's cave above the beach. They watched the soldiers climb the cliff wall and crawl into an opening almost invisible to the eye. They followed thee distant mouth of the cave through the mists.

Pistola thought, for God's sake, let the mists conceal José, or let the *Zweena* blow her whistle and distract the soldiers."

CHAPTER XL

Falcon's whistle blew its sound at first muffled in the rising mist, and then echoed off cliff and mountains. The reverberation on his ear tapped his ear drum and awakened him from troubled sleep. José was exhausted from his night of running and hiding from the soldiers. He threw off the woven rug soaked with dampness and from the window of Pistola's cave looked out onto the quay. Soldiers and passengers awaited the approaching tugboat. He'd missed *Zweena!*

He rubbed his eyes. Across the beach in the mist, a crowd of peasants chattered and pointed at the smuggler's cave. Village boys played football on the beach, yelling and laughing at the soldiers.

He searched his bed for his knife and in his rush he missed it lying under the blankets. His head ached and he shook it and rubbed his ears and forehead. He rolled up the blankets and threw them into the storage. He peeled a banana and stuffed half of it in his mouth. He worried about the weather and eyed the mists and the white capped waves. He buttoned his ragged jacket and pulled his knitted cap down over his ears. He saw the soldiers climb the cliff side and disappear into the smuggler's cave.

He ran from the mouth of Pistola's cave. The sentries stood on the cliff overlooking the beach. The soldiers, greater in number than the day before, were spread out at intervals across the beach and José looked for an opening to evade them and make his way to the dory. The villagers were on the beach with the soldiers and staring up at the mouth of the smuggler's cave. He'd run across the beach and into the rocks. From the rocks, he would push the dory into the surf and surprise the soldiers. He hurried up the path under the cover of the trees. He walked across the bridge over the riverbed swollen by winter rains. The crowd stared at the mouth of the smuggler's cave, their necks craned, intent on two soldiers standing at the entrance of the cave on the cliff side. A soldier with a rifle leaned against the parapet of the bridge. He slid his fingers through the dew on the bridge-rail.

Pistola, Father Domingo, the militia captain and the Senhorio huddled a few meters from two dogs wrestling on the rocks and waited for the tugboat. The militia hooted and encouraged the men that searched the cave.

José calmly walked behind the soldier guarding the bridge and moved slowly down the cart road toward the pebbled beach.

The rising sun heated the mists and they slowly lifted, rising off the sea. The horizon was patches of blue sky and masses of mountain-like clouds.

He strolled down to the pebbled beach toward the water's edge where Joachim the younger had combed the pebbles and debris for treasures from the sea, bottles, colored glass, shells, and feathers. He looked about and no one observed him. All attention was directed at the approaching tug when he prepared to dash along the rocks and into the dory. He hesitated and listened. The waves splashed against the rocks and one after the other broke into foamy white sheets.

The soldier at the bridge saw him and yelled something to his comrades. One shot in the leg and he lost the race. One in the arm and he'd row the dory in a circle! The soldier waved to the soldiers at the smuggler's cave.

José was closer to the dory. Rosa and her mother were somewhere in the crowd of intent faces. What happened between her and the Senhorio? He'd never know. The hour of the morning was later than he realized. Whether the steamship sailed from Funchal or not he'd row into the mists and out in the gray and white water.

Then he ran across a smooth expanse of pebbles and a hectometer into the rocks. The soldiers were in view and if he slipped, they'd catch him two or three dekameters, one hundred feet, from the sea.

From the rocks he jumped down toward the waterside less than a dekameter, thirty feet, away and lost sight of the soldiers. The dory was hidden from them at that distance. His dropping from sight was sudden.

José breathed deeply and pushed the murmur of the crowd out of his mind. The soldier on the bridge aimed his rifle. He squinted and a gleam of sunlight shone off the barrel.

José ran.

The first half of his sprint went well and silently except for the crack of the pebbles under his feet. Then he heard the soldiers on the cliff-side shouting to the soldiers on the quay. He tucked his chin in and leaned forward, gave a burst of speed, slipped and lurched a little and lost his balance.

"We found a corpse," yelled a soldier from mouth of the smuggler's cave.

"Whose?"

"An old woman's," said the soldier, "fully clothed at the back of the cave."

José scrambled up the loose rocks on his hands to keep his balance. His left food slipped and he pitched forward, pushed away from the rock with his hand and regained his balance.

"José, wait. José, wait for me," Rosa yelled.

He ran toward the dory and rolled part-way down to the water's edge. He pulled the painter out of the ring and gave the dory a heave into the waves and guided it into the deep and stepped in.

"Halt in the name of the King," said the captain.

José launched the dory and pulled at the oar, when the captain yelled to the sentries, "Fire, commence firing!"

The soldier on the bridge knelt and fired. The sentries on the beach raised their rifles. A girl ran down the beach, her beautiful hair streaming behind her, across the pebbles on her bare feet, her figure revealed by the onshore breeze against her blouse. The soldiers ceased firing and watched Rosa run into the shallow water.

José feathered and pulled the oars in short delicate strokes. The folk on the quay stared up at the cave and paid little attention to Rosa, alone on the pebbled beach.

He rowed and didn't stop rowing until the dory hit a large wave and a little water spilled over the gunwale. He paused and the wave swept by and moved on toward the shore and then he pulled hard.

Years later, he heard that Father Domingo was surprised when the villagers demanded to know who buried the old aunt in the cave.

Esquerda and Mandado chased Rosa to the water's edge to keep her from going into the sea and their comrades stopped firing for fear of hitting them.

"Take me with you," she yelled to José.

"Shut up," said Esquerda. "He won't turn back."

Blackeye and Twenty-Seven ran down and grabbed her to keep away Esquerda and Mandado.

The first shot hit two meters from the dory. The soldier was surprised it didn't hit the runaway in the face. He reloaded and rested the rifle on the parapet and aimed.

Three soldiers on the quay raised their rifles and fired, the reports resounded off the cliff, the gulls rose into the mist their cries dwarfed by firing of rifles and jeering peasants. Esquerda raised his rifle and squeezed off a round as its sight came down on the dory.

José laughed and laughed. One slug tore his trouser and gouged his thigh, blood, water and shredded cloth.

"I'll row down the coast," he thought and rowed easily.

The priest, the captain and the Senhorio stood on the water's edge waving their arms.

"Come back. You'll drown," said the *Senhorio*.

"The rock-spire, the *campanário,* you'll break on the rocks," said the captain.

He saw their mouths saying something but whatever they said he couldn't hear their figures grew small, their sounds, tiny and faint.

Pistola walked along the beach toward the quay, showing no interest or concern for his agitated neighbors. Small boys ran out on the end of the quay to meet the tug. *Falcon* appeared out of the mist and blew her horn and the soldiers stopped firing.

Once out of the range of their rifles, José rested on his oars and splashed seawater onto his thigh.

More Soldiers ran onto the quay and the wherrymen edged their lighters close to the tug. They refused to take the soldiers and give up their fares.

The soldiers gave off firing and lined up along the beach, across the bridge and onto the quay. The captain engaged a wherry and rowed to *Falcon* with three other men.

José rested on his oars and thought; they may come after me soon. *Falcon* blew her whistle and moved off toward Ribeira Brava.

Mists blew off the sheer granite of the campanário, its massive rock faces towering above the waves. He used this spire as his landmark and checked his drift toward Cabo Girão, and headed west in the offshore current. The dory moved well beyond the wave action of the shore. Sunlight etched the tall pines on the lower ridges of the village and the features of the island itself, rocky cliffs, precipices and headlands showed more distinctly through the rising mist.

Rowing tired him and his strength died. He rowed slower until he had to stop. The mist seaward was low-lying, the further he drifted on the current. He lost sight of *Falcon* and listened. Soon, he heard her pounding boilers move toward him. Her whistle blew signaling her departure for Ribeira Brava.

The tug-boat moved closer. Enough mist covered the waters to conceal the dory. He rowed again cocked his ear for the throb of the tug. The captain may have convinced the pilot to look for him, though he thought sailors were independent of land officials and known for their individuality.

The wake from the larger vessel swelled and his dory rolled and bounced, and flung him about. He righted the dory, and the surge went off.

He concentrated on the oars, stretched his legs and leaned his shoulders into each stroke. He counted each stroke, his eye followed the oars to adjust them sp they struck the surface together. He felt the chill sea air on his ears and neck and the side of his face.

The only sound was the waves against the dory and the slap of oars. Where was *Zweena*? He prayed for the mists to rise and clear the surface of the sea. Looking toward the island, he saw the campanário, the island high in the background, green forests and below red, gray, and brown cliffs. The orange-tiled roofs of white cottages in the village were brilliant in shafts of sunlight. The church spire soared above the cottages. He turned the dory toward shore and the view of village was beautiful. He wanted to reach out through the mists and touch it.

His feet burned and his ankles ached from the cold water in the dory. He pulled the oars and churned water in an attempt to move the dory forward.

Water rose in the bottom of the dory. He looked along the seams near the bow and caught a glimpse of tiny rivulets seeping in. The more he forced the hull ahead, the more water leaked through the seams. He knew the wherrymen used the dory for gathering limpets and repairing the quay. They needed it to deliver messages to a boat standing off the *campanário* when the wherries were unavailable.

José rested and then rowed until the water rose about half a meter. He had no bail unless he pulled off his shirt and knotted it. He'd bail and drift closer to shore and sheer rocks that had no landings. He'd row as long as possible and make a bucket with his shirt.

The mist cleared and suddenly before his eyes, way off, he saw the *Zweena*, a cloud of black smoke pouring from her stack, a dark line along the horizon.

He waved one oar. He stood on the bow until the dory sunk and water reached his armpits. Then he kicked off from the sunken dory and swam with no hope of reaching the steamship.

He tried to keep his head above the waves, but they were high. He headed into one with his eyes closed and arms stretched out over his head.

The sun broke through the clouds, a beautiful day for climbing in the mountains with Henrique, the breeze blew and a kestrel rode on the current of air. Over green walls of water, rising and falling far below the winged shadow, swiftly the bird soared in glee, slipping, rising to hover, the cry muffled, the wild eye staring down at the waves.

A white sail appeared beyond Cabo Girão, tacked and set a course for *Zweena*. The sloop was rigged fore and aft with one mast and a single headsail jib. It moved under full sail, hauled straight into the wind, with two dark figures aboard.

The *Zweena* stopped and changed course. A bell sounded and José heard voices. The slap of a hull cutting like a knife through the waves reached his ear. He raised his head.

The loveliness of the white sail, full in the sunlight! His heart leapt at the sight.

"*Aqui, ca estou*, Here, here I am," he yelled and raised his hand.

Jenkins leaned forward and pointed so Talbot could see their prize barely visible in the waves, their crests blown by freshening wind. The sloop circled and cut through its wake to pluck him from the sea.

He gagged and vomited and lay shivering in the bow. Jenkins brought a blanket from below and wrapped him in it. Talbot stood at the tiller and guided the craft toward *Zweena*.

The men aboard the steamship waved and cheered. They let down a cradle and as fast as José blessed them, they hauled him up over the rail. The men at the winch, laughed, and shook his hand. Three bells rang and the mate waved good-bye to the sloop as she slipped off and away. The steamer belched smoke as she changed course and headed out into the sea. He smelled the soot from her stack. The sailors nodded and went back to duty. José stood silent at the rail and waved to Jenkins and Talbot.

A sailor with a red beard took him by the arm, and took him below to Jorge the Greek who spoke Portuguese, showed him his bunk and took him into the galley for breakfast.

The cook was a small man with a large gut covered with a filthy apron. He smelled of garlic and olive oil.

"I'm glad you made it. Senhor Talbot's an old friend. He knew Captain Taylor in the South African campaign, sailed with him out of Southampton." The other cook Gordo was Brazilian, with a strange accent and picked his teeth as he spit out friendly words.

They wrapped him in a blanket and gave him a mug of hot coffee. They helped him into his bunk and he closed his eyes and slept. The sound of the ship's bell awakened him. He opened his eyes and stumbled onto the deck. The crew came forward to meet him. He thanked Captain Taylor for taking him aboard.

The island lay under bright sunshine, a plume of clouds rising over her highest mountains, great headlands, strips of green pine forest, a jewel in the sea. At that moment he saw the island through his tears. He would remember that sight of Madeira as long as he lived.

"I pray thee, Father, to watch over my family, protect Maria and Rosa from harm," he said, thanking God and King Carlos that he was going to Brazil.

The island grew small in the distance, the size of Tia Nita's hand. As it changed color, green to blue to gray and then black as a sea dragon, he lost sight of his island in the line of where the sea meets the sky.

The sailors beckoned him to come below, but he stood staring out over blue waves, seeing white caps, bright in the sunlight. The sun warmed him at *Zweena's* rail and he watched the clouds disappear over the sea. The land faded away and with it the magic of the evil one, breath of Tia Nita.

He remembered standing on the mountain top, the wind in his ears, blowing over the fields where the shepherds tended their flocks in the setting sun, leading them through the rocky pastures to the enclosure where they lay down and were safe for the night. He loved Madeira its terraced land, its sugar cane leaning before the wind, a light, green wave with the sunlight moving over it, and the dappled vines with a white shirt bent over fruit, the man tending his vines. The great white clouds over Madeira moved toward the sea. José spread his hands open and felt the light on his palms as he searched the horizon for one last glimpse of Campanário. That vision of the island would remain with him wherever he traveled over the earth.

"Abreu," called a voice from below. "You're wanted in the galley."

The steward called him *piloto* and the Greek showed him how to make coffee and set the table to Captain Taylor's standard.

CHAPTER XLI

The sun burst through the clouds, its rays flooding the pebbled beach in light. The villagers pulled down their caps and kerchiefs over their heads and stared beyond the *campanário*. A sloop under full sail headed out to sea.

"I shot him," said Esquerda.

"Where's his body?" said Direito.

"It'll come ashore on the high tide."

"He's gone from this island."

The soldiers at the end of the quay stared out at the sea and the stream of dark smoke on the horizon. Pistola and the priest joked about the captain in the wherry in his pursuit of José, though the priest smiled through grim lips.

"That's Talbot off on his cruise to Tenerife," said Pistola.

"You can laugh. The wild bird would be caged but for you."

"I don't know what you're talking about," said Pistola.

"You spoke with the young rebel for months. I was told of your acquaintance with him and his visits to Maçapez," said Father Segundo.

The Senhorio cursed and spit. "That Rosa secreted the key out of my bedroom and freed him. She deserves stoning and sea burial."

Pistola laughed.

"Laugh, my dear shopkeeper, we live with vicious mockery of authority," said the priest. "Your business has different hardships. There's trouble in the land. The soul of the people awakens. They pay no tax or tithe after the harvest. They scoff at King Carlos. Their hearts are cold and they doubt God."

"Our village will one day be only widows and women with husbands in the New World, like villages in the Minho," said the Senhorio. "When the young flee the land dies."

"I sold more *bacalhau* this year than last," said Pistola. "Tomorrow, I'll order more beef from my agent in Santa Maria. The sugar cane harvest was excellent driving down prices. Let's plant garlic. Spring's coming."

"You arranged his baptism disguised as a girl. His name was not on the Militia's roll," said the priest.

"He wanted to serve the church. You didn't teach him his letters. You'll catch other fish in your net."

"His family rebels against authority. My men keep watch on Silvino, João and that mountaineer Henrique," said the *Senhorio*.

The sloop sailed away from the steamship on the horizon. The wherry returned to land and the captain climbed onto the quay and sent Mandado off to the telegraph office. He hastened to Pistola and Father Segundo, unsmiling.

"I sent a telegraph message to Ribeira Brava and Câmara De Lobos, to be on the lookout for this man and arrest him."

"I don't think *Falcon* picked him up," said Pistola. "I'll speak with Talbot when he returns from his cruise. You better collect your conscripts and ship them to Funchal, before they run off."

Pistola waved away the villagers. They had remained silent. They were saddened by the discovery Tia Nita's corpse in the cave and awaited Father Domingo's word. He was silent until evening prayer.

Pistola bought a Blandy ticket for Rosa. She was going to Funchal.

"Father Domingo, please speak with Senhora Castagna. Her daughter will work for the Talbots in Funchal-town. I'll write to the Mother Superior at Saint Catherine's," said Pistola.

The priest turned to the *Senhorio*. "I ordered the body of the witch left in the cave. It's not necessary to throw it into the sea. The lineage of Abreu is ancient. It will endure. They that carry the old name worship God in three persons."

"A few worship the old ways. They'll die out. I was born from the tail of the pig but I believe in Christ," said the *Senhorio*.

"The corpse's better off buried in the smuggler's cave than in the sea. The villagers will forget her."

"Father, will you give me the baptismal list during my summer march?" said the captain.

"Yes sir. You missed one recruit. Few of them escape the island. He'll return, if he doesn't die. We have patience, and we'll wait for him."

Pistola laughed.

"I'll buy you gentlemen a drink, a salute to wisdom. You've sealed the well against ignorance and taken the young men off to serve the King. You're thirsty. Wine will refresh us and give us patience until the day we die and have forgotten the events of this day. The young appear again and again in our lives, like the pebbles tossed up by the tides."

"On that future day, no men will serve the King," said the Captain.

The sky cleared blue as far as their eyes could see across the surface of the aquamarine sea where the *Zweena* sailed for Brazil.

Glossary of Portuguese words used in the story

A missa: the Mass
Á sua saude: to your health
Achada: plateau
Água de giro: irrigation schedule
Aguardente: rum
Amoreira: mulberry-tree
Anona: custard apple
Bacalhau: codfish
Basta: enough
Bastardo: bastard
Bema: Latin word for the Sanctuary platform for church services
Bola da Berlim: German cake, ball-shaped, filled with cream
Cais: wharf
Calçada: pavement
Campanário: steeple, steeple-shaped rock formation
Cantina: canteen
Carapuça: knitted cap
Cisterna: water holding-tank
Dineiro: money
Enxada: hoe
Espada: scabbard fish
Espatada: barbcued beef
Estrangeiros: strangers, foreigners
Estrela: star
Faca: knife
Favas: broad beans
Festa: festival
Fogo: kindling
Francelho: kestrel, sparrow-hawk
Freguesia: parochial district with a number of parishes
Lapa: limpet, marine mollusk
Laranja: orange (fruit)
Levada: water channel
Linguiça: sausage

Machete: ukulele, small four-stringed guitar
Maracuja: passion fruit
Marranos: Jews (derogatory)
Milho: maize, cornmeal
Minho: region of northern Portugal
Morgado: landowner by inheritance
Muito obrigado: thank you
Nêsperas: loquats,
Nossa Senhora: Our Lady, mother of Jesus
Nosso Senhor: Our Lord
O Senhor: sir
Pargo: sea bream
Pastelaria: pastry shop, sweet shop
Piloto: guide, pilot
Praça: town-square
Preto: black
Quinta: estate, manor house
Reis: crowns (currency) plural of **Real,** worth $.75 in 1900
Saudade: longing, nostalgia
Senhorio: feudal landlord
Sesta: nap after the midday meal
Sítio: a section of town or village
Taberna: pub, barroom
Tatara: caterpillar (nickname)
Traseiros: buttocks
Uveira da Serra: Madeiran blueberry
Vinho verde: green wine (newly-made)
Zé Povinho: Little Joe (cartoon hero)

About the Author

Don Silva writes stories set on the the Island of Madeira. His family has lived on the island since the 15th century. His grandparents emigrated to New England over a century ago. He first lived in Madeira in 1970. Silva has lectured at the *Museo Frederico da Freitas* in Funchal for the last three years. He is a writer, poet, mountaineer, and swimmer. Silva taught English at the University of New Hampshire. He is the author of *An Annotated Bibliography and Internet Guide for the Madeira Islands,* Lampeter, Wales: The Edwin Mellen Press, 2005.

Printed in the United States
117734LV00007B/167/A